ICE STATION NAUTILUS

ALSO BY RICK CAMPBELL

The Trident Deception
Empire Rising

ICE STATION
NAUTILUS

RICK
CAMPBELL

ST. MARTIN'S PRESS NEW YORK

ICE STATION NAUTILUS. Copyright © 2016 by Rick Campbell. All rights reserved. Printed in the United States of America. For information, address St. Martin's Press, 175 Fifth Avenue, New York, N.Y. 10010.

www.stmartins.com

Designed by Steven Seighman

Library of Congress Cataloging-in-Publication Data

Names: Campbell, Rick (Navy Commander) author.
Title: Ice Station Nautilus / Rick Campbell.
Description: New York : St. Martin's Press, 2016.
Identifiers: LCCN 2016003700 | ISBN 978-1-250-07215-3 (hardback) |
    ISBN 978-1-4668-8355-0 (e-book)
Subjects: LCSH: Submarines (Ships)—Fiction. | BISAC: FICTION / Sea Stories. |
    FICTION / Technological. | FICTION / Espionage. | GSAFD: War stories. | Spy stories. |
    Sea stories.
Classification: LCC PS3603 .A48223 I29 2016 | DDC 813/ .6—dc23
LC record available at http://lccn.loc.gov/2016003700

Our books may be purchased in bulk for promotional, educational, or business use. Please contact your local bookseller or the Macmillan Corporate and Premium Sales Department at 1-800-221-7945, extension 5442, or by e-mail at MacmillanSpecialMarkets@macmillan.com.

First Edition: June 2016

10 9 8 7 6 5 4 3 2 1

To Lynne—our thirty-year journey together has been amazing. I couldn't have chosen a better partner.

ACKNOWLEDGMENTS

Many thanks are due to those who helped me write and publish this novel:

First and foremost, to my editor, Keith Kahla, for his exceptional insight and recommendations to make *Ice Station Nautilus* better. To others at St. Martin's Press—Hannah Braaten, Justin Velella, and Paul Hochman, who I relied upon in many ways as *Ice Station Nautilus* progressed toward publication. And finally, thanks again to Sally Richardson and George Witte for making this book possible.

To those who helped me get the details in *Ice Station Nautilus* right: to Navy Captain Tom Monroe, former Commanding Officer of PMS 391, Escape and Rescue Program Office, along with his deputy, Dave Wunder, who walked me through the submarine search and rescue process. To Commander Andrew Kimsey and Lieutenant Commander Jonathon Gibbs, Commanding Officer and Engineer Officer of the Undersea Rescue Command, who showed me the submarine rescue equipment and explained its operation.

To U.S. Navy public affairs officers Lieutenant Matthew Stroup, Lieutenant Ryan de Vera, Colleen O'Rourke, Brie Lang, Olivia Logan, and Stan Weakley, who arranged the meetings with the above organizations and assisted getting those sections of *Ice Station Nautilus* reviewed by the appropriate subject matter experts.

To Director Larry Estrada and ice pilot Howard Reese at the Arctic Submarine Laboratory, for walking me through Arctic ice camp operations and the unique differences in submarine operations while in the Marginal Ice Zone and under the polar ice cap.

To Lieutenant Commander Stephen and Nicole Hunt, for helping translate legacy submarine operations into how Virginia class submarines operate, as well as explaining the hardware differences between Virginia class and older submarines.

And finally, to the men and women who have served in our armed services. My heart and thoughts will always be with you.

I hope you enjoy *Ice Station Nautilus*!

MAIN CHARACTERS

(COMPLETE CAST OF CHARACTERS
IS PROVIDED IN ADDENDUM)

UNITED STATES ADMINISTRATION
CHRISTINE O'CONNOR, national security advisor
STEVE BRACKMAN (Captain), senior military aide

USS *NORTH DAKOTA* (VIRGINIA CLASS FAST ATTACK SUBMARINE)
PAUL TOLBERT (Commander), Commanding Officer

USS *MICHIGAN* (OHIO CLASS GUIDED MISSILE SUBMARINE)
MURRAY WILSON (Captain), Commanding Officer
JOHN MCNEIL (Commander), SEAL team commander
JAKE HARRISON (Lieutenant), SEAL platoon officer-in-charge

UNDERSEA RESCUE COMMAND
NED STEEL (Commander), Commanding Officer
PETER TARBOTTOM, lead contractor for Phoenix International

ARCTIC SUBMARINE LABORATORY
VANCE VERBECK, technical director
PAUL LEONE, ice pilot

RUSSIAN FEDERATION ADMINISTRATION

Yuri Kalinin, president
Boris Chernov, minister of defense

RUSSIAN FLEET COMMANDERS

Georgiy Ivanov (Fleet Admiral), Commander-in-Chief, Russian Navy
Oleg Lipovsky (Admiral), Commander, Northern Fleet

K-535 *YURY DOLGORUKY* (BOREI CLASS BALLISTIC MISSILE SUBMARINE)

Nicholai Stepanov (Captain First Rank), Commanding Officer

K-157 *VEPR* (AKULA II CLASS NUCLEAR ATTACK SUBMARINE)

Matvey Baczewski (Captain Second Rank), Commanding Officer

K-329 *SEVERODVINSK* (YASEN CLASS NUCLEAR ATTACK SUBMARINE)

Josef Buffanov (Captain Second Rank), Commanding Officer

ICE CAMP BARNEO / *MIKHAIL RUDNITSKY*

Julius Raila, Chief of Search and Rescue Services

POLAR SPETSNAZ UNIT

Josef Klokov (Captain First Rank), Commanding Officer
Gleb Leonov (Captain Second Rank), Executive Officer

ICE STATION
NAUTILUS

USS *MICHIGAN*-BARENTS SEA

"Torpedo in the water, bearing two-five-zero!"

Captain Murray Wilson acknowledged Sonar's report, then examined the geographic display on the nearest combat control console. A red bearing line appeared, radiating from Sierra eight-five, forty degrees off the port bow. He needed to turn away.

"Helm, ahead flank. Right full rudder, steady course three-four-zero. Launch countermeasure."

The Helm rang up ahead flank and twisted his yoke to right full, and the Officer of the Deck launched one of *Michigan*'s decoys. Wilson turned his attention to getting a torpedo into the water. His crew was still at Firing Point Procedures, but his Executive Officer hadn't determined an adequate target solution. With *Michigan* increasing to ahead flank, they would likely lose Sierra eight-five due to the turbulent flow of water across *Michigan*'s sensors. They needed to launch a torpedo soon.

Wilson stepped from the Conn and stopped beside his Executive Officer, examining all three consoles. With the frequent maneuvering by both submarines, the target solutions were all over the place, failing to converge on a similar course, speed, and range. As Wilson evaluated his options, he was interrupted by another announcement by the Sonar Supervisor.

"Torpedo in the water, bearing two-four-five!"

A purple bearing line appeared on the geographic display. Their adversary had launched a second torpedo. Wilson responded immediately.

"Check fire. Quick Reaction Firing, Sierra eight-five, tube One."

Wilson canceled their normal torpedo firing process, implementing a more urgent version that forced his Executive Officer to send his best solution to the torpedo immediately.

Lieutenant Commander Sparks shifted his gaze between the three consoles, then tapped one of the fire control technicians on the shoulder. "Promote to Master."

Sparks announced, "Solution ready."

The Weapons Officer followed up, "Weapon ready."

"Ship ready," the Officer of the Deck reported.

"Shoot on generated bearings," Wilson ordered.

Wilson listened to the whirr of the submarine's ejection pump impulsing the torpedo from the tube. Inside the sonar shack, the sonar techs monitored the status of their outgoing weapon.

"Own ship's unit is in the water, running normally."

"Fuel crossover achieved."

"Turning to preset gyro course."

Michigan's torpedo was headed toward its target.

Wilson examined the red and purple lines on the geographic display, with new lines appearing every ten seconds. The red torpedo bearings were marching slowly forward, which eased Wilson's concern until he evaluated the purple lines. The bearing to the second torpedo remained constant. The Russian captain had fired a torpedo salvo, with a *lead* torpedo fired slightly ahead of *Michigan* and a *lag* torpedo fired behind. When Wilson turned away, he had unwittingly put *Michigan* on an intercept course with the second torpedo.

"Helm, right standard rudder, steady course zero-seven-zero. Launch countermeasure."

Michigan turned toward the east as the Officer of the Deck launched another torpedo decoy. Wilson watched intently as the second torpedo closed on *Michigan*.

TWELVE DAYS EARLIER

NORFOLK, VIRGINIA

Andy Wheeler, seated at his desk inside the Atlantic Submarine Fleet's head-quarters, worked his way down the inbox on his computer display. He took a sip of his morning coffee as he clicked through the emails, stopping to review the daily Naval intelligence report. In addition to the standard infor-mation, it contained something unexpected. Russia's new Borei class ballistic missile submarine was preparing for its first patrol.

He placed the coffee mug on his desk and opened the attachment of time-lapsed satellite photographs. A moment later, he called Commander Joe Ruscigno, seated at his desk at the back of the room.

"Look at these photos," Wheeler said as Ruscigno stopped behind him.

He cycled through the satellite images. Russia's first Borei class ballistic missile submarine, *Yury Dolgoruky*, had conducted a torpedo and supply load-out, then entered the missile handling facility.

"It's about time," Ruscigno said. "She's been delayed for years."

"We'll need to assign someone to shadow *Dolgoruky* during her patrol," Wheeler said. "Is *Annapolis* still on the northern run?"

"No, she just got relieved by *North Dakota*."

"Perfect. I'll draft a message while you brief the Admiral."

Wheeler pulled up the message template and entered the pertinent data. *Yury Dolgoruky* was about to embark on her maiden patrol.

North Dakota would be there to greet her.

GADZHIYEVO, RUSSIA

Along the snow-covered shore of Yagelnaya Bay, a cold Arctic wind blew in from the Barents Sea as Captain First Rank Nicholai Stepanov emerged from the back of his black sedan. The icy wind bit into his exposed face, and he pressed the flaps of his ushanka fox-fur hat tighter against his ears. The month-and-a-half-long polar night had finally ended, and Stepanov welcomed the faint warmth of the early-morning sun, hovering in a clear-blue sky just above the snow-covered hills to the east.

Stepanov stood beside his car, taking in the scene. Tied up along the center pier of Gadzhiyevo Naval Base, its curving shoreline forming a semicircular bay, was the pride of the Russian fleet—K-535 *Yury Dolgoruky*, the Navy's first new ballistic missile submarine in seventeen years. The sun glinted off the sides of the 170-meter-long submarine, the ship's black hull trapped in a thin layer of coastal ice. Nearby, the nuclear-powered icebreaker *Taymyr* waited patiently for orders to clear a path to sea.

A second sedan pulled up and two Russian Admirals emerged. Stepanov saluted his superiors—Rear Admiral Shimko, commander of the 12th Submarine Squadron, and Admiral Lipovsky, commander of the Northern Fleet. The two Admirals returned Stepanov's salute, but no words were exchanged. Stepanov already knew Admiral Lipovsky desired to speak with him, in private, following this morning's ceremony.

Stepanov turned and strode onto the pier toward his submarine. The two Admirals joined him, their feet crunching through a fresh layer of snow deposited by the weekend storm. As the three men headed down the long pier, Stepanov's eyes went to a podium on the pier across from his submarine. The sides of the temporary ceremonial stand were draped in red, white, and blue striped bunting that matched the colors of the Russian Federation flag.

Yury Dolgoruky's crew was already assembled on the submarine's missile deck; 107 men—55 officers and 52 enlisted—were standing in formation with the seven battle department commanders in front of their respective men. Stepanov's First Officer, Captain Second Rank Dmitri Pavlov, stood at the head of the formation. On the pier, in front of the podium and facing *Yury Dolgoruky,* were assembled the three submarine staffs under the purview of Rear Admiral Shimko—his own 12th Squadron staff, plus those of the 24th and 31st Submarine Divisions.

Stepanov and the two Admirals climbed the wooden stairs onto the platform, and Rear Admiral Shimko approached a lectern while Stepanov and Lipovsky settled into chairs behind him. Shimko greeted his staff and Stepanov's crew, and, after a short introduction, relinquished the lectern to Lipovsky. The Commander of the Northern Fleet stepped forward, studying *Dolgoruky*'s crew before beginning his speech. As Lipovsky spoke, Stepanov's mind drifted. He had heard it all before. *Yury Dolgoruky* was a symbol of the Russian Navy's bright future, not unlike the sun climbing into the sky after the long polar night.

Like Gadzhiyevo, the Russian Navy had emerged from dark times. In the years that followed the collapse of the Soviet Union, the once proud Soviet Submarine Fleet had decayed, submarines rusting alongside their piers due to inadequate funding for even the most basic repairs. But the economy finally gained traction and the government had begun the task of rebuilding the Navy, committing to two new nuclear attack submarines per year, plus eight Borei class submarines to replace the aging Akyna, Kal'mar, and Delfin class submarines—called Typhoon, Delta III, and Delta IV by the West.

The rusting hulks had been towed to nearby Guba Sayda, a holding pen for submarines awaiting dismantling, or had already been scrapped at nearby shipyards. The submarines that remained at Gadzhiyevo Naval Base in addition to *Yury Dolgoruky*—six ballistic missile and a half-dozen nuclear attack submarines—were fully operational.

Yury Dolgoruky was also operational. *Finally.* It had slipped from its floating dock at the Sevmash shipyard into the White Sea six years ago, and the submarine and its new nuclear warhead–tipped ballistic missile, the Bulava, had been plagued with countless design and material issues. After a seemingly endless series of sea trials, shipyard repairs, and test missile firings, *Yury Dolgoruky* was finally ready to commence her first patrol.

After almost forty minutes, Admiral Lipovsky finished his speech and retreated from the lectern. It was Captain Stepanov's turn to inspire his crew. He approached the lectern, resting his hands along the edges as he surveyed his men. They had been standing in formation in the bitter cold for almost an hour, assembling topside twenty minutes before the two Admirals and their Captain arrived. Stepanov decided to keep his speech short.

"Station the underway watch."

He could see the faint smile on his First Officer's face as his second-in-command saluted crisply. Stepanov returned the salute, and Captain Second Rank Pavlov turned to address the battle department commanders. A moment later, the formation dissolved into a mass of men moving toward the submarine's three hatches. One by one, the men disappeared down the holes.

Rear Admiral Shimko wished Stepanov good luck, then headed down the pier with the three squadron staffs, leaving Admiral Lipovsky and Stepanov behind.

"Your stateroom," the Admiral said.

A few minutes later, the two men entered Stepanov's stateroom, a three-by-three-meter room containing only a narrow bed and a table seating two persons. Lipovsky closed the door, then settled into one of the chairs, motioning Stepanov into the other with a wave of his hand. The Admiral kept his coat and gloves on; their discussion would not take long.

"You are a man of few words," the Admiral said as Stepanov took his seat. "I should learn from you. I sometimes like to hear myself speak."

"The men appreciate your visit," Stepanov replied.

"And I appreciate your dedication," Lipovsky said. The Admiral fell silent, his eyes probing Stepanov until he finally spoke again.

"How many men know what *Yury Dolgoruky* carries?"

It was Stepanov's turn for silence, reviewing in his mind the images of the loadout three days ago in the missile handling facility.

"The entire crew knows," Stepanov replied. "Missile Division assisted with the loadout, and you cannot keep something like this a secret."

Lipovsky leaned forward. "You *must* keep it a secret. No one besides your crew and the personnel in the missile handling facility can know."

Stepanov nodded. "I have already spoken to my men. They know not to speak about this to others. Not even family members."

"Good," Lipovsky replied. "We cannot underestimate our peril if others learn of our deception. The *Rodina* itself would be at risk." Lipovsky paused before continuing, expressing his fear more distinctly. "The Americans cannot discover what you carry."

3

USS *NORTH DAKOTA*

Just off the coast of Russia's Kola Peninsula, USS *North Dakota* cruised at periscope depth, the top of its photonics mast sticking above the ocean's surface. Seated at the command workstation near the front of the Control Room, the submarine's Officer of the Deck, Lieutenant Scott Molitor, studied the left display on the dual-screen console, examining the image from the photonics mast as he rotated it clockwise with a tilt of the joystick. Molitor paused on each revolution to study Kola Bay to the south, the exit point for warships stationed in the Northern Fleet ports along the shores of the Murmansk Fjord, searching for their target of interest.

Yury Dolgoruky.

The latest INTEL message reported the Russian ballistic missile submarine was preparing for her first patrol. If things went as planned, *North Dakota* would accompany her.

Molitor had only one hour left on watch, but so far had nothing to show for his effort. After five hours of scrutinizing the shore and surrounding ocean, he had detected only a few merchant ships far out to sea. He commenced another sweep with the photonics mast, shifting to the low-power Wide-Field view with a push of a button on the joystick. He was thankful *North Dakota* had photonics masts instead of periscopes. He couldn't imagine going round and round on his feet for six hours straight, *dancing with the Gray Lady*—the senior officers' phrase for countless hours spent circling with one of the mechanical periscopes on older submarines.

As Molitor continued his clockwise rotation, the Sonar Supervisor, standing only a few feet away, spoke into his headset, his report coming across the speakers in Control.

"Conn, Sonar. Hold a new surface contact on the towed array, ambiguous bearings designated Sierra three-two and three-three, bearing one-nine-zero and one-one-zero. Analyzing."

North Dakota's towed array was a valuable asset, detecting contacts at longer ranges than the submarine's other acoustic sensors. However, the array was an assembly of hydrophones connected in a straight line, which meant it could not determine which side the sound arrived from, resulting in two potential bearings to the contact—one on each side of the array.

Molitor acknowledged and rotated the photonics mast to a bearing of one-one-zero, shifting to Narrow-Field view. There were no contacts. He swung to the south. As he examined Kola Bay, he spotted a small speck on the horizon. He called to the Electronic Surveillance Measures watch. "ESM, Conn. Report all radar contacts to the south."

"Conn, ESM. I hold no contacts to the south."

Molitor reached for the ICSAP handset and pressed the button on the touch-screen display for the Captain's stateroom. A few seconds later, Commander Paul Tolbert answered.

"Captain."

"Captain, Officer of the Deck. Hold a new surface contact, designated Sierra three-two, bearing one-nine-zero, exiting Kola Bay. Hold no navigation radar."

"Very well," the Captain replied. "I'll be right there."

Commander Tolbert entered the Control Room a moment later, his arrival announced by the Quartermaster. "Captain in Control."

Commander Paul Tolbert stopped behind the command workstation, examining both displays over the shoulder of his junior officer. Molitor had resumed his visual search routine, and the photonics mast was rotating slowly clockwise.

"Show me what you've got," Tolbert directed.

Molitor swung the photonics mast to a bearing of one-nine-zero, then shifted to Narrow-Field view. The speck on the horizon was larger now, but was still difficult to classify. It was *hull-down*—only the top of the distant ship was visible due to the curvature of the earth. All Tolbert could see was the contact's boxy superstructure. Since it was transiting through coastal ice, it had to be an icebreaker. *Breaking the ice for what?*

Tolbert ordered, "Take an observation using the laser range-finder."

Lieutenant Molitor repeated back the order, then pressed a soft key on his command workstation, activating the laser range-finder on *North Dakota*'s photonics mast.

Molitor called out, "Prepare for observation, Victor one, Number One mast."

One of the two fire control technicians manning the starboard consoles reported, "Ready."

Molitor aligned the photonics mast to the contact, then announced, "Bearing, mark," and squeezed the trigger on the joystick.

The fire control technician called out, "Bearing one-nine-zero, range ten thousand yards." Lieutenant Molitor added, "Angle on the bow, zero."

If the icebreaker was clearing a path for a warship, Tolbert now knew its range. It would trail close behind the icebreaker, traversing the clear water before ice chunks floated back into the open channel. However, the ice-breaker's large superstructure blocked *North Dakota*'s view, making the detection of a ship behind it impossible. They needed to move off the ice-breaker's track so they could see behind it. Tolbert decided to turn perpendicular to the icebreaker's course.

"Come to course zero-nine-zero."

The Pilot tapped in the ordered course, and as *North Dakota* turned to port, Tolbert suppressed an involuntary shudder. It had taken a while to get used to the Virginia class design. Although he was now comfortable with a Control Room containing sonarmen but no periscopes, and calling the Helm a Pilot, he still got the willies from normal course and depth changes.

On older submarines, the Officer of the Deck would give a rudder order when changing course more than ten degrees, and when changing depth, the Diving Officer would order a specific up or down angle for the boat. On Virginia class submarines, however, "the ship" made those decisions. The Officer of the Deck would order a new course or depth and the Pilot would enter it into the Ship Control Station, and the ship's computer would automatically adjust the submarine's rudder, bow, and stern planes to the optimal angles. If desired, manual control could be taken by ordering a specific rudder or ship angle. But it was normally a "hands-off" operation.

North Dakota steadied on the ordered course and the ship's computer returned the rudder amidships. They were at periscope depth traveling at only five knots, and Tolbert's submarine moved slowly off the icebreaker's track. Tolbert and Molitor studied the photonics display, searching behind the icebreaker. Slowly, a black rectangle appeared—a submarine sail.

"Sonar, Conn," Molitor called out. "Hold an outbound submarine behind Sierra three-two. Report additional contacts in vicinity of Sierra three-two."

"Conn, Sonar," the Sonar Supervisor replied. "The only thing we hold is Sierra three-two. It's masking anything behind it."

Tolbert studied the submarine's sail. Based on its size and shape, he discarded one submarine class and then another, leaving only one. *Yury Dolgoruky* was headed to sea.

Plumes of water spray jetted into the air from the submarine's bow and stern. It was diving, venting the air in its main ballast tanks.

Tolbert turned to his Officer of the Deck. "Come down to one-five-zero feet and increase speed to ahead two-thirds. Station the Fire Control Tracking Party."

Three minutes later, *North Dakota* was at 150 feet and ten knots, the photonics mast lowered. Every console in the Control Room was manned, with supervisors standing behind the men at their workstations. The submarine's Navigator had relieved Lieutenant Molitor as Officer of the Deck, and Molitor now occupied a console on the starboard side, one of three workstations configured to determine the contact's solution—its course, speed, and range.

Tolbert assumed the Conn, leaving the Navigator with responsibility for the Deck—handling routine evolutions and monitoring the navigation picture, ensuring *North Dakota* stayed clear of dangerous shoal water. Tolbert stopped behind Molitor and examined the geographic plot on the upper display of his dual-screen workstation. It contained a map of the southern Barents Sea, with *North Dakota* in the center and the Kola Peninsula and Kildin Island to the south. Sonar hadn't detected *Yury Dolgoruky* yet; it was still being masked by the icebreaker.

Finally, the Sonar Supervisor's report came across the speakers. "Conn, Sonar. Gained a fifty-Hertz tonal on the towed array, designated Sierra three-four and three-five, bearing zero-eight-zero and one-seven-zero. Analyzing."

A discrete frequency with no broadband meant whatever was generating the noise was designed to be quiet.

Dolgoruky.

The Russian Captain had turned to the east, hugging the shore of Kildin Island in an attempt to slip by anyone awaiting them.

Tolbert announced, "Sierra three-five is our contact of interest. Designate Sierra three-five as Master One. Track Master One."

The Fire Control Tracking Party began determining Master One's course, speed, and range. Tolbert's Executive Officer, Lieutenant Commander George Sites, studied the geographic plot on Molitor's console. After examining the distance to the shoals surrounding Kildin Island, Sites announced into his headset, "Maximum range to Master One is six thousand yards."

It didn't take long for the two fire control technicians and Lieutenant Molitor to converge on similar solutions. The Executive Officer examined the three consoles, then tapped one of the fire control technicians on the shoulder. "Promote to Master."

Tolbert examined the solution on the display. Master One was on *North Dakota*'s starboard beam, on course one-zero-zero, ten knots, range four thousand yards. He would normally fall in behind the Russian submarine. However, if he turned south, toward shallow water, his towed array would drag on the bottom, damaging it. Tolbert couldn't retrieve the array either, since it was the only sensor they held *Dolgoruky* on. That meant *North Dakota* would remain in deeper water to the north, setting up a dicey situation.

"Attention in Control," Tolbert announced. The twenty watchstanders in the Control Room ceased their conversations, turning toward Tolbert as he continued. "I expect Master One will eventually turn north. We're in a bad position, on Master One's port beam. We're going to slow and open range, pulling as far back as possible. Carry on."

Tolbert followed up, "Pilot, ahead one-third."

The Pilot tapped the appropriate symbol on the Ship Control Station screen, and *North Dakota* slowed. Tolbert monitored the narrowband display on one of the sonar consoles, watching the tonal's signal strength fade. When *North Dakota* opened range to five thousand yards, the Narrowband operator spoke into his headset.

"Sonar Sup, Narrowband. I've lost the automated tracker on Master One. Buzzing bearings manually to fire control."

Tolbert overheard the report. *North Dakota* had dropped back as far as possible, and they now needed to match Master One's pace. "Pilot, ahead two-thirds."

The Pilot entered the command as Tolbert examined the geographic display on Molitor's console again. *North Dakota* was trailing forty-five degrees behind *Dolgoruky,* in her aft port quarter. They would watch Master One closely now, waiting for her turn to the north.

4

BARENTS SEA

YURY DOLGORUKY

Captain First Rank Nicholai Stepanov leaned over the navigation table in the Central Command Post, examining his submarine's position on the electronic chart. Seated beside him was the Electric Navigation Party Technician, wearing the enlisted rank of Michman on his uniform collar. Erik Glinka was busy verifying the operation of the submarine's two inertial navigators. It would be a long patrol with infrequent trips to periscope depth to obtain satellite position fixes. Satisfactory operation of their inertial navigators was critical.

Glinka looked up. "Both navigators are stable and tracking together, Captain."

Stepanov acknowledged Glinka's report, then turned his attention to the center of the Command Post, where the submarine's most experienced Watch Officer, Captain Lieutenant Mikhail Evanoff, supervised his watch section, his eyes scanning each display and the men at their consoles.

Yury Dolgoruky's First Officer, Captain Second Rank Dmitri Pavlov, entered the Command Post, joining Stepanov at the navigation table. "Everything is satisfactory, Captain. All equipment is functioning normally."

"Very well," Stepanov replied as his eyes settled on his second-in-command.

Dmitri Pavlov was a rising star in the Russian Navy—smart and capable, lacking only in experience. Pavlov had joined the Navy after the fall of the Soviet Union, and like many of his contemporaries, had spent little time at sea. Pavlov had been assigned to *Dolgoruky* to glean as much knowledge as possible from Stepanov, who was Russia's most experienced commanding officer. He had just completed a three-year tour in command of *Gepard,* the most advanced Project 971 nuclear attack submarine, and had taken command of *Yury Dolgoruky* upon her commissioning. As *Dolgoruky* headed to its patrol area, Stepanov focused on the training of his First Officer.

"First Officer Pavlov," Stepanov began. "If you were captain of *Yury Dolgoruky,* what would you do next?"

Pavlov glanced at the electronic chart. Kildin Island was sliding by to the south, and thus far, they had detected no submerged contacts; only several merchants to the north. But they had not yet deployed their towed array, their most capable hydroacoustic sensor.

Dolgoruky's First Officer answered, "We have completed our two-hour transit to the east, and should turn north toward our patrol area, deploying our towed array once we reach water deep enough."

"Correct," Stepanov replied, then turned toward his Watch Officer. "Captain Lieutenant Evanoff, prepare to deploy Number One Towed Array."

Evanoff relayed the command to Hydroacoustic, and Stepanov returned his attention to his First Officer. "As we begin the journey to our patrol area, what is your most significant concern?"

"That we might be trailed by an American submarine," Pavlov answered. "But that is highly unlikely," he added. "*Yury Dolgoruky* is the quietest submarine in our Navy."

"You must always assume worst-case," Stepanov countered. "An American submarine could have detected our surface transit and tracked us once we submerged." Pavlov looked at Stepanov skeptically as the older man continued, "If so, where would the Americans be?"

Pavlov examined the navigation chart, studying the outline of Kildin Island and the half-dozen bottom-contour lines circling the island.

He answered, "If an American submarine has detected us, they would likely be tracking us on their towed array. Under normal circumstances, they would trail us from behind. However, we are still operating in shallow water, and the Americans would have to shadow us in water deep enough for their towed array. Assuming their array droop characteristics are similar to ours, at ten knots they could not deploy it in water shallower than one hundred fifty meters."

Pavlov studied the bottom contour curves, then placed his finger on the

150-meter curve, on *Dolgoruky*'s port quarter. "That would put them some-where around here."

"Excellent deduction," Stepanov said. "Station yourself as Command Watch Officer. If there is an American submarine following us, find it."

Pavlov announced to the watchstanders that he was stationed as the Com-mand Watch Officer, with the authority to direct shipboard operations as if he were the commanding officer. He then pointed to the spot on the navi-gation chart.

"Michman Glinka. What is the course to intercept a contact at this position, headed east at ten knots?"

Glinka entered the parameters into the navigation chart and a line ap-peared. "Bearing three-two-five."

Pavlov turned toward the Watch Officer. "Captain Lieutenant Evanoff. Come to course three-two-five and deploy the towed array."

USS *NORTH DAKOTA*

North Dakota's Sonar Supervisor, standing behind the sonar consoles on the port side of Control, evaluated the changing parameter of their contact, then made his report.

"Possible contact zig, Master One, due to upshift in frequency."

The fire control technicians and Lieutenant Molitor examined the time-frequency plot on their displays, watching the frequency of the tonal rise. Lieutenant Commander George Sites stopped behind the consoles, and after the frequency steadied up, he announced, "Confirm target zig. Contact has turned toward own-ship. Set anchor range at five thousand yards."

Tolbert stopped beside his Executive Officer, examining the displays. *Dolgoruky* had turned toward the north as expected. In the worst-case scenario, *Dolgoruky* and *North Dakota* could be headed directly toward each other. Although submarine collisions were uncommon, they did occur. In these very same waters, USS *Baton Rouge,* a Los Angeles class fast attack submarine, had collided with a Russian Sierra class submarine.

Tolbert planned to ensure there was no repeat of that incident. He had to maneuver *North Dakota,* but needed to know *Dolgoruky*'s course so he didn't make the situation worse.

"I need a solution fast, XO."

Sites nodded and scanned the combat control consoles, his eyes squinting as the three operators slowly converged on a common solution. A minute later, Sites informed the Captain, "I have a solution. Master One is on course three-two-five, speed ten."

Damn. *Dolgoruky* was on an intercept course. They either knew they were being followed or had guessed where *North Dakota* was with incredible accuracy. Tolbert had to get off *Dolgoruky*'s track.

"Pilot, come to course zero-four-five. Ahead standard." They would move out of *Dolgoruky*'s way, let her pass, then fall in behind.

The Pilot entered the commands and as *North Dakota* turned to the northeast, Petty Officer Second Class Reggie Thurlow, stationed as the Broadband operator, pressed his headphones to his ears, listening to the unusual sound.

"Sonar Sup, Broadband. Picking up mechanical transients from Master One."

Chief Bob Bush donned the Broadband headphones and listened to the distinctive sound. It was much quieter than on other Russian submarines, but recognizable nonetheless.

Bush reported, "Fire Control Coordinator, Sonar Supervisor. Picking up mechanical transients from Master One. Sounds like towed array deployment."

Commander Tolbert listened to the report with concern. Range to *Dolgoruky* had decreased to four thousand yards. The United States had scant data on the new Borei class submarines, and he had no idea at what range *North Dakota* would be detected.

YURY DOLGORUKY

Stepanov checked the red digital clock at the front of the Command Post. They had deployed their towed array ten minutes ago, enough time for Hydroacoustic to check all sectors. Captain Lieutenant Evanoff must have been watching the clock as well, because he slipped the microphone from its holster.

"Hydroacoustic, Command Post. Report all contacts."

The Hydroacoustic Party Leader's reply came across the speakers. "Hydroacoustic holds three contacts. All three contacts are merchants to the north."

Stepanov joined Pavlov in front of the hydroacoustic display, searching for patterns within the random specks. Pavlov was not yet convinced. Narrowband detections were not instantaneous like broadband. The algorithms needed time to generate. As the two men examined the display, a narrow vertical bar rose from the bottom of the display. The Hydroacoustic Party Leader's report arrived a moment later.

"Command Post, Hydroacoustic. Hold a new contact on the towed array, a sixty-point-two-Hertz tonal, designated Hydroacoustic five, ambiguous bearings zero-one-five and two-six-zero. Sixty-point-two-Hertz frequency correlates to American fast attack submarine."

Pavlov and the submarine's Watch Officer turned in their Captain's direction. Stepanov announced, "Man Combat Stations silently."

The two Command Post Messengers sped through the submarine, and three minutes later, *Dolgoruky*'s Central Command Post was fully manned. Stepanov caught Pavlov's attention and nodded.

"This is the First Officer," Pavlov announced. "I have the Conn and Captain Lieutenant Evanoff retains the Deck. The target of interest is Hydroacoustic five, classified American fast attack submarine. Track Hydroacoustic five."

The men at their consoles focused on their duties, and with Pavlov taking the Captain's position, Stepanov assumed his First Officer's role of Tracking Party Leader. Stepanov moved behind the two fire controlmen, and it wasn't long before they converged on the same solution. The American submarine had crossed in front of them and was now traveling down *Dolgoruky*'s starboard side in the opposite direction.

As the range between the two submarines began to open, Hydroacoustic made the report Stepanov expected, "Loss of Hydroacoustic five."

Stepanov asked his First Officer, "An American submarine has detected us and is moving into position behind us. What is your recommendation?"

Pavlov studied the geographic display, then replied, "We should deploy a mobile decoy, then engage the electric drive to reduce our sound signature and turn to break contact."

Yury Dolgoruky was equipped with a quiet electric drive propulsion system, able to propel the submarine at up to ten knots.

"No," Stepanov replied. "Our advantage is that the American Captain does not know we have detected him. I don't want to alert him."

"You are going to let him trail us?" Pavlov asked.

"For the time being. We will let him work around behind us."

"*Then* we engage the electric drive and deploy a decoy?"

"No."

"I do not understand."

"Patience, First Officer. Let us see what the American Captain does when we enter the Marginal Ice Zone, and then I will decide."

USS *NORTH DAKOTA*

Commander Tolbert studied the geographic plot. *Dolgoruky* was to the west, and *North Dakota* had worked its way around the Russian submarine. In a few minutes, they would be directly behind her. Thus far, there was no indication *North Dakota* had been detected; *Dolgoruky* remained steady on course and speed, headed northwest at ten knots.

Tolbert waited until *North Dakota* intersected *Dolgoruky*'s trail, then ordered, "Pilot, come to course three-two-five. Ahead two-thirds."

North Dakota turned right and slowed, steadying up five thousand yards behind the Russian submarine, matching its course and speed. Tolbert was pleased with his crew's performance. They had dodged a bullet, successfully skirting around *Dolgoruky*. He hoped their luck held out; the Russian submarine would conduct many baffle clears during its patrol. Each time, there was the potential they would detect *North Dakota*.

The Sonar Supervisor called out, "Possible contact zig, Master One, due to upshift in frequency."

Lieutenant Commander Sites stood behind the combat control consoles, his eyes shifting between the displays. A moment later, he announced, "Zig confirmed. Set anchor range at five thousand yards. Master One has turned north and remains at ten knots."

Tolbert examined the geographic display. In a few minutes, *North Dakota* would also turn north, staying in *Dolgoruky*'s baffles.

Sites turned toward Commander Tolbert. "If *Dolgoruky* continues north, she'll enter the Marginal Ice Zone."

Commander Tolbert nodded. "Where the Russians go, we go."

5

MOSCOW, RUSSIA

The Moscow Kremlin—a "fortress inside a city"—spreads across sixty-eight acres in the heart of Moscow. Comprised of five palaces, four cathedrals, and the enclosing Kremlin wall with its twenty towers, the Kremlin has been the seat of Russian grand dukes and tsars since the fourteenth century, and today it is home to Russia's presidential administration. The green dome of the triangular-shaped Kremlin Senate, the Russian version of the White House, overlooks Red Square to the east and the merchant district of Kitai-gorod in the distance.

On the third floor of the Kremlin Senate, inside a twenty-by-sixty-foot conference room, a polished ebony conference table capable of seating thirty persons was occupied by only four. On one side sat Christine O'Connor, America's national security advisor, opposed by Maksim Posniak, director of security and disarmament in Russia's Ministry of Foreign Affairs. An interpreter sat on each side of the table, though thus far they had not been needed. Posniak's accent was thick, but his English understandable.

They were engaged in the first round of negotiations for the successor to New START, the current nuclear arms treaty between the two countries. As they approached the end of their weeklong negotiations, Christine's mood could not have soured further. They had made progress while discussing long-range bombers and ICBM silos, but had reached a stalemate concerning Navy launch systems. Sitting across from her, Posniak was a formidable adversary—six feet, three inches tall and 250 pounds—almost a foot taller and weighing twice as much as Christine.

Nonetheless, Christine leaned toward him, adding emphasis to her response. "This is unacceptable."

"Our position is firm, Ms. O'Connor," he replied. "No inspectors will be allowed on our Borei class submarines."

Christine pulled back. "Under the current treaty, we have authorization to inspect all nuclear weapon storage and launch sites. Our satellites detected the loadout of *Yury Dolgoruky* two days ago, which means we already have authorization to board her under New START."

"We differ in the interpretation of the treaty," Posniak replied. "The Borei class submarines were not operational when New START was signed and are not listed in the authorized inspection sites. We have no intention of adding them or including them in the follow-on treaty."

"Then how do we verify the number of warheads on your Bulava missiles?"

"We will have to use another method. I suggest we count the number of launchers and eliminate warhead verification."

"Launchers are only one part of the equation. How many warheads each missile can deploy is an essential element that must be verified."

"This issue is not negotiable. Either we work around this stipulation, or there will be no follow-on treaty."

"This is a deal-breaker for us," Christine said. "President Kalinin publicly announced his intention to craft a follow-on treaty with the United States, further reducing the number of warheads in each country's arsenal. I don't think he'll be pleased with our inability to craft a new deal. Is he aware of the *stipulation* you're making?"

"He is aware."

"I'd like to have a few minutes with President Kalinin. Is he available today?" Christine checked her watch. She was due to fly back to the United States in six hours. However, her stay could be extended to accommodate the Russian president's schedule.

"You are in luck, Ms. O'Connor. President Kalinin plans to stop by this morning to see how negotiations are progressing." It was Posniak's turn to check his watch. "He should be here any moment."

As Posniak finished speaking, the mahogany French doors behind him opened and two men entered. Christine recognized the man on the right as President Yuri Kalinin and the man on the left as Boris Chernov, Russia's minister of defense. Christine and the three men at the table rose to their feet as Kalinin and Chernov entered.

Chernov eyed Christine oddly, the same way Posniak stared at her when they first met four days ago. Christine was used to stares from men, but there was something unusual about the way Posniak, and now Russia's minister of defense, studied her. Christine's attention turned to President Kalinin, and as their eyes met, he almost stopped in his tracks. His complexion paled as he continued into the room, leaving his eyes on her until he turned abruptly and headed toward one end of the conference room, with Chernov following behind.

Kalinin turned toward his minister of defense, looking over his shoulder at the American woman.

Chernov spoke first. "I am sorry, Yuri. I should have warned you about how closely she resembles Natasha."

"That would have been wise," Kalinin replied. "She could be Natasha's twin." He was silent for a moment as he stared at the woman. "What is her heritage? Is she Russian?"

"Her last name is O'Connor," Chernov replied. "Irish descent."

"She looks Russian," Kalinin countered. "She could have Russian blood."

Chernov placed his hand gently on the president's shoulder. "I know how close you and Natasha were, and how difficult those last few months were. Do not let this woman's likeness to her affect you. When you are ready, I will find you a suitable *Russian* woman."

Kalinin grinned. "No doubt a close relative of yours."

"No doubt." Chernov matched Kalinin's grin, then dropped his hand as he glanced at the American woman. "Come, we should introduce ourselves."

Christine extended her hand as the two men approached. "Mr. President. It's a pleasure to meet you."

Kalinin shook her hand firmly. "It is my pleasure," he said with only a slight accent. "If I may ask," he added, "what is your heritage? You remind me of . . . someone I once knew."

"I'm half Irish and half Russian."

"Russian?"

"I am Boris Chernov," the minister of defense interjected, speaking in a heavy accent as he extended his hand. "Are you enjoying your time in Moscow?"

"Yes," Christine replied. "Although I haven't seen as much as I'd like. We've been working long hours. Your director of security and disarmament drives a hard bargain and, unfortunately, we've reached an impasse. Director Posniak says you want to remove missile warhead inspections from the next nuclear arms treaty."

"Only regarding our Bulava missile," Kalinin explained. "You may inspect our older weapon systems, but not our newest strategic submarine or its missile."

"That will be a problem, Mr. President. The treaty must be approved by our Senate, and without the ability to count warheads, I doubt there will be enough votes."

"Perhaps you can use your influence to ensure the new treaty passes," Kalinin replied. "I think we can agree that a significant reduction in nuclear weapons is a worthwhile goal."

"I *do* agree, Mr. President, but without the ability to verify every weapon system is in compliance, I won't recommend we sign a new treaty."

Kalinin's expression hardened as he replied, "Then we *do* have a problem." He turned toward Posniak, speaking to him in Russian.

Posniak nodded. "Da," was his response.

Kalinin turned back to Christine and said briskly, "It was a pleasure meeting you, Ms. O'Connor." He forced a smile onto his face.

"Likewise, Mr. President." Christine did not reciprocate the smile.

Kalinin and Chernov exited the conference room, and Christine settled into her chair across from Posniak. "If you don't mind me asking," Christine said, "what did the president say to you?"

Posniak stared at her for a moment, then answered, "Americans will set foot on one of our Borei class submarines when the crayfish sings on the mountain."

As Christine tried to decipher the last part of Posniak's response, he added, "It is a Russian idiom. It translates in English to—*when Hell freezes over.*"

6

BARENTS SEA

YURY DOLGORUKY

Captain Nicholai Stepanov ducked his head as he stepped through the watertight doorway into Compartment One, closing the heavy metal door carefully to prevent a transient from being transmitted into the surrounding water. A day ago, they had detected a 60.2-Hertz tonal during their port egress, and a few hours ago, Stepanov had ordered an aggressive baffle clearance maneuver to the south. They had picked up the 60.2-Hertz tonal again, which faded after only a few minutes as it had done the first time. The American submarine was still following *Dolgoruky*.

Inside the Torpedo Room, Stepanov spotted Senior Lieutenant Ivan Khudozhnik—Torpedo Division Officer, and Senior Michman Andrei Popovich—Torpedo Division's senior enlisted. Although neither man was on watch, Stepanov was not surprised to find them in the Torpedo Room, verifying everything was in working order. An American submarine was within firing distance, and they might soon be handling weapons. Considering what happened to *Kursk*, this was not an insignificant matter.

Kursk, an Oscar II cruise missile submarine, sank in the Barents Sea while her crew was preparing to fire a Type 65 exercise torpedo. Although what happened could never be known with certainty, the official Navy report concluded the torpedo, fueled partly by High Test Peroxide—a concentrated form of hydrogen peroxide—developed a crack at a weld, and the HTP leaked into the torpedo casing, coming into contact with a catalyst. The HTP rapidly expanded to five thousand times its original volume, rupturing the torpedo's kerosene fuel tank and producing an explosion equivalent to 100 kilograms of TNT, killing everyone in Compartment One.

Two minutes later, several warshot torpedoes detonated due to the high heat in the Torpedo Room. The explosion ruptured the bulkheads between the first three compartments and blew a mammoth hole in the bow. All but twenty-three crew members were killed, with the surviving men trapped in Compartment Nine, the farthest one aft. Rescue efforts were hindered by weather and malfunctioning submarine rescue equipment, and the twenty-three men also perished. Following the tragedy, heightened attention was given to torpedo maintenance and weapon handling.

Standing near the forward bulkhead, Khudozhnik and Popovich were supervising a junior Torpedoman who was taking measurements inside an electric panel with a multi-meter. The men turned toward Stepanov, and Khudozhnik greeted the submarine's commanding officer.

"Good morning, Captain."

Stepanov nodded his acknowledgment. "What is the problem?"

"Number Two Tube is out of action," Khudozhnik replied. "The firing panel failed its weekly check, and we're determining which circuit card has gone bad."

"What is the status of our spares?" Stepanov asked.

"We have two of every card in the firing panel," Khudozhnik replied. "As long as the same fault doesn't develop in more than two firing panels, we will be fine."

Stepanov nodded again, then headed back toward Compartment Two, confident his men would identify the fault and return Number Two Torpedo Tube to service.

Upon entering Compartment Two, Stepanov returned to the Central Command Post. Captain Lieutenant Evanoff was on watch again, and First Officer Pavlov was also present, supervising the watch section. As long as an American submarine was in the vicinity, either he or his First Officer would be in the Command Post. Stepanov stopped beside Pavlov at the navigation table and examined the chart. According to the latest oceanographic report, they were approaching the edge of the Marginal Ice Zone.

Stepanov turned to his Watch Officer. "Captain Lieutenant Evanoff. Slow to ten knots and station the Ice Detail."

USS *NORTH DAKOTA*

Commander Tolbert leaned against the navigation plot in Control, monitoring Master One's course with concern. *Dolgoruky* was headed into the Marginal Ice Zone, a hazardous area for submarine operations. At the fringe of the polar ice cap, wave action and ocean swells broke off edges of the ice floes, creating a zone of broken ice extending outward over a hundred miles.

It wasn't the ice floating on the surface that concerned Tolbert. It was the random icebergs scattered throughout the Marginal Ice Zone. Over three thousand icebergs were produced each year in the Barents Sea, breaking off glaciers on Svalbard, Franz Josef Land, and Novaja Zemlja, accompanied by the calving of glaciers on the east coast of Greenland. Most of the icebergs were small, but the larger ones descended several hundred feet, occasionally deep enough to ground on the bottom of the shallow Barents Sea.

Tolbert called to his Weapons Officer, Lieutenant Mark Livingston. "Officer of the Deck, set the Arctic Routine."

Livingston repeated back the order and issued commands to his watch section. After settling in behind *Yury Dolgoruky*, Tolbert had returned *North Dakota* to a normal watch section rotation, with each watch augmented with a Section Tracking Party comprised of an additional fire control technician to monitor the plots, a Contact Manager, and a Junior Officer of the Deck. By setting the Arctic Routine, Tolbert had ordered additional sonar consoles manned and the Deck and Conn split, with Tolbert and the XO alternating as the Conning Officer.

After a briefing from the Weps, Tolbert relieved him of the Conn, announcing to watchstanders in Control, "The Captain has the Conn, Lieutenant Livingston retains the Deck."

The Quartermaster acknowledged and continued preparations for entering the Marginal Ice Zone. He energized the submarine's topsounder and fathometer. The topsounder would send sonar pings up from one of four hydrophones mounted on top of *North Dakota*'s hull: two on the sail and one each on the bow and stern. The topsounder would detect ice above and provide warning if an ice keel descended toward them. To help avoid the occasional small iceberg, *North Dakota* would run deep, closer to the bottom than usual, using the fathometer to ensure they didn't run aground.

One of the sonar watchstanders shifted consoles, preparing to energize *North Dakota*'s High Frequency Array, the forward-looking under-ice sonar mounted in the front of the sail, which would detect ice formations ahead. The sonar technician entered the requisite commands, bringing the console on-line, then cast furtive glances toward the ship's Captain.

Tolbert knew what he was thinking. *North Dakota*'s topsounder and fathometer weren't detectable, emitting narrow high-frequency beams that bounced back to *North Dakota* after reflecting off the ocean's surface or bottom. That was not the case with the High Frequency Array, which sent pulses out in front of the submarine. Having set the Arctic Routine, Tolbert had to make the decision he'd been putting off—whether to energize the under-ice sonar and risk being detected.

Commander Tolbert announced his decision. "Attention in Control. We will not use our under-ice sonar. We'll let the Russians pick a path through the Marginal Ice Zone, and follow directly behind. Carry on."

Tolbert added, "Pilot, come to course three-five-five."

The Pilot entered the new course and *North Dakota* turned slightly left. Tolbert had been trailing the Russian submarine with an offset to starboard, but needed to trail directly behind while in the Marginal Ice Zone.

After *North Dakota* eased into position behind the Russian submarine, Tolbert turned back to the north. Moments later, the Quartermaster looked up from the electronic chart and announced, "Entering the Marginal Ice Zone."

7

MARGINAL ICE ZONE

YURY DOLGORUKY

Yury Dolgoruky continued her steady trek north at ten knots. Thus far, the topsounder had detected only sporadic chunks of sea ice floating above them, while the bottomsounder reported the smooth, shallow bottom of the Barents Sea, averaging only 230 meters in depth. However, Stepanov was focused on *Dolgoruky*'s Ice-Detection Sonar display, which displayed objects in front of them as a colored blotch. Different colors represented the intensity of the sonar return, with red indicating a large, deep, or dense formation.

Unfortunately, ice-detection sonars were not very good at determining the depth of the object, which is what ultimately mattered. The color of the ice was key. As *Dolgoruky* closed on the object, shallow ice keels would recede upward and exit the top of the ice-detection beam. As it receded, the color would change from bright red to darker, cooler colors until it faded to black.

The Ice-Detection Sonar used a simple geometry algorithm to determine if the obstacle was a threat. If the ice didn't change from red to another color within a certain distance—the Minimum Allowable Fade Range—Stepanov would have to turn or go deeper. The display was black; there were no ice formations ahead.

Several hours after entering the Marginal Ice Zone, Stepanov approached his First Officer.

"If an American submarine is following us, where are they?" Stepanov asked.

Pavlov answered, "They are directly behind us."

"Why?"

Pavlov replied, "They are not using their under-ice sonar, afraid we will detect it. They are using us to chart a safe path through the Marginal Ice Zone."

"Correct," Stepanov replied. "That is what I needed to determine."

When Stepanov did not amplify, Pavlov asked. "What is your plan?"

Stepanov replied, "We will use their lack of under-ice sonar against them."

"How do we do that?"

Stepanov smiled. "We continue north, under the polar ice cap."

USS *NORTH DAKOTA*

As *North Dakota* continued north, Tolbert stopped by the navigation plot, examining the multicolored curves on the display. They were midway through the Marginal Ice Zone, passing between the archipelagos of Svalbard to the west and Franz Josef Land to the east. If *Dolgoruky* held her northern course, she would slip beneath the polar ice cap in a few hours.

"XO." Tolbert summoned his Executive Officer, who joined him at the navigation plot. "Draft a message to CTF-69, advising them we're tracking *Yury Dolgoruky* and might proceed under the polar ice cap."

Lieutenant Commander Sites acknowledged and headed into Radio. The message was quickly drafted and Tolbert reviewed it, releasing it for transmission.

"Officer of the Deck, prepare to proceed to periscope depth. We have one outgoing."

8
WASHINGTON, D.C.

Seated at her desk in her West Wing office, National Security Advisor Christine O'Connor looked up from her computer display. Through her windows, she could see the Eisenhower Executive Office Building. Called the *wedding cake* by some due to its layered, palatial facade, the building housed the vice president's ceremonial office. A heavy snow had started falling this morning, and a thick blanket was already coating the ornate building.

The white landscape reminded Christine of the scenery around Moscow, which pulled her thoughts back to the document on her computer monitor; her report on nuclear arms reduction negotiations between the United States and Russia. The report detailed the agreements reached to date, the differences to be resolved, and the one issue Russia was unwilling to negotiate. She had her suspicions as to why, which she would lay out during her 9 a.m. meeting with the president.

Her thoughts were interrupted by a firm knock on her door. "Enter," she said, and the door opened, revealing a Naval officer in dress blues, with four gold stripes on each sleeve.

Captain Steve Brackman was the president's senior military aide. There was no one on the president's staff she had worked more closely with, agreeing on almost every issue. When engaging in battle with other staff over national security issues, it helped having the military on her side. A few months ago, when Brackman approached the end of his two-year tour, she had talked him into extending, not wanting to risk dealing with a replacement with opposing viewpoints.

"Good morning, Christine. The president's schedule has changed and he'd like to meet with us now."

Christine glanced at the document on her computer. She'd have to finish and send it to the president later. After grabbing the notepad from her desk, she joined Brackman and headed down the seventy-foot-long hallway and entered the Oval Office. The president was seated at his desk, and Kevin Hardison, the president's chief of staff, occupied one of three chairs facing him. Christine settled into the middle seat while Brackman sat beside her.

The president closed the folder on his desk and looked up at Christine. "How was your trip?"

"We made a lot of progress," Christine replied, "but there are many items left to resolve." She spent the next few minutes briefing the president, concluding with the one item upon which the United States and Russia completely disagreed.

"For some reason, they refuse to allow inspections of their new Bulava missiles or the Borei class submarines that carry them. They want to count launchers and not warheads."

Hardison interjected. "They want to go back to the way warheads were counted in the original START I treaty?"

"Correct. At least for their Bulava missile."

The president frowned. "Do you think it's because it can carry more warheads than we expect?"

"Exactly."

The president turned to Brackman. "What do you think?"

Brackman replied, "It could be that, or because it can decoy or even destroy incoming anti-ballistic missiles."

The president said to Christine, "Their Bulava missile *must* be subject to inspection. It's not negotiable."

"Under the New START treaty," Hardison reminded him, "we already have authorization to inspect missiles and board their Borei class submarines once they make their first deployment."

"That isn't their interpretation," Christine replied. "They maintain the treaty does not allow inspections of missiles or submarines that were not operational when the treaty was signed."

"Peel this onion apart," the president replied, looking at Christine. "Give me your appraisal of what we're allowed to inspect under New START and include an intelligence analysis of the Bulava missile."

"Yes, Mr. President. I'll meet with ONI tomorrow." Turning to Brackman, she said, "You should join me." Having a former ballistic missile submarine commander accompanying her might be useful.

9

ARCTIC OCEAN

YURY DOLGORUKY

Nicholai Stepanov leaned over the navigation table next to his First Officer, examining the topography of the surrounding water. *Yury Dolgoruky* was two hundred kilometers under the polar ice cap, steady on a northern course. Water depth was two hundred meters, leaving only a thin column of water to operate in, made even narrower by the random ice keels. Even though the underside of the polar ice cap was mostly flat, ice keels descended at unpredictable locations. The ice cap was not a solid sheet of ice, but a piecemeal collection of ice floes jammed together by the wind, currents, and waves. Where the edges met, they frequently buckled upward, creating surface ridges, and downward, creating ice keels that could descend sixty meters.

The ice floe edges did not always meet, creating leads, narrow gaps covered by a foot of slush, within which submarines could surface. There were also polynyas, ice-free holes the size of a small lake, often large enough for two or more submarines to surface. They were rare, however, with submarines almost always surfacing in leads or punching through a thin section of ice. As a result, submarines monitored the ice thickness during their transit, annotating locations where the ice was thin enough to break through.

Although the ice above was thick, they could still receive radio messages. Stepanov had deployed *Dolgoruky*'s VLF—Very Low Frequency—antenna, a one-inch-thick cable trailed behind the submarine several hundred meters. But the floating wire antenna could only receive; it could not transmit. As *Dolgoruky* headed deeper under the polar ice cap, Stepanov recalled his operational directives. He could not go much farther north.

The topsounder operator's report pulled Stepanov from his thoughts. "Ice thickness, ten meters." He listened intently as the Starshina Second Class announced, "Ice thickness, twenty meters," followed rapidly by "forty meters," then "sixty meters."

The ice stabilized at sixty meters, then receded. This was the deepest ice ridge they had passed; deep enough to suffice.

Stepanov addressed his First Officer. "When we detected the American submarine, you wanted to shift to the electric drive and launch a mobile decoy. I said then was not the right time. Remember?"

Pavlov nodded and Stepanov continued, "Now is the right time." He turned to the Command Post Watch Officer. "Load a mobile decoy in tube One and man Combat Stations."

USS *NORTH DAKOTA*

In the fast attack submarine's Control Room, Lieutenant Commander Sites, who had been stationed as Command Duty Officer for the midwatch, finished briefing Commander Tolbert.

"Contact is steady on course north, speed ten, range five thousand yards."

"You are secured as CDO," Tolbert said.

Not much had changed in the last six hours. *Dolgoruky* was still plodding along at ten knots, headed north. As Tolbert considered the Russian captain's intentions, traveling so deep under the polar ice cap, he surveyed the activity in the Control Room. The Navigator was on watch as Officer of the Deck this time, along with Lieutenant "JP" Vaugh as Junior Officer of the Deck, in charge of the Section Tracking Party. It was quiet in Control, not much going on. Tolbert settled into the Captain's chair in front of the navigation plot, preparing for a long, but hopefully uneventful day.

YURY DOLGORUKY

"All compartments report ready for combat."

Stepanov acknowledged, and Captain Lieutenant Evanoff added, "A mobile decoy has been loaded in tube One."

To evade the American submarine following them, Stepanov would launch one of his two mobile decoys. The decoy had a "swim-out" feature—it would propel itself out of the torpedo tube instead of being ejected. This was critical for two reasons: the swim-out capability eliminated the loud torpedo tube launch transient, which would alert the American submarine that *Dolgoruky* was up to something. Secondly, if the Americans detected the launch transient, it was possible they would conclude a torpedo was being fired at them and counterfire.

Captain Lieutenant Evanoff followed up, "Request decoy presets."

"Set course one-eight-zero," Stepanov replied, "ten knots, depth one hundred and forty meters. Set under-ice sonar transmissions—on."

Evanoff relayed the settings to the fire control Michman, who entered the parameters into his console. Stepanov checked the clock. It had taken four minutes to man Combat Stations and load a decoy.

Stepanov made the announcement loudly, so everyone in the Command Post could hear. "This is the Captain. I have the Conn. Steersman, left ten degrees rudder, steady course one-eight-zero." He turned to his Watch Officer. "Open muzzle door, tube One."

USS *NORTH DAKOTA*

"Sonar, Conn. Possible contact zig, Master One, due to upshift in frequency."

Tolbert noted the Sonar Supervisor's announcement, then stood and moved behind Petty Officer Tom Phillips, assigned as the Plots Operator for the Section Tracking Party. Phillips studied the time frequency plot, watching the tonal slowly increase, then steady up.

Phillips spoke into his headset, "All stations, Plots. Twenty knot upshift in frequency. Contact has either reversed course or is more broad and has increased speed. Analyzing."

Lieutenant Vaugh, seated at the command workstation as Junior Officer of the Deck, examined the time-bearing plot on his display. After noting the bearings to Master One were drifting left, he announced, "Confirm target zig, Master One. Set anchor range five thousand yards. Contact has turned to port and is on a closing trajectory."

A moment later, the Sonar Supervisor reported, "Receiving high-frequency ice-detection pulses from Master One."

Dolgoruky was definitely headed toward them.

YURY DOLGORUKY

"Steady on course one-eight-zero," the Steersman announced.

Stepanov acknowledged the report, then checked the geographic display on the fire control console. He had turned with a ten-degree rudder, putting *Dolgoruky* on a reciprocal course with a slow turn to the west. The last thing he wanted was to run into a submarine trailing them. The water column was very narrow, with only 140 meters between the ocean bottom and the lowest ice keels. After taking into account safety margins to the bottom and ice above, Stepanov figured both submarines were traveling at the same depth or close to it.

It would not be long before they would learn if the American submarine was still following them. He waited for a report from Hydroacoustic, but the Command Post speakers were silent. Another minute passed without a report, then a voice broke the silence.

"Command Post, Hydroacoustic. Hold a new contact on the towed array, designated Hydroacoustic seven, a sixty-point-two-Hertz tonal, ambiguous bearings one-six-zero and two-zero-zero."

Stepanov responded immediately—they were approaching the sixty-meter-deep ice ridge.

"Prepare to Fire, tube One."

His crew executed the order quickly, and in less than a minute, Stepanov received the report from Captain Lieutenant Evanoff. "Ready to fire, tube One."

"Launch decoy, tube One."

The fire control Michman announced, "Decoy launched from tube One."

Stepanov ordered, "All stop. Shift to electric drive." He glanced at the under-ice sonar. The ice keel was five hundred meters away. Stepanov followed up with, "Secure all sonars."

The watchstanders complied and the Steersman soon announced, "Propulsion has been shifted to the electric drive."

Dolgoruky had gone quiet, securing its main engines and sonars. There was one thing left to do. "Steersman, back one-third. Compensation Officer, set Hovering to fifty meters."

Dolgoruky slowed, rising toward the ice.

USS *NORTH DAKOTA*

"Conn, Sonar. Picking up transients from Master One."

"What kind of transients?" the Navigator asked.

The Sonar Supervisor answered, "We detected a faint broadband transient, which lasted for ten seconds. It wasn't metallic—it sounded more like cavitation. But there's been no change in Master One's frequency that would correlate to a speed increase."

As Tolbert tried to figure out what *Dolgoruky* was up to, he examined the sonar screens. *Dolgoruky*'s fifty-Hertz tonal was coming in stronger than ever now that *Dolgoruky* had turned toward them and was closing. How close would she get? He examined the geographic plot on Petty Officer Phillips's display. *Dolgoruky* was headed south at ten knots, with a CPA of two thousand yards.

Tolbert had a problem. At two thousand yards, *North Dakota* would likely be detected. But to open CPA range, he'd have to turn away, no longer following in *Dolgoruky*'s track. There was no way he was going to travel blindly under the ice cap, yet at the same time, he didn't want to activate his under-ice sonar, giving away *North Dakota*'s presence.

That was his dilemma. Activate his under-ice sonar and ensure counter-detection, or let *Dolgoruky* close to two thousand yards and hope for the best. Neither was a good option, but he chose the lesser of two evils. He would stay on course.

However, he could improve the odds *North Dakota* passed by undetected. "Pilot, all stop."

North Dakota's main engine turbines, reduction gears, and propulsor stopped spinning. Slowly, *North Dakota* coasted to a halt.

YURY DOLGORUKY

As *Dolgoruky* rose slowly toward the ice canopy, Stepanov monitored his submarine's depth and speed. They had risen to ninety meters, approaching zero knots.

"Steersman, all stop."

The sixty-meter-deep ice keel would soon be between *Dolgoruky* and the

American submarine. For Stepanov's plan to work, the American submarine had to stay on the other side of the keel, and that depended on whether *Dolgoruky*'s decoy fooled them.

As *Dolgoruky* rose to seventy meters, the Hydroacoustic Party Leader made the report Stepanov hoped for. "Command Post, Hydroacoustic. Ten knot downshift in frequency from Hydroacoustic seven. Contact is slowing or turning away."

The American submarine had either stopped or turned ninety degrees. When the decoy passed by, the American captain would hopefully turn and follow, staying on the other side of the ice keel.

The Steersman called out, "Depth, sixty meters, zero knots." *Dolgoruky*'s ascent slowed, and a moment later, Stepanov received another welcome report. "Command Post, Hydroacoustic. Loss of Hydroacoustic seven."

The ice keel was now between the two submarines, and if *Dolgoruky* could no longer track the American submarine, the Americans could not detect *Dolgoruky*.

"On ordered depth, fifty meters," the Steersman announced.

Dolgoruky hung motionless beneath the ice.

USS *NORTH DAKOTA*

Tolbert watched tensely as Master One approached its CPA of two thousand yards. As the contact closed, Sonar reported a detection of Master One on the spherical array and then the port Wide Aperture Array on *North Dakota*'s hull. It was quiet in the Control Room. Every watchstander realized how close the Russian submarine would come.

The contact's course and speed remained steady as it reached CPA, then passed by. When Master One opened to four thousand yards, Tolbert resumed trailing. "Pilot, ahead two-thirds. Left five degrees rudder. Steady course one-eight-zero."

North Dakota picked up speed and reversed course, and a few minutes later settled back into *Dolgoruky*'s wake. Master One remained steady on course and speed, giving no indication *North Dakota* had been detected.

As the tension eased from Tolbert's body, the Sonar Supervisor spoke into his headset. "Conn, Sonar. Request the Captain at Sonar."

Tolbert joined Chief Bob Bush on the port side of Control.

"We may have an issue," Bush began. "Master One passed by at two thousand yards, but we didn't pick up propulsion or steam-plant-related broadband. Additionally, we should have picked up other tonals, but we didn't. We held only the fifty-Hertz tonal and *Dolgoruky*'s ice-detection sonar."

Tolbert considered Chief Bush's report. The contact was too *clean*. Nuclear-powered submarines had dozens of pumps, electrical generators, and spinning turbines creating noise. At long distances, only strong, low-frequency tonals were detected. But as the range decreased, higher-frequency tonals as well as broadband would normally be heard. Either *Dolgoruky* was an incredibly quiet contact, or . . .

"We could be following a decoy," Bush said.

Tolbert was quiet. If they were following a decoy, it was no bigger than a torpedo. There was an easy way to determine whether they were following a small decoy or a large submarine—go active and measure the size of the object. But that would give away *North Dakota*'s presence. However, if they were following a decoy, they needed to figure it out fast before *Dolgoruky* slipped away.

"Transmit on MFA," Tolbert ordered, "Forward sector only, five-thousand-yard range scale."

A moment later, *North Dakota* transmitted on their Mid-Frequency Active sonar and the return lit up the sonar screen; directly ahead was a small white blip. Chief Bush reported, "Contact width is less than five feet."

Tolbert gritted his teeth. He'd been fooled into following a decoy. The Russian captain was good. But the game wasn't over. They hadn't been following the decoy very long and could still regain track on *Dolgoruky*. Tolbert recalled the short burst of cavitation they'd detected. That must have been when the decoy was launched. An examination of the navigation plot determined that spot was ten thousand yards to the north.

"Pilot, come to course north," Tolbert ordered. "Sonar, Conn. Prepare to transmit MFA, forward sector, ten-thousand-yard range scale."

North Dakota swung back to the north, and as she steadied up, Bush reported, "Conn, Sonar. Ready to transmit MFA."

"Transmit."

North Dakota transmitted, but this time, instead of a single contact, there was a wide band of white running across the screen.

"Ice keel at ten thousand yards," the Sonar Supervisor announced. "No contacts between us and the ice keel."

Tolbert immediately discerned what the Russian captain had done. He had gone shallow to place the ice keel between the two submarines, and was slipping away as *North Dakota* followed his decoy south.

There was no time to lose. Tolbert ordered, "Pilot, ahead full," then turned to the Officer of the Deck. "Station the Fire Control Tracking Party."

A few minutes later, the Fire Control Tracking Party was stationed, returning the Control Room to full manning as *North Dakota* sped north.

YURY DOLGORUKY

Captain Stepanov checked the clock in the Command Post. *Dolgoruky* had hidden behind the ice keel for thirty minutes. At ten knots, the American submarine would have traveled far enough for *Dolgoruky* to slip away.

"Set Hovering to one hundred and forty meters," Stepanov ordered. They were pointed directly at the ice keel, and would need to drop beneath it before restoring propulsion.

The Compensation Officer dialed in the depth, and valves in the variable ballast tanks opened, flooding water into the tanks. *Dolgoruky* began its descent.

Stepanov added, "Resume transmitting on top- and bottomsounders."

The two sonars started transmitting again, measuring the distance to the ice and bottom. As *Dolgoruky* dropped beneath the ice keel, offering a clear view of the water to the south, a report blared from the speakers. "Command Post, Hydroacoustic. Regain of Hydroacoustic seven, bearing one-seven-eight. SNR has increased nine decibels!"

Stepanov didn't need to do the calculations to know they were in trouble. They had previously held the American submarine at four thousand meters, which meant it was now only five hundred meters away.

Hydroacoustic followed up with, "Detecting broadband propulsion noises from Hydroacoustic seven. Contact is operating at high speed!"

Stepanov was no longer worried about detection. The American crew had discovered they were following a decoy much quicker than he expected, and their captain had run back up the decoy's track, directly toward *Dolgoruky*.

Assuming the American submarine was traveling at twenty knots, it would close the remaining distance in forty-five seconds.

Dolgoruky was at all stop. They could not turn out of the way. That left only two options—up, or down. An Emergency Blow would send *Dolgoruky* surging toward the ice, crushing the conning tower and maybe even puncturing the pressure hull. However, *Dolgoruky* was already descending, and maybe they could drop below the American submarine in time.

Stepanov shouted out, "Disengage Hovering! Flood all ballast tanks!"

USS *NORTH DAKOTA*

Commander Tolbert leaned over the navigation plot, examining the white dot representing *North Dakota*. They were on course three-five-eight, approaching the point where the Russian captain had launched the decoy, but they had not yet regained *Yury Dolgoruky* on any sensor. However, they were traveling at ahead full, blunting the range of their acoustic sensors, and Tolbert decided to slow and take a look around.

"Pilot, ahead two-thirds."

The Pilot entered the new propulsion order and as *North Dakota* slowed, the Sonar Supervisor announced, "Conn, Sonar. Hold a new broadband contact on the spherical array, designated Sierra three-seven, bearing three-five-eight. Analyzing."

Tolbert acknowledged the unusual report. Initial broadband gains were almost always merchant ships, and there were no merchants under the ice.

Chief Bush followed up, "Conn, Sonar. Hold the contact at zero elevation. SNR has increased threefold since we gained contact and continues to rise."

The Sonar Supervisor's report made no sense. How could Signal-to-Noise Ratio triple in only twenty seconds? He glanced at the MFA display on one of the sonar consoles, noting the white-banded return from their active pulse, painting the image of an underwater ice ridge. A ridge they were passing under now.

It was at that moment that Tolbert understood. The broadband contact they had picked up was *Dolgoruky,* dropping below the ice keel she had been hiding behind. They had picked her up on broadband, which meant she was close, and if signal strength had tripled in twenty seconds, that meant—

North Dakota jolted upward, knocking Tolbert off balance. He grabbed on to the navigation plot as a metallic screech tore through the air. Seconds later, everyone in Control was thrown forward as *North Dakota* slowed suddenly and the bow tilted downward.

10

USS *NORTH DAKOTA* • K-535 *YURY DOLGORUKY*

USS *NORTH DAKOTA*

The second jolt was more violent than the first, knocking every watchstander not buckled into their chairs to the deck and launching every unsecured item toward the forward bulkhead. The loose items crashed to the deck as the metallic screeching ceased, and *North Dakota*'s bow swung up to an even keel. The silence lasted for only a few seconds. The Flooding Alarm sounded, followed by a report blaring from the emergency 4-MC system.

"Flooding in the Engine Room! Flooding in Shaft Alley!"

The Co-Pilot reached toward the Ship Control Station and turned toward Commander Tolbert, awaiting direction to Emergency Blow. As Tolbert caught the Co-Pilot's eyes, he realized an Emergency Blow would send them careening toward the surface in an uncontrollable ascent, smashing into the ice cap.

"Do *not* Emergency Blow!" Tolbert shouted.

The Pilot announced another crisis. "Maneuvering reports all stop!"

A 7-MC report from the Engineering Officer of the Watch followed. "Conn, Maneuvering. The shaft has seized. Unable to answer bells."

Tolbert acknowledged, then called out, "Secure the Fire Control Tracking Party." He turned to Lieutenant Commander Sites. "Take charge in the Engine Room."

As the XO headed aft, accompanied by the Engineer Officer, *North Dakota*'s bow began tilting upward. They were taking on water aft. Tolbert checked *North Dakota*'s depth on the Ship Control Station. They were at three hundred feet and sinking. The Co-Pilot had lined up the drain pump to the Engine Room bilges, but more water was flooding in than was being pumped off.

Tolbert ordered, "Co-Pilot, line up the trim pump to take a suction on the drain system."

The Co-Pilot complied and both pumps began dewatering the Engine Room. Tolbert checked the ship's depth again. They were at 350 feet, still sinking.

The lights flickered in Control, and Tolbert realized Maneuvering had split the vital and non-vital electrical buses. That meant they were about to lose the turbine generators.

The 7-MC report explained. "Control, Maneuvering. Loss of all condensate pumps due to flooding."

The condensate pumps sent water from the turbine hotwells into the feed system, where it was sent into the steam generators to be turned into steam. No condensate pumps meant no steam, and no steam meant no propulsion or electricity. As *North Dakota* sank toward the bottom of the Barents Sea, Tolbert realized the situation was spiraling out of control.

YURY DOLGORUKY

Stepanov knew instantly they were in dire straits. The Compensation Officer was flooding all variable ballast tanks to increase *Dolgoruky*'s descent rate when Stepanov felt the first impact. A metallic grinding from above pierced the Central Command Post, and Stepanov concluded the top of *Dolgoruky*'s conning tower had impacted the underside of the American submarine, gouging the bottom of its hull as it passed by. Then a second jolt hit, accompanied by a horrible wrenching sound as Stepanov and the other watchstanders were knocked to the deck. *Dolgoruky*'s conning tower must have caught the edge of the American submarine's propulsor. As Stepanov landed on the deck, water flooded into the Command Post from around the periscope barrels.

Water sprayed in every direction, bouncing off bulkheads and equipment consoles. Stepanov wiped the cold water from his eyes as he pulled himself to his feet, assessing the damage. The tops of both periscope barrels were deformed. The conning tower must have been severely damaged and the periscopes bent.

They could not stop the flooding. Their only hope was that the flooding was within the capacity of the drain pumps. As Stepanov tried to make that assessment, the submarine's flooding alarm sounded, followed by reports from Compartments Two and Three. There was flooding from hatches to the escape pod in the conning tower.

As First Officer Pavlov headed aft to check on the escape pod, Stepanov knew this was a disastrous scenario. There was no way to stop the flooding, and an Emergency Blow under the ice would do them no good. He glanced at the depth gage. They were at 160 meters and sinking, and the bow began tilting downward due to the water flooding into the two forward compartments. The drain pumps were not keeping up. Confirming Stepanov's assessment, water surged into the Command Post from the level below.

They had to abandon the Central Command Post, and in the process, abandon hope they would gain control of the situation. He shouted as loud as he could, hoping he was heard over the roar of the inrushing water.

"Evacuate to Compartment One!" The watchstanders turned toward him and he shouted again, pointing toward the watertight door.

As the frigid water swirled around their knees, the watchstanders abandoned their posts, trying to maintain their balance as *Dolgoruky*'s down angle increased. Stepanov was the last to leave the Command Post, and as he did, he realized *Yury Dolgoruky* was lost.

USS *NORTH DAKOTA*

Four hundred feet and still sinking.

It was surprisingly quiet in Control; there was little more Tolbert and the Control Room watchstanders could do. They needed to stop the flooding, and *North Dakota*'s fate would be determined by personnel in the Engine Room. As Tolbert awaited the outcome, there was a modicum of good news. The submarine's up angle had steadied. Now that the trim and drain pumps were dewatering the Engine Room bilges, they were keeping up with the flooding. However, *North Dakota* was still negatively buoyant and continued sinking.

"Passing five hundred feet," the Co-Pilot announced.

Tolbert tried to imagine what it was like in the Engine Room. At a depth of five hundred feet, pressure was fifteen times greater than at sea level, and the water would shoot into the submarine with such force that personnel could not risk crossing paths with the high-pressure streams, which could cut through flesh and bone. The water would bounce off bulkheads and equipment, making it difficult to see, and the approach toward the flooding would be treacherous.

Lieutenant Commander George Sites leaned back against the hot surface of the port main engine, taking cover from the high-pressure water spraying in too many directions to count. Beside him was the Engineer, along with a phone talker wearing a sound-powered phone headset, while Sites held a WIFCOM radio in his hand. The three men were pinned down by the flooding, unable to get a clear look at the source or approach any closer. On the other side of the Engine Room, Sites spotted Chief Machinist Mate Tony Scalise, head of Machinery Division, and two other machinist mates.

Sites shouted into the WIFCOM so he'd be heard over the inrushing ocean. "Chief Scalise, XO. Have you determined the source of flooding?"

"XO, Scalise. The flooding is from shaft seals."

A pit formed in Sites's stomach. That was the one place they could not afford to have flooding. Other hull penetrations had primary and backup valves that could be shut, isolating breaches. The shaft had elaborate seals instead. If they failed, there was no valve to shut, but older submarines had an emergency "boot," which could be inflated around the shaft to stop flooding. Unfortunately, NAVSEA engineers, in their infinite wisdom, had not designed an inflatable boot into Virginia class submarines.

They were screwed.

Movement on the other side of the Engine Room caught Sites's attention. Chief Scalise and the two mechanics were moving aft, working their way between the high-pressure streams ricocheting throughout the Engine Room. The two Petty Officers each carried a green tool kit.

Sites shouted into his WIFCOM again. "Scalise, XO. What is your plan?"

Scalise replied, "Our shaft seals are designed so they can be tightened down, mating with the shaft. We just have to get there."

Scalise and the other two mechanics disappeared as they worked their way aft. A few minutes later, the torrent of water streaming into the Engine Room abated, then slowed to a trickle before ceasing altogether.

"Control, Maneuvering. The flooding is stopped."

Tolbert acknowledged the report, and he felt the submarine's deck returning to an even keel as the trim and drain pumps dewatered the Engine Room bilges. Depth was six hundred feet. They were still sinking, but the rate was slowing.

North Dakota returned to an even keel at the same time the submarine stopped sinking, then the numbers on the depth gage reversed. *North Dakota* began rising toward the surface.

"Co-Pilot," Tolbert ordered. "Hover at three hundred feet."

YURY DOLGORUKY

As *Dolgoruky* headed toward the ocean floor, Stepanov pulled himself into Compartment One. There was no one behind him and he ordered the watertight door sealed. As the door swung shut, he spotted three men in Compartment Two—Michman Glinka and the submarine's senior enlisted man, Chief Ship Starshina Egor Lukin, dragging their unconscious First Officer. As the rising water began surging through the opening into Compartment One, Stepanov assessed whether they could shut the door if he waited. He ordered the door kept open.

"Hurry!" Stepanov shouted.

When Glinka and Lukin reached the doorway, Stepanov helped drag his First Officer, who was bleeding heavily from a head laceration, into the compartment. Glinka and Lukin followed and Stepanov ordered the door shut. As water surged through the doorway, their feet slipped on the wet, sloping deck. Stepanov lent a shoulder and the door inched shut. Once closed, Stepanov spun the handwheel, engaging the lugs.

Dolgoruky shuddered and Stepanov and the others flew backward, bouncing off equipment, while water burst from the ventilation vents. Lukin clambered to his feet and shut the ventilation isolation valve, completely sealing Compartment One. A moment later, the lights in the compartment extinguished, enveloping Stepanov and his men in darkness.

11
USS *NORTH DAKOTA*

As *North Dakota* hovered at three hundred feet, Tolbert assessed the condition of his crew and ship. The flooding had been stopped and the Engine Room bilges were being dewatered. A dozen watchstanders in Control had been knocked to the deck by the second impact, but they had picked themselves up and no one appeared injured. The situation could have been far worse.

Lieutenant Commander Sites entered Control. He was soaked through and shivering.

"Damn, that water is cold," he said as he stopped beside Tolbert.

"Well done, XO," Tolbert replied.

"The credit goes to Chief Scalise and M-Division. They tightened the shaft seals."

Tolbert nodded. "I'll thank them when I get a chance. What's the status of the Engine Room?"

"Main propulsion is out. The propulsor must have been damaged in the collision, bending the shaft, which caused the flooding."

"Let's hope the Outboard still works," Tolbert said. "It won't move us fast, but two knots is better than zero knots."

"We've got bigger problems," the XO replied. "The Engine Room is down hard. Both condensate pumps were submerged in seawater and their controllers are soaked as well. Engine Room Forward has been dewatered and the Engineer and E-Division are checking things out, but even if we can restore the condensate system and resume steaming, it's not going to happen any time soon. Probably a couple of days, and the battery won't last that long."

Tolbert assessed the grim scenario. *North Dakota* was running on the battery now. Unfortunately, nuclear-powered submarine batteries lasted hours instead of days. Once power ran out, they wouldn't be able to operate their atmosphere control equipment. Even worse, if power ran out before the condensate pump repairs were complete, they wouldn't be able to start up the Engine Room. It was a paradox—they needed power to restore power.

Under normal circumstances, they would proceed to periscope depth and start the emergency diesel generator. But the diesel generator was a combustion engine. It needed air. The problem was, there was a layer of ice between them and the surface.

Tolbert replied, "Let's see if the ice is thin enough to break through." He turned to the topsounder watch. "Report ice thickness."

Petty Officer Bob Hornsey repeated back the order, then set the topsounder to detect the return from the bottom of the ice and the surface reflection from the top. By measuring the time difference between the two returns, the topsounder calculated the thickness of the ice. Additionally, the topsounder hydrophones could determine if the ice was flat or if there was an ice keel that could damage the submarine.

Hornsey activated the topsounder, then reported, "Ice thickness is ten feet, flat surface."

Tolbert didn't respond. Ten feet was too thick to break through. "Measure it again."

Hornsey acknowledged and sent another set of high-frequency pings toward the surface. His report was the same.

Tolbert stood with his hands on the navigation plot, evaluating the situation. If the repairs to the Engine Room took several days, they were toast.

"We're going to try to break through anyway," he announced. "Pilot," Tolbert ordered, "hover at one-eight-zero feet."

The Pilot complied, and *North Dakota* drifted upward.

"Co-Pilot, establish a three-degree up-angle." To crack the ice canopy, Tolbert would hit it with the reinforced forward edge of the sail. "Line up Emergency Blow to Main Ballast Tanks One-Alpha and Five-Bravo."

The Co-Pilot pumped water from Forward Trim to After Trim, and a few minutes later, *North Dakota* was hovering at 180 feet with a three-degree up-angle. The Co-Pilot reported, "Emergency Blow is lined up to One-Alpha and Five-Bravo."

Tolbert announced, "All stations, Conn. Vertically surfacing the ship. Co-Pilot, establish upward velocity of four-zero feet per minute."

The Co-Pilot pumped water off, and *North Dakota* rose toward the ice. "Four-zero feet per minute upward velocity," he announced.

The Pilot called out, "One hundred feet," then started reporting depth in ten-foot increments. After passing seven-zero feet, *North Dakota* shuddered when its sail hit the ice.

"Co-Pilot, Emergency Blow," Tolbert ordered. Hopefully the sail had cracked the ice and the buoyancy from the Emergency Blow would force the sail through.

As high-pressure air flowed into the ballast tanks, Tolbert waited for the first indication of success or failure. The bounce. When submarines hit the ice canopy, the sheet of ice flexed upward. If the attempt to break through the ice was unsuccessful, the ice canopy flexed back, pushing the submarine down about five feet.

North Dakota bounced downward.

Tolbert continued the Emergency Blow anyway. If the ice was especially thick, sometimes the submarine would bounce and still break through. *North Dakota* surged upward and hit the ice again, but then depth stabilized. The sail wasn't pushing through.

Air started spilling from the main ballast tanks, so Tolbert secured the blow. He waited a few minutes with the faint hope the sail would push through, but depth remained stable.

Lieutenant Commander Roger Swenson, the submarine's Engineer Officer, entered Control with a grim look. He joined Sites and Tolbert.

"The condensate controllers are fried," he said, "and both pumps are severely damaged. The backup pump kicked on when the primary went down, leaving us with two bad pumps."

"How long before one is repaired?" Tolbert asked.

"Not sure yet. We're checking supply for spares. We'll cannibalize anything else we need from the controller and pump in the worst shape. My best guess is it will take a few days. I've got more bad news," the Eng added. "The Outboard won't lower. It looks like the Russian submarine hit us along the keel and jammed the fairing."

They were stuck under the polar ice cap. Even if they restored power, they could not restore propulsion. Additionally, Tolbert couldn't inform anyone about their predicament. They couldn't transmit radio messages through the ice, and their high-frequency emergency SEPIRB buoys had the same problem. No one would become aware of *North Dakota*'s plight until they missed their reporting deadline in two days, and then what? How would they find them under the polar ice cap?

They had enough food for several months, but needed electricity to make water and keep the air breathable. Without power, they could last a week, no more. They had to snorkel or figure out how to make the battery last until they restored the condensate pumps and a turbine generator.

Tolbert decided to give it another try. "We're going to try to break through the ice again. "Co-Pilot, vent all Main Ballast Tanks. Pilot, hover at three hundred feet."

As the Pilot tapped in the ordered depth, the XO asked, "Why three hundred?"

"We're going to come up faster than authorized and hit the ice with more force."

"How fast?"

"Eighty feet per minute."

The XO ran his hand through his wet hair. "If we don't break through, we'll damage the sail and most, if not all, of our masts and antennas."

"If we don't break through, we've got bigger problems."

The Co-Pilot opened the Main Ballast Tank vents and *North Dakota* descended, steadying up at three hundred feet.

"Co-Pilot, increase up-angle to five degrees." Tolbert hoped to spare the aft section of the sail, where the snorkel mast was located, from damage.

Tolbert ordered, "Line up Emergency Blow to all Main Ballast Tanks." This time, they would create the maximum buoyancy to push the sail through the ice.

Shortly after the submarine's angle increased to five up, the Co-Pilot reported, "Lined up Emergency Blow to all Main Ballast Tanks."

Tolbert slipped the 1-MC microphone from its clip and informed the crew. He finished by directing all hands to brace for impact, then surveyed the faces of his XO and Engineer. They had nothing to add, so he turned toward the front of the Control Room.

"Co-Pilot, establish an eight-zero-feet-per-minute ascent rate."

The Co-Pilot began pumping water from the variable ballast tanks, and *North Dakota* started rising.

The Pilot announced, "Two hundred feet," then, "one hundred feet."

After passing seven-zero feet, *North Dakota* hit the ice hard, the impact accompanied by a metallic crunching sound. There was no doubt the sail had been damaged, but hopefully they had cracked the ice this time.

"Co-Pilot, Emergency Blow," Tolbert ordered.

As the high-pressure air flowed into the ballast tanks, Tolbert watched the depth gage. *North Dakota* bounced down again, this time ten feet. The submarine surged upward, hitting the ice again. As the Emergency Blow increased the submarine's buoyancy, Tolbert heard metallic groans from above. *North Dakota* was straining, pushing against the ice canopy.

Air spilled out of the ballast tanks again and Tolbert secured the blow. The groans from above were louder now, no longer masked by the sound of the high-pressure air. The sail was deforming. Thankfully, *North Dakota* didn't have hull-penetrating periscopes and Tolbert didn't need to worry about flooding into the Forward Compartment from around periscope barrels.

He checked the depth gage. There was no change.

Tolbert waited a few minutes before concluding their second attempt had failed. The ice was too thick. His shoulders slumped in defeat as he ordered the Co-Pilot to vent all Main Ballast Tanks. The Co-Pilot opened the vents, and as air escaped, reducing *North Dakota*'s buoyancy, the metallic groans ceased.

"Co-Pilot. Maintain the submarine five-zero thousand pounds positively buoyant."

Rather than pick a depth and float there, Tolbert decided to stay where they were, pressed against the polar ice cap. It was as good a place as any.

Having failed to break through the ice, Tolbert's thoughts turned to *Dolgoruky*. "Sonar Supervisor, do you have any indication of what happened to the Russian submarine?"

Chief Bush replied, "We'll pull up the broadband recording and see what we've got."

Petty Officer Thurlow selected the point where the two submarines collided, then hit play. The sounds of scraping and twisting metal were soon replaced with silence. Tolbert listened as the recording played on, and about a minute later, there was a deep rumbling sound that lasted a few seconds. Bush looked toward Tolbert, the conclusion evident in his eyes.

The Russian submarine had plowed into the ocean floor.

It was quiet in Control again, and the Engineer broke the uncomfortable silence. "The reactor is still up, but it's not doing us any good without the ability to steam the Engine Room. I recommend we shut down and secure as much equipment as possible."

"I concur," Tolbert said. "Shut down the reactor. As far as securing equipment, we're turning off everything. And I mean *everything*. All tactical systems and even atmosphere control equipment. That's the only way the battery will last long enough to repair a condensate pump. For atmosphere control, we'll bleed oxygen from the banks and scrub carbon dioxide using emergency CO_2 curtains."

The Engineer acknowledged, and as he headed aft, Tolbert realized their predicament was grim, but the resolution simple. They had to repair a condensate pump before the battery ran out.

It was a race against time.

12

K-535 *YURY DOLGORUKY*

In the yellow emergency lighting, Captain Stepanov picked his way through the crowded compartment, checking on his men as he evaluated his submarine. *Dolgoruky* had settled on the bottom of the Barents Sea at a twenty-degree down-angle, its bow buried in the silt, with a fifteen-degree list to port. The compartment had shifted to emergency lighting, indicating the Engine Room was down. The good news was the battery was still functioning and hadn't been shorted out by the flooding.

Stepanov stopped beside Senior Michman Andrei Popovich, the Torpedo Division Leading Petty Officer, who had donned a set of sound-powered phones, establishing communications with the rest of the submarine. Compartments Two and Three were flooded, but Compartments Four through Nine, in addition to Compartment One, were habitable.

The reactor had shut down upon impact with the bottom, and Reactor Department personnel were determining the extent of damage. However, it didn't matter. The Engine Room condensers had fouled after *Dolgoruky* settled on the ocean bottom, after the Main Seawater pumps sucked in too much silt. They could not start up the reactor.

There was a modicum of good news, however. They had completed a muster of *Dolgoruky*'s crew. There were fifty-seven personnel in the aft compartments, and forty-five men in Compartment One, which meant Stepanov's entire crew had evacuated to safety. There was only one serious injury—Stepanov's First Officer. Pavlov was lying on a makeshift bed on the empty torpedo decoy stow, where *Dolgoruky*'s Medical Officer, Captain of the Medical Service Ivan Kovaleski, was tending to him. His head was wrapped in white gauze to stop the bleeding, but a red stain had already seeped through.

"How is he?" Stepanov asked.

"Stable, for now," Kovaleski replied. "However, I cannot determine the extent of his injury. Hopefully it's only a severe concussion and not a fractured skull with internal bleeding. Time will tell."

As Stepanov nodded his understanding, his Chief Ship Starshina, Egor Lukin, joined Stepanov and Kovaleski. "The inventories are complete," Lukin said. "Food is not an issue and we have enough water for one week."

"What about the air regeneration units?" Stepanov asked.

Lukin replied, "We have enough potassium superoxide cartridges in Compartment One to sustain us for eight days, assuming the battery will power the regeneration units for that long. The men aft have enough cartridges to last ten days, since they have access to the cartridges in Compartments Five and Nine."

Stepanov ordered, "Pass the word to secure all unnecessary equipment. We need to ensure the battery can power the air regeneration units until we run out of cartridges. Also, I want every man to minimize his activity to reduce the amount of oxygen consumed and carbon dioxide produced."

"There is one more issue," Kovaleski added. "Hypothermia. The water temperature under the polar ice cap is minus two degrees Centigrade, below zero because salt water freezes at a lower temperature than pure water. It won't be long before temperature in the compartment drops below freezing."

"We can don our survival suits," Lukin replied. "They're designed to protect us during an escape into frigid waters. We have one hundred and sixty-five suits split evenly between the compartments with escape hatches. There should be fifty-five suits in Compartment One, which means we have enough for everyone here."

"Good idea, Chief Ship."

They had enough air regeneration cartridges to last eight days, assuming they didn't freeze to death in the meantime. However, no one would miss *Dolgoruky* until they failed to report in at the end of patrol. It would be two months before the Fleet realized disaster had befallen them. They would be dead by then.

"What do we do now, Captain?" Lukin asked.

"We wait," Stepanov answered, "and pray the American submarine also sank and their Navy comes looking for it."

"If the Americans reach us first, what then? We cannot abandon *Dolgoruky* and let them board her."

Stepanov contemplated Lukin's assertion, then replied, "We will deal with it when the time comes."

13

SUITLAND PARK, MARYLAND

Established in 1882, the Office of Naval Intelligence is the United States' oldest intelligence agency. Tasked with maintaining a decisive information advantage over America's potential adversaries, ONI's focus on naval weapons and technology was why Christine O'Connor, along with Captain Steve Brackman in the passenger seat of her car, were entering the forty-two-acre compound of the National Maritime Intelligence Center, only a short drive from the White House. Christine stopped in visitor parking, and after retrieving a notepad from her briefcase on the backseat, she and Brackman approached the four-story building.

Waiting inside the lobby was Pam Bruce, a supervisor in the three-thousand-member organization. After introducing herself, she said, "We have the appropriate experts waiting upstairs."

Pam escorted Christine and Brackman to a third-floor conference room occupied by two men in their fifties. "Greg Hartfield"—Pam pointed to the man on the left—"is our senior expert on Russia's Borei class submarines, and Stu Berman is our premier expert on the Bulava missile."

After introductions were complete, Christine spent several minutes providing the background on the new nuclear arms reduction treaty being negotiated with Russia, culminating with Russia's refusal to allow U.S. inspectors to board their Borei class submarines or inspect the Bulava missile. When she finished, she asked, "Why would the Russians take this position?"

"I'll go first," Hartfield said, "and provide an overview of the submarine, then Stu can follow up with the Bulava missile." Christine opened her notepad as Hartfield continued, "Russia has eight active ballistic missile submarines: one Typhoon, a Delta III, and six Delta IVs. All are approaching their end of life, with three slated for retirement in the next eighteen months.

"Enter the new Borei class. Russia plans to build eight total, and the last five will be an improved version with twenty missile tubes instead of sixteen. The first Borei class submarine, *Yury Dolgoruky,* was launched several years ago, but has been plagued with material problems and software issues with its missile launch system, which delayed its commissioning for five years. Even after it was commissioned, her initial patrol was postponed repeatedly by issues with its new Bulava missile, which is Stu's area of expertise."

Greg Hartfield fell silent and Berman began. "Originally, the Borei submarines were supposed to carry an upgraded version of the R-39 missile designed for the Typhoon class. However, after the first three test firings resulted in catastrophic failures, the R-39 upgrade program was terminated. Instead, Russia developed the Bulava, an entirely new missile. It too was plagued with problems, due to the shortened timeline to develop a new missile quickly enough to support the Borei class submarines.

"Each missile has a range of six thousand, two hundred miles, and can be equipped with up to ten warheads, although there is some debate on the maximum number. The warheads are fully shielded against electromagnetic pulse damage and have a yield of one hundred fifty kilotons each. The Bulava is highly advanced, and we believe it is capable of evasive maneuvering and may have decoys that can be deployed to fool anti-ballistic missiles.

"As I mentioned, the Bulava missile was plagued with problems, with six of the first twelve test launches being failures. It appeared they had resolved the problems, because the next six launches were successes, and the Russian Navy accepted the missile into service two years ago. However, missile production was suspended eighteen months ago and all missiles were recalled."

"Why did they halt production?" Christine asked.

"Most likely for an upgrade. What type, we don't know. They must be back in production, however, because they loaded missiles aboard *Dolgoruky,* which raises some concerns."

"What concerns?" Christine asked.

"Missile production hasn't resumed at their manufacturing facility, yet *Dolgoruky* was able to load out. That means there is a second production facility we know nothing about, and without the ability to target it for intelligence gathering, we're completely in the dark as to what kind of modifications they've made and what type of payload is installed."

"That would certainly explain why they don't want us to inspect the

Bulava missile," Christine said. Turning toward Hartfield, she asked, "Do you know of any reason why the Russians wouldn't want START inspectors aboard Borei class submarines?"

Hartfield answered, "It's possible the launch system displays the number and type of warheads loaded on each missile, as well as its countermeasures, so operators can monitor their status as the missile is spun up and target packages are assigned. That'd be my guess."

Christine asked Captain Brackman, "Do you have any questions?"

Brackman shook his head. "I think we've covered everything."

Christine turned back to the two men. "Thank you, gentlemen. You've been very helpful."

14

K-535 *YURY DOLGORUKY*

After two days, the emergency lanterns in Compartment One were starting to dim. Stepanov had divided them into four sets, so that all together, they would last eight days. As the light decreased, so had the temperature. It was just above freezing. Although their survival suits guarded against hypothermia, it was still painfully cold. Thankfully, the air regeneration canisters generated heat as they produced oxygen and absorbed carbon dioxide, and Stepanov's men took turns gathered around the air regeneration unit.

Stepanov was in the midst of a round through the compartment, checking on his men. His First Officer was still unconscious, and Medical Officer Kovaleski was worried he might not recover. Stepanov stopped by Starshina First Class Oleg Devin, who was taking air samples. He broke the tips of the glass tube and inserted it into the handheld pump, then squeezed it five times, drawing air through the tube. This tube measured oxygen, and read 17.2 percent.

Stepanov moved on, stopping by Senior Lieutenant Ivan Khudozhnik, the Torpedo Division Officer, whose men were taking turns manning the sound-powered phones, staying in communication with the men in Compartments Four through Nine. Stepanov found it both odd and comforting; this was the Torpedomen's compartment, and it was their duty to man the phones during emergencies. It was as if they were oblivious to the fact that their submarine was wrecked, that they would likely not survive. The adherence to their obligation to man the phones, however, provided a sense of normalcy.

"How is everyone doing?" Stepanov asked.

"It is quiet," Khudozhnik replied.

Khudozhnik's response was as close to *all is well* as one could expect.

15

USS *NORTH DAKOTA*

Commander Tolbert headed aft, stepping from the freezing Forward Compartment into the welcome warmth of the Reactor Compartment Tunnel. Even though the reactor was shut down, it was still generating heat from the decay of fission by-products. It was probably only sixty degrees in the passageway, but compared to the other two compartments, it was downright balmy. It was now thirty-five degrees inside the Forward Compartment and Engine Room.

Tolbert stepped through the watertight doorway into the Engine Room. Inside the near-freezing compartment, his breath condensed into white mist. Several crew members wore the orange "pumpkin suits," thick full-length foul-weather gear worn by personnel on the Bridge in harsh weather. However, the ship had only ten suits, and the rest of the crew had donned Submarine Escape Immersion Equipment suits to preserve body heat. The insulated SEIE suits, also orange, came with flexible black neoprene gloves and a polar fleece head mask.

Upon entering the Engine Room, Tolbert took in the scene. It was a virtual rain forest. As the temperature plummeted, the water vapor in the air condensed on the cold metal surfaces, and water was dripping from piping, machinery, and walkways. Tolbert entered Maneuvering, a ten-by-ten-foot control room. Normally occupied by an officer and two enlisted, there was only one man present. Petty Officer Second Class Allen Terrill manned the Electric Plant Control Panel, monitoring battery discharge rate and voltage.

"What do you think?" Tolbert asked.

"It doesn't look good, Captain," Terrill replied. "The battery is already down to thirty percent; enough power for one more day. It's probably the low temperature, reducing capacity."

The battery was draining faster than expected. They needed to return a condensate pump to service soon. He had headed aft to get an update, and the answer better be—within a day.

Tolbert left Maneuvering and descended to Engine Room Forward, where he found the Engineer Officer, Lieutenant Commander Roger Swenson; the Electrical Division Chief, Mike Moran; and two first class electrician's mates, Art Thompson and Tim Brandon. Thompson was working on a condensate pump controller, while Brandon was repairing one of the pumps.

The covers were off both controller cabinets, and as Chief Moran aptly described it, they were a hot mess. Almost every circuit card had been damaged, some with charred components, while other cards were more difficult to diagnose. Even the smallest component gone bad could prevent operation. Supply didn't have a spare for every card in the controller, forcing Thompson to triage the cards with no spares. He had picked the best one between the two controllers, and was now diagnosing which components had been damaged. The cards were laid on a rubber mat, keeping them away from dripping water, and he was taking measurements with a multimeter.

Brandon was working on the pump. Normally, a wetted pump had a decent shot of returning to service. However, Number One Condensate Pump had been running for several hours, and when its hot internals had been doused with twenty-nine-degree salt water, the pump had turned into a rotating molten fireball. Number One Condensate Pump was unrepairable.

That left the second pump. Unfortunately, Number Two Condensate Pump had turned on when its partner tripped off-line, starting up at the same time it was submerged in seawater. It had fared much better, but its stator had been damaged. There was little Brandon could do to fully repair it, but he was giving it his best shot.

Chief Moran was supervising the two first class Petty Officers, studying the controller schematic in the tech manual. At the end of the day, they didn't need to fully repair a controller and pump. The pump just had to run. Moran was figuring out how to circumvent the bad components that could not be replaced.

Moran had his four best electricians working the problem. Thompson and Brandon had this twelve-hour shift and Bowser and Radek the other. By the time the electricians were done, the controller and pump were going to look like little Frankensteins, pieced back together. Tolbert didn't care as long as they came alive when the switch was flipped, and that the repairs were completed before the battery was expended.

The Engineer Officer wasn't much help when it came to controller and pump repairs, but there was nothing more important than restoring the condensate system, so he hovered in Engine Room Forward like an expectant father.

"Eng, how much longer?" Tolbert asked.

The Engineer looked at Moran. The chief must have felt eyes on him, because he looked up from the schematics. "Three, maybe four days."

Moran's response hit Tolbert in the gut. The battery would be drained in one day.

"You've got twenty-four hours, Chief," Tolbert said. "Make it happen." Tolbert often challenged his subordinates to meet tight schedules. This time, however, it didn't work.

"It can't be done, Captain," Moran replied. "We're going as fast as we can. Three or four days is what it's going to take."

Tolbert looked to his Engineer, but Swenson confirmed his Chief's assessment. "It's the best we can do, sir."

"Then we need to solve the battery problem," Tolbert said.

The Engineer replied, "We need to preserve enough power to complete a reactor and engine room start-up. I recommend we open the battery breaker."

Tolbert considered his Engineer's suggestion. *North Dakota* would become completely dead—a cold metal carcass beneath the polar ice cap. However, he could think of no alternative.

"All right," he said. "I'll let the crew know what's going on. In the meantime, you'll need to set up to continue repairs using emergency battle lanterns."

A few minutes later, Tolbert entered the Control Room. Even though the tactical systems had been deenergized, he had left the normal underway watches stationed; they were performing an important task. Moisture was condensing on the metal surfaces, including the sonar and combat control consoles, navigation plot, Radio Room equipment—everything. It was one thing for water to drip from piping and machinery in the Engine Room, another to allow it to seep inside the tactical consoles. Each watchstander was armed with Kimwipes, the Navy version of lint-free paper towels, and the men were wiping down the consoles.

Tolbert stopped beside Lieutenant Molitor, who was stationed as the Officer of the Deck, and explained the plan. Molitor passed the word to all spaces, and a few minutes later, he retrieved an emergency battle lantern mounted in the overhead, then gave the order.

"LAN Technician, open the battery breaker."

The Petty Officer repeated back the order, then headed to lower level, where the battery was located. Shortly thereafter, the Control Room went dark. There was no electronic life aboard the submarine, not even a solitary indicating light. Molitor flicked on his battle lantern, and a bright shaft of light pierced the darkness.

Tolbert reached up and retrieved a second lantern. As he debated where to head next, he realized he had lost track of time. He turned on his lantern and checked his watch. It was 0855 Greenwich Mean Time. *North Dakota's* next report was due in five minutes.

16

NORFOLK, VIRGINIA

In the U.S. Navy compound off Terminal Road, Petty Officer Second Class Vince Harms sat at his console in the Communication Center. It was approaching 4 a.m., but as usual, the message traffic was brisk this time of day. With submarines synchronizing their day to Greenwich Mean Time, it was almost 0900 on every American submarine on deployment. The workday had begun, and those authorized to transmit had uploaded their radio messages.

Harms checked the printout listing the submarines due to report in during his watch. It was only a few minutes before *North Dakota*'s deadline, but Harms wasn't worried. She was on a northern run, and submarine crews in trail often pushed it to the limit as they waited for an opportune time to come to periscope depth and transmit, without losing contact of their adversary.

He busied himself with additional message traffic, then checked the message queue again at exactly 0900. No message from *North Dakota*. He waited another minute to be sure, then looked around the Communication Center, spotting Chief Marc Arsenault, the supervisor during tonight's midwatch, standing behind another radioman on duty.

"Chief," Harms called out. Chief Arsenault looked over as the junior radioman added, "We've got an issue. *North Dakota* is overdue."

The Chief stopped behind Harms and examined the printout by his console, then glanced at the time displayed on the Communication Center wall.

"Yep," Arsenault replied, "we got a problem. Draft a message to *North Dakota,* directing her to report in ASAP, and a SUBLOOK message for all commands. I'll brief the Watch Officer and get authority to release."

———

Later that afternoon, sitting at his desk in COMSUBLANT's headquarters, Vice Admiral Bob Tayman waited impatiently for word from *North Dakota*. She was now twelve hours overdue. It wasn't the first time a submarine had failed to report in, the crew engrossed with the tactical situation, unaware the clock had struck midnight and they had turned into a pumpkin. However, the probability that something had happened to *North Dakota* was increasing with each passing hour.

A SUBLOOK had been issued, but the timeline to implement SUBMISS procedures wasn't written in stone. It was a judgment call, depending on the situation. Twelve additional hours would normally be enough time to convince him something had gone wrong. But *North Dakota* had gone under the ice, and her ability to transmit would be affected by the availability of open leads or polynyas, or ice thin enough to surface through. Still, *North Dakota*'s commanding officer would have taken that into account.

If he initiated SUBMISS procedures, he would expend millions of dollars in the effort, perhaps for nothing more than a false alarm. However, if *North Dakota* was in distress, there was no time to waste. His head hurt as he thought about the implications—a submarine sunk under the polar ice cap. How would they find it? The 406 MHz transmission from their emergency SEPIRB buoys wouldn't penetrate the ice.

There was a knock on the door and Tayman acknowledged. Captain Rick Current, his chief of staff, entered. It was the end of the day and time to make a decision.

Tayman gave the order. "Initiate SUBMISS procedures for *North Dakota*."

17

NORTH ISLAND, CALIFORNIA

It was mid-afternoon in San Diego as Commander Ned Steel leaned back in his chair, taking a break from reviewing the paperwork in his inbox. Steel was the commanding officer of the Navy's Undersea Rescue Command, located on the western shore of North Island, across the water from Naval Base Point Loma, home to Squadron ELEVEN's fast attack submarines.

Steel's second-story window overlooked the test pool, a twenty-by-fifty-foot pool used to train pilots for the Atmospheric Diving Suit, and Steel took a moment to observe the latest training dive as the launch system lowered the suit into the water. Built from forged aluminum with sealed rotary joints, and attached to an umbilical for power and communications, it could descend to two thousand feet.

Because the inside of the ADS was maintained at normal surface pressure, it wasn't a diving suit at all. It was actually a deep submergence vehicle, operated by the pilot inside the contraption. Maneuvered by two thruster packs and with a light and camera on one shoulder and a sonar transducer on the other, the ADS's primary mission was to determine the condition of a sunken submarine and clear off any debris from the hatch area so the rescue vehicle could mate.

As the command's name implied, rescuing a distressed submarine's crew was what the Undersea Rescue Command was all about. Although the ADS could investigate a sunken submarine, the rescue effort fell to the Submarine Rescue System. Steel's eyes shifted to the SRS, staged not far from the test pool. The SRS consisted of three main components: the Pressurized Rescue Module, the Launch and Recovery System, and two hyperbaric decompression chambers.

Steel's BlackBerry vibrated at the same time his personal cell phone and desk phone rang. He checked his BlackBerry as the two phones continued ringing. It was a text message from the Squadron ELEVEN Operations Center. Steel answered his desk phone and, as expected, heard an automated message. A SUBMISS message had been sent. He turned to his computer, where another prompt was displayed on screen. He pulled up his email, and the unclassified message was at the top of his inbox.

Steel read the message quickly, and as he finished, his XO and lead contractor arrived. Lieutenant Commander Marlin Crider and Peter Tarbottom had their cell phones in hand. Tarbottom was an Australian expatriate who made America his home when he joined Phoenix International twenty years ago. The fifty-year-old with the colorful language was the senior supervisor for the contingent of contractor personnel supporting the Undersea Rescue Command.

"What are the details?" Steel's XO asked.

"*North Dakota* is twelve hours overdue."

"All right," Tarbottom said as he interlocked his fingers and cracked his knuckles. "I'll get the men packing. What port will we be loading out from?"

"I don't think we'll be loading out from a port," Steel said, as he tried sorting through the implications of *North Dakota*'s location.

"What do you mean?" Tarbottom asked. "We have to load onto a ship somewhere."

"I don't think a ship is going to take us where we need to go."

"And where might that be?"

"*North Dakota* is under the polar ice cap."

"Aw, crikey!" Tarbottom exclaimed. "Under the ice?"

Tarbottom had summarized the problems facing them in one succinct question. Could the ADS and SRS function in subfreezing temperatures? How would they get the equipment onto the ice cap? Five C-5s or fifteen C-17s were required to transport the equipment to an airport, where it would be trucked to a nearby port and loaded aboard an awaiting ship. However, there was no ship that could transport the equipment to the rescue location and serve as a base of operations.

Even if they got the equipment onto the ice, what would they anchor the Launch and Recovery System to? The hydraulic lift system was normally bolted to supports welded to the deck of the surface ship, holding the A-frame in place as it lifted the twenty-ton PRM and lowered it into the water.

Without being secured to something, the A-frame would topple over when it tried to lift the PRM.

"We've got our challenges," Steel replied, "but the Navy has an even bigger problem."

"What's that?" Tarbottom asked.

"How are they going to find *North Dakota*?"

18

POINT LOMA, CALIFORNIA

The conversation had been short, and Director Bobby Pleasant hung up the phone with a single thought.

It was an impossible task.

Pleasant was the director of the U.S. Navy's Arctic Submarine Laboratory. Located in warm San Diego, California, the Arctic Submarine Lab was responsible for developing and maintaining the skills, equipment, and procedures enabling the United States Submarine Force to operate safely and effectively in the Marginal Ice Zone and under the polar ice cap.

Before *North Dakota* departed for its northern run, Arctic Submarine Lab personnel had trained the crew to operate safely in the unique Arctic environment. Had Pleasant known the submarine was headed under the polar ice cap, he would have recommended they take an ice pilot, which was the normal protocol. However, *North Dakota* wasn't supposed to head under the ice; whatever the crew was trailing must have taken her there.

In addition to training and assigning ice pilots to submarine crews during under-ice missions, the Arctic Submarine Lab was responsible for planning and executing periodic ice exercises, or ICEXs, which included the establishment of Arctic ice camps, especially when submarines were shooting exercise torpedoes under the ice. Exercise torpedoes floated to the surface after completing their run, where the multimillion-dollar weapons were retrieved and sent back to a maintenance facility for refurbishment. However, under the ice cap, the torpedoes didn't float to the surface; they bumped up against the ice. So Arctic ice camps were established with the personnel and equipment to locate the exercise torpedoes and retrieve them.

It was the Arctic Submarine Lab's experience in establishing ice camps, as well as locating torpedoes under the ice, that resulted in the phone call

Pleasant had just received. However, locating a sunken submarine was a far different task than finding a torpedo. Exercise torpedoes had end-of-run pingers that were detected by a sonar array laid on top of the ice, plus the ice camp personnel already knew the area in which the torpedoes would be fired; typically only a few square miles. *North Dakota's* location was unknown. At this time of year, the polar ice cap was at its maximum extent, and the submarine could be anywhere beneath six million square miles of ice.

Pleasant picked up his phone and called two men. A moment later, Vance Verbeck, the Arctic Submarine Lab's Technical Director, and Paul Leone, the Lab's most experienced ice pilot and a retired submarine commanding officer, entered his office.

"What's up?" Verbeck asked.

"There's a SUBMISS on the broadcast. *North Dakota* is twelve hours overdue."

Verbeck was silent for a moment, then said, "Since you called us in here, I take it *North Dakota* went down under the ice cap."

Pleasant nodded.

"Do we know where she sank?"

"I'm afraid not," Pleasant replied.

"What *do* we know?"

Pleasant located the SUBMISS message on his computer, then read aloud the pertinent details. *North Dakota* was last located eighty-five hours ago in the Marginal Ice Zone in the Barents Sea, headed north. Pleasant read off the latitude and longitude, and the three men turned to a laminated map of the Arctic on Pleasant's far wall.

Paul Leone pulled the cap off a dry-erase marker and put an X on the LAT/LONG position. Directly north was the gap between Svalbard and Franz Josef Land. He sketched a narrow wedge, widening out from *North Dakota's* last known position, constrained by the shores of Svalbard to the west and Franz Josef Land to the East. Once past the two archipelagos, he drew a larger wedge expanding outward at forty-five degrees.

"Let's assume an average speed of ten knots," Leone said. "If she was trailing a ballistic missile submarine, it's unlikely they were traveling any faster. Assuming she went down somewhere between her last position and seventy-two hours later when she missed her reporting deadline, that gives us a maximum distance traveled of seven hundred and twenty nautical miles."

He drew a straight line north from *North Dakota*'s last known position, then marked off the distance in one-hundred-nautical-mile increments. When he reached 720, he drew a curved top to the wedge and then cut off the bottom, marking the maximum extent of the ice cap at this time of year, then stepped back.

Leone had drawn an area resembling a slice of pie with the crust at the top, and a bite taken off the bottom. It was approximately six hundred miles long with an average width of two hundred miles.

"She's somewhere in here," Leone said.

Pleasant did the math. Assuming Leone was correct, they had narrowed the search area from six million to 120,000 square miles. However, the sonar array they laid over the ice covered only four square miles. It would take at least a day to transport, set up, and listen in each of the four square miles. That meant it would take thirty thousand days—more than eighty years—to cover the 120,000 square mile area.

"Well," Pleasant said, "it's a start."

He looked up at his technical director. "We need to expand the area we can search with the tracking array. Let's combine the two arrays we have and add our spare hydrophones. Find a spot for the ice camp as close to the center of the search area as possible, and we'll start from there. We'll need multi-year ice, the thickest we can find."

Verbeck examined the map. "Let's stage out of Svalbard. We can fly everything into the airport at Longyearbyen, then transport it to the ice camp from there."

"Sounds good," Pleasant replied.

He turned to Leone. "Find out what aircraft the submarine rescue equipment is transported in, and what the aircraft weighs fully loaded, so we can figure out if it can land on the ice, or we'll have to get the equipment there another way. Also, if we locate *North Dakota,* we'll need to lower the rescue vehicle through the ice. This won't be as easy as cutting a three-foot hole for torpedo retrieval. Coordinate with the Undersea Rescue Command and NAVSEA and come up with a way to cut a hole in the ice, large enough for the submersible."

Pleasant turned back to Verbeck. "This ice camp will be different than a normal one. For starters, we're going to need more berthing hooches for the submarine rescue personnel, and who knows who else will be up there.

More food, more fuel, more heating oil, more cold-weather gear, more transportation—you get the picture. Get everyone moving and start figuring things out."

"Got it," Verbeck said.

He headed out the door, but Leone didn't move. He was contemplating something.

"What is it?" Pleasant asked.

"We need a backup plan. Even if we find *North Dakota*, there's no guarantee the submarine rescue equipment will work in sub-zero temperatures or we'll be able to cut through the ice fast enough."

"Your backup plan is . . . ?"

"What if we try to rescue *North Dakota* from below the ice?"

"Below the ice? How would we do that?"

Leone took a moment to outline his plan.

19

WASHINGTON, D.C.

It was almost 6 p.m. and Christine O'Connor was about to call it a day. Sitting at her desk, she flipped the next page of the document in front of her. She had spent the last few hours reviewing the New START Treaty, which incorporated many improvements over START I. In addition to reducing the number of deployed nuclear warheads by two-thirds, it also required counting the warheads on each deployed ICBM and SLBM, rather than relying on an assumed number of warheads per launcher. What the Russians proposed in Moscow was a return to START I methodology.

New START gave the United States the authority to conduct a Type One inspection on all deployed and nondeployed strategic offensive arms sites, giving the United States the ability to verify the number of warheads. There was one fly in the ointment, however. Russia's new Bulava missile and Borei class submarines were not yet listed in the latest biannual exchange of data. Russia had deliberately kept them off the list. If they were not on the list, they could not be inspected. However, by not including them on the list of strategic arms, Russia was in direct violation of New START.

As she leaned back in her chair, evaluating how to address the flagrant violation, there was a knock on her door. Christine acknowledged and Captain Brackman entered.

"The president wants us in the Situation Room."

"What's up?" Christine asked.

"Richardson and N97 are on the way over from the Pentagon to brief the president."

Christine wondered what could be so important as to warrant a visit by the secretary of defense and the Director of Undersea Warfare at 6 p.m. Before she could ask, Brackman added, "Admiral McFarland and Dawn Cabral are on the way too."

Something was brewing. The CNO was joining them, and the secretary of state's presence meant the issue had international implications.

"Do you know what the topic is?"

"Yes," Brackman replied, and Christine could sense the concern in his voice. "They think USS *North Dakota* has sunk beneath the polar ice cap."

Christine and Brackman were the first to arrive in the Situation Room, joined shortly by Secretary of State Dawn Cabral, Press Secretary Lars Sikes, and Chief of Staff Kevin Hardison. The president arrived moments later, followed by SecDef Don Richardson and two Admirals: Michael McFarland, the Chief of Naval Operations, and Rear Admiral Gary Riley, the Director of Undersea Warfare. The president took his seat at the head of the table, joined by the eight other men and women in the Situation Room.

"For those who haven't been prebriefed," Richardson began, "we believe one of our fast attack submarines, USS *North Dakota,* has sunk beneath the polar ice cap. Admiral Riley is here to brief us."

Admiral Riley passed around a stack of PowerPoint briefs. As the president received his copy, he asked, "What was the submarine doing up there?"

Riley replied, "*North Dakota* is on a northern run in the Barents Sea, tasked with tracking Russian submarines." He flipped to the first page of the brief, which showed a map of the Arctic Ocean and the northern shore of Russia. "Russia's first Borei class submarine, *Yury Dolgoruky,* departed Gadzhiyevo Naval Base five days ago for her first strategic patrol, and *North Dakota* was assigned to collect intel. We know very little about Borei class submarines—their sound characteristics and operating patterns. *North Dakota* began tracking *Dolgoruky* once she entered the Barents Sea, and her last transmission placed both submarines in the Marginal Ice Zone, headed north. We believe *North Dakota* followed *Dolgoruky* under the ice, where something happened to *North Dakota.*"

"Are we certain *North Dakota* sank?" the president asked.

"No, sir," Riley replied. "That's why we've issued a SUBMISS instead of a SUBSUNK. There are three submarine rescue alert levels," he explained. "A SUBLOOK message gets issued when a submarine fails to report in on time. Once there's reason to believe a submarine has sunk or is in distress, a SUBMISS goes out and we begin mobilizing rescue resources. Once we've confirmed a submarine has sunk, we issue a SUBSUNK."

Riley continued, "It's possible *North Dakota*'s crew is okay and unable to report in for some reason, but the likelihood they have suffered a serious casualty increases with each hour."

Captain Brackman asked, "Have we detected any explosions or other acoustic events that might provide a clue as to what happened?"

"We've heard nothing so far," Riley replied. "Which at least means no torpedoes have exploded, either deliberately or by accident."

"How long can the crew survive?" the president asked.

"They have enough emergency supplies to keep the air viable for seven days. In the worst case, if *North Dakota* went down shortly after her last transmission, the crew has three days left. In the best case, if something happened just before she was due to report in, they have six days left. However, if they have electrical power and can run their atmosphere control equipment, they'd be okay for several months, until they run out of food. For now, we're assuming they have no power and time is critical."

Riley flipped to the next page of his brief, which showed a map of the Barents Sea and the pie-shaped area drawn by Paul Leone, the ice pilot from the Arctic Submarine Lab.

"This is where we think *North Dakota* sank. We'll focus our search over the Barents Shelf, where the water is shallow. If *North Dakota* went down in the north, in the Nansen Basin, the crew is lost. Water depth in the basin is over twelve thousand feet, and the pressure hull would have imploded. We haven't detected any implosions, so that means if she's on the bottom, she's on the Barents Shelf.

"Which gets me to the next issue. Our rescue plans." Riley flipped the page.

He began with the resources most people were familiar with. "We used to have two Deep Submergence Rescue Vehicles, or DSRVs—*Avalon* and *Mystic,* which attached to a mother submarine for transit to the rescue location. However, *Avalon* was decommissioned in 2001 and *Mystic* was retired in 2008. Their replacement is the Submarine Rescue Diving and Recompression System, located at the Undersea Rescue Command in San Diego.

"Our Arctic Submarine Lab will establish a base camp on the ice cap, where we'll begin our search efforts. Once we locate *North Dakota,* we'll transport the rescue equipment onto the ice." Riley continued, "There are a lot of details still to be worked out, but we have a plan.

"Additionally, we have a Plan B," he added. "Our rescue equipment wasn't designed to operate in the Arctic environment and was also built to deploy from the deck of a support ship, not atop the ice. Even if we find *North Dakota* and the rescue equipment arrives in time, there's the possibility it won't function properly or be too heavy for the ice. Our backup plan is to send one of our guided missile submarines under the polar ice cap. Deployed SSGNs carry two platoons of SEALs and an equal number of Navy divers. If necessary, they may be able to ferry emergency supplies to *North Dakota* and escort personnel off in small groups. The nearest SSGN will be receiving orders on her next trip to periscope depth."

"What do we tell the public?" Press Secretary Sikes asked. He looked to the president, who referred the question to Riley.

"For now," Riley answered, "I recommend we say nothing. It's not uncommon to issue a SUBLOOK, and on rare occasions we issue a SUBMISS and begin mobilizing rescue assets. The last U.S. submarine that sunk was USS *Scorpion* in 1968. Every SUBMISS since then has been a false alarm. Until we're confident *North Dakota* has sunk, I recommend we not mention anything unless we're queried."

"I agree," the president said. "Draft something for my review," he instructed Sikes, "in case the story breaks."

"There's one other thing to consider," Brackman said. "If *North Dakota* was trailing *Dolgoruky,* there's the possibility they collided. If that's the case, the Russian submarine may have also sunk. You might want to call President Kalinin to inform him we're initiating rescue efforts and they should verify their submarine is okay."

"The Russians already know," Admiral McFarland said. "They're a member of ISMERLO, the International Submarine Escape and Rescue Liaison Office, which is a consortium of every country that operates submarines. They know we're mobilizing to rescue one of our submarines beneath the polar ice cap."

The president replied, "I'll call President Kalinin first thing in the morning, Moscow time."

Admiral Riley concluded his brief with sober words. "This is a nightmare scenario—a submarine sunk under the polar ice cap, with no ability to escape to the surface or let anyone know where they are. We've narrowed the search area to a hundred and twenty thousand square miles. However, that's almost as big as California. The probability we'll find *North Dakota* in time is slim to none."

20

USS *MICHIGAN*

It was just before midnight aboard the guided missile submarine USS *Michigan,* outbound from the Trident submarine base in Bangor, Washington. Seated in the Captain's chair on the Conn, Captain Murray Wilson surveyed the watchstanders in the Control Room as they completed preparations for a trip to periscope depth. The submarine's Officer of the Deck, Lieutenant Barbara Lake, stood on the Conn between the two lowered periscopes, waiting for the towed array to steady after the submarine's baffle clearance maneuver.

Michigan was halfway across the Pacific Ocean, headed to its operating area along China's coast. After China's recent transgression, attacking Taiwan and Japan, the United States was keeping as much firepower as possible within striking distance. Loaded aboard *Michigan,* in eighteen of her twenty-four missile tubes, were 126 Tomahawk missiles, seven per tube. Also aboard *Michigan* tonight were two platoons of Navy SEALs as well as two SEAL Delivery Vehicles inside dual Dry Deck Shelters attached to the submarine's Missile Deck.

Lieutenant Lake had ordered *Michigan* shallow, to 180 feet, preparing to head to periscope depth to catch the broadcast, turning to check for contacts in the baffles.

"Sonar, Conn. Report all contacts."

A few minutes later, Sonar reported, "Conn, Sonar. Hold no contacts."

Wilson was not surprised; they had not held a contact for over a day as *Michigan* traversed the Northern Pacific, not far from Alaska's Aleutian Island chain.

After obtaining permission to proceed to periscope depth, Lake announced, "Raising Number Two scope," then reached up and twisted the periscope ring above her head clockwise. After the periscope finished its silent ascent, Lake snapped the handles down and adjusted the optics, selecting low power with her right hand and maximum elevation with her left. She twisted the periscope left and right, verifying it rotated freely.

"All stations, Conn," Lake called out. "Proceeding to periscope depth."

Sonar, Radio, and the Quartermaster acknowledged as Lake placed her right eye against the eyepiece. "Helm, ahead one-third. Dive, make your depth eight-zero feet."

The Diving Officer repeated Lake's order, then directed the two watchstanders in front of him, "Ten up. Full rise fairwater planes."

Michigan tilted upward and rose toward the surface.

"Passing one-five-zero feet," the Dive announced.

As *Michigan* ascended, the Dive called out the submarine's depth in ten-foot increments, and Lake gradually rotated her left wrist forward, tilting the scope optics down toward the horizon. As the Dive called out *eight-zero feet,* the scope broke the surface of the water and Lake circled with the periscope, searching for nearby contacts. After several revolutions, she announced, "No close contacts."

Conversation in Control resumed, and Radio reported over the 27-MC, "Conn, Radio. Download in progress." The Quartermaster followed with, "GPS fix received."

Lake acknowledged the reports, and a moment later, Radio reported *Michigan* had received the latest round of Naval messages. "Conn, Radio. Download complete."

With both objectives completed, Lake called out, "All stations, Conn. Going deep. Helm, ahead two-thirds. Dive, make your depth two hundred feet."

Each station acknowledged and *Michigan* tilted downward, leaving periscope depth behind. "Scope's under," Lake announced, then turned the periscope until it looked forward. She snapped the handles back to their folded positions, then reached up and rotated the periscope ring counterclockwise, lowering the scope into its well.

As *Michigan* leveled off at two hundred feet, a radioman entered Control, delivering the message clipboard. Wilson reviewed the messages, studying one in particular. They had received new orders.

He was surprised *Michigan* had been selected. But after reviewing the locations of the other three SSGNs—USS *Florida* was in the Persian Gulf, and *Ohio* and *Georgia* were in standard maintenance periods—he realized they were the closest submarine with SEALs and Navy divers. He would need to brief the crew on *Michigan*'s new task, and have the Navigator prepare the charts and plot a course through the Bering Strait.

Wilson turned to Lieutenant Lake. "Come down to five hundred feet, course north. Increase speed to ahead flank."

21

MOSCOW

With the morning sun streaming through tall Palladian windows behind him, President Yuri Kalinin looked across his desk at his minister of defense, Boris Chernov.

"Mr. President," Chernov began, "an American submarine has sunk in the Barents Sea, somewhere beneath the polar ice cap."

"Have they requested our assistance?" Kalinin asked.

"No, Mr. President. The United States is mobilizing their rescue assets."

"Is there some way we can assist?"

"We do not believe so. The Americans have a robust rescue system, which can be quickly transported where they need it."

"If we have not been asked for assistance and cannot provide any, then why the urgent meeting?"

"There is a . . . wrinkle in the situation," Chernov replied. "*Yury Dolgoruky* departed on patrol five days ago. American submarines deploy to the Barents to trail ours, and there is no target more desirable than *Dolgoruky*. It is not unreasonable to assume the Americans were trailing her, and if that is the case, there is the possibility the two submarines collided."

"Do we have any indications they collided?"

"No, Mr. President, but unless *Dolgoruky* reports in, we cannot be sure. That is why I am here, to request permission to order *Dolgoruky* to break radio silence."

Before Kalinin could respond, his phone rang. His executive assistant would not interrupt a meeting with his defense minister unless it was important.

"What is it?" Kalinin said as he answered the phone.

"The American president is on another line. He wishes to speak to you."

Kalinin glanced at Chernov as he raised an eyebrow. "Put him through."

The American president offered a perfunctory greeting, then got straight to the point. An American submarine had gone down under the polar ice cap. He offered what little he knew, then addressed the sensitive issue.

"We believe our submarine trailed *Yury Dolgoruky* under the ice, and the two submarines may have collided."

Kalinin eyed his defense minister as he replied, "I am sorry, Mr. President, but you are misinformed. *Yury Dolgoruky* is not on patrol in the Northern Barents. She is in local waters off the Kola Peninsula for crew training. However, if you need our assistance, do not hesitate to ask."

He hung up the phone, then directed Chernov, "Order *Dolgoruky* to report in."

ST. PETERSBURG, RUSSIA

The Admiralty building, built in Russian Empire style with a quarter-mile-long facade, served as the headquarters of the Imperial Russian Navy under the tsars until 1917, becoming the seat of power for the Russian Navy again in 2012. Sitting atop the building's 240-foot-high golden spire, the sailing warship weather vane is one of the city's most recognizable symbols.

On the third floor of the building, Fleet Admiral Georgiy Ivanov stood behind Michman Danil Krasinski, seated at his console in the Communications Center. As the young man scrolled through the messages on his display, Ivanov could tell the radioman was nervous; his supervisor peered over his left shoulder, while the highest-ranking officer in the Russian Navy peered over his right. Krasinski scrolled through the radio messages received from Northern Fleet units in the last week, searching for transmissions from *Yury Dolgoruky*.

The Communications Center had been transmitting for the last twenty-four hours over every circuit, including VLF and ELF in case *Dolgoruky* went under the ice, ordering the submarine to report in. Ivanov had grown nervous, the probability that disaster had befallen *Dolgoruky* becoming more likely with each passing hour. Even if Captain Stepanov had taken *Dolgoruky* under the ice for some reason, he was far too experienced to have taken her so deep that he couldn't transit to open water within the required time frame.

Upon reaching the end of the queue, Krasinski announced, "There is nothing, Admiral. *Dolgoruky* has not transmitted since she left port."

Ivanov turned to Krasinski's supervisor. "Initiate Signal Number Six procedures."

MOSCOW

Yuri Kalinin was reviewing the daily intelligence briefing when he heard the heavy knock on his door. He acknowledged, and Russia's minister of defense entered, striding briskly across the thirty-foot-wide expanse of open space. Chernov stopped in front of the president's desk, and Kalinin could tell he brought news. He gestured toward a chair.

As Chernov settled into his seat, Kalinin asked, "You have word of *Dolgoruky*?"

"She has not reported in," Chernov replied. "The Navy has concluded she has sunk, most likely in a collision with the American submarine. Northern Fleet has initiated Signal Number Six procedures."

Kalinin was silent for a moment, then asked, "Do we know where she sank?"

"No," Chernov replied. "*Dolgoruky*'s operating area is extremely large; over one million square kilometers. Once our ballistic missile submarines reach their operating areas, they can travel in any direction, even under the ice."

"How do we find her?"

"Northern Fleet is sortieing every ship to look for her, but our ship and submarine sonars are not equipped for bottom searches. We will be lucky to stumble across her. A more likely scenario is that the Americans find her for us. They have a rough idea of where their submarine sank. Once they locate it, we will know where to look for ours."

"Therein lies the problem," Kalinin replied. "If the Americans find their submarine, they will likely find ours."

"But the Americans won't be looking for *Dolgoruky*," Chernov replied.

A confused expression worked its way across Kalinin's face. "Why not?"

"Because we're not going to tell them *Dolgoruky* sank. Let them look only for their submarine, and if they find it, we will set up a base camp nearby, ostensibly to assist. But we will be preparing to rescue *Dolgoruky* instead. Without America looking for her, the odds we reach her first will increase."

"I understand," Kalinin replied. "But what if the Americans *do* reach her first?"

Chernov studied Kalinin carefully before he answered. "You know what we must do."

Kalinin evaluated Chernov's assessment, then pulled a stationery pad from his desk. Chernov waited as Kalinin wrote and signed the directive, then placed it in an envelope and sealed it. He handed it to Chernov.

"Deliver this to Fleet Admiral Ivanov."

As Boris Chernov closed the doors to the president's office, an idea began to take hold. Tragedy had befallen the Russian Navy again. Yet it was also an incredible opportunity, and it didn't take long to decide the risk was worth it.

He headed to the Kremlin basement.

Moments later, Chernov entered the Intelligence Center. The senior officer on watch, Captain Second Rank Eduard Davydov, looked up from his console. "Good morning, Defense Minister. How can I help you?"

"Which American submarine is in the Barents Sea?"

Davydov entered several commands at his console, and maps of the Atlantic Ocean, Mediterranean Sea, and Persian Gulf appeared on the monitor at the front of the Intelligence Center. Overlaid on the maps were five blue areas and one green.

"America's Atlantic Fleet has five attack submarines and one guided missile submarine on deployment. By analyzing underway dates, transit times, and port calls, we can determine where each submarine is deployed. The blue areas indicate the locations of their fast attacks, while their guided missile submarine is in the green area. As you can see, their guided missile submarine and two fast attacks are in the Persian Gulf, with another two fast attack submarines in the Mediterranean. The fifth fast attack is on a northern run. We detected her passing our surveillance arrays near Iceland, which puts her in the Barents Sea."

Davydov moved the pointer on the display onto the blue area covering the Barents Sea. A text box popped up, displaying the relevant data. Davy-dov read it aloud. "The American submarine in the Barents is *North Dakota*."

Chernov suppressed a smile.

North Dakota was America's first Block III Virginia class submarine, armed with the latest tactical systems.

It could not have been more perfect.

24

ST. PETERSBURG, RUSSIA

After a short flight from Moscow, Boris Chernov entered the office of Fleet Admiral Georgiy Ivanov, prepared to discuss not only the directive he was carrying in his suit pocket, but another, more dangerous effort that would require the Admiral's cooperation.

Chernov settled into the chair across from Ivanov. "These are difficult times," he began. "Another Russian submarine has sunk, and the challenge we face is more difficult than *Kursk*. We do not know where *Dolgoruky* is."

Ivanov replied, "You are not telling me anything I don't already know. Get to the point."

Chernov was taken aback by the Admiral's brusque response, which he excused, given the circumstances. "I have discussed the situation with President Kalinin," Chernov replied, "including what to do if the Americans reach *Dolgoruky* first." He pulled the sealed envelope from his pocket and handed it to the Admiral.

Ivanov opened the envelope and read the instructions.

"I understand," he replied. "I will draft the order myself and send it today."

Chernov held out his hand. There could be no record of what Kalinin had ordered.

Ivanov hesitated, then folded the directive and placed it back in the envelope. "I could destroy it for you," he said as he returned it.

Chernov said nothing as he slid the envelope into his pocket. There was a strained silence before he broached the second, more sensitive topic.

"There is something else I wish to discuss with you, Admiral."

Ivanov said nothing, waiting for Chernov to continue.

"The American submarine that sank is their first Block III Virginia class, outfitted with their newest tactical systems. If we reach it first and evacuate the crew, we can harvest the submarine's technology." Chernov leaned forward in his chair. "We cannot let this opportunity slip through our fingers."

Admiral Ivanov stared at Chernov dispassionately, giving no indication he was moved by Chernov's plea. "What do you want, Boris?"

Chernov took a few minutes to explain his plan, finishing with, "If we are successful, all will be forgiven."

The Admiral considered Chernov's proposal. The assets required for the operation were under Ivanov's command. If he failed, it would be his head on the chopping block.

Chernov tried to assure Ivanov there was no threat of incarceration. "I believe there is no risk to you other than your career. If things do not turn out well, I have no doubt Kalinin will fire you. But that will be the extent of the ramifications. Whether we succeed or fail, Kalinin will publicly deny our involvement while assuaging the Americans."

After a long silence, Ivanov replied, "You are correct. We cannot let this opportunity pass. I will give the necessary orders."

25

K-329 *SEVERODVINSK*

Captain Second Rank Josef Buffanov made his round through his submarine's Central Command Post, stopping to review the last entry in the Deck Log.

Course: 000, Depth: 100 meters, Speed: 35 knots

Severodvinsk had been in the Barents Sea, headed to the Mediterranean for deployment, when Buffanov received new orders. They were now headed north at maximum speed, preparing to slip beneath the polar ice cap in search of *Yury Dolgoruky*.

K-329 *Severodvinsk* was a fourth-generation nuclear-powered submarine, the first of the new Yasen class. Built as a replacement for the Project 971-A attack and 949-A guided missile submarines, dubbed Akula and Oscar by the West, *Severodvinsk*'s technology was state-of-the-art. Outfitted with a new spherical array sonar, *Severodvinsk* was also equipped with upgraded flank arrays on the hull and more capable towed arrays. While the sensor suite of the Yasen class submarine was vastly improved, so was her armament. With ten torpedo tubes and eight vertical launchers, each of the latter carrying five antiship or land-attack cruise missiles, *Severodvinsk* was a formidable ship.

Severodvinsk's First Officer, Captain Third Rank Anton Novikoff, entered the Command Post, joining Buffanov at the navigation table. *Severodvinsk* was approaching the Marginal Ice Zone, and they had to slow and set the ice watches before proceeding.

Captain Lieutenant Dmitri Ronin, the Watch Officer, approached the two men, addressing the submarine's Captain. "I intend to slow and set the Ice Detail," he said.

Buffanov gave his concurrence and Ronin ordered the submarine to slow to ten knots. As *Severodvinsk* slowed, its streaming antenna floated toward the ocean's surface and they regained sync with the message broadcast.

"Command Post, Communication. Have received a Commanding Officer Only message."

Buffanov entered the Communications Post and stopped by the two printers. "Ready."

The radioman hit the print button and a message emerged from the left printer.

Buffanov read the message, then reread it. He glanced at the radioman, who was processing the rest of the messages they had downloaded. Buffanov folded the paper and slid it inside the breast pocket of his coveralls.

"Senior Michman," Buffanov called out. The radioman turned in his direction. "Have we received new waterspace assignments?"

The radioman scrolled through the messages on his display. "Yes, Captain." He selected the message and hit the print button, and a second sheet of paper slid from the printer.

Buffanov took the message and returned to the Command Post, without revealing his emotions. No doubt, his First Officer and the watchstanders were wondering about the Commanding Officer Only message. The time would come when he would reveal *Severodvinsk*'s new mission. Meanwhile, they would loiter just outside the Marginal Ice Zone.

"Watch Officer, slow to ahead one-third. We will not be heading under the ice." He turned to his First Officer and handed him the new waterspace assignment. "Have the Navigating Officer plot our new operating area."

As his First Officer reviewed the message, Buffanov reflected on their new order. Until a few minutes ago, he had planned to put *Severodvinsk*'s new sonar systems to use, scouring the ocean for *Yury Dolgoruky*. Now, his submarine's armament was being called into service.

26

USS *MICHIGAN*

Lieutenant Mark DeCrispino swung the periscope around, then steadied up for another observation on the contact of interest.

"Iceberg off the port bow. Bearing, mark!"

As Captain Wilson watched from his chair on the Conn, DeCrispino pressed the red button on the periscope handle, sending the bearing to combat control. Petty Officer Chris Malocsay, manning one of the combat control consoles, determined the range by setting the iceberg's speed to zero and analyzing its bearing rate.

"Range, five thousand yards. CPA range—three thousand, two hundred yards."

Malocsay had calculated the iceberg's Closest Point of Approach as it passed down the port side of the submarine. It would remain sufficiently far away; no course change was required.

USS *Michigan* was in the Marginal Ice Zone just north of St. Lawrence Island, headed toward the polar ice cap. Before slipping under the ice, Wilson had ordered his submarine to periscope depth for a final GPS fix for their inertial navigators.

The Quartermaster reported. "Both inertial navigators have accepted the GPS fix."

A moment later, DeCrispino called out from the Conn, "Captain, radio download is complete and GPS fix obtained. I intend to go deep."

"Very well," Wilson replied. "Deploy the floating wire when you are steady on depth."

Once *Michigan* slipped beneath the polar ice cap, she could not head to periscope depth to copy the broadcast. Instead, they would trail the floating wire antenna, monitoring message traffic over the VLF broadcast.

Lieutenant DeCrispino gave the necessary orders and *Michigan* tilted downward. Their journey beneath the ice would be treacherous, transiting over the shallow Chukchi Shelf in the Pacific and the Barents Shelf in the Atlantic. The ice keels were deep during the late winter months, leaving little room for safe transit. *Michigan* settled out at two hundred feet, and as Wilson prepared to head beneath the ice, he knew he wouldn't get much sleep until they reached the deep-water basins of the Arctic Ocean.

27

ARCTIC OCEAN

Dawn was breaking across a white, barren landscape as a Cessna 182 sped north, skimming a few hundred feet above the ice. In the front passenger seat, Vance Verbeck leaned against the window, binoculars to his eyes, scanning the snow-covered ridges rippling across the otherwise flat landscape. The technical director of the Arctic Submarine Laboratory was looking for an ice floe strong enough to support an ice camp. The thickness of the surface ridges, where the edges of the ice floes buckled upward, was a good indicator. However, rescue from atop the ice might not even be possible, considering the weight of the rescue equipment.

Three hundred tons!

He nearly fell out of his chair when the commanding officer of the Undersea Rescue Command told him the weight of the fully assembled system, sitting inside a footprint smaller than a basketball court. *North Dakota* had better be stuck under some pretty thick ice. Luckily, based on his observations this morning, the ice was sufficiently thick this winter. After convincing himself the nearby floes were no thicker than the one he had selected, Verbeck directed the pilot to turn around and head back. The pilot banked the Cessna to the right, then steadied on a course returning to the GPS marker they had tossed onto the candidate ice floe.

A few minutes later, the ski-equipped Cessna glided to a halt atop the polar ice cap. Verbeck stepped from the aircraft, joined by Paul Leone, their most experienced ice pilot, hauling a duffle bag of equipment and an auger. They needed to determine the thickness of the ice and whether it was first-year ice or multiyear. First-year ice was prone to breaking apart.

Leone began drilling with the auger. The first indication was good; he had to attach several extensions to continue drilling. Finally, he broke through. By measuring the length of the auger drill, Leone determined the ice was six feet thick.

Based on the thickness, Verbeck was almost positive it was multiyear ice. But he had to be sure. The way to assess the age of sea ice was to measure its salinity. As seawater freezes, the salt water concentrates into brine, which stays liquid and gets trapped within the ice crystals. Over time, the heavy brine migrates down through the ice and eventually back into the ocean. As a result, the top of multiyear ice is nearly salt free and drinkable.

Leone scraped a chunk of ice from inside the hole and deposited it in a glass beaker, then placed it inside the warm Cessna. After the ice melted, he checked the salinity with a test strip, followed by a sip of the water. Both confirmed the water was salt free. After Leone informed him of the results, Verbeck pulled an iridium phone from his pocket, sending the GPS coordinates back to Svalbard Airport, where the rest of their gear was staged.

It wasn't long before the next aircraft appeared, and the ski-equipped C-130 flown by the 109th Air Wing of the New York Air National Guard touched down nearby. The rear ramp of the C-130 lowered, and the first piece of equipment out was a bulldozer, used for building a landing strip suitable for aircraft without skis.

Next onto the ice were a half-dozen men from the Applied Physics Laboratory, University of Washington, along with six men from the Arctic Submarine Lab, who unloaded stacks of the special triple-layer plywood used to build the ice camp huts; two layers of plywood sandwiched around an inner layer of Styrofoam insulation. The huts weren't fancy—nothing more than six-sided plywood boxes.

The first building constructed would be the command hut, where the communication gear, both satellite and underwater, would be installed. One of the floor panels had a precut two-foot-diameter hole, which would provide access to the ice beneath the hut. A hole would then be cut in the ice for the Remote Acoustic Transmission System, the same type of underwater transmitter submarines used. Once the building was constructed, the electronic gear would be installed inside and antennas mounted on the top.

Other teams were assembling the remaining components of an ice camp, beginning with the berthing hooches. As more men and equipment arrived, the galley and generator tents would be set up, and of course, no ice camp would be complete without outhouses and pee boxes.

Leone approached Verbeck. "You still haven't picked a name for the ice camp."

Verbeck had been too busy, overseeing the hundreds of details involved with establishing an ice camp. "Any suggestions?"

"How about Nautilus?"

USS *Nautilus* was the first nuclear-powered submarine, and the first to transit from the Pacific to the Atlantic Ocean beneath the polar ice cap.

"I like it," Verbeck said. "Ice Camp Nautilus it is."

Verbeck checked on the bulldozer. It had finished the landing strip with no time to spare. To the southwest, a half-dozen aircraft were headed their way, small dark specks on the horizon.

They had a long day's work ahead of them.

SEVEROMORSK, RUSSIA

It was just after sunrise on the northern shore of the Russian province of Murmansk, the sun climbing slowly into a clear blue sky. Standing on the afterdeck of *Mikhail Rudnitsky,* Julius Raila pulled his black wool watch cap down farther over his ears, the edges of his cap mating with his thick gray beard. *Rudnitsky's* deck was a flurry of activity, and Raila brought his hand to his forehead, shielding his eyes from the bright winter sun as he watched his men unbolt the submarine rescue equipment from its foundations.

Rudnitsky, mother ship to AS-34, a Priz class Deep Submergence Rescue Vehicle, was tied to a wharf in the Northern Fleet port of Severomorsk. In addition to the DSRV, *Rudnitsky* was outfitted with the handling gear for the submersible, plus decompression chambers for the submarine crew once they were rescued. Thankfully, the equipment was far less integrated into the ship than the new Divex system aboard *Igor Belousov,* and could be disassembled and transported with relative ease.

Rudnitsky's crane swung AS-34 over the side and deposited it onto one of ten flatbed trucks waiting on the wharf. Personnel strapped the DSRV down for its trip to Murmansk Airport, where several Anatov 124s, the Russian equivalent of American C-5 cargo transports, were waiting. Raila ran his fingers through his beard. The disassembly was the easy part. Once the Russian ice camp was set up and his equipment arrived, he would begin the painstaking process of reassembling everything, not to mention carving a hole through the ice big enough for AS-34. Whether the heavy Anatov 124s could land on the ice was beyond his expertise. However, getting the equipment onto the ice was someone else's problem. He had enough of his own.

GADZHIYEVO, RUSSIA

In the normally crowded Northern Fleet base of Gadzhiyevo, only a single submarine remained tied to the pier. The banner affixed to the ship's brow identified the submarine as K-157 *Vepr,* a third flight Shchuka-B nuclear attack submarine, dubbed Akula II by NATO. Inside the officers' mess, Captain Second Rank Matvey Baczewski sat at the head of the table, flanked by twelve of his officers as they gathered for lunch.

It was unusually quiet during the meal, his officers sulking over their lack of orders. Every other attack and guided missile submarine had sortied to sea yesterday in search of *Dolgoruky.* But *Vepr*'s orders had been canceled without explanation. Northern Fleet had singled her out for some reason, deciding she, and she alone, was not worthy. It flew in the face of reason. *Vepr* was the most capable submarine in their squadron, consistently earning all departmental and ship awards.

Baczewski noticed the furtive glances from his officers, wondering if their Captain's Polish heritage had anything to do with their canceled order. But Baczewski had done well in the Navy thus far; his ethnicity had not been an issue.

"Fleet Admiral, arriving."

The announcement from topside over the submarine's communication system caught Baczewski by surprise, and the Duty Officer almost choked as he swallowed a mouthful of tea. Lieutenant Chaban grabbed the napkin from his lap, wiping his face as he stood, almost knocking his chair over in the process. He looked toward his Captain, belatedly requesting to be excused from the table. Baczewski nodded and Chaban left the wardroom, hurrying topside to greet the Russian Navy's highest-ranking Admiral.

The other officers at the table stared at their Captain, some with their soup spoons suspended in the air, awaiting direction.

"Eat," Baczewski said.

His officers remained frozen. An unannounced visit by the Fleet Admiral after canceled orders did not bode well. "Eat," Baczewski repeated, adding a warm smile this time. "Admiral Ivanov and I are old friends. He was my commanding officer on my first submarine."

The officers followed their Captain's order and resumed eating. Baczewski pushed back from the table, then headed forward.

Baczewski waited in the upper level of Compartment One as Fleet Admiral Ivanov climbed down from topside.

"Welcome aboard *Vepr*, Fleet Admiral," he said as Ivanov stepped off the ladder.

Ivanov did not reply. Instead, his eyes swept the compartment, examining the weapons in their stows and the condition of Baczewski's ship. Baczewski repressed a smile. In twenty years, Ivanov hadn't changed; he had been a demanding commanding officer. Finally, Ivanov's eyes met Baczewski's. But there was no warm greeting.

"Your stateroom," was all he said.

Ivanov followed Baczewski into his stateroom, then closed and locked the door.

"To what honor do we owe your visit?" Baczewski asked, attempting to break the ice.

"It is no honor," Ivanov replied. "Be seated."

Baczewski took his seat as Ivanov settled into his. The Admiral reached into his overcoat and retrieved a sealed envelope, which he placed on the table between them. "Your orders."

Vepr's commanding officer opened the envelope, and as he read the letter, signed by the Admiral, mixed emotions surged through him—fear, and excitement. After a moment of reflection, he decided his reaction was as it should be for someone heading into battle.

"It is only a contingency measure," the Admiral said. "And you may decline the order."

Baczewski read the order again, evaluating the possible scenarios. There was no way to predict the risk to his crew. However, Ivanov would not have made the request without good reason. Baczewski folded the letter and placed it back into the envelope.

"I have no reservations, Admiral. I will do as you instruct."

Ivanov nodded. "How soon can you get underway?"

"The reactor is shut down. By the time we start up, it will be dark. Unless it's imperative we get underway tonight, I recommend we get underway first thing tomorrow morning."

"You will depart tonight," Ivanov answered.

The Admiral stood, and before turning toward the door, he said, "Keep the envelope in a safe place. If you are called into service and survive, you will need it to absolve yourself."

Ivanov's sedan was parked on the pier, not far from *Vepr*'s brow, the back door held open by his driver. Ivanov slid into the back seat of the warm sedan—the car engine and heater had been left running. The driver shut Ivanov's door and climbed into the front seat a moment later. He looked at the Admiral through the rearview mirror. "Back to the airport, sir?"

"No," Ivanov replied as he took his gloves off. "Pechenga."

"Yes, Admiral."

He put the car in gear and guided it down the narrow pier. Not long thereafter, the sedan pulled onto Route E105, headed northwest toward the far corner of the Kola Peninsula.

30

PECHENGA, RUSSIA

In the northwest corner of the Kola Peninsula, not far from the Norwegian and Finnish borders, Fleet Admiral Ivanov looked out his sedan window at the sprawling base in the Pechengsky District. Originally part of the Swedish Empire, the district was annexed by Russia in 1533, then ceded to Finland in 1920 after the Finnish civil war. However, after five million tons of nickel deposits were discovered in the region, the land was seized by the Soviet Union during 1939's Winter War, then reclaimed by Finland during the Continuation War, joining Nazi Germany's assault on Russia. The Soviet Union prevailed, however, and with tremendous underground wealth and a tumultuous history, it was not surprising there was a Russian military base in the remote rural district.

It was late in the afternoon, with the sun slipping toward the craggy peaks of the Pechenga Mountains, when Ivanov's sedan reached the installation. The guard at the security gate checked the identification of the driver, then waved them through. The driver followed Ivanov's directions, and pedestrian and vehicular traffic thinned as they headed deeper into the base, until no cars or soldiers were visible.

"Stop here," the Admiral commanded.

The sedan ground to a halt in front of a four-story redbrick building. Ivanov stepped from the car and entered the facility. The quarterdeck watch saluted briskly, holding his salute until the Admiral dropped his.

"Inform Captain First Rank Klokov that Fleet Admiral Ivanov is here."

The Starshina Third Class picked up the phone, and after speaking into the handset, hung up. "Captain Klokov is on his way."

Captain First Rank Klokov was the commanding officer of Russian military unit 10511. Its official title was the 585th OMRP, which stood for Otdel'nyy Morskoy Razvedyvatel'nyy Punkt and translated in English to "Detached Naval Reconnaissance Point." Outside Russia, however, the unit was known as Spetsnaz.

Spetsnaz were elite special forces, with several units being Marine Commandos, the equivalent of America's Navy SEALs. There were over one hundred Spetsnaz units spread throughout the Russian military and intelligence organizations, but only a few met Ivanov's needs. Marine Commandos would have been a suitable selection. However, those units were under the direct control of the military's Main Intelligence Directorate, or GRU. Ivanov needed a unit under his command, and there was one unit that met the specifications for the mission Boris Chernov had outlined. The Polar Spetsnaz unit, based in Pechenga.

The Polar Spetsnaz brigade was trained and equipped for warfare in Arctic conditions, with DT-30P Vityaz tracked vehicles. However, against their potential adversary, they would not need their armored vehicles. Their training, small arms weapons, and helicopters would suffice.

Captain Klokov arrived at the quarterdeck and the two officers saluted each other. After the required greetings, Klokov led the Admiral down a hallway and into his office. Ivanov settled into a chair across from Klokov's desk, then Klokov took his seat.

Klokov began with the expected pleasantries, but Ivanov interrupted him. "I have an assignment for your unit."

Ivanov laid out the unit's assignment and timeline. When he finished, Klokov said nothing while he worked through the various scenarios. He finally responded, addressing a critical issue.

"There will be many witnesses."

"Minimize the casualties," Ivanov replied, "but mission success is paramount."

Ivanov departed without ceremony, then stepped into the back of his sedan. His driver awaited guidance, and Ivanov said, "Murmansk Airport."

As the car headed toward the base exit, Ivanov reflected on what he had done today. The plan had been put in motion, but he could not predict the outcome or his fate if it failed. His career had been distinguished, guiding

Russia's Navy through its darkest times, and he'd been Fleet Admiral longer than anyone. As he leaned back, sinking deeper into the leather upholstery, he told himself again that the potential gain was worth risking what was left of an old man's career.

31

USS *NORTH DAKOTA*

Commander Paul Tolbert stood in the deserted Control Room, the light from his battle lantern cutting through the darkness and reflecting off ice-coated consoles. Without power to run the ventilation heaters, temperature had stabilized at twenty-nine degrees Fahrenheit, matching that of the ocean beneath the polar ice cap. The watchstanders had wiped away the moisture condensing on the submarine's metal surfaces, but now that temperature had dropped below freezing, everything was coated in a thin sheen of ice.

As the temperature fell, hypothermia became an issue, and after conferring with *North Dakota*'s corpsman, Tolbert secured all watches except the essential ones in the engineering spaces, and sent everyone to their racks, where they were hibernating in their SEIE suits beneath every available blanket. Tolbert shined his light on the dead Ship Control Station. He had no idea what depth the ship was at, but was confident they had pumped off enough water to keep them pinned against the bottom of the ice cap.

He was about to head aft to check on Electrical Division's progress again, but decided otherwise. There had been little else to do the last three days, and repairs were proceeding even slower than Chief Moran had predicted. As the temperature plummeted, the electricians lost dexterity in their fingers, affecting their ability to conduct the delicate repairs. Even though the SEIE suits came with flexible neoprene gloves, they were of no use since the work required bare hands.

Tolbert spotted a yellow glow creeping his way. A moment later, the Chief of the Boat, Master Chief Paul Murgo, entered the Control Room, a battle lantern in hand. Like Tolbert, he conducted frequent tours, checking on the condition of the men and ship.

Murgo shined his light across the frozen consoles.

"Ahh, there's no place like home." The Alaskan native seemed unfazed by the frigid temperatures. "What I wouldn't give for a hundred and thirty pairs of red slippers, though," he said. "Just click three times . . ."

"We're not in Kansas, anymore, Toto," Tolbert replied.

Murgo grinned.

Two more beams of light appeared, and the Engineer Officer and Auxiliary Division Chief entered Control. They joined Tolbert and Murgo around the navigation plot. In the dim light, Tolbert noticed worried looks.

"We've got another problem," Lieutenant Commander Swenson said. "The potable water tanks have frozen. We can't get any more water."

Of all the things they'd been worried about, Tolbert thought—air, power, and temperature—who would have thought water would be an issue? But submarines weren't designed to operate at three degrees below freezing, and they had never had to think through the implications. He reviewed the different fluids aboard—seawater, pure water, diesel fuel, hydraulic fluid, and battery acid, and figured the only issues were the pure water–based systems.

The reactor plant water would be fine. Even though the reactor was shut down, heat was still being generated from the radioactive decay of fission by-products, and Tolbert could feel the welcome warmth emanating from the bulkheads as he passed through the Reactor Compartment Tunnel. That left the Engine Room systems.

"If potable water is freezing," Tolbert said, "the Condensate and Feed systems will also freeze, if they haven't already done so."

Swenson replied, "I just checked Condensate and Feed by opening some of the drains. The feedwater piping near the Reactor Compartment is still above freezing, but everything else is frozen."

They had realized the problem too late. As water froze, it would expand and potentially crack piping or separate joints.

"Any evidence of damage?" Tolbert asked.

"Nothing so far. I think we're okay in the Feed System, as that piping is designed for high pressure so it can force water into the steam generator, but the Condensate System is low pressure. We could have some issues there. We won't know for sure until we thaw everything out. Which brings up another problem. We have to thaw everything out *before* we start up."

Tolbert realized the implication immediately. They couldn't start up with frozen Condensate and Feedwater systems, nor did he want to start spinning a turbine with ice formations inside. He would have to warm everything up first, placing an additional drain on the battery. His decision to open the battery breaker had been wise, preserving the remaining energy. They were going to need every bit of it.

"We'll restore the ventilation heaters and warm up the Engine Room before start-up," Tolbert said. "Our immediate problem, however, is water. Any recommendations?"

"Chief Johnson has one," Swenson replied.

Tolbert turned to Larry "Big Red" Johnson, the tall A-Gang Chief with red hair and a temper to match. Johnson answered, "As the Eng said, the metal near the reactor is still warm and some feedwater hasn't frozen. I had Chief Scalise check, and the Pure Water Tank hasn't frozen either."

Tolbert considered Johnson's idea. Pure Water was used as reactor coolant. But as its name implied, it was pure water, nothing more. "Great idea, Chief. Use the Pure Water Tank for drinking water. Check the tank temperature with a surface pyrometer every hour, and if it drops to thirty-three degrees, drain the remaining water into containers and store them in the Reactor Compartment Tunnel."

With the water problem solved, Tolbert turned to Master Chief Murgo, "How are we doing on carbon dioxide?"

"We've got one more day of CO_2 absorbers left," Murgo replied. "After that, we'll have to start a scrubber, whether we've got a turbine generator up or not. It's your call as to when, but Doc recommends we keep CO_2 below one percent."

Tolbert wasn't looking forward to the decision. Running a scrubber would drain the battery, leaving insufficient power for start-up, which was their only hope of long-term survival. It was a Catch-22 situation. Start a scrubber to save their lives, but seal their fate in the process.

They needed to restore power, which was held up by the Condensate System repairs.

"How much longer, Eng?"

Swenson replied, "My best guess is . . . twenty-four hours."

32

K-535 *YURY DOLGORUKY*

In the upper level of Compartment One, Captain Nicholai Stepanov pulled himself to his feet, leaving behind his Chief Ship Starshina, asleep on the deck beside him with his back against a torpedo. He retrieved a water bottle from inside his survival suit and took a small sip. Now that temperature in the compartment had dropped below zero degrees Centigrade, he kept the bottle inside his suit to keep the water from freezing. He took a small sip for good reason; they had enough water bottles for each man to receive one more.

Stepanov surveyed the dimly lit compartment. Aside from the faint glow from Captain Kovaleski's flashlight, tending to Stepanov's still unconscious First Officer, it was dark in upper level. Had he checked his watch, it would have told him it was 7 a.m., time to begin a new day. But only a few men were stirring. He figured that was best, minimizing the production of carbon dioxide. They had enough air regeneration cartridges to last another day.

Stepanov reached for his lantern and began his round. He dropped down to middle level, where the men huddled around the air regeneration unit. He checked each man, talking for a moment with those awake. He did his best to project a positive outlook, but had few encouraging words. He could not hide the obvious facts from his men; Russia would not notice *Dolgoruky* was missing for another two months, and so far, there was no sign anyone was looking for the American submarine or that it had even sunk nearby.

He finished his round, then returned to upper level and checked on his First Officer, still in his makeshift bed on an empty torpedo stow. Kovaleski was tending to him, and as the Medical Officer turned to greet the approaching light, Stepanov could see the dark circles under his eyes. Unlike the rest of *Dolgoruky*'s crew, Kovaleski was exhausted. He made constant rounds through the compartment, checking on the men and deciding who needed more time around the air regeneration unit based on their symptoms.

"How is he doing?" Stepanov asked.

Kovaleski glanced at Pavlov before answering, "There is no change."

"Is that good or bad?"

"Without knowing the extent of his injuries, I cannot tell."

Stepanov sensed the helplessness in his Medical Officer's voice. He and Kovaleski were in similar situations; both were responsible for the crew, and each knew the almost certain outcome.

"You are doing an excellent job," Stepanov said. "We are fortunate to have you as our Medical Officer."

Kovaleski simply nodded.

Stepanov returned to his spot beside his Chief Ship Starshina and slid down to the deck, placing his back against the cold metal skin of the torpedo again, and his emergency lantern beside him. He zipped his exposure suit tight around his face, then turned off the light.

ICE CAMP NAUTILUS

The bright afternoon sun reflected off the white landscape, but Vance Verbeck didn't notice inside the windowless plywood command hut. He was leaning over Alyssa Martin's shoulder, examining the display for the above-ice sonar array, spread atop the polar ice cap a few miles to the north. Sitting beside Alyssa, Scott Walworth spoke into his microphone, transmitting again over RATS, their Remote Acoustic Transmission System, lowered through the hole in the command hut floor, then listened for a response.

They had been transmitting on the command hut RATS throughout the night and into the morning, as well as on a second RATS deployed with the above-ice array, its hydrophone lowered through a hole drilled in the ice each time the array was moved. After transmitting on RATS, they would listen for a response on the array.

The size of their above-ice array had been quadrupled for this trip to the polar ice cap, cobbling together their primary and backup arrays and adding in the spare hydrophones, expanding their search area from four to sixteen square miles. Still, they had 120,000 miles to cover, which would take a mere 7,500 searches. At their current pace, they could conduct six searches a day, which meant it would take three and a half years to search the entire area. Quite an improvement from their original eighty-year estimate, but a sobering fact nonetheless.

Verbeck checked the map taped to the command hut wall. Their plan was to advance the array straight north from *North Dakota*'s last known position until they reached the edge of the Barents Shelf, then head back toward Camp Nautilus on either the east or west side.

Alyssa looked up at Verbeck. "There's no response. I'm ready to move the array."

USS *NORTH DAKOTA*

Paul Tolbert stepped into the Reactor Compartment Tunnel, picking his way through the mattresses jammed on the passageway deck. After temperature stabilized at three degrees below zero, hypothermia had become an issue, and the Doc recommended the most affected personnel sleep in the warmest compartment. Tolbert examined his men as he passed through; they were bundled in SEIE suits and green foul-weather jackets, then layered beneath as many blankets the rest of the crew could spare. So far so good, though. No one had suffered permanent injuries.

Tolbert entered the Engine Room, then climbed down into Engine Room Forward. He stopped beside the Engineer and Chief Moran as Petty Officers Brandon and Thompson completed the final assembly of the controller and condensate pump. The repairs had been completed none too soon; they had just expended their last carbon dioxide absorber.

Thompson stepped back from the controller. He didn't bother trying to close the cabinet cover. With the number of jumpers installed, bypassing bad circuit cards and cutting in crude replacements, the cover wouldn't close. Brandon finished assembling the condensate pump, then stood, stretching out his back. All eyes turned to Chief Moran, who had inspected the work as it progressed.

"We're ready to give it a whirl, Captain."

They couldn't run the pump for long, because the condensate system was still frozen and there was no water to pump, but they could determine if it worked.

Tolbert turned to the Engineer. "Shut the battery and port condensate breakers."

The Engineer gave the order to Petty Officer Brandon, who donned a sound-powered phone headset and relayed the orders to Engine Room Upper Level and the Forward Compartment, where electricians were standing by to shut the breakers.

A moment later, Brandon reported, "The battery and port condensate breakers are shut."

The three electricians turned to examine the controller, hoping for a lack of smoke. There was no visible problem, so Brandon approached the condensate pump switch, turning to his Chief for direction.

Tolbert felt the tension in the air.

"Put it in slow speed," Moran ordered.

Brandon reached out and rested his hand on the switch for a moment, as if saying a silent prayer, then twisted it to SLOW.

The pump lurched to life with a squeal that quickly faded, replaced by a steady whirr. After thirty seconds, Moran said, "Secure the pump."

Brandon switched the pump off and it coasted to a halt.

"Well done, men," Tolbert said. "Once we get the ice cream machine up, you guys get first dibs."

The other men grinned.

"I'll take a long hot shower," Brandon said.

"You got it," Tolbert said. "Speaking of hot"—he turned to Lieutenant Commander Swenson—"restore Engine Room ventilation and heaters. Let me know once everything has thawed and you're ready to commence start-up."

The Engineer acknowledged, and Tolbert left Engine Room Forward, stopping in Maneuvering to check on the battery. Electrician's Mate Second Class Allen Terrill was the sole person on watch again, seated at the Electric Plant Control Panel with a worried look. Tolbert followed his eyes to the battery meters, and was shocked at the low voltage.

Tolbert's bubble of excitement over repairing the condensate pump had been burst. Battery capacity had dropped from thirty percent when they opened the battery breaker to only fifteen percent now.

"We've lost capacity because the battery cooled down after we open-circuited it," Terrill said. "Maybe it will recover as it warms back up, giving us a few more hours than it appears."

Tolbert hoped Terrill was right.

35

USS *NORTH DAKOTA*

Eight hours later, Tolbert returned to the crowded Engine Room, shielding his eyes from the light as his pupils adjusted. They were getting close to commencing reactor start-up, so essential equipment had been energized, along with a portion of the Engine Room lights. Now that the ventilation heaters in the compartment had been restored, every member of *North Dakota*'s crew congregated in the warm compartment, thawing out after living in a sub-zero climate for the last week. However, even though the Engine Room had been heated to eighty degrees, it was taking longer than expected to melt the ice in the Condensate and Feed systems. As he reached Maneuvering, he almost didn't want to receive the update on the battery's status.

Tolbert entered a fully manned Maneuvering this time, with the most experienced personnel on watch. With the battery draining ever faster as voltage lowered, they might have to take a few shortcuts during the Engine Room start-up, so the Engineer Officer had stationed his most senior personnel in Maneuvering and throughout the Engine Room. Lieutenant Vaugh, the most experienced Engineering Officer of the Watch, sat at his console behind the two enlisted watchstanders: Electrician's Mate Art Thompson as the Electrical Operator, and Electronics Technician Joe Hipp, who was seated at the Propulsion Plant Control Panel.

Lieutenant Commander Swenson joined Tolbert in Maneuvering, his eyes focusing on the battery voltage and discharge rate. Battery capacity was down to five percent.

He turned to Tolbert, "The Feed System is ready to go, but Condensate is still frozen in a few spots." He glanced at the battery meters. "We can't wait any longer. I recommend we start up now, and by the time we're ready to open the steam stops, Condensate should be ready."

Tolbert concurred. "Commence reactor start-up."

Swenson passed the order to the Engineering Officer of the Watch, who initiated the procedure.

Once all prerequisites were verified, the Propulsion Plant Operator announced, "Latching Group One rods," then he twisted the shim switch to the IN position while applying latching current. A moment later, he announced, "Withdrawing Group One rods," then shifted the shim switch to the OUT position.

Tolbert watched the battery discharge rate rise as the Control Rod Drive Mechanisms atop the reactor pulled the control rods upward. Petty Officer Hipp alternated between control rod groups, withdrawing each set in stages as he monitored reactor start-up rate.

A short while later, he announced, "The reactor is critical," meaning the fission rate inside the reactor had become self-sustaining, no longer overcome by control rod neutron absorption. Hipp continued withdrawing the control rods, and a few minutes later announced, "The reactor is in the power range."

Power had been increased to one percent and the reactor was now generating heat. But they still had a long way to go. They needed to heat the plant several hundred degrees to its normal operating temperature, but could heat up only so fast. Submarine reactors were pressurized water reactors, meaning the water inside was kept at extremely high pressure to keep it from boiling, which would interfere with heat transfer from the fuel cells.

Because of the high pressure, submarine reactors were built with one-foot-thick Inconel walls. At extremely low temperatures, the reactor vessel could brittle-fracture if the thermal stress across the metal was too great. They had to warm the reactor vessel slowly. From a temperature this low, it would be several hours before the plant was hot enough to generate steam.

Tolbert's eyes went to the battery meters. It was going to be close.

It was barely an hour later when Tolbert received the bad news. He was still in Maneuvering with the Engineer when the Electrical Operator reported, "Battery cell reversal has begun."

North Dakota's battery was comprised of 126 cells connected in series. There were minor manufacturing differences in the four-foot-tall, two-thousand-pound cells and some would deplete faster than others. When a cell depleted, it would *reverse,* and begin charging itself at the expense of others. They needed to disconnect reversed cells quickly to minimize the power drained from the remaining good cells.

The Engineer Officer ordered, "Get me a readout of all cells." A minute later, Vaugh handed the Engineer a printout. Swenson circled a few readings with his pen, then handed it to Tolbert. Cell eighty-nine had reversed, and there were six other cells whose voltage was lower than the rest and wouldn't be far behind.

"I recommend we jumper out these seven cells."

Tolbert agreed. However, they had a problem. The battery breaker was usually opened before jumpering a cell, to eliminate current flow while personnel were inside the cramped Battery Well. Unfortunately, the battery was their only source of power, which meant he would have to send someone into the Battery Well with the breaker still shut.

The Engineer reached the same conclusion. "Request permission to jumper out cells without opening the battery breaker."

In Forward Compartment Lower Level, Chief Moran held the battle lantern in the darkness while Petty Officer Tim Brandon stripped the SEIE suit from his body, then removed all metal accoutrements from his clothing. No belt buckles, metal-framed glasses, military insignia—nothing metal would go into the Battery Well aside from the tools and cables needed to jumper out the bad cells. However, the tools and cables were rubber coated, with bare metal exposed only at the ends, so he could handle them without getting electrocuted.

Brandon folded the paper Moran had given him, listing the cells to be jumpered out, and slid it into his pocket, then inventoried his tools and jumper cables. "I'm ready," he said.

Moran spoke into his headset. "Maneuvering, Forward Compartment Lower Level. Request permission to enter the Battery Well. The battery breaker is still shut."

Seconds later, Moran replied, "Enter the Battery Well, aye."

Moran passed the order to Brandon, who donned a pair of plastic goggles. He was entering the Battery Well with 126 lead-acid cells filled with sulfuric acid, potent enough to eat through flesh. Skin would heal, but eyes were a different matter. Brandon pulled the hatch open, then lowered himself into the cramped compartment, his feet hitting wooden support plates on top of the cells three feet down.

Brandon grabbed his tool bag, several cables, and a flashlight, then crouched down and crawled through the dark well toward cell eighty-nine. Upon reaching it, he retrieved a pair of insulated pliers from his tool bag and loosened the nuts attaching the cables on both sides of the cell. He had to be careful, jumpering out the cell in the correct sequence so as not to open circuit the battery in the process, which would interrupt power to every piece of equipment, spelling disaster for the reactor start-up.

It took only a few minutes to jumper out the cell, then Brandon moved to the next one.

"Maneuvering, Forward Compartment Lower Level. All seven cells have been jumpered and Petty Officer Brandon has exited the Battery Well."

Tolbert's eyes went to the battery voltage and current meters. Three of the other six cells had reversed while Brandon was in the Battery Well, with the remaining three on the verge. They had gained valuable time for the Engine Room start-up.

The reactor plant heat-up was continuing, with the rate pegged at the maximum permissible. At the current heat-up rate, it would take another two hours before they could commence Engine Room start-up.

It was only an hour later when the Electrical Operator reported, "Engineering Officer of the Watch, multiple battery cell reversals."

Tolbert checked the Electric Plant Control Panel again; he had never seen battery voltage so low. They were running out of time. He glanced at reactor temperature on the Propulsion Plant Control Plant. They were still a ways from normal operating temperature, but at three hundred degrees, it was hot enough to generate steam. It was against procedure, but he had no choice.

"Engineer, open the port Main Steam Stop and start up the port side of the Engine Room."

They would bring steam into the Engine Room, but start up only one side to minimize the drain on the battery as additional Engine Room systems were brought on-line.

Lieutenant Commander Swenson gave the order to the Engineering Officer of the Watch, and orders went out to the Engine Room watchstanders, who raced to bring the systems on-line. Tolbert concentrated on battery voltage while he waited. The battery was almost depleted, and voltage began dropping like a rock when the report came over the Maneuvering Room speakers.

"Maneuvering, Engine Room Upper Level. The port turbine generator is ready for electrical loading."

Thompson didn't wait for the order. The Electrical Operator shut the port turbine generator breaker and unloaded the port converter, which had been pulling energy from the battery to supply the Vital bus. A few more clicks and the turbine generator was supplying both sides of the electric plant.

Tolbert turned to Swenson. "Bring up the starboard side of the Engine Room, then commence an equalizer battery charge."

An hour later, Tolbert looked around the brightly lit and crowded Control Room. The Engine Room had been fully restored aside from the main engines, and the electric plant was in a Normal Full Power Line-Up with both turbine generators operating. Their repaired condensate pump was chugging along, giving no indication it was worse for the wear, but Tolbert had no idea how long it would hold out. They had commenced an equalizer battery charge—a heavy-duty version done after a deep discharge—and the atmosphere control equipment was running, making oxygen and purifying the air.

The rest of the submarine systems were slowly returning to life, but the Control Room was still dead. The watchstanders had wiped down the equipment as the sheen of ice melted, preventing moisture from seeping inside. However, moisture had frozen on the inside of the consoles as well, and the tactical systems could not be brought up until they were confident nothing would short out.

The electrical cabinets and consoles in the Control Room had been opened, and the sonar techs were using heat guns to dry out the internals of the sonar consoles and computer servers. Tolbert had focused on Sonar first, expediting its recovery. Although *North Dakota*'s crew was no longer in extremis, the last thing they had heard on sonar was *Yury Dolgoruky* plowing into the ocean bottom. Due to sitting on the silted ocean floor, Tolbert doubted their engine room was operational, and if not, *Dolgoruky*'s crew had no power and was running out of time.

Tolbert figured the U.S. Navy was looking for *North Dakota* by now, but they had an almost insurmountable challenge, locating a submarine under the ice. Tolbert planned to help.

The Sonar Division Chief made another round, inspecting the Sonar equipment, then directed the cabinet and console panels shut. He approached Commander Tolbert.

"All Sonar gear is dried out," Chief Bush said. "Request permission to restore Sonar."

"Start up Sonar."

Chief Bush ordered a cold start-up, and had a sonar tech standing by with a CO_2 fire extinguisher in case a short-circuit started an electrical fire. The servers and consoles energized and the sonar screens flickered to life. There was no indication of anything abnormal.

It took a few minutes for the system to complete its start-up and diagnostics, then Bush called out, "Conn, Sonar. Cold start-up of Sonar is complete. Hold no contacts."

Tolbert ordered his Officer of the Deck, "Transmit MFA OMNI, maximum range scale."

A moment later, *North Dakota* sent a powerful sonar ping into the water.

36

K-535 *YURY DOLGORUKY*

Without the ship's routine to remind him, Nicholai Stepanov lost all sense of time and day. He continued his rounds through the submarine, doing his best not to stumble. He was numb from the cold, and his movements were uncoordinated. He probably should have told the Medical Officer, but decided it didn't matter. They had inserted their last cartridge into the air regeneration unit, and it wouldn't be long before the air could no longer support human life. He figured the toxic air would claim him before the low temperature.

There was only one emergency lantern on in middle level, and the single source of light drew him toward the air regeneration unit. A dozen men were gathered around, sharing a package of the submarine's emergency rations. The men opened a spot, and Stepanov joined them. As he settled onto one of the makeshift chairs they had created from toolboxes and other equipment, the man beside him handed him an open package of food.

Stepanov took a bite of the *galeta,* a hardtack cracker made from flour and water, a common ration in navies around the world. The Russian version was softer than most, not that he could tell. At minus two degrees Celsius, the crackers were rock hard, and he had to let the wafer warm up in his mouth before it became soft enough to chew. He was about to take another bite when he heard the distinctive sound penetrate the submarine's hull.

All eyes turned toward him. He hadn't imagined it.

He stood abruptly, the open package of crackers falling to the deck. Someone was out there, looking for *Dolgoruky* or the American submarine. It might even be the American submarine itself, returning to the location of the collision.

Stepanov shouted, "Grab tools and bang on the hull and piping!"

The men scrambled in the darkness, additional lanterns flicking on as the men searched for suitable items. First one, then another man, banged on the hull and piping, the vigorous pounding knocking off chunks of ice that had frozen on the metal surfaces.

37

USS *NORTH DAKOTA*

"Conn, Sonar. Hold a new broadband contact on the spherical array, designated Sierra one, bearing one-seven-zero."

Tolbert listened as Lieutenant Livingston replied, "Sonar, Conn. Aye. Do you have a classification?"

"Conn, Sonar. No. It doesn't sound like a ship."

"What does it sound like?" Tolbert asked.

Chief Bush directed the Broadband operator, "Put Sierra one on audio."

Petty Officer Reggie Thurlow put the contact on the speakers, and Tolbert listened to the unusual cacophony of metallic tings. After a moment, the sound died down.

"Transmit MFA OMNI," Tolbert ordered. "Maximum range scale."

Bush complied, and a few seconds later, another powerful sonar ping was transmitted.

The metallic tings commenced again.

"Are you thinking what I'm thinking?" Tolbert asked.

"Yes, sir," Bush said. "It's *Dolgoruky*."

A moment later, the metallic tings died down again, and Tolbert ordered, "Send three consecutive pings, one second apart."

The three pings were sent, met again by the unusual noise.

"Line up the WQC for underwater comms," Tolbert ordered.

A moment later, Tolbert placed the WQC microphone to his mouth. "*Dolgoruky*. This is United States submarine. If you can hear me, bang on your hull."

There was no response, so Tolbert tried again. Still no response.

As he slid the microphone into the holder, he said, "They either don't have access to their underwater comm system or don't have power. Either way, we need to establish communications with them somehow."

"How about Morse code?" Thurlow asked. "We can send long and short pulses."

"Don't tell me you know Morse code," Tolbert said.

"Nah," Thurlow said with a grin. "Only the CO of *Dallas* in *The Hunt for Red October* does. I guess he got trained up when they installed the flashing light on his periscope."

The sonar technician was referring to the movie version of *The Hunt for Red October*. Submarine periscopes didn't have flashing lights, and no one besides a radioman on a ballistic missile submarine would know Morse code.

Thurlow added, "But I'm sure it's in Radio's publications somewhere."

"Sounds like a plan," Tolbert said. He turned to Lieutenant Livingston. "Get a few sonar techs schooled up on Morse code and devise a plan to communicate with *Dolgoruky*. In the meantime, continue pinging at one-minute intervals."

Livingston acknowledged, and as he conferred with Chief Bush, Tolbert's thoughts went to *Dolgoruky*'s crew, wondering how much time they had left. The Russian crew had heard *North Dakota*'s pings. The critical question was—had anyone else?

38

ICE CAMP NAUTILUS

Inside the command hut, Alyssa Martin energized the above-ice sonar display after completing its latest move sixteen miles to the north. Shortly after the monitor flickered to life, a small white blip appeared on the screen. She studied the unusual artifact, wondering if a glitch in the system had been created during the array's move. The white blip faded from the screen, then reappeared again.

Alyssa turned to Scott Walworth, operating the RATS. "You hear anything unusual? I'm picking up something to the north."

Walworth pressed the earphones against his ears.

A third blip appeared on Alyssa's screen. "Now," she said.

Walworth squinted, as if that would help him hear, then shook his head. "Nothing."

Alyssa picked up the handheld radio and summoned Verbeck and Leone, who arrived a moment later. As the two men studied the display, the white blip appeared again.

"There," Alyssa said.

Verbeck turned to Leone, who was a former submarine commanding officer. "What do you think?"

"What's the frequency?" Leone asked.

Alyssa pulled up another display and analyzed the blip, reporting the frequency.

"That's her," Leone replied. "That's a Mid-Frequency Active transmission."

"Locate the source," Verbeck directed.

Alyssa selected the farthest row of hydrophones to the north, aligned on an east-west axis, then used the bearings from each hydrophone to determine the blip's location.

"Fifty-seven miles away on a bearing of three-five-seven."

"Convert that to a LAT and LONG," Verbeck said, "then get packing."

Verbeck checked his watch. It was 8 a.m. It would be tight, but they should be able to break down the camp and get the essential sections up and running at the new location by nightfall. He glanced at Alyssa and Walworth, who were wrapping things up with no sense of urgency.

"Hop to, fellas. Daylight's burning."

ST. PETERSBURG, RUSSIA

It was mid-morning in the Russian Navy's headquarters when Fleet Admiral Ivanov's phone rang. As he answered, a glance at the number told him it was the Operations Center.

The Watch Officer introduced himself, then made his report. "The Americans have reported on ISMERLO that they found their submarine. They detected an active sonar transmission this morning."

"Where is it located?"

As Ivanov wrote down the latitude and longitude, the Watch Officer asked, "Do you want to vector one of our submarines to the area?"

"Have the Americans sent other submarines under the ice?"

"Yes, Admiral. One of their guided missile submarines is on its way from the Pacific. If their rescue efforts from the ice camp fail, they will assist using their SEALs and Navy divers."

Ivanov replied, "Pull all submarines from under the ice."

The Watch Officer repeated back Ivanov's directive. "Do you have any other orders, sir?"

"Inform Admiral Lipovsky at Northern Fleet to move our rescue equipment onto the ice. Set up camp as close to the Americans as possible."

Ivanov hung up the phone, then studied the coordinates. The Americans had found their submarine. It was time to put Chernov's plan in motion.

MURMANSK, RUSSIA

Julius Raila stared through the window of the second-floor office at Murmansk Airport. Near the runway were a dozen Antonov AN-74s, loaded with equipment for Ice Camp Barneo. In addition to the AN-74s, three AN-124s were parked nearby, their ramps lowered to the concrete, waiting to be loaded with equipment stripped from Raila's deep-sea rescue ship *Mikhail Rudnitsky*. The heavy AS-34 Priz submersible and its handling gear required the larger AN-124s.

Once a landing strip was prepared, the AN-74s would land on the polar ice cap and off-load the men, equipment, and supplies for Camp Barneo. Since the AN-124s were too heavy to land on the ice, Raila's equipment would be flown to the nearest airport, then ferried to the camp using Russia's MI-26 heavy-lift helicopters, which could lift twenty metric tons at a time.

The Priz class submersible was still loaded on a flatbed truck, undergoing last-minute maintenance. Personnel were checking the status of the submersible's new batteries, developed after the disastrous *Kursk* sinking. The two Priz submersibles employed in the *Kursk* rescue attempts had barely enough power to complete a round trip to the disabled submarine, leaving insufficient time to overcome the challenges of docking with a submarine resting on the ocean bottom with a heavy list and down angle. If they'd had more time that first day, before the heavy storm moved in, they might have successfully mated with the stricken submarine and saved the twenty-three men in Compartment Nine.

Raila's cell phone vibrated. He answered and received the news he'd been awaiting. They had located the American submarine. Camp Barneo would be established one kilometer away from the new American base camp, and the AN-74s would be taking off within the hour, followed by the AN-124s once Raila's equipment was loaded. The AN-124s would land at Svalbard Airport in Norway, where his equipment would be ferried to the camp.

He hung up the phone, and as he surveyed his men completing final maintenance checks on AS-34, he realized they were fortunate to have developed new batteries. Unlike the American deep-submergence rescue vehicle, Russia's Priz class submersibles had a range of thirty-eight kilometers. They didn't need to establish an ice camp directly over the disabled submarine. Anywhere close would suffice.

41

USS *MICHIGAN*

Depth: 600 feet.

Speed: Ahead Flank.

Captain Murray Wilson leaned over the navigation plot in Control, examining their transit across the Arctic Ocean. In the deep-water basins, *Michigan* could proceed at maximum speed without fear of hitting the ocean bottom or ice keels descending from above.

In front of Wilson stood Petty Officer Second Class Pat Leenstra, on watch as Quartermaster. The electronics technician was analyzing the ship's two inertial navigators for error. Once *Michigan* passed eighty-four degrees north latitude, both had been shifted to Polar Mode to compensate for the reduced effect of the Earth's rotation. Traveling across the top of the world was always touchy when relying on inertial navigators. For example, when at the North Pole, no matter which direction you turned, you were headed south.

"How are we doing, Leenstra?"

"Good, sir. Both inertial navigators are tracking together."

Wilson nodded at the good news, then glanced around the quiet Control Room. It was 6 a.m. and watch turnover was in progress. The enlisted watchstanders had already relieved, and the oncoming Officer of the Deck was reviewing the ship's status with the off-going OOD. Per custom, the oncoming officer was the last member of his watch section to relieve, the turnover occurring as close to the hour as possible.

The two men completed their turnover and Lieutenant DeCrispino announced that he had the Deck and the Conn. As Petty Officer Leenstra entered the event into the ship's log, Wilson began his tour through the submarine, swinging first through Radio and Sonar.

The tour through Radio was uneventful, aside from the Radioman of the Watch noting they were approaching the end of their broadcast window. Wilson had accounted for that in his Night Orders, which laid out the schedule for the next day. Lieutenant DeCrispino would slow and come shallow, allowing their floating wire antenna to rise close enough to the ice to receive VLF transmissions. A quick stop in Sonar confirmed what Wilson already knew. They held no contacts, and hadn't since they'd entered the Bering Strait.

With his tour of Operations Compartment Upper Level complete, Wilson dropped down one level to the officer staterooms. The XO's door was closed, as were the doors to the three-man staterooms shared by the other twelve officers. Wilson continued to Operations Compartment Third Level, where the cooks were wrapping up breakfast, and after a quick tour through the Torpedo Room in Lower Level, Wilson felt the submarine tilt upward and the vibrations in the deck ease. Lieutenant DeCrispino was slowing and coming shallow to copy the broadcast.

Wilson continued his tour, heading aft toward the Missile Compartment. In *Michigan*'s previous life, he would have stopped in Missile Control Center, reviewing the status of the ship's twenty-four nuclear warhead–tipped missiles. But MCC was now outfitted with the Attack Tomahawk Weapon System, and there would be no missile launches while under the ice. Wilson bypassed MCC and entered the Missile Compartment on the port side, by Missile Tube Two.

Tubes One and Two had been converted into access hatches to the Dry Deck Shelters attached to *Michigan*'s Missile Deck. In the other twenty-two tubes, Tomahawk seven-pack launchers had been installed, arming *Michigan* with 154 Tomahawk missiles. However, each of the Dry Deck Shelters covered two of the Tomahawk tubes, reducing *Michigan*'s available arsenal to eighteen tubes. The Tomahawk launchers took up only the top one-third of each tube, and the remaining space had been configured for various uses. Two of the missile tubes had been converted into magazines, which stored over sixty tons of ordnance—every type of weapon and explosive a SEAL team could require.

In the level beneath Wilson, the bulk of the crew slept in nine-man bunkrooms between the missile tubes, while the SEALs and Navy divers slept in berthing installed in second level during the submarine's conversion to SSGN. Wilson headed down the port side of the submarine toward the Engine

Room, spotting yellow light leaking from one of the SEAL bunkrooms. He stopped and rapped his knuckles on the side of tube Twelve, then pulled back the dark brown curtain covering the entryway. In the top of three bunks, Lieutenant Jake Harrison laid prone, the light above his bunk illuminating a book in his hands.

Harrison looked over. "Good morning, Captain."

He swung his feet over the edge of his bunk and dropped onto the deck. The forty-two-year-old prior-enlisted SEAL was an imposing physical specimen; six feet, two hundred pounds, with deep blue eyes set within a chiseled face. Over the last few days, Wilson had met with Harrison and Commander John McNeil, who was in charge of *Michigan*'s SEAL detachment. They had discussed the capabilities of McNeil's SEALs and Navy divers and how to rescue *North Dakota*'s crew, or at least transfer emergency supplies aboard, should the rescue from topside fail.

"Morning, Lieutenant," Wilson replied. "You're up early."

"I just finished working out," he replied, "then I decided to read a while before the day got started."

Wilson was about to head aft when he spotted the photos taped to the top of Harrison's rack; pictures of his wife and daughter, plus one of another woman. She had one arm in a sling and a crutch under the other.

"Is that Christine O'Connor?" Wilson asked.

Harrison followed Wilson's gaze. "Yes, sir. That's when we were in Guam, waiting for *Michigan* to pull in."

Christine had accompanied the SEAL team into Beijing, and she and Harrison were the only two who survived, neither without injury. Wilson's eyes went to Harrison's shoulder. "How's the arm?"

"Good as new."

There was an awkward silence as Wilson debated whether to ask Harrison about his relationship with O'Connor. Having a photo of another woman taped to your rack, beside your wife's, was unusual. Finally, he decided to ask.

"Rumor has it you and Christine were engaged."

"We were," Harrison replied. "But that was twenty-four years ago, and we've gone our separate ways. She's a good friend now. Nothing more."

There was another awkward silence, interrupted by the Messenger of the Watch, who pulled to a halt behind Wilson, almost passing by the Captain in his haste. He handed Wilson the message board. "New orders, sir."

Wilson flipped through the OPORD, reading the pertinent details. They had located *North Dakota,* and *Michigan* had been directed to rendezvous at prescribed coordinates.

As he handed the board back to the Messenger, *Michigan* tilted downward and Wilson felt the vibration in the deck return. Lieutenant DeCrispino had ordered the submarine deep again, and back to ahead flank.

42

K-329 *SEVERODVINSK*

With his nuclear attack submarine at periscope depth just outside the Marginal Ice Zone, Captain Second Rank Josef Buffanov sat at his desk in his stateroom, reviewing the weekly reports. Since receipt of the Commanding Officer Only message three days ago, he had reflected on the mission he had been assigned. It was only a precautionary measure, he told himself, and hopefully the plan would not be executed. If the order was received, however, *Severodvinsk* was well armed for the task.

There was a knock on his stateroom door, and after Buffanov acknowledged, the door opened to reveal the Communication Post Messenger.

"Captain," the young senior seaman began, "we have received another Commanding Officer Only message."

Buffanov arrived in the Communication Post a moment later, stopping by the printers as the radioman looked up. Buffanov announced, "Ready," and a single sheet of paper emerged. As he read it, his fear was confirmed. *Severodvinsk* was being called into service.

He left Communications and entered the Command Post at the same time his First Officer, Captain Third Rank Anton Novikoff, arrived. Novikoff had obviously been informed of the second Commanding Officer Only message. There were few things Buffanov kept from his First Officer. Buffanov eyed Novikoff as the younger man waited by the navigation table. At the proper time, he would seek his counsel. Until then, he would not reveal their mission.

Buffanov ripped off the bottom of the message and handed it to Novikoff. "Have the Navigating Officer plot a course to this position."

Novikoff read the coordinates, no doubt realizing they were headed deep under the polar ice cap. He looked up at Buffanov, waiting for him to explain why. Buffanov did not amplify.

"Yes, Captain. I will have the Navigating Officer plot our new course. When will we head under the ice?"

Buffanov considered his First Officer's question. The timeline for *Severodvinsk* was fluid and uncertain. However, the sooner they arrived, the better.

"Come down from periscope depth and station the Ice Detail. Inform me when we are ready to enter the Marginal Ice Zone."

43

K-157 *VEPR*

Captain Second Rank Matvey Baczewski sat in the Captain's chair in the Officers' Mess, with a half-dozen of his senior officers flanking each side of the table. *Vepr's* Weapons Officer was at the front of the Mess, standing beside a flat panel monitor, reviewing the features of their 533-millimeter torpedoes and the optimum settings. Shooting torpedoes under the ice was challenging, and over the shallow Barents Shelf, even more so. The torpedo would receive many false returns. The surface reflections from the ice canopy would be strong, and there would also be bottom bounces. If the settings were improper, their torpedoes could follow the reflections and smash into the surface ice or ocean bottom.

Complicating matters were the random ice keels. Even if the settings were optimal, their torpedoes might interpret an ice keel as a valid target. Of course, they could instruct their torpedoes to ignore immobile objects, but then they would also ignore a submarine playing possum against the ice.

The communication panel on the bulkhead buzzed, and a glance at the red light told Baczewski it was from the Communication Post. *Vepr* was at periscope depth just outside the Marginal Ice Zone, monitoring communications as directed. An important message must have been received for officer training to be interrupted.

Baczewski picked up the handset. Another Commanding Officer Only message had been received; one he had been waiting for.

A moment later, Baczewski was in the Communication Post, standing by one of the printers. "Ready," he said, and the message slid out. As he read it, he realized the basic plan hadn't changed. Their target, however, was a surprise. And she was heavily armed. Baczewski thought for a moment on the potential reasons they would engage this target, then decided it didn't matter. He had accepted the mission from Fleet Admiral Ivanov, and *Vepr* would not fail.

Baczewski pulled a blank sheet of paper from the printer and wrote down the coordinates, then headed into the Command Post.

"Station the Ice Detail," he said to his Watch Officer as he handed him the sheet of paper. "Plot a course to this position."

PECHENGA, RUSSIA

In the northwest corner of the Kola Peninsula, not far from the coast and only ten kilometers from the Norwegian border, Captain First Rank Josef Klokov took a break from reviewing paperwork, gazing out his window at the sprawling military base. For the sake of external appearances, Klokov's unit was a component of the 200th Independent Motor Rifle Brigade, and his men wore the same uniform with no special designation. However, they were no ordinary soldiers. His unit was one of two highly trained Polar Spetsnaz brigades.

Klokov's Executive Officer, Captain Second Rank Gleb Leonov, entered Klokov's office with a message folder in hand. Klokov accepted the folder and read the directive. His unit was being deployed. The Russian ice camp setup had commenced and suitable habitats were being constructed for his men.

"Your orders, Captain?" Leonov asked.

The message was deliberately vague, but Admiral Ivanov had explained the details during his visit. If the Americans won the race to rescue the two submarine crews, Klokov's unit would be employed to . . . *rectify* the situation.

The American ice camp would likely not be armed, aside from the polar bear watches. A single Spetsnaz platoon of twenty-four men would be sufficient for the task. However, they would also need to board the American submarine, so he decided two platoons would be required. As far as timing went, the Russian ice camp accommodations would be ready by nightfall.

"Prepare two platoons," Klokov said. "We deploy tonight at dusk."

ICE STATION NAUTILUS

"*North Dakota* is directly beneath us."

Standing atop the ice floe with Paul Leone, Vance Verbeck acknowledged the report from his ice pilot. Earlier this morning, after detecting the sonar pulse from the American submarine, personnel had flown north to determine a more accurate position, drilling holes in the ice every five hundred yards, dropping hydrophones to listen for *North Dakota*'s sonar pulse. After cutting three holes, they triangulated the submarine's position, and Verbeck was now standing directly over the disabled submarine.

He had already confirmed the ice flow was ten-feet-thick multiyear ice, capable of supporting an ice camp and even more important, the three-hundred-ton Submarine Rescue Diving and Recompression System. To differentiate between the two camps during the transition, Verbeck had decided to give the new ice camp a different name. He was partial to the name Nautilus, America's first nuclear-powered submarine, and seeing how the new installation would be much larger than a typical camp, with over one hundred additional submarine rescue personnel, Verbeck decided to name the new location Ice Station Nautilus.

Verbeck shielded his eyes from the mid-afternoon sun as he examined the activity on the ice floe. Their bulldozer had been airlifted to the new camp and was busy plowing a landing strip, and a dozen helicopters hovered nearby, all but one carrying a plywood hut strapped in slings, with the last helicopter carrying a payload of electronic equipment they would need right away.

"Put the command hut there," Verbeck said, pointing to the nearest ice hole they had drilled, a few hundred feet to the west. The command hut needed access through the ice to lower the RATS hydrophone, plus the ice above *North Dakota* had to be left free for the submarine rescue equipment.

Leone relayed the order over his radio, and the command hut descended from the sky. A layer of light snow billowed toward them, driven by the helicopter's rotor wash. After lining up the command hut floor with the ice hole, the hut landed and men scrambled atop the plywood building and disconnected one end of each sling. After extracting the slings from under the hut, the helicopter tilted and headed south for another round of ferrying equipment from the old camp, as did the other helicopters after they deposited their berthing huts.

Verbeck inspected the outside of the command hut, then stepped inside. He nodded with satisfaction. His assessment that the huts would survive the short trip in good weather had not been wrong. The smaller berthing huts would be no problem, although the galley and generator tents would have to be dissembled and reassembled, but that was not a difficult task. The rest of the equipment and supplies would be brought north once the landing strip for the C-130s was ready.

For now, Verbeck focused on establishing communications with *North Dakota*. If time was running out, he needed to know what that timeline was. He stepped outside the command hut to check on the electronic equipment. It was carried by the last helicopter, and Leone directed it to land nearby. The RATS gear was the first equipment to arrive at the hut, and the hydrophone was lowered through the ice hole and the equipment connected to a portable generator outside.

As Scott Walworth energized the RATS, the rhythmic beat of helicopter rotors greeted Verbeck's ears. Their helicopters could not have returned with another load so soon. Verbeck opened the command hut door and peered outside. The sky was filled with a hoard of helicopters headed toward them from the southwest, carrying loads suspended from slings. The rotor tempo was deeper than the helicopters the United States used, and as they grew larger in the sky, Verbeck realized they were Russian MI-26 helicopters, the most powerful cargo helicopters in existence.

The swarm of helicopters skirted Ice Station Nautilus, then continued northeast a half-mile before they slowed to a hover and deposited their loads onto an adjacent ice floe. The Russians had apparently decided to help, or perhaps someone in the administration had requested their assistance. Still, it was unusual for another country to appear on scene without prior coordination. Once he sorted out the details with *North Dakota*, he would include the information about the new Russian ice camp in his next report to COMSUBFOR.

"I'm ready," Walworth yelled from inside the command hut.

Verbeck stepped inside and gave the go-ahead, and Walworth spoke into the microphone. A hundred feet below the ice, his voice was transmitted by the RATS hydrophone.

"USS *North Dakota,* this is Ice Station Nautilus. Do you read me?"

46

USS *NORTH DAKOTA*

Sonar Technician Second Class Reggie Thurlow propped his elbows on his console as he pressed the headphones against his ears. *North Dakota* had resumed its underway watch rotation, and normalcy had returned to the submarine. The lights were on and all tactical systems had been restored. Temperature had returned to normal, and he had shed the SEIE suit and green foul-weather jacket; he was back to wearing just the standard blue coveralls. There was no indication that less than a day ago *North Dakota* had almost become a dark, icy tomb.

North Dakota had just transmitted another sonar pulse, and Thurlow listened intently for a sign someone had heard them. He wasn't exactly sure what he was listening for, though. But at least it was quiet under the ice cap, devoid of shipping noise and the chatter of biologics—the especially noisy shrimp were absent.

Although it was quiet under the ice cap, there were all sorts of weird noises, and more than one sonar tech had reported a contact with diesel lines. Further analysis determined the sound was low-frequency tonals produced by the edges of the ice floes as they ground against each other. Thurlow was nearing the end of his watch, and his mind was playing tricks on him. A few minutes ago, he thought he heard the faint beat of helicopter rotors, but then it disappeared. The next sound Thurlow heard, however, left no doubt—it wasn't his imagination. It was a man's voice, clear as day.

USS North Dakota, *this is Ice Station Nautilus. Do you read me?*

"Officer of the Deck!" Thurlow shouted, bypassing the Sonar Supervisor in his excitement. "I've got something!"

Lieutenant Molitor, seated at the command workstation, turned toward Thurlow as the Sonarman put the audio on speaker.

USS North Dakota, *this is Ice Station Nautilus. Do you read me?*

"Energize the WQC," Molitor ordered as he grabbed the 1-MC micro-phone at his workstation. "Captain to Control."

Tolbert arrived as another transmission emanated from the speakers.

USS North Dakota, *this is Ice Station Nautilus. Do you read me?*

He stopped by the forward port console, and a quick glance told him the WQC was lined up to transmit. He pulled the microphone from the holder and replied, trying to conceal his excitement.

"Ice Station Nautilus, this is *North Dakota*. Read you loud and clear, over."

"*North Dakota,* we are establishing an ice camp above you. What is your condition?"

Tolbert spent the next few minutes explaining *North Dakota*'s status. As their conversation wound down, Tolbert informed the ice station that the Russian submarine had sunk after the collision, and *North Dakota*'s crew had determined through Morse code communications that *Dolgoruky*'s crew had less than thirty-six hours of viable air remaining.

A rescue would indeed be required, but not for *North Dakota*.

47

WASHINGTON, D.C.

Christine O'Connor was seated in the Oval Office across from the president, along with Chief of Staff Kevin Hardison and Captain Brackman. The president was on the phone with SecDef Don Richardson, and Christine watched several emotions play across the president's face. It was clear from the one-sided conversation that they had located USS *North Dakota* and the crew was okay. However, Christine was unable to discern the reason for the president's surprised, then concerned, expression toward the end of the call.

"Thank you, Don," the president said. "Keep me informed."

After he hung up, he addressed his staff. "We've located *North Dakota* and the crew is safe. They have power and life support, and enough food to last several months. The issue is propulsion. They collided with a Russian submarine and damaged their main and backup propulsion systems and are stuck under the ice. The Navy is working on a plan to tow the submarine to a shipyard for repairs."

The president paused, and Christine waited for him to explain the reason for his expressions during the end of the call.

"The Russian submarine was also damaged and sank nearby," the president continued. "Two of the compartments are flooded and they've lost power, and they're using emergency supplies to provide oxygen and remove carbon dioxide from the air. The best estimate is that they have a day and a half left before the air becomes toxic.

"We've shifted the focus of our rescue effort to the Russian crew," the president added. "However, the Russians are also setting up an ice camp a half-mile from ours, preparing for a rescue attempt of their own. The peculiar part is that they started setting up camp before we learned the Russian submarine sank nearby. It's apparent they've known all along their submarine sank and haven't told us."

"I thought the Russians learned their lesson after the *Kursk* debacle," Hardison said. "Why would they keep the sinking of their submarine a secret and risk not only the crew, but another public affairs nightmare?"

"The submarine is *Yury Dolgoruky*?" Christine asked.

"It is," the president said. "*North Dakota* trailed her under the ice cap."

"The Russians act oddly whenever their Borei class submarine or Bulava missile is involved. They're hiding something from us," Christine said. "The last thing they want is for us to rescue *Dolgoruky*'s crew, then take a walkabout aboard their submarine, loaded with Bulava missiles."

"I agree," the president replied. "Your task is to figure out what they're hiding. In the meantime, I'll inform Kalinin that we've found their submarine and will do our best to rescue its crew."

Hardison asked, "How are you going to broach the issue of whether they've known their submarine sank and kept it from us?"

The president replied, "I'll state the facts and see what he says, then take it from there."

He checked his watch. It was 5 p.m. in Moscow, and Kalinin would likely still be in the Kremlin. The president picked up the phone and directed his secretary to put him through. A moment later, the call was connected, and the president put it on speaker.

The two men exchanged pleasantries, and then the president said, "Yuri, I'm sorry to call you unexpectedly, but I have important information to share."

"It is not a problem," Kalinin replied with the same light accent Christine remembered from their meeting in Moscow. "What is the issue?"

"We've located our submarine under the ice cap. It collided with one of your submarines, which sank nearby."

"I am already aware," Kalinin replied. "We have been monitoring ISMERLO and learned of the collision an hour ago. We are preparing to rescue our crew."

Christine was surprised at Kalinin's matter-of-fact response. No accusations. An American submarine had been following *Dolgoruky* and disaster had occurred, but the expected finger pointing had not commenced. However, there was no way Russia learned only an hour ago that their submarine had sunk. The president decided to press the issue.

"I noticed you established an ice camp near ours before we learned your submarine had sunk. Why is that?"

Kalinin replied without hesitation, "We were preparing to help. Our submarine rescue equipment is designed to handle the harsh Arctic temperatures, and we were uncertain of your equipment. There must have been a breakdown in communication, and our offer of assistance was not relayed."

The president looked at Christine, who overrode her impulse to mouth the words, "He's lying."

"Thank you," the president replied. "I appreciate your assistance. We will do the same. If we complete preparations first, we will rescue *Dolgoruky*'s crew."

This time, there was hesitation on Kalinin's end. After a few seconds, he replied, "Your assistance is not required. I will contact you if circumstances change. Thank you for the call."

Without another word, Kalinin hung up.

The president turned off the speakerphone. "That was interesting," he said.

And consistent, Christine thought. Any time *Dolgoruky* was involved in the conversation, the Russian response was irrational. There was only one way to figure out what was going on. She would need help, though. Greg Hartfield and Stu Berman, the ONI experts on the Borei class submarine and Bulava missile, would be a start. Plus Brackman. As a former commanding officer of a ballistic missile submarine, his insight might prove valuable.

"Mr. President," Christine said. "I'd like to visit our ice camp, and bring Captain Brackman and two ONI experts with me."

"What would you do once you got there?" the president asked.

"A walkabout." Christine smiled, then added, "If we complete preparations first and rescue the Russian crew, we could then return and . . . take a look around."

As the president considered Christine's request, Hardison said, "That's not a bad idea. If the opportunity presents itself, I recommend we have a team of experts board *Dolgoruky*."

After a long moment, the president replied, "Coordinate with ONI to assemble a team, and if we rescue *Dolgoruky*'s crew, go back aboard and check things out. I want to find out what they're hiding."

48

ICE CAMP BARNEO

Darkness had descended over the wintry landscape, temperatures dipping into the negatives as Julius Raila, Russia's Chief of Search and Rescue Services, took a sip of hot tea. He was seated in his berthing hut, reviewing his notes scribbled on sheets of paper scattered across the table's surface. There were no manuals for stripping the rescue equipment from *Mikhail Rudnitsky* and reassembling it atop the polar ice cap. As he scratched his cheek through his thick gray beard, he realized there was an American term for what he was doing. He was winging it.

Once the equipment was reassembled, he was confident it would work properly, even in the subzero temperatures. What concerned Raila was lowering their submersible through the three-meter-thick ice after digging a five-by-fifteen-meter wide hole. They had to excavate over two hundred tons of ice.

As Raila wondered whether the equipment could withstand the rigors of digging through multiyear ice as hard as concrete, his attention was captured by the whirr of helicopter rotors. But unlike the heavy beat from the MI-26 cargo helicopters, the sound was a soft purr. He donned his jacket and opened the door, examining the heliport on the east side of camp.

As the helicopters approached, the bright lights around the landing pad were extinguished. In the faint illumination from the remaining ice camp lights, Raila watched the first of four white helicopters land and a dozen soldiers in white Arctic gear exit. It took only fifteen seconds and the helicopter lifted off, settling to rest in the snow twenty meters to the east. One by one, the three other helicopters landed, each off-loading another dozen men, although the fourth helicopter off-loaded two extra soldiers, whom Raila assumed were the unit's senior officers, for a total of fifty.

Raila watched the camp director, Demil Poleski, greet the men and direct them toward their berthing huts. When Raila returned his attention to the heliport, he had difficulty locating the white helicopters blending into the landscape. As he closed the door, he wondered why a Polar Spetsnaz unit had been sent to Camp Barneo.

49

SVALBARD, NORWAY

Christine leaned back in her seat aboard the C-32 executive transport, the military version of Boeing's 757, looking out the window as the aircraft descended. The C-32, normally used by the vice president, was designated Air Force One whenever the president was aboard, or Air Force Two when the vice president was being flown. However, with only Christine, Brackman, and twelve ONI personnel as passengers today, neither call sign applied.

Seven hours earlier, Christine had departed Joint Base Andrews just outside Washington. Pam Bruce at ONI had assembled a team of experts on short notice; there was no lack of volunteers. Stu Berman and Greg Hartfield sat behind Christine and Brackman, with both men gazing out the window while Brackman sat in an aisle seat beside Christine, his eyes closed.

They were flying over Spitsbergen, the largest and only permanently inhabited island in the Norwegian archipelago of Svalbard. Through a break in the clouds, Christine spotted the town of Longyearbyen, the world's northernmost city, with a population of two thousand. In Norwegian, Longyearbyen translated to Longyear City; the town was founded by John Longyear, an American who established a mining operation on the archipelago in 1906. A more appropriate name, however, would have been Long*night* City.

In late October, the sun sets for the last time each year, remaining below the horizon and shrouding Longyearbyen in the Arctic night for almost four months. Thankfully, it was mid-March and the sun rose at the respectable time of 6 a.m. In another month, the Arctic day would begin, the sun not setting until late August.

As they prepared to land and begin the final leg of their journey to the polar ice camp, Christine figured the first-class seats would be the last creature comforts she would experience for a while. A few minutes later, the C-32 touched down at Svalbard Airport and coasted to a halt opposite the terminal and adjacent hangar. While she waited for the staircase, she examined the scenery through the cabin window. The airport was running out of parking space.

Lining one side of the runway were fifteen C-17 aircraft, their ramps down and cargo bays empty, while a CH-53E Super Stallion, the U.S. military's most powerful cargo helicopter, hovered above the pavement, attached to the last load of equipment. In addition to the American aircraft, a dozen Russian Anton AN-74s were parked alongside the runway, their ramps also lowered and cargo bays empty. It looked like Svalbard Airport had become a staging point for both countries establishing ice camps.

Christine nudged Brackman and his eyes opened. After a glance out the window, he stood and pulled Christine's luggage from the overhead, then his. They donned their coats and Christine headed toward the front of the cabin, followed by Brackman and the ONI team. The cabin door opened and a blast of frigid air hit Christine. As she descended the staircase, several four-person transporters approached, stopping near the base of the stairs. The driver exited the first vehicle and greeted Christine as she stepped onto the tarmac.

"Good morning, Ms. O'Connor," he said loudly over the whine of the C-32's jet engines. "I'm Bobby Pleasant, director of the Arctic Submarine Lab. I'll get your team geared up for your stay at the ice camp and send you on your way."

Christine thanked him and climbed aboard with Brackman and Berman, and the vehicle took off with a jolt. Pleasant spoke into a handheld radio as the transporter curved toward the hangar, and the forty-foot-tall double doors slid open. Inside, men were placing equipment on cargo pallets and rolling fifty-gallon drums toward awaiting aircraft. There was a row of offices on the left side, and along the back wall, arranged on hanging racks and shelves, was an assortment of winter clothing. Pleasant stopped beside a rack of black jackets, each with a fur-lined hood, an American flag on the left shoulder, and the Arctic Submarine Lab patch on the right breast. After they exited the vehicle, Pleasant eyed Christine, then pulled a jacket from the rack and handed it to her.

"Try this on."

Christine removed her coat and slipped into the thick insulated jacket. The arm length was right, but it was loose fitting otherwise.

"It's a little big," she said.

"It's perfect," Pleasant said. "Once you're bundled up in the rest of your gear, there won't be extra room."

He handed jackets to Brackman and Berman, who tried them on. After a nod of satisfaction, Pleasant sorted through a box and retrieved three black leather name tags with gold lettering on the front and Velcro on the back. He pressed one tag onto Berman's jacket, over the corresponding Velcro patch on the left side, then slapped the second onto Brackman's jacket. He stopped by Christine and was about to press her name tag onto her jacket when he pulled up short and handed the tag to her instead. The Velcro patch was over her left breast.

"You should probably put this on," he said.

Christine smiled. "No problem."

Pleasant led them down the line of clothing, explaining what the items were as he piled them in their arms. "On the polar ice cap, you'll wear three layers of clothing: the parka and bib overalls, a mid-layer fleece pullover and pants; and a base layer of thermal underwear."

He added a balaclava to keep her head and neck warm, gloves, and four pairs of wool socks. Finally, he stopped by a bin and pulled out three green duffle bags.

"Stow your gear in these," he said, "then put on two pairs of socks."

After donning the socks, Christine tried on a pair of boots Pleasant provided, which were a perfect fit.

"There's an empty office where you change into your gear. Hop in."

The transporter took off with a jolt again, leaving the rest of the ONI team behind as they accumulated their clothing, and Pleasant pulled up to the empty office.

"When you change," he said, "turn your cell phones off. They won't work on the ice cap. No signal. We use special Iridium phones."

Once Christine and the two men were properly clad, Pleasant guided them toward an aircraft with its rear ramp lowered, explaining the Casa C-212 twin turboprop cargo plane would take them to the ice camp. There were no executive transports; everything hauled cargo. Inside the aircraft were a dozen fifty-gallon drums, six on each side, leaving the center aisle clear. At the front of the cargo bay were two bench seats facing rearward.

Pleasant disappeared into the cockpit and reemerged with a man who looked like a backwoodsman, with a bushy beard, knit cap, sweatshirt, and coveralls.

"This is Frank Salimbene, your pilot."

"Make yourselves comfortable," Salimbene said, breaking into a grin as he gestured to the bench seats, outfitted with thin, worn pads. "We've got a two-hour trip. If you want," he added, "I've got an extra seat in the cockpit, if anyone wants to join me.

Stu Berman immediately perked up but didn't say anything, and Christine could tell he was waiting for her to accept or decline.

"Why don't you join Frank?" Christine said.

Berman smiled. "Thanks, Ms. O'Connor."

"Well," Pleasant said, "that wraps things up on my end. You'll be in good hands from here on out. The rest of your team will follow in additional aircraft."

Pleasant shook everyone's hands, then headed down the cargo bay ramp. Christine and Brackman deposited their duffle bags on the bench seats on one side of the aircraft, then settled into their seats on the other side, with Christine by the window and Brackman along the aisle again. A moment later, the ramp lifted upward, and she felt the vibration in the deck as the twin turboprops began spinning. There were six small portals on each side of the cargo bay, and Christine looked out the nearest one as the Casa exited the hangar, then taxied onto the airstrip and took off.

This time of year, the Svalbard archipelago was ice-locked, and it was only a few minutes before the island of Spitsbergen faded in the distance, leaving nothing but a white landscape. As far as she could see, there was nothing but flat ice, interrupted only by ragged ridges that marked where the edges of the ice floes met. From their altitude of only a few hundred feet, the ridges looked like raised ant trails, wandering randomly across the polar ice.

The drone of the Casa's turboprop engines filled Christine's ears as it plodded steadily northeast toward the ice camp. In the unheated cargo bay of the aircraft, Christine's left shoulder began to ache. She tried massaging it through her thick jacket, but her efforts had no effect. Brackman noticed and watched for a while, then spoke.

"Does it always hurt?"

"Only when it's cold and my muscles tighten up."

Brackman glanced at her legs. "How's the thigh?"

"It's fine."

The aching in her shoulder and Brackman's questions pulled Christine's thoughts into the past, when she had been trapped in Beijing's Great Hall of the People during China's war with the United States. She had left a trail of six bodies, but the seventh and final death had always been difficult to reconcile. With bullets in her thigh and shoulder, and blood running down her face from a gash in her head, she had been in no mood for negotiation. Christine knew she was impulsive and it sometimes got her into trouble, but this time she had put a bullet in the head of a defenseless man who knelt at her feet.

She had replayed the scene in her mind a thousand times, wondering how different choices would have turned out. As she relived the encounter, a lump formed in her throat. She glanced at the hand that pulled the trigger, then looked out the small window, trying to divert her mind from what she had done.

Christine felt Brackman's hand on hers, and she turned and met his eyes.

"You did the right thing," he said. "Stop second-guessing yourself."

Brackman had somehow known where her thoughts were. In the heat of the moment, it had seemed justified; the lives of many Americans were at stake. In hindsight, she wasn't sure. It was murder, despite the justification.

"I can't," she replied.

Brackman left his hand on hers, and Christine wondered if there was something more to his gesture. She recalled his kiss in the Pentagon when USS *Kentucky*'s last warhead was destroyed, a kiss that lingered too long for a simple congratulation. However, Brackman had given no other indication he was interested in her. That was fine with Christine. A romance with another member of the president's staff would have complicated her life.

As she looked at his hand, she remembered the first time she met him; there had been a faint tan line on his left ring finger. Brackman had been a recent widow, his wife and daughter killed in an accident a few weeks before arriving at the White House. Brackman had never talked about it, and up to now, she had never asked.

Christine peered around the corner, into the cockpit. Berman was chatting with the pilot, and she could see a GPS display in the console. They still had a ways to go; plenty of time to kill. She decided to broach the subject.

"What happened to your wife and daughter?"

Brackman's head snapped toward her and she felt his body tense as he pulled away his hand.

"You don't have to talk about it," Christine added quickly. "I was just wondering."

Brackman stared at her for a long moment, then leaned back against the bulkhead, but the tension in his body didn't ease. He answered, "They were killed in a car accident. They got rear-ended at a traffic light and their car burst into flames. They were trapped inside."

It was Brackman's turn to look away, staring out one of the windows on his side. Christine reached over and squeezed his hand. He gave no indication he noticed. They completed the rest of the flight in silence.

Her stomach dropping signaled the aircraft's descent, and Christine peered out the window as the plane turned in preparation for landing. She spotted the ice camp in the distance, a hodgepodge of buildings and tents, with a depot of supplies to one side.

They landed with a gentle bump and the aircraft coasted to a halt. The aircraft ramp lowered and Stu Berman and the pilot emerged from the cockpit. After collecting her duffle bag, Christine stepped onto the hard-packed snow and shielded her eyes from the bright sunlight reflecting off the white surface.

A man approached and said, "Good morning, Ms. O'Connor. I'm Vance Verbeck, technical director of the Arctic Submarine Lab. Welcome to Ice Station Nautilus."

50

ICE STATION NAUTILUS

"I take it your trip was uneventful?" Verbeck asked as he escorted Christine, Brackman, and Berman from the airstrip toward the cloister of buildings.

Christine answered, "No issues."

As they approached the camp, she noticed the clear blue sky and calm air; not what she had imagined atop the polar ice cap. "Do you get many storms?" she asked.

"Very few," Verbeck said. "The Arctic is actually classified a desert. The air is so cold that it doesn't hold much water vapor, so it rarely snows. Clear days like this are the norm." Verbeck continued, explaining the layout of the camp when they reached the outer buildings. "The camp contains three dozen berthing hooches, a command hut, galley, and generator tent. Plus there's the rescue equipment that arrived last night. I'll take you to your berthing hooch first, where you can drop off your stuff. You'll be staying in Tahiti."

"Tahiti?"

"Each ice camp has a theme for berthing hooch names," Verbeck explained. "Submarines, naval battles, famous hotels. You could have been in the Ritz, but the theme for this camp is tropical islands. Your hooch is over there."

Verbeck pointed toward a plywood hut with TAHITI stenciled on the side in black spray paint. "It's the most luxurious accommodation this side of eighty-north." Verbeck grinned as he stopped by the hut and opened the door.

The inside was no more elegant than the outside. The windowless box included six bunks built from two-by-fours and plywood. The only items not made of wood were the mattresses and bedding, two white plastic chairs and a small table, and a circular metal heater with a hose running through the wall to a fuel tank outside, plus a couple of metal hooks on the wall to hang their gear. Verbeck pointed to one of the bunks, which was neatly made up with the linen tucked in. "That's yours."

Christine placed her duffel bag on the bed and Verbeck led them to the hooch Brackman and Berman were assigned to, letting them drop off their gear as well, then continued the tour. Next up was the command hut.

It was the largest hut in the camp, the size of two berthing hooches mashed together. An assortment of antennas were mounted to the roof, so it was easy to spot from anywhere in the camp. Inside, two senior naval officers were reviewing a timeline posted on the wall. The older man was Vice Admiral Eric Dahlenburg, Fleet Forces Deputy Commander for Fleet and Joint Operations, and the other was Captain Mike Naughton, Commodore of Submarine Squadron ELEVEN.

Admiral Dahlenburg extended his hand to Christine. "It's a pleasure to meet you. I've heard a lot about you."

Christine shook hands as she gave the Admiral an inquisitive look. "How's that?"

"Actually, I read about you. Captain Brackman provided your bio. Very impressive, especially your handiness with a pistol."

Christine cast a steely glance at Brackman, who seemed not to notice.

She turned back to the Admiral. "My ex-husband taught me how to shoot."

"He did a good job."

Christine didn't reply, so Dahlenburg continued. "Has Vance explained the command structure here?"

"Not yet, Admiral."

"As far as the ice camp goes, Vance Verbeck is the Officer-in-Charge, and he's responsible for day-to-day operations. For submarine rescue operations, there are three echelons of command. I'm the On-Scene Commander, Captain Naughton here is Coordinator, Rescue Forces, and Commander Ned Steel, who is out earning his paycheck, is the Rescue Element Commander.

"In plain English," Dahlenburg added, "Commander Steel is supervising the assembly of the submarine rescue equipment, Naughton is here to supervise Steel, and I'm doing a fine job supervising Naughton. Standard military operation." The Admiral grinned, then added, "Our command structure is designed for an at-sea rescue, where several Navy and civilian ships and even other nations could be involved. It's redundant on the polar ice cap, but we've had a number of challenges to work through, and as they say, three heads are better than one."

"I understand," Christine said. "Speaking of challenges, where do we stand on the rescue attempt?"

The Admiral deferred to Captain Naughton, who answered, "The submarine rescue system is being assembled, and we expect everything will be ready by nightfall. The biggest challenge is cutting an access hole large enough for the rescue vehicle. The Pressurized Rescue Module is twenty-five feet long, so we plan to create a thirty-foot-diameter hole. That's an enormous amount of very hard ice to dig through. We're taking an innovative approach, though, and the equipment will arrive this afternoon. Once we're through the ice, we'll commence rescue operations."

"How are we doing on time?" Christine asked.

"We have until morning," Dahlenburg replied. "At least for the men in *Dolgoruky*'s bow compartment. The men trapped aft have more air regeneration canisters and the air should last another day or two."

"Have you been briefed on the plan after we rescue *Dolgoruky*'s crew?" Christine asked.

"I have," the Admiral said. "Assuming we complete rescue efforts before the Russian submersible is in operation, we'll send you, Captain Brackman, and the ONI team down for a look around, assuming the atmosphere in the submarine is suitable." Dahlenburg added, "Do you mind if I join you? It's hard to pass up an opportunity to explore Russia's newest ballistic missile submarine."

"Not at all," Christine said.

Captain Naughton joined in. "We're pretty much in a holding pattern while the Submarine Rescue System is being assembled. I'll have Commander Steel walk you through the equipment this afternoon if he has a free moment."

"Thank you, Captain," Christine replied.

"In the meantime," Verbeck said, "we're in communication with *North Dakota* via our RATS underwater communication system, and they've been relaying information about *Dolgoruky*. They're communicating via Morse code, with *North Dakota* sending out sonar pulses and *Dolgoruky*'s crew banging on metal surfaces."

Stu Berman, who'd been eyeing the communication and above-ice sonar equipment, asked, "Do you mind if I chat with the operators?"

"I'm sure they'd enjoy your company," Verbeck replied. He turned to Christine. "Ready to continue the tour?"

"If it's okay with you, ma'am," Brackman said, "I'd like to talk with Admiral Dahlenburg and Captain Naughton for a while."

"That's fine, Captain."

Verbeck led Christine from the command hut and continued the camp tour, pointing out the diesel generator hut before heading toward a large tent.

"Most important," Verbeck said, "is the galley. While we're there, I'll introduce you to one of your roommates, Sally Firebaugh." He had a slight smirk as he added, "Don't be concerned. Her bark is worse than her bite."

They entered the galley, which was a double-insulated tent in the shape of a half moon, attached to a plywood hut in the back. There were a dozen white plastic tables in the tent, surrounded by matching plastic chairs. Verbeck headed to the back of the tent, approaching one of the cooks behind a counter in the plywood hut, a woman in her fifties preparing lunch.

"Good morning, Sally," Verbeck said.

Sally looked up and when she spotted Verbeck, a scowl formed on her face. "What's so good about it?"

"I'd like you to meet your roommate, Christine O'Connor, the president's national security advisor."

Sally turned to Christine and a smile replaced her scowl. "A pleasure to meet you." To Verbeck, she said, "Can she cook?"

Verbeck sighed. "Not again, Sally."

Sally gestured to the other cooks in the galley as she turned back to Christine. "We're busier than one-legged men in an ass-kicking contest. There's twice as many people here compared to a normal ice camp, but the same number of cooks. You'd think whoever was in charge of this operation could've done the math." She glared at Verbeck.

"We couldn't find any cooks willing to freeze their butt off on such short notice," Verbeck replied. "Besides, no one boils water like you do."

Sally smiled and placed her hand over her chest, "Aww, that just melts my heart." She grabbed an ice pick on the counter, then thrust it toward Verbeck. "Speaking of water, why don't you make yourself useful and dig up some?"

Verbeck reached for the ice pick. "Not a bad idea," he said as he put the ice pick in his pocket. He turned to Christine. "Want to dig up some water?"

Christine wasn't sure what that entailed, but it sounded interesting. "I'm game."

She followed Verbeck out of the galley and around back, where he climbed onto a snowmobile with a black bin attached behind it. "Hop on."

Christine slid behind him and Verbeck hit the accelerator. They headed out of camp, past one of the polar bear watches, a man with binoculars hanging from his neck and a 12-gauge shotgun cradled in one arm. Verbeck explained there were polar bear watches stationed on each side of the camp to protect everyone from the curious and sometimes hungry denizens of the Arctic.

The snowmobile stopped a hundred feet away from the ice camp, well within sight of the polar bear watch, near a patch of ice where the snow had been cleared and a small pit dug. Lying beside the pit was a pick ax. Verbeck hopped off the snowmobile and grabbed the ax, using the blade to crease an outline in the ice that matched the size of the black bin. He started hacking at the ice, explaining things between each whack.

"We don't ship water to the camp. We melt ice cut from the ice cap. Which might sound strange," he said, "since polar ice is frozen seawater." Verbeck explained how the brine migrated downward over time, resulting in the surface of multiyear ice being drinkable.

After a few minutes, Verbeck paused, stretching out his back. "Do you want to take a turn? It's sort of a rite of passage around here."

"Sure," Christine said.

He handed her the pick ax and she began chopping where he left off, and it wasn't long before a block of ice broke off. Verbeck picked it up and placed it in the bin. It didn't quite fit, and he used the ice pick Sally gave him to chip away at the edges until the block fell into the bin. He put the ice pick into his pocket and they headed back to camp.

Verbeck parked the snowmobile behind the galley, then opened a door at the back of the hut and yelled inside. "I've got your water. Come and get it!"

As he closed the door, his radio squawked, and he pulled it from his parka.

"Verbeck," he answered.

"We need you at the command hut," a voice said. "There's a third submarine beneath us."

51

USS *MICHIGAN*

"*North Dakota,* this is *Michigan.* Do you copy? Over."

Standing in the Control Room, Captain Wilson released the microphone switch and listened for a response over the submarine's underwater telephone. Technically, he was supposed to use call signs for both submarines, which changed periodically and disguised which submarines were communicating in case a foreign ship was eavesdropping. However, the entire ISMERLO community knew *Michigan* had been sent under the ice to assist *North Dakota.* He figured he wasn't giving anything away.

Hours earlier, Wilson had slowed from ahead flank as they approached the Barents Shelf, where the bottom rose rapidly from a depth of fourteen thousand feet to less than seven hundred. *Michigan* was now at all stop, hovering at three hundred feet a thousand yards away from *North Dakota*, well within range of the WQC in the quiet waters beneath the polar ice cap. This was Wilson's second transmission over the WQC, and this time there was a response.

"*Michigan,* this is *North Dakota* actual. Read you Lima Charlie, over."

Wilson's transmission had been heard *Lima Charlie*—Loud and Clear, and the *actual* commanding officer of *North Dakota* was speaking. Joining Wilson in Control was Commander John McNeil, commanding officer of *Michigan*'s SEAL detachment. *Michigan* had been tabbed as "Plan B" in case the topside submarine rescue mission failed, and that plan would involve McNeil's unit. In the meantime, *Michigan*'s SEALs could inspect *North Dakota* to see if there was an easy fix for her propulsion problem. Wilson relayed his thoughts to *North Dakota*'s commanding officer, who concurred with the plan. As their conversation wound to a close, another voice broke into the conversation.

"*Michigan*, this is Ice Station Nautilus. Welcome to the Arctic."

Whoever was on the other end had been listening to the conversation, because Wilson was given further instructions. If *North Dakota*'s inspection revealed anything useful, he was directed to find a lead or polynya where *Michigan* could surface and transmit photographs of the issue. After the conversation wrapped up, Wilson turned to McNeil.

"How long before you're ready to deploy?"

"Any time now. I already ordered a team to suit up."

Lieutenant Jake Harrison stepped through the circular hatch in the side of Missile Tube One, joined by a second SEAL, Special Warfare Operator First Class Tim Oliver. The two men stood on a metal grate in the second level of the missile tube, containing a steel ladder leading up two levels to another hatch. Harrison climbed the ladder, passing through the hatch into the relative darkness of the Dry Deck Shelter, bathed in diffuse red light.

The Dry Deck Shelter was a conglomeration of three chambers: a spherical hyperbaric chamber at the forward end, a spherical transfer trunk in the middle, which he had just entered, and a cylindrical hangar containing the SEAL Delivery Vehicle, a black mini-sub twenty-two feet long by six feet wide. The hangar was divided into two sections by a Plexiglas shield dropping halfway down, with the SDV on one side and hangar controls on the other.

There were five Navy divers inside the hangar; one on the forward side of the Plexiglas shield to operate the controls, and four divers in scuba gear on the other side. Oliver followed Harrison as he ducked under the Plexiglas shield, stopping beside the SDV, which was loaded nose first into the Dry Deck Shelter. The SDV had two seating areas, one in front of the other, each capable of carrying two persons.

Oliver, who was a sniper and the SEAL team's unofficial photographer, placed his waterproof camera and a wide-angle dive light into the SDV. Harrison lifted a rebreather from a rack and helped Oliver into it, then Oliver returned the favor. The two men climbed into the front seat of the SDV and Harrison manipulated the controls. The displays energized and Harrison entered *North Dakota*'s location into the navigation console. The two men put their face masks on, then Harrison rendered a thumbs-up to the diver on the other side of the Plexiglas shield.

Water surged into the hangar from vents beneath them, and the chamber was soon flooded. The door behind them opened with a faint rumbling sound, and the two divers on each side of the SDV glided out with a kick of their fins. The divers pulled rails out from the hangar onto the submarine's Missile Deck, and the SDV moved backward out of the Dry Deck Shelter. Harrison manipulated the controls, and the SDV lifted off its rails and moved forward, passing along the side of *Michigan*'s sail, then over the submarine's bow into the dark water ahead.

At this depth beneath the polar ice cap, it was pitch dark. Harrison turned the SDV toward *North Dakota*'s position, while Oliver activated the dive light, illuminating the water ahead. A few minutes later, a large object materialized, slowly taking the shape of a submarine. They were approaching the bow, and Harrison angled the SDV for a pass down the port side. The beam of Oliver's dive light scanned back and forth across the side of the submarine, and there was no detectable damage. When they reached the stern, however, it was clear *North Dakota* had collided with something.

The bottom of the propulsor shroud was mangled, with the leading edge bent backward.

Harrison slowed the SDV, allowing for a more thorough inspection, and Oliver began taking pictures. The welds attaching the bottom of the propulsor to *North Dakota*'s hull had broken and the entire propulsor tilted upward a few degrees.

Oliver gave Harrison a thumbs-up and Harrison maneuvered the SDV for a look at the other side of the submarine. There was no damage, and Harrison made a pass beneath *North Dakota*, starting from the bow. There was a ten-foot-wide gash running along the keel. The Outboard fairing was mangled and jammed into the adjacent section.

Between the bent propulsor and damaged Outboard fairing, there was no quick fix for *North Dakota*'s propulsion problem; repairs in a drydock would be required. Harrison turned the SDV around and headed toward *Michigan*.

Harrison lined up for an approach from astern, gliding over the submarine's Missile Deck. The SDV coasted to a hover behind the Dry Deck Shelter, slowly sinking until it came to rest with a gentle bump on the rails. Two divers on each side latched the SDV to the rails, and Harrison and Oliver exited the mini-sub. The SDV was retracted inside, and once the divers joined Harrison and Oliver in the shelter, the large chamber door shut with a faint thud. Red lights flicked on and an air pocket appeared at the top of the chamber, the water level gradually lowering.

When the water level fell below their necks, the two SEALs removed their face masks and rebreathers and Harrison led the way into the transfer trunk and down into the missile tube, exiting into Missile Compartment Second Level. Wilson and McNeil were waiting for them in the Battle Management Center behind the Control Room, where Oliver extracted the memory card from his camera and inserted it into one of the SEAL laptops.

Wilson and McNeil reviewed the images, agreeing with Harrison's assessment; *North Dakota*'s propulsion was down hard. Wilson entered Control and picked up the underwater telephone microphone, relaying what he had learned to *North Dakota* and Ice Station Nautilus.

52

K-157 *VEPR*

"Underwater communications, bearing zero-zero-five, designated Hydroacoustic two-four."

Captain Second Rank Matvey Baczewski, seated in the Captain's chair in the Central Command Post, listened intently to Hydroacoustic's report. As the announcement faded from the speakers, his Watch Officer, Captain Lieutenant Dolinski, responded as he was trained.

"Steersman. Left full rudder, steady course two-seven-five."

They had detected an underwater transmission almost dead ahead. The range was unknown, but underwater communications did not travel far. It was prudent to turn away and give fire control an opportunity to determine how close they were.

"Hydroacoustic, Command Post. Send bearings manually to fire control," Dolinski ordered. As *Vepr* turned to port, Dolinski followed up. "What language is the underwater communication in?"

"English."

Baczewski stood and joined his First Officer, Captain Third Rank Petr Lukov, at the navigation table. They were four kilometers from the American ice camp.

"Command Post, Hydroacoustic. Detect a second transmission of underwater communications, bearing zero-one-eight, designated Hydroacoustic two-five."

Dolinski acknowledged the report, then Baczewski called out, "Hydroacoustic, Captain. Put the communications on speaker."

The Hydroacoustic Party Leader complied, and the warbly sound of underwater communications filled the Central Command Post air. Although Baczewski didn't understand English, his First Officer did, and Petr Lukov listened carefully to the transmission, then informed the submarine's captain of its content.

There was a second American submarine under the ice—a guided missile submarine carrying Navy SEALs. They had inspected *North Dakota*, reporting that the submarine's propulsion was severely damaged and would require drydock repairs.

So far, everything was correlating with the intelligence Baczewski had been provided. He checked his submarine's speed and depth. *Vepr* had slowed to five knots as they approached the American ice camp, and was at 150 meters, well below the ice keels. He had secured their under-ice sonar, and the only emissions they were making were an occasional ping from their secure bottomsounder.

No one would detect *Vepr*'s approach.

53

K-329 *SEVERODVINSK*

"Central Command Post, Hydroacoustic. Hold a new submerged contact on the towed array, designated Hydroacoustic four-seven, bearing three-three-zero. Classified Shchuka-B nuclear attack submarine."

The Hydroacoustic Party Leader followed up a moment later, "Command Post, Hydroacoustic. Contact tonals match K-157 *Vepr.*"

Captain Buffanov stood at the back of the Central Command Post, appreciating the advanced tactical systems of his Yasen class submarine. The sonar on older submarines would not have detected the quiet third flight Shchuka-B submarine to the northwest.

While traveling under the ice, Buffanov had received a third Commanding Officer Only message, informing him of *Vepr*'s presence and assigning the waterspace around the American ice camp to *Vepr. Severodvinsk* would remain at the boundary until the prescribed time. He checked his submarine's speed and position; they had slowed to five knots and were less than a kilometer from *Vepr*'s water.

According to the last satellite image received, there was a surface ridge a few hundred meters ahead. Where there was a surface ridge, there would also be an ice keel, although without his under-ice sonar running, he would not know how deep it went. That wasn't critical, however. It was almost assuredly deep enough to hide behind.

Buffanov addressed his Watch Officer. "Prepare to ice pick."

Captain Lieutenant Ronin initiated the process. "Steersman, all stop." As *Severodvinsk* coasted to a halt, he gave the next order. "Topsounder, determine distance to ice canopy."

The Michman energized the topsounder, sending a single ping from the conning tower hydrophone toward the ice. He reported, "Distance to ice is one hundred twenty meters."

Ronin followed up. "Compensation Officer, engage Hovering. Set depth to thirty meters."

Severodvinsk rose toward the ice, settling out at a depth of thirty meters. He turned to his commanding officer. "Captain, we are ready to ice pick."

"Very well," Buffanov replied. "Set Hovering to twenty meters. Limit vertical velocity to five meters per minute."

Ronin relayed the order and *Severodvinsk* rose slowly upward, impacting the ice with a dull thud two minutes later. He checked the status of the equipment in the conning tower; as expected, there was no damage.

Severodvinsk's floating wire drooped and they lost sync with the radio broadcast. "Communication Post, Captain. Shift to the conning tower VLF antenna."

Radio acknowledged, and moment later reported, "Command Post, Communications. In sync with the VLF broadcast."

Buffanov settled into his chair in the Command Post. *Severodvinsk* was resting against the polar ice cap, just outside *Vepr*'s waterspace, in continuous communications.

The only thing left to do now was wait.

54

K-157 *VEPR*

"Your orders, sir?"

Vepr's Watch Officer, Captain Lieutenant Dolinski, stood behind the fire control consoles, waiting for the expected order from Captain Baczewski. The tactical situation could not have been more ideal. Both American submarines were motionless, hovering beneath the ice cap, and would be easy prey for a salvo of torpedoes.

While *Vepr* loitered outside the Marginal Ice Zone, Baczewski had drilled his officers on the capabilities of their potential adversaries, but after receiving the second Commanding Officer Only message, he had concentrated on only one class of submarine. Their target was the SSGN, the less capable of the two submarines.

During the conversion of the first four Ohio class submarines into SSGNs, the United States had modernized their tactical systems. From a weaponry standpoint, the guided missile submarines were as capable as other American submarines, carrying MK 48 Mod 7 torpedoes and the new BYG-1 combat control system. Their sonar systems had been upgraded as well, but only the hardware and software inside the ship. The legacy components outside the submarine, particularly the bow array hydrophones, had not been upgraded. With her towed array either stowed or useless due to the vertical droop, the guided missile submarine's ability to detect *Vepr* was impaired.

Dolinski waited for the order from his Captain. However, Baczewski spoke to the Electric Navigation Party Leader instead. "Display the latest satellite map."

An image of the polar ice cap, with latitude and longitude lines overlaid, appeared on the screen beside the navigation table. Baczewski studied the map, identifying the feature he desired. He would not need to find thin ice. There was an open lead of water three kilometers to the northwest.

He gave the order to Dolinski, but not the one his Watch Officer expected. "Come to course three-one-zero. Prepare to surface."

55

ICE STATION NAUTILUS

Inside the crowded command hut, Christine stood between Verbeck and Brackman, listening to the underwater communications between Vice Admiral Dahlenburg and the American submarines. As the communications drew to a close, Dahlenburg directed *Michigan* to remain on station and monitor the WQC. If the attempt to rescue *Dolgoruky*'s crew from topside was unsuccessful, *Michigan* would be called into service.

Verbeck turned to Christine. "Why don't we check on the status of rescue preparations?"

Christine glanced at Brackman and Berman, to see if they wanted to join her.

"I'll come along," Brackman said, as did Berman.

Verbeck led Christine and the two men from the command hut toward an assortment of metal objects, explaining they were components of the Submarine Rescue Diving and Recompression System. Verbeck headed toward two men standing near a twenty-five-foot-long cylindrical submersible that resembled a giant yellow medicine capsule. An umbilical cord and two metal cables led from the top of the submersible to an immense metal A-frame structure over the vehicle.

The two men turned toward them as they approached. Name tags identified the man on the right as Commander Ned Steel from the Undersea Rescue Command, and the other as Peter Tarbottom from Phoenix International. Verbeck led a round of introductions, and Christine noticed Tarbottom's Australian accent. Verbeck then asked Steel to explain the SRDRS and provide an update on rescue preparations.

"No problem," Steel replied. "We've got fifteen minutes before the first milestone." He turned to Tarbottom. "Let me know when you're ready."

Tarbottom acknowledged, then headed toward men climbing over the A-frame, and Christine listened as Steel explained that the SRDRS, or Submarine Rescue Diving and Recompression System, was actually two systems. The first was the Assessment and Underwater Work System, which was a pilot in an Atmospheric Diving Suit, along with its launch and recovery system. The pilot would be the first in the water, descending to the disabled submarine, where he would inspect the hatch and clear any debris.

The other half of SRDRS was the Submarine Rescue System, which had three main components. The yellow submersible was the Pressurized Rescue Module, or PRM. The second component was the Launch and Recovery System, or LARS, a large hydraulically operated A-frame, which would lift the PRM from the deck cradle and outboard it over the ocean, then lower and retrieve it. The third main component consisted of two decompression chambers for the crew after they were rescued.

The Pressurized Rescue Module was named *Falcon,* in honor of ASR-2 USS *Falcon,* which participated in the first successful rescue of men trapped aboard an American submarine: USS *Squalus* in 1939. *Falcon* was a remotely operated vehicle guided by a pilot from topside, and could transport eighteen persons—two attendants and sixteen sailors—rescuing them from a depth of up to two thousand feet. The PRM could mate with a submarine resting on the ocean floor at up to a forty-five-degree angle or list due to a skirt on the bottom of *Falcon,* which could be adjusted to match the angle of the submarine while the PRM remained level.

Falcon could gain access to a submarine pressurized up to five atmospheres absolute due to flooding. Although five ATAs corresponded to a depth of only 132 feet, oxygen toxicity became a problem above five atmospheres, and the crew would die before the SRDRS could arrive on scene. The next component, the Launch and Recovery System, was being assembled, and they would test it momentarily.

The last major component was the Surface Decompression System, which included two hyperbaric chambers that could hold thirty-four persons each: thirty-two rescued sailors plus two attendants to assist personnel during the decompression process. The SRS was the first American system capable of rescuing an entire crew from a pressurized submarine.

Peter Tarbottom approached the group, stopping beside Steel. "We're ready to outboard unmanned."

Steel led everyone toward the LARS as he explained, "This is the first test of the system to see if it will operate in the Arctic."

Before the giant A-frame could be extended over the ocean, or in this case over the hole in the ice yet to be created, they had to solve the problem of what to attach the LARS to so the contraption didn't topple over when it tried to outboard the PRM. It was normally bolted to supports welded to a ship's deck, but there was no ship here. So they bolted the LARS directly to the ice. Or rather, through the ice. Holes had been drilled in the ice underneath each LARS mount, and NAVSEA had manufactured long bolts with spring-loaded flanges on the end, essentially giant hollow-wall anchors, which had been inserted through the ice cap. They had just tightened the last bolt and finished connecting the LARS electrical and hydraulic systems.

Steel gave the order and the A-frame's two lift winches began retracting their cables attached to the top of the PRM. The PRM rose slowly in the air, and when it reached the top of the A-frame, two bayonet spikes snapped into the A-frame, locking the PRM in place. Two massive pistons on each side of the LARS tilted the A-frame outboard until the PRM was extended over the ice. All eyes shifted between the PRM, swaying gently in the air at the top of the A-frame, to the base of the LARS. It remained firmly affixed to the ice.

The bayonet spikes were retracted, and the lift winches slowly lowered the PRM. When the PRM was only a few feet from the ice, Tarbottom's men stopped the descent, and after a ten-minute hold time, the Australian joined Steel and the rest of the group.

"So far, so good," he said. "We're ready to inboard."

Commander Steel issued a second order, and the winches lifted the twenty-ton submersible upward, then the pistons on each side of the LARS pivoted the PRM back to the inboard position. The evolution was completed flawlessly, and Christine could sense the tension ease as the men congratulated each other.

Steel continued his explanation of the Submarine Rescue System. With the PRM in the inboard position, the hatch on the end of the submersible mated with what looked like a man-sized hamster habitrail. A pressurized flexible manway connected the PRM to the two-story deck transfer lock, which had three exits, one to each of the decompression chambers through

additional habitrail tunnels, and a deck access so the PRM could be provi-
sioned between dives.

Tarbottom stopped beside Commander Steel. "The only thing left is the
final assembly of the Transfer Under Pressure system"—Tarbottom pointed
to the habitrail—"and everything should be squared away by nightfall."

Steel and Tarbottom seemed pleased with their efforts, but Christine's
eyes went to the patch of ice the PRM had been suspended over. Being able
to inboard and outboard was great, but what good would it do them without a hole in the ice?

"What's the plan for the ice hole?"

Tarbottom and Steel looked to Verbeck, who answered, "That's my
department. We've got lots of experience cutting holes in the ice to retrieve
torpedoes. Those holes are only three feet wide, while we need a thirty-foot-
wide hole for *Falcon,* but the same process should work. We just need the
right equipment, which will arrive soon."

The radio in Verbeck's pocket squawked, then called his name. It was the
polar bear watch on the west side of the ice station. Something peculiar had
appeared on the horizon.

Verbeck bid farewell to Commander Steel and Tarbottom, then led Christine, Brackman, and Berman to the west edge of the camp. The polar bear
watch was examining something through his binoculars. He handed them
to Verbeck, who scanned the horizon.

"That's interesting," he said, then handed the binoculars to Christine.

She surveyed the flat, white landscape, moving slowly to the right until
an object appeared. She adjusted the optics and a black, rectangular shape
came into focus. She had an idea of what it was, but handed the binoculars
to Brackman for him to confirm. It took him a few seconds to locate the
object and a few more to come to a conclusion.

"It's a submarine sail," he said.

There were only two American submarines under the ice cap, and they
were both hovering beneath Christine's feet. The submarine in the distance
was Russian.

56

ICE CAMP BARNEO

Julius Raila stepped from the warm galley after lunch, pulling the hood of his parka over his head as he headed toward the sound of metal crunching into ice. It wasn't long before he reached the five-by-fifteen-meter-wide ice hole, with an excavator on each side of the oval depression, breaking apart chunks of ice and lifting them to the surface in their buckets.

As Raila stopped beside the hole, one of the four excavators swiveled around and lowered its bucket onto the ice cap. In the subzero temperatures, metal became brittle, and half of the bucket's teeth had broken off. It was only a minute before a cargo transporter headed toward the excavator with a replacement bucket. They had worked out the kinks in the process, and a new bucket would be installed and the excavator back in operation in an hour. Still, that was another hour lost, and at least one other excavator would break down in the meantime. This was their seventh bucket replacement today, and it was just past noon. Raila peered over the edge into the ice hole. They had been at it for over a day and were only halfway through. At the current pace, they would be too late to save the men in *Dolgoruky*'s Compartment One.

However, AS-34 Priz was ready. It had been easy to transport the submersible onto the polar ice cap, and Raila decided to forgo installing the handling equipment at Camp Barneo. Since Priz was an autonomous vehicle with no attachments to the surface, they would simply use an MI-26 heavy-lift helicopter to lower the submersible through the ice hole. A hole that was taking far too long to dig.

Raila turned to the west, toward the American ice camp. He was confounded by the American approach. From the edge of Ice Camp Barneo, Spetsnaz soldiers kept watch on the American ice camp activity. The

American rescue system was much more complex than Russia's Priz class submersible, and while he understood the Americans' focus on assembling the equipment, he didn't understand their failure to tackle the most difficult challenge. They hadn't started digging an ice hole, and there were no excavators standing by, either.

As Raila wondered what their plan was, the faint sound of helicopter rotors greeted his ears and several gray specks appeared to the southwest. He watched as two U.S. Navy Super Stallion helicopters towed a large spider-like contraption, while a third Super Stallion carried a giant metal ring. He scratched his beard, wondering what the Americans were up to.

57

ICE STATION NAUTILUS

Christine was seated at a table in the galley with Brackman, Verbeck, and Berman savoring hot chicken noodle soup when she heard the beat of the heavy-lift helicopters. Verbeck stepped from the galley for a look, and Christine and the other two men followed. She spotted several specks in the clear blue sky, growing slowly into three CH-53E Super Stallions. Two of the helicopters carried an oval structure about forty feet wide and eighty feet long, with sixteen giant legs dangling from the perimeter, while the third helicopter transported a large metal ring about thirty feet in diameter.

Verbeck led Christine and the others to the east side of the camp, where the first two Super Stallions slowed to a hover, gently landing the spiderlike object next to the submarine rescue equipment. The third helicopter deposited the large metal ring onto the ice next to the Launch and Recovery System. Men and equipment converged on the ring, which was six inches thick and had several threaded ports on top, evenly spaced along its circumference.

A snowmobile towing a cart pulled up, and men extracted six-foot-tall metal poles, screwing one into each threaded port until there were ten poles evenly spaced around the ring, sticking straight up into the air. Four more snowmobiles approached, each one dragging a sled with a metal contraption on it, and after the snowmobiles pulled to a halt, men attached two hoses from each machine to additional ports in the metal ring. It took only ten minutes to hook everything up, then one of the men approached Verbeck.

"We're ready to go," he said.

Verbeck took a moment to introduce the man. "Ms. O'Connor, this is Paul Leone, the senior ice pilot at the Arctic Submarine Lab. He's my right-hand man here at the camp."

Verbeck continued, explaining the plan. "As I mentioned earlier, we cut holes in the ice to recover exercise torpedoes after their run, but we don't dig a hole, we melt one. Those contraptions are melters." He pointed to the equipment pulled by the four snowmobiles. "They heat water and pump it through the metal ring. The water heats the metal, which melts the ice."

The ice pilot ordered the four melters fired up, and a moment later hot water started running through the metal ring. The ice beneath the ring began melting, and a man stationed at each of the ten poles pressed the ring downward. As the ice melted, the ring sank slowly into the ice. The poles became shorter as the ring descended, until only a foot of each pole extended above the ice.

Leone shouted a command and the men stopped pushing the ring downward. Each man retrieved a second six-foot-long pole from the cart, then screwed it into the end of the first, extending the pole another six feet skyward. After another command from Leone, the men pushed down again. A few minutes later, with only two feet of pole remaining, the men lurched forward as the resistance eased, and the thirty-foot-diameter section of ice popped up half a foot. Christine finally realized what they were doing. They had created a giant ice cork, and all they had to do now was lift it out of the way.

Verbeck explained that lifting the ice cork was the real challenge. For a three-foot-wide torpedo-sized hole, they drilled a hole in the center of the cork and dropped a hollow-wall anchor through the hole, then lifted it manually using a tripod and chain fall. However, a three-foot-wide ice cork weighed only a few thousand pounds. The thirty-foot-wide ice cork they had created weighed over two hundred tons. It would take a dozen Super Stallions to lift the ice cork, and connecting that many helicopters to the ice plug was asking for trouble.

Instead, Verbeck asked NAVSEA to construct the spiderlike contraption, a sixteen-leg monstrosity rising twenty feet into the air. The thick metal legs bent ninety degrees at the top, in toward the middle of the oval, where they connected to a central section with tracks running its length. A flanged anchor, its edges folded up, hung from one end of the central section.

The two Super Stallions placed one end of the oval structure around the ice plug, with the metal legs positioned around its perimeter and the flanged anchor over the center of the ice cork. The tow cables were released and the

Super Stallions landed in the distance while men climbed onto the ice plug and began drilling a two-foot-wide hole in the center. When they finished, the flanged anchor at the top of the contraption, which was connected to a thick metal cable, was lowered through the hole and the flanges were released.

"Cross your fingers," Verbeck said, "and pray we don't end up with a pile of metal parts."

Slowly, the cable retracted, lifting the ice plug until it cleared the surface, then the ice plug moved along the center track to the other end of the contraption, where it was lowered onto the polar ice cap. The effort had taken only two hours, and Christine was staring at a thirty-foot-diameter Arctic swimming pool, through which the PRM could be lowered.

The two Super Stallions moved in again, moving the contraption aside, clearing the way to outboard the PRM over the ice hole. On the other side of the hole, personnel from the Undersea Rescue Command were hooking up a pilot in an Atmospheric Diving Suit to its launch and recovery system. The ADS would be sent down first, to inspect *Dolgoruky*'s hatches.

It wasn't long before the ADS was suspended over the ice hole, then began its descent. Christine watched the pilot, his face visible through the bulbous glass vision dome of the ADS helmet, disappear into the cold Arctic waters.

ICE CAMP BARNEO

Captain First Rank Josef Klokov had watched in curious fascination, finally deciphering the American plan. It had taken them two hours to accomplish what would take Julius Raila's men over two days. He looked at the half-finished ice hole they'd been digging. Russia had lost the race, which meant Klokov's men would intervene.

The Spetsnaz unit's Executive Officer, Captain Second Rank Gleb Leonov, approached with Julius Raila in tow. The discussion was short. Raila was relieved *Dolgoruky*'s crew would be rescued in time, but Klokov sensed his pride was damaged. Russia would have to rely on another country to rescue their crew. Klokov didn't care. The only thing that mattered was how long until the Americans commenced rescue operations. Raila explained they would be ready shortly after dark.

Klokov excused Raila, who left to inspect the ice hole. They would continue their efforts in case something went wrong with the American rescue. Klokov turned to his Executive Officer.

"Prepare both platoons. We depart one hour after sunset."

Leonov acknowledged Klokov's order, then addressed the most critical issue. "Once the mission is complete, what will we do with the witnesses?"

Klokov reflected on his discussion with Fleet Admiral Ivanov when the man had visited him in Pechenga. Ivanov had directed Klokov to keep the loss of life to a minimum. However, *minimum* was a subjective term. Klokov's men were Spetsnaz, and they did not leave evidence behind, especially the talking kind.

Klokov answered his Executive Officer. "We will leave no witnesses."

USS *NORTH DAKOTA*

It was late afternoon aboard *North Dakota* when Commander Paul Tolbert stepped into the relatively quiet Engine Room. The submarine's two electrical turbine generators were running, but the main engines were silent. Petty Officer Third Class Scott Turk looked up from his clipboard as the submarine's Captain descended into Engine Room Forward, and his face brightened. He was three hours into his watch, and aside from the occasional pass-through by the Engine Room Supervisor and Engineering Watch Supervisor, there was no one to talk to in the bowels of the Engine Room. He stood as Commander Tolbert approached.

"How's it going?" Tolbert asked, glancing at the condensate pump.

"Sounds a little funny, sir," Turk replied, "but it runs okay."

"Is it getting worse?"

"No, sir," Turk replied. "It's sounded funny since E-Div repaired it."

"Got it," Tolbert said. He wasn't surprised their little Frankenstein sounded odd. But he figured it was a good sign as long as the sound remained the same. "Anything else unusual?"

Turk thought for a moment, then replied, "No, sir. With no propulsion orders and the turbines in a full-power line-up, there's not much going on down here."

Tolbert bid Petty Officer Turk good-bye, then ascended to Engine Room Upper Level and stopped in Maneuvering. The Engineering Officer of the Watch had nothing significant to report, and Tolbert headed forward. It was the same throughout the ship. *North Dakota* had resumed hovering at two hundred feet, and aside from the sonar techs who kept in communication with *Dolgoruky*, the watchstanders had settled into a routine one could best describe as boring.

Still, after a week of stress following the collision and flooding in the Engine Room, followed by a frantic race to restore power before the battery ran out, the calm aboard the submarine was welcome. However, Tolbert figured it was anything but calm aboard the Russian submarine. Their air was becoming toxic, and they had only a few hours left.

60

K-535 *YURY DOLGORUKY*

In the dark, frigid compartment, Nicholai Stepanov tilted his head back, lifting the water bottle to his parched lips. The few remaining drops of water dribbled into his mouth, then he placed the empty bottle on the deck beside him and prepared for another round through the compartment. The air regeneration unit, which had been a welcome source of warmth over the last week, was now a hunk of cold metal; they were out of air regeneration canisters.

The oxygen level was falling, while the concentration of carbon dioxide rose. As *Dolgoruky's* Medical Officer predicted, oxygen was not the issue; it was still at fifteen percent. Carbon dioxide level, on the other hand, had reached four percent. Stepanov could feel the effects of the high CO_2 level. He was tired despite plenty of sleep, his head pounded from a severe headache, and his respiration was shallow and rapid.

He looked around the dark compartment. There were no emergency lanterns on. There were only a half-dozen left with good batteries. He had one of them and turned it on, the faint yellow glow illuminating a radius of a few meters. He pulled himself to his feet, supporting himself on a nearby torpedo, then flexed his stiff hands inside his gloves. Reaching down, he retrieved the lantern and aimed it around the ice-coated compartment.

Stepanov moved slowly, checking first on the men in upper level, huddled in small groups between the torpedo stows. The men who were awake murmured greetings to their Captain as he stopped for a moment. At the aft end of the compartment, Stepanov stopped near the sealed watertight door to Compartment Two. Starshina First Class Oleg Devin, one of Stepanov's Torpedomen, manned the sound-powered phones.

"How are the men aft?" Stepanov asked.

"They have one more day of air regeneration canisters," was the reply.

In the faint illumination, Stepanov could see the despair in the young man's eyes. Devin knew that he, along with the other men in Compartment One, had only a few hours left. Stepanov squeezed the man's shoulder, conveying what support he could. Devin placed his hand over Stepanov's, holding it in place. He could feel the tremors in Devin's hand.

Devin released Stepanov's hand and Nicholai squeezed the young man's shoulder again. "Do not give up hope."

The young man nodded, then replied, "Yes, Captain."

Stepanov continued his round through upper level and spotted his Medical Officer, Captain Kovaleski, examining a patient in a makeshift bed on one of the torpedo stows with a small flashlight. Kovaleski turned toward Stepanov, and as the lantern illuminated his features, Stepanov noticed a smile on his doctor's face.

Stepanov almost lurched to a halt, wondering if his Medical Officer had become delusional in the high-CO_2 air, or if the bitter cold was impairing him.

"Captain," Kovaleski said. "I was about to come get you."

Stepanov approached his Medical Officer, who pointed toward the patient on the torpedo stow. It was Stepanov's First Officer, who had been knocked out during the flooding and had remained unconscious for the last week. Pavlov's eyes were open, and they were looking at Stepanov. Relief washed through him. For some reason, despite their impending doom, knowing his First Officer had survived buoyed his spirit.

"Captain," Pavlov said groggily. "How bad is it?"

Stepanov looked to Kovaleski, wondering what the two men had discussed.

"He just awoke," Kovaleski said. "I have not told him anything."

Pavlov had clearly deduced, from the dark, frigid surroundings, that *Dolgoruky* was in dire straits. Stepanov decided not to withhold anything.

"Compartments Two and Three are flooded, and we have sunk to the bottom." Stepanov paused, then forced the bitter words from his mouth. "*Dolgoruky* is lost."

"How long do we have?" Pavlov asked.

Stepanov pulled the end of his glove back, exposing his watch. The sun had set an hour ago atop the ice cap.

"A few hours."

61

ICE CAMP BARNEO • ICE STATION NAUTILUS

ICE CAMP BARNEO

Captain Klokov stood beside the helicopter fuselage in the darkness, beneath the downdraft of the rotor wash, as the first squad of men boarded the transport. Fifty feet to his left, Klokov's XO did the same as another squad boarded, and not far away, the second platoon boarded their transports. After the twelfth and final man in Klokov's squad climbed into the Ka-60 Kasatka, painted white to match the Arctic landscape, he grabbed a handrail inside the fuselage and swung himself aboard. The helicopter lifted off immediately.

The four Russian helicopters skirted the edge of Camp Barneo, then turned west, skimming fast and low, fifty feet above the ice, toward the lights in the distance.

ICE STATION NAUTILUS

They were almost ready. Christine stood in the cold under the bright ice camp lights, watching final preparations for the PRM launch. Standing beside her was Captain Brackman, his eyes likewise locked on the submersible about to be lowered into the ocean. All that remained was a final checkout by the pilot, who operated the PRM from the control van—a metal Conex container on top of the starboard Surface Decompression Chamber—and a briefing by Commander Steel. He stood not far from Christine, in front of a small team of personnel who would journey to the ocean bottom.

Although the eighteen-person-capacity PRM was normally manned by only two attendants, they would be joined on the first trip by the Disabled Submarine (DISSUB) Entry Team, who would remain aboard *Dolgoruky* to assist until the last survivor was evacuated. The DISSUB Entry Team included a submarine independent duty corpsman to assess the crew's health, an Auxiliary Division chief to assist with entering the submarine and monitoring atmospheres, and a Russian translator.

While Christine waited for Steel to complete his brief, she admired the aurora borealis—the Northern Lights, illuminating the night sky in a diffuse green glow. As she wondered about the atmospheric conditions that created the phenomenon, she heard the sound of helicopters approaching the camp. Choppers had been coming and going all day, but why would helicopters arrive in the dark?

The sound faded, returning the camp to relative silence. Not long thereafter, a dozen armed men, wearing white Arctic uniforms and with their weapons drawn, emerged from the darkness at the ice camp perimeter, advancing toward them. One of the men shouted, "Lie down on the ground!"

Shocked expressions worked their way across everyone's faces as three more groups of soldiers appeared, each from a different direction, searching the huts they passed by as they approached. The polar bear watches were at the front of each formation, with soldiers carrying their shotguns.

The first man shouted again, "Down on the ground. Now!"

One by one, everyone complied. Christine lay down and watched the soldiers inspect each person as they were pulled to their feet. Two men approached her, pulling her upright, then checked her pockets and unzipped her parka to check for weapons. Satisfied she was unarmed, they moved on, leaving her standing beside Brackman, who had also been pulled to his feet and searched. As Christine zipped her parka back up, she noted the soldiers spoke Russian. They were Spetsnaz. But why would they assault Ice Station Nautilus?

The Spetsnaz finished inspecting the ice station personnel, then forced everyone into a line, with Brackman on one side of her and Peter Tarbottom on the other. The Spetsnaz walked down the line, examining name tags. Senior Navy personnel were pulled forward, forming a second line in front of another Spetsnaz soldier, whom Christine concluded was the unit commander. The four Americans in line were Vice Admiral Dahlenburg, Captain Naughton, Captain Brackman, and Commander Steel.

The Spetsnaz commander moved in front of Vice Admiral Dahlenburg.

"This is the plan," he said. "My men are going to take a trip in your rescue vehicle. You need to supply the personnel to operate the equipment. Under-stand?"

The Admiral did not respond.

The Spetsnaz commander continued, "All you have to do is give the order."
Dahlenburg stared back.

The Spetsnaz pulled a pistol from its holster and pointed it at the Admiral's head. "Do not make this difficult," he said. "You have until the count of three."

Admiral Dahlenburg said nothing.

"One."

It didn't take long for Christine to figure out where the Russians were headed once they boarded the PRM. The unsuspecting crew aboard *North Dakota* would be taken by surprise. Admiral Dahlenburg apparently came to the same conclusion.

He remained silent.

"Two."

The Spetsnaz commander had his arm extended, his pistol pointed at Dahlenburg's head. The Russian waited an extra second, then spoke again.

"Three."

A gunshot rang out in the still Arctic air and Dahlenburg's head snapped back, then he collapsed onto the ice. Blood poured from the wound in his forehead, soaking into the snow.

The Spetsnaz examined the name tags of the two Navy Captains in front of him: Captain Mike Naughton, Commodore of Submarine Squadron ELEVEN, and Brackman, the president's senior military aide. The Russian correctly deduced Naughton was the next man in the undersea rescue chain of command, and he stepped in front of the Commodore.

"As you can see," the Spetsnaz said, "I do not count to four." He raised his pistol, pointing it at Naughton's head. "Order your men to operate the equipment, or you will suffer the same fate as your Admiral."

Naughton's eyes darted to the Admiral's body in the snow, then to the Spetsnaz commander's pistol, then to Commander Steel.

"One."

Naughton's eyes went back to the pistol, then to the Spetsnaz command-er's face.

"Two."

The Commodore's posture stiffened, then he finally spoke.

"Go to Hell."

"Three."

A second gunshot rang out, and this time Captain Naughton crumpled to the ice. The Russian commander stepped in front of Brackman, placing the pistol against his forehead.

"It is only a matter of time," the Russian said. "Someone will give the order. Save yourself."

Brackman stared ahead, giving no indication he would comply.

"One."

Christine's heart began to race. She knew Brackman would not give the order. She wasn't even sure he *could* give it. Although he was senior to Commander Steel, the Commander wasn't in Brackman's chain of command. Christine's eyes went to Steel, but he was staring directly ahead, just like Brackman.

"Two."

Brackman remained silent, and Christine panicked.

She stepped forward. "Stop it!"

Tarbottom grabbed her arm and yanked her back in line, but it was too late. The Spetsnaz commander's head snapped toward Christine, his cold eyes locking on to her.

He stepped in front of Christine, examining her for a moment. Then he grabbed both sides of her face, his gloved hand under her jaw, and tilted her head up. "What is a beautiful Russian woman doing with the likes of these men?"

Christine slapped his hand away. "I'm not Russian. I'm American."

The Spetsnaz commander smiled and said something loudly in Russian, and several of his men laughed.

"I like you," he said in English.

He pointed the pistol at her head. "Unfortunately, Miss American, you will be dead by the time I count to three if I do not get the assistance I need."

Christine realized she hadn't thought things through, and her impulsive nature had gotten her in trouble again.

"One."

She looked at Brackman and then Commander Steel, then back to the Russian. "I don't have the authority," she said, hoping the Russian would understand.

"It does not matter," he said. "If someone gives the order, I will spare your life."

"Two."

Things were moving too fast. She could feel her heart pounding in her chest as she searched frantically for a way out of her predicament.

"I will give the order."

The pistol fell away from her head as the Spetsnaz commander turned to the man beside her. Peter Tarbottom had spoken.

Tarbottom added, "Most of the operators are civilians who work for me. They will follow my direction."

The Spetsnaz commander examined Tarbottom's name tag. "A wise decision, Peter. How long until you are ready to deploy the submersible?"

Tarbottom replied, "Fifteen minutes."

"How many men can the submersible carry?"

"Eighteen, but two of them are attendants. They're normally Navy divers, but I have two men who can operate the equipment and gain access to the submarine."

The Spetsnaz commander shouted in Russian again, and sixteen of his men assembled into a group while Tarbottom gave orders to his men. Each contractor who departed was escorted by one of the remaining Spetsnaz soldiers.

"I need assistance with one more item," the Spetsnaz commander said. "I need someone who can operate your underwater communication system." His eyes scanned the remaining men and women in the group. "Anyone?"

He waited a few seconds, then placed the pistol to Christine's head again.

Scott Walworth, one of the RATS operators, raised his hand. "I can help."

Another soldier escorted Walworth to the command hut, and the Spetsnaz pulled plastic tie wraps from their pockets and tied the hands of the remaining Americans behind their backs. The Spetsnaz commander holstered his pistol and turned Christine around roughly, then her wrists were bound by one of his men.

The Spetsnaz divided the Americans into groups of eight and led them toward the berthing hooches. Christine was in the last group, comprised of only her and Brackman. They were likewise led to a berthing hooch, where one of the soldiers shoved her inside. She tripped over the door threshold and landed hard on her side, then a tie was placed around her ankles. The door was shut, enclosing her and Brackman in darkness.

62

USS *NORTH DAKOTA* • ICE STATION NAUTILUS

USS *NORTH DAKOTA*

Commander Tolbert was in his stateroom, catching up on paperwork when the ICSAP beeped. He picked up the handset. "Captain."

Lieutenant Molitor was on the other end. "Captain, Officer of the Deck. We're receiving underwater comms. Request your presence in Control, sir."

"I'll be right there."

Tolbert hung up and headed to the Control Room, entering as another transmission was received. "*North Dakota,* this is Ice Station Nautilus. Repeat, Vice Admiral Dahlenburg from Fleet Forces Command is on his way down. Do you copy? Over."

One of the sonar technicians handed Tolbert the WQC microphone.

"Ice Station Nautilus," Tolbert replied slowly, so his words would be heard clearly over the underwater comms, "this is *North Dakota*. Understand all. What is the purpose of the Admiral's visit? Over."

"*North Dakota,* Ice Station Nautilus. Admiral Dahlenburg desires a tour of your submarine, and a review of any damage you have sustained. Over."

"Ice Station Nautilus, *North Dakota*. What is the Admiral's E-T-A? Over."

"*North Dakota,* Ice Station Nautilus. One-five mikes. Over."

Tolbert glanced at the nearest clock. The Admiral would arrive in fifteen minutes.

"Ice Station Nautilus, *North Dakota*. Understand Admiral will arrive in one-five mikes. Which hatch will the submersible attach to? Over."

"*North Dakota,* Ice Station Nautilus. Wait."

Tolbert waited patiently for whoever was on the other end of the WQC comms to run down the desired information. A minute later, the WQC comms resumed.

"*North Dakota,* Ice Station Nautilus. *Falcon* will attach to the forward escape trunk. Out."

Tolbert slid the WQC microphone into its holder and retrieved the nearest 1-MC mike. "XO, COB, lay to Control."

Lieutenant Commander Sites was the first to arrive, joined a few seconds later by Master Chief Murgo. Tolbert explained the Vice Admiral's pending arrival, leaving it to the XO and COB to have appropriate personnel at the forward escape trunk and the officers and chiefs standing by in their respective spaces.

PRM-1 *FALCON*

"Close the hatch."

Standing inside the PRM with the other fifteen Spetsnaz, Captain Second Rank Gleb Leonov ordered the attendant beside him to shut the forward hatch. The attendant, Bob Ennis, nervously closed the hatch, sealing himself inside with sixteen Spetsnaz soldiers and another attendant. At the other end of the rescue vehicle, Art Glover sat at a control station where he monitored the submersible's atmosphere and communicated with the pilot topside.

Between the two attendants, fifteen Spetsnaz sat; eight on one side and seven on the other. Leonov settled into the final seat, fingering the pistol inside his jacket pocket. There would not be much space to maneuver aboard the submarine, and each man carried a PSS Silent Pistol, along with additional magazines in their parka pockets. Underneath their parkas, PP2000 close-combat submachine guns hung from slings, as backup for the small-caliber pistols.

"Standby for Launch," Glover announced.

A moment later, the submersible lifted upward, then came to a halt with a loud thunk as the bayonet spikes locked into the A-frame. The PRM lurched forward as the massive A-frame arms began pivoting outboard, coming to a halt once the A-frame reached a thirty-degree tilt. *Falcon* swayed in the air directly over the ice hole.

Once *Falcon* steadied up, Glover announced, "Coming out of the latches."

Leonov felt the bayonet spikes retract, and the PRM began its descent. There was a gentle impact as the vehicle hit the water, followed shortly by the high-pitched whine of the PRM's hydraulic pumps. Not long thereafter, Glover began calling out the vehicle's depth. Leonov located a video display above Glover's left shoulder. The submersible's lights were energized, and the camera on the vehicle was panning back and forth, illuminating the water below them.

As the submersible descended, Leonov reviewed the plan in his mind. In a few minutes, the PRM would attach to the American submarine and its hatch would open. He would leave one Spetsnaz behind, guarding the attendants in the PRM, leaving him with fourteen men for the assault. The main issue was entering the submarine quickly enough, before the American crew could arm themselves. His men would have to climb down through the hatch one by one, then gain control before the crew was alerted.

As the PRM descended deeper beneath the ice cap, the pilot in the control van atop the ice reported they had gained sonar contact on *North Dakota,* and a few minutes later, a dark object appeared on the display, growing slowly larger until a submarine materialized from the haze. The submersible slowed its descent, and Leonov felt the thrusters kick in, maneuvering *Falcon* toward a hatch in front of the submarine's conning tower.

USS *NORTH DAKOTA*

Commander Tolbert stood beneath the Forward Escape Trunk, waiting for the arrival of the submersible carrying Vice Admiral Dahlenburg. The COB and XO were also there, while the rest of the officers and chiefs were standing by in their respective spaces. The cooks were already whipping something up to serve the Admiral after his tour. Tolbert had no idea what they would come up with, but was confident his Culinary Specialist Chief would concoct something worthy.

Seaman David Lorms was standing by with a WIFCOM radio in his hand, in communication with Control in case anything went wrong. It wasn't often one opened a hatch while at two hundred feet. Auxiliary Division Chief Larry Johnson was standing by to drain the cavity above the hatch and open it. In the few minutes since they were notified over the WQC, everyone had scrambled into position.

A loud clank from above announced the PRM's arrival. There were a few other metallic sounds and then silence, except for a faint humming. Several minutes passed, and then Tolbert heard the metallic tap code. Nine taps; the DSRV had formed a seal with *North Dakota*'s hull and pumped out most of the water in the transfer skirt connecting the two vessels.

Chief Johnson opened the hatch drain, and the residual water above the hatch flowed from the drain pipe at the standard rate, indicating the pressure on the other side was normal atmospheric, rather than pressurized to two hundred feet. After thirty seconds, the water ebbed to a halt and four taps were heard; it was safe to open the hatch. Johnson climbed the ladder to within reach of the hatch handwheel, then looked down to Tolbert for direction.

"Open the hatch," Tolbert ordered.

Johnson turned the handwheel, and once the hatch lugs disengaged, he pushed the heavy, spring-loaded hatch up until it latched in the vertical position. Tolbert peered through the opening; the submersible hatch was open and men were climbing down. Chief Johnson dropped down from the ladder and moved out of the way, and the first man descended the ladder. He was wearing white Arctic gear instead of Navy foul-weather gear, but that wasn't surprising given their location. The man dropped onto the deck and turned toward Tolbert.

He had never met Admiral Dahlenburg, but knew what he looked like. The first man wasn't him. Nonetheless, Tolbert greeted his guest. "Welcome aboard *North Dakota*."

The man said nothing as he took a step forward. His eyes scanned the confined space, shifting rapidly from one person to the next. The second man landed on the deck and took a step aft as a third man descended swiftly behind him.

When the third man hit the deck, he said something Tolbert didn't understand, and the three men pulled pistols from their pockets.

Tolbert reacted immediately. "Repel boarders!"

Seaman Lorms brought the WIFCOM to his mouth, but before he could say anything, he was shot between the eyes and collapsed to the deck. Tolbert turned back toward the man in front of him, who was swinging his pistol toward his head. He tried to duck, but was too slow. He felt a hard crack against his skull, and his world went black.

———

Fifteen minutes later, Captain Second Rank Leonov stood in the empty Central Command Post of the Virginia class submarine, marveling at the technology. There were so many displays, consoles, and computer servers that he had difficulty grasping how much equipment they were dealing with. His order had been simple: strip all hardware of value. That amounted to pretty much the entire damn submarine.

Leonov turned as his platoon leader and six other Spetsnaz entered the Command Post.

"What is the status?" Leonov asked.

Captain Lieutenant Erik Topolski replied, "We have control of the entire ship. The crew is bound in their berthing compartment, with the exception of three watchstanders in their engineering control room. I thought it best to leave them on watch, but guarded, while the submarine's nuclear reactor was in operation."

Leonov nodded his approval. He had expected to board a disabled submarine, with the crew clinging to life as its atmosphere became toxic. Instead, the ship appeared fully operational. Leonov's eyes swept around the Command Post, locating a depth indication. The submarine was hovering at two hundred feet, and he was uneasy leaving the Command Post unmanned. "Select a crew member who can control the submarine's depth and angle, and station him at the proper position."

Topolski acknowledged the order as Leonov examined the Command Post again. There was a lot of equipment to strip, and they had until daylight to complete their mission and return to Camp Barneo, vacating the American ice camp before implementing the last phase of their plan. They would need to move fast. Fortunately, many of the consoles were identical.

"Begin here in the Command Post," Leonov directed. "Gut one of each type of console, and strip all servers." He added, "Be careful with the equipment. It must be functional when it is reassembled." He surveyed the consoles again. They were energized. "Find a crew member who can deenergize their equipment. Kill however many men you need until someone complies."

"Yes, Captain," Topolski replied.

Topolski issued the order to one of his men, then followed up with the rest. They removed their parkas in the warm submarine as they prepared to disassemble the Command Post equipment.

Leonov addressed Topolski again. "I will inform Captain Klokov of our status, then return with the material to complete the mission."

Topolski acknowledged as Leonov left the Command Post and headed toward the submarine's open hatch, then climbed the ladder into *Falcon*. The two attendants were at the far end of the submersible, still under the surveillance of the Spetsnaz left behind. Leonov directed the Americans to establish communications with the Spetsnaz commander in the PRM control van and Glover complied, then handed his headset to Leonov. Captain Klokov was quickly updated.

Leonov handed the headset back to Glover, then grabbed a white duffel bag they had loaded aboard *Falcon* on the surface. He slung the heavy bag over his shoulder, then descended the ladder into the submarine.

63

ICE STATION NAUTILUS

Captain First Rank Klokov stood at one end of the control van beside Peter Tarbottom, with another Spetsnaz at the other end and three Americans manning the panels between them. As he handed the microphone back to the nearest operator, the control van door opened and another Spetsnaz entered, along with a gust of Arctic air. Captain Lieutenant Kiril Boganov, head of Second Platoon, reported, "All American prisoners are bound and locked in their berthing huts, except for one man at the launch and recovery station and the four men here."

Klokov examined the four civilians in the control van. The three men at their stations—the pilot, who maneuvered the submersible; the co-pilot, who operated the submersible's sonar and video systems, and a third man monitoring life support aboard the submersible—appeared essential. Their boss, however, was not.

"Take Tarbottom to one of the berthing huts," Klokov directed.

Before leaving the control van and settling in for the night, Klokov evaluated the situation at the ice camp. He had thirty-three men left on the surface, far more than were necessary. He would leave one man in the control van and another at the launch and recovery system, and station two men outside to keep an eye on things. "Send Second Platoon back to Barneo," Klokov ordered. "Leave eight men from First Platoon here, divided into two groups for shifts through the night."

The platoon leader acknowledged the order, then Klokov added, "I'm in the mood for celebration tonight. Have something appropriate sent over from Barneo." Then he ordered, "Bring the American woman to my hut."

Christine lay on her side, her hands and feet bound, not far from Brackman. During their discussions in the darkness, she had not mentioned it. Tarbottom, and not Brackman, had given the order that saved her life. She tried to view things through a logical and not emotional prism, but had difficulty reconciling her close friendship with Brackman and his refusal to save her life. It had become clear, in that last frantic second before the Spetsnaz officer counted to three, that Brackman's responsibility as a Naval officer was more important than her life.

The door opened and a man with his hands tied behind his back was shoved into the berthing hooch. In the illumination from the ice camp lights, Christine recognized Peter Tarbottom. Once inside, his feet were bound by one of the Spetsnaz soldiers. Christine expected the Russians to leave, sealing them in darkness again, but instead, the two Spetsnaz lifted her to her feet, then cut the ties around her wrists and ankles.

"What are you doing with her?" Brackman asked.

He was answered with a kick to his stomach.

Christine decided not to ask.

The Spetsnaz who kicked Brackman shoved her toward the open door and she tumbled through the doorway. Her boots slipped on a patch of ice and she landed face first in the snow. The two Spetsnaz grabbed under her shoulders, lifting her to her feet. The Spetsnaz who shoved her moved in front and brushed the snow from her face and hair. "You must be presentable," he said with a lewd grin.

He turned and headed toward Vance Verbeck's berthing hooch, and a gentle shove from the second Spetsnaz prodded Christine into following. When they reached Verbeck's hut, the lead Spetsnaz turned and spoke. "I recommend you enjoy yourself tonight."

"Why is that?" Christine asked.

He answered, "Because this will be your last night alive."

Before Christine could process his comment, three more Spetsnaz arrived at Verbeck's hut. One of the men handed a white backpack to the lead Spetsnaz, then the three men continued toward an adjacent berthing hooch. The lead Spetsnaz knocked on Verbeck's hut and the door opened, revealing the Spetsnaz commander. He had removed his jacket and outer pants, revealing his green thermal garments. He spoke in Russian to the two Spetsnaz, and the lead Spetsnaz handed the backpack to him, then took station outside the hooch, while the second man headed to the adjacent berthing hut, joining the other three Spetsnaz.

"Come inside, Miss American," the Spetsnaz commander said, "where it is warm." He offered a genuine smile, with no hint of what awaited her.

Christine hesitated. Nothing good would happen inside the hut, but she didn't seem to have any choice. After a moment of indecision, she stepped inside and the Spetsnaz behind her closed the door.

The Russian officer extended his hand. "First," he said, "proper introductions are required." He glanced at the name tag on her jacket. "I am Captain First Rank Josef Klokov, Christine. It is a pleasure to meet you."

Christine declined to shake Klokov's hand. "And what is *second* on your agenda tonight?"

Klokov stood with his hand extended for a moment, then turned and headed toward a small table with two chairs. He settled into the chair facing her, placing the backpack on the table.

"Second," he replied, "I invite you to drink with me." He pulled a bottle of clear liquor and two shot glasses from the bag.

"And then?" Christine asked.

The Russian officer studied her for a moment, then answered, "We both know why you are here. However, I am not the type of man who forces himself on a woman. I prefer a willing partner. It is my intent to persuade you into participating."

"You mean you plan to get me drunk and take advantage of me."

Klokov grinned. "It is the oldest trick known to man. What are my odds of success?"

Several responses flashed through Christine's mind, and she settled on something appropriate for the setting. "A snowball would have a better chance in Hell."

"Ah," Klokov said. "Then there is a chance, however slim." He gestured toward the empty chair. "Please join me."

Christine decided to make her position clear enough so even a Spetsnaz could understand. But before she did, assuming Klokov would release her, she wanted to know if what the guard outside said was true; that this would be her last night alive.

"What are you going to do with the ice station personnel when you are finished?"

"You will be released once we have accomplished our objective," Klokov answered.

Despite his reassuring words, Christine was convinced he was going to murder everyone at the ice station and aboard *North Dakota* once he was finished.

"Surely," Klokov added, "spending time with me, even just for conversation, is preferable to being bound and locked in the darkness."

Christine stared at Klokov, contemplating his assertion. She was about to decline and request she be returned to the berthing hut when she noticed an object over Klokov's shoulder. Lying on a wood beam framing the wall behind him was the ice pick Verbeck used when they went digging for water.

She smiled warmly. "You're right. I prefer to be here." She unzipped her parka and shrugged out of it, then removed her balaclava, boots, and waterproof pants, leaving her mid- and inner thermal layers on. She took her seat, opposite Klokov, as he filled her shot glass, then his.

"I'll drink with you on one condition," Christine added.

"And that is?"

"That you take two drinks to my one. You weigh twice as much as me—it's only fair. I don't want your task of taking advantage of me to be too easy."

Klokov answered without hesitation. "Agreed."

He held up his shot glass. "Za zda-ró-vye!" Christine gave him a blank stare, and he translated to English, "To your health!" There was a darkness in his eyes as Christine raised her glass and clinked it against his. He downed the liquid in a single swallow. Christine brought the glass to her lips, then tilted her head back and dumped the contents into her mouth, swallowing quickly to minimize the taste. Surprisingly, it was very smooth. Not surprisingly, it was vodka.

"What kind is this? It's very good."

"You are drinking one of Russia's finest. *Kauffman* vodka!"

Klokov poured himself a second glass, which he downed quickly, then a second drink for Christine and another for himself. She raised her glass in the air, trying not to think about what would soon happen. Drinking with Klokov was a dangerous tactic. However, considering what she was planning, she was going to need some liquid courage.

64

USS *NORTH DAKOTA*

In the fast attack submarine's Torpedo Room, Captain Second Rank Leonov knelt on the deck beside one of the twenty-four green warshot torpedoes. He reached into his white duffel bag, retrieving a rectangular block measuring one inch thick, two inches wide, and ten inches long. He removed the olive-green wrapping, exposing a white, claylike material, then slid his hand into the gap between the nearest torpedo and the stow above, pressing the explosive onto the torpedo's warhead. Another reach into the bag retrieved a detonator. He extracted a thin, silver initiating tube from a compartment and inserted it into the C-4 explosive, then removed the covering over the adhesive strips on the back of the detonator and pressed it onto the torpedo shell, beside the C-4.

He moved to the next torpedo, replicating his actions until all but one weapon was wired with explosives. After approaching the last torpedo, he retrieved a detonator of a different design—programmable, with the initiator built into its underside. Leonov extended the initiator, then pressed the detonator firmly atop the C-4.

Captain Lieutenant Topolski entered the Torpedo Room, stopping beside Leonov. "The submersible is full, and we are not finished stripping the equipment."

"Send it to the surface," Leonov directed, "and have the two American attendants off-load the equipment. We'll make as many trips as possible before sunrise."

After Topolski acknowledged the order and left the Torpedo Room, Leonov programmed the detonator with a one-hour delay, giving them sufficient time to return to the surface and depart the American ice camp.

Finally, he set the detonator to Master. It would communicate with the others, detonating all twenty-four simultaneously.

It would be an American version of the *Kursk* disaster, the submarine destroyed by a faulty torpedo. There would be nothing left of the submarine, and the shock wave from an explosion that large would fracture the ice floe above, and the American ice camp would be swallowed by the Arctic Ocean. There would be no trace of what Russia had done, and America would have no idea their tactical systems had been harvested.

65

ICE STATION NAUTILUS

Christine leaned forward with both elbows propped on the table, an empty shot glass dangling from one hand and a half-empty bottle of vodka gripped in the other. She refilled the shot glass, some of the vodka spilling over the rim, then handed the bottle to Klokov. She tilted her head back and downed the cool liquid, then slammed the glass on the table. A flick of her finger sent the glass sliding toward Klokov, where it coasted to a halt beside his glass.

"Your turn."

Klokov grinned. She had to admit he was an attractive man, with a charismatic personality. He was also an animal, who in a few hours would slaughter every inhabitant of the ice station and *North Dakota*'s crew. He and his men had to be stopped. She needed to contact someone, let them know what was going on. But first, she had to get past Klokov and the guard outside.

While seated across from Klokov, she had not looked at the ice pick resting on the ledge behind him. She was afraid he would follow her eyes, giving away her plan. As she stared at Klokov, however, she could see the ice pick in her peripheral vision, over his left shoulder and two feet behind him. She would have to get close enough to grab it without him noticing. She had to act soon, too. She couldn't keep drinking.

They had consumed half a bottle of vodka, and there was no way she could finish it. She could already feel the effects, and there was more alcohol in her system to metabolize. Klokov, however, appeared unaffected. She had wanted to dull his mental faculties, but hers were deteriorating faster. She decided it was now or never.

Christine stood and walked over to Klokov and sat down in his lap, her thighs straddling his waist. "It's getting warm in here," she said as she pulled her mid-layer thermal top off.

"It is part of my plan," Klokov replied as he grinned again. "The heat is on high."

Christine pulled her inner fleece over her head and tossed it on the floor, then placed her hands on Klokov's shoulders. The ice pick was almost within reach. Klokov ran his hands up her slim waist, then along her rib cage toward her white-laced bra. His eyes devoured every inch of her body, but then his gaze shifted to her left shoulder and the distinctive small round scar. As a Spetsnaz, Klokov undoubtedly recognized the bullet wound.

He leaned back, examining her body more critically, identifying another bullet scar on her right bicep, and then the thin, vertical knife scar on her neck.

"There is more to you than there appears," he said.

"I'm just unlucky," she replied. "I keep ending up in the wrong place at the wrong time."

Christine could feel Klokov's body tensing. His smile was gone and he was becoming suspicious. She needed to distract him and get the ice pick while she had the opportunity. She reached behind her back with both hands and undid her bra, then slid it from her shoulders and dropped it on the floor. Klokov's eyes went to her breasts and his hands soon followed.

Now was as good a time as any.

She leaned forward, smothering his face between her breasts. She could feel his hot mouth on her flesh as she reached with her right hand toward the ice pick, but it was a few inches too far away. She leaned forward even more, pushing Klokov's head back as she pressed her body tightly against his. She heard muffled sounds of enjoyment as her fingers wrapped around the ice pick handle.

Christine pulled back, resting her forearms on Klokov's shoulders, the ice pick firmly in her grip. She was ready to strike. However, she had to kill Klokov quietly, so the guard outside wasn't alerted. She was nervous, and began trembling. She couldn't delay any longer.

"You like my body?" she asked.

"It is wonderful. You are a beautiful woman."

Christine smiled. "I hope you enjoy this."

She leaned forward again, pressing her left breast into his face as she ran her fingers through his hair, then cradled his head in the crook of her left arm. As his mouth opened to take in her nipple, she clamped down tightly with her left arm and pulled her right hand back, then jammed the ice pick into Klokov's temple.

Christine kept his face squeezed tightly against her breast, muffling his scream as she worked the ice pick back and forth, slicing through his brain. Blood spurted from his head, coating her arm and splattering onto her shoulder and face as Klokov started convulsing.

His body finally went slack, his arms dropping to his side. She kept his face clamped against her breast until the blood spurting from his head slowed to an ooze, then she gradually released him from her embrace. His head tilted back; his mouth was open, as were his eyes, staring at the ceiling.

Christine pulled the ice pick from his head, then wiped the blood from it with the front of his shirt. She cleaned herself off, then placed the ice pick on the table and donned her clothing. Next, she searched for a firearm. She found a pistol in a harness hanging from a peg on one of the walls, but there was no silencer on the barrel. She had to kill the guard outside without alerting the four Spetsnaz in the adjacent hut, or any others in the camp.

Her search of the hut produced no other weapons, nor a silencer for the pistol. She slid the pistol into her parka pocket, then grabbed the ice pick and headed for the door. She stopped when she reached it, thinking through how to kill the guard outside. The Spetsnaz had taken station on the left side of the door, so she kept the ice pick in her right hand, against her thigh so its view was blocked by her body. She took a deep breath, then opened the door.

The Spetsnaz was to her left, as expected. He turned toward her, looking past her briefly for a sign of Klokov. Christine stepped onto the hardened snow beside the Spetsnaz. She answered his questioning look with a smile, then swiveled toward him and jammed the ice pick through his throat. However, he didn't die quickly like Klokov.

He grabbed her hand holding the ice pick, and then her throat with his other hand, slamming her against the hut. Christine tried to twist the ice pick to the side, ripping a gash in the man's neck, but with her body pinned against the hut and his hand firmly around hers, she could barely move the ice pick. Blood was spurting from the puncture wound, but he seemed unaffected. His gloved hand around her neck tightened like a vise, cutting off her air. He tried calling for help, but the only sound that came out was a sick, wet gurgle. His eyes narrowed and his hand around her neck clamped down even harder.

Christine tried to pry his hand from her throat with her left hand, but he was too strong. She thought about releasing the ice pick, giving her two hands to break his grip, but decided it was a bad idea. Once she released the ice pick, he'd extract it, and it'd come her way a second later. It was a standoff. Blood spurted from the puncture wound with every heartbeat, and it was only a matter of time before he lost too much blood. But time was counting down for her as well; she could live without oxygen for only so long.

She thought about Klokov's pistol. Unfortunately, the pistol was in her right pocket, and her right hand was stuck holding the ice pick. Her eyes moved to the pistol strapped to the man's waist. It was just out of reach. If he reached for the gun, however, she was ready. The instant he released her, she'd twist her body and rip the ice pick through his neck. It seemed the man understood his peril, because he kept her immobile, pinned against the hut, cutting off her air.

Christine started to feel light-headed. She redoubled her effort to pry his hand from her neck, even for just a second—long enough to gasp for air— but he was too strong. Her vision started to narrow, blackness creeping in from the periphery, when the man's grip weakened. She pried his fingers loose and sucked in a breath of cold air. His grip went flaccid a moment later and he dropped to his knees. His eyes closed and his hands fell limp to his sides.

She laid his body on the snow and extracted the ice pick. She looked around, and seeing no one, tossed the ice pick into the hut, then dragged the man inside. She searched his pockets and located the wire snips he used to cut her plastic ties, then retrieved his pistol. After exiting the hut and closing the door, she covered the red stain on the ground with a layer of fresh snow. Stepping back, she assessed the scene. There was no indication there were two dead Spetsnaz inside.

With the guard's pistol in her hand, she ran to the berthing hut where Brackman and Tarbottom were held, and slipped inside.

"It's me," Christine whispered.

Brackman replied, "What did they want you for? Are you okay?"

"I'm fine."

"Where are the Spetsnaz?"

"They have no idea I'm here. I killed the Spetsnaz commander and another one."

"How did you do that?"

"Ice pick."

Christine was relieved when Brackman didn't ask her to elaborate. Pulling the wire snips from her pocket, she knelt down and cut the two men free. "We need to contact someone so they can send help," she said. "Any ideas?"

Tarbottom answered, "There should be an Iridium phone in the command hut. We can contact the Arctic Lab in Svalbard, and if we're lucky, help will arrive tomorrow."

"We don't have until tomorrow," Christine replied. "The Spetsnaz plan to kill everyone at the ice camp before sunrise to cover their tracks, and I think they're going to kill everyone aboard *North Dakota*, too. We need help tonight."

"We can contact *Michigan* and have them send SEALs," Brackman said. "They should be monitoring underwater comms. If we can get to the command hut, we can use the RATS."

"What about *North Dakota*?" Christine asked. "If *Michigan* can hear us, will the Spetsnaz on *North Dakota* hear us too?"

"It's possible," Brackman replied. "But if the Spetsnaz have taken over the submarine, I doubt anyone is monitoring underwater comms."

"Sounds like a plan."

"We need to get to the command hut without being seen," Brackman said. "Do you know how many Spetsnaz are at the camp and where they are?"

Brackman had directed his question at Christine, but Tarbottom answered. "I saw one platoon board their helicopters and head to the Russian camp. I think there are eight left here at Nautilus, not counting Klokov. There's one in the PRM control van and another at the LARS operating station. I don't know where the other six are."

"I know where five of them are," Christine replied. "Four are in the berthing hut beside Verbeck's, and a fifth is dead inside Verbeck's hut, along with Klokov. That leaves one."

She pulled Klokov's pistol from her jacket and handed it to Brackman. He took the gun, then moved to the door, cracked it open, and peered outside. "I don't see anyone," he said, then opened the door and led Christine and Tarbottom into the cold night air.

66

USS *MICHIGAN*

"Captain to Control."

Wilson's first indication something was amiss was the 1-MC announcement, requesting his presence in the Control Room. He was touring the submarine's spaces and had just returned to the Operations Compartment. He ascended the nearest ladder, reaching the Control Room seconds later.

Lieutenant Barbara Lake was on the Conn, holding the WQC microphone, wearing a worried look. "We've been contacted by Ice Station Nautilus," she began. "The station has been taken over by Russian Spetsnaz, who have also taken control of *North Dakota*."

"What?" Wilson said as he reached Lake. "Give me the mike."

Wilson brought it to his mouth. "Ice Station Nautilus. This is *Michigan* actual. Say again, over."

A response over the WQC followed. "*Michigan,* this is Captain Steve Brackman, the president's senior military aide. The ice station has been assaulted by Russian Spetsnaz, and they have also taken control of *North Dakota*. Request immediate assistance, over."

Wilson connected the dots. The Russians wanted the tactical hardware and software aboard a Block III Virginia class, and were willing to resort to nefarious means.

He activated the WQC. "Ice Station Nautilus, this is *Michigan*. Understand all. Wait, over." He turned to the Chief of the Watch, "On the 1-MC, request Commander McNeil's presence in Control."

The Chief of the Watch passed the word and a moment later, the head of *Michigan*'s SEAL detachment arrived. Wilson brought McNeil up to speed.

"How many Spetsnaz are we talking about?" McNeil asked.

Wilson relayed the question over the WQC, which was followed by the response, "There are seven Spetsnaz at Ice Station Nautilus, sixteen aboard *North Dakota,* and twenty-four at the Russian ice camp. Over."

"May I?" McNeil gestured toward the microphone, and Wilson handed it to him. The SEAL asked his next question. "Ice Station Nautilus, *Michigan.* Do you know where the Spetsnaz at Nautilus are deployed?"

McNeil listened intently as Brackman informed him there were two Spetsnaz at the submarine rescue equipment control stations, four in a berthing hut, and one on patrol.

"Understand all. Will send assistance," McNeil replied. Brackman explained they would wait at the edge of the PRM ice hole, then McNeil handed the WQC microphone back to Wilson. "Request you pass on the 1-MC, SEAL platoon OICs report to Control."

A moment later, Lieutenants Jake Harrison and Lorie Allen arrived. McNeil explained the situation, then instructed Harrison, "Take a squad in the two SDVs and head to the surface ASAP. The rest of us will follow via mass lockout."

67

K-157 *VEPR*

Captain Second Rank Matvey Baczewski made his way through his Shchuka-B attack submarine, assessing the readiness of his ship and crew. He was in Compartment One, checking the status of his eight torpedo tubes and forty torpedoes. Although *Vepr* carried twelve 650-millimeter-diameter wake-homing torpedoes, designed to chase down American aircraft carriers, Baczewski focused on the twenty-eight 533-millimeter-diameter, multipurpose torpedoes, with both wake and active/passive sonar homing capability. If *Vepr* was called into action beneath the ice, they would use their smaller, but still deadly, sonar homing torpedoes.

In preparation, Baczewski had already ordered tubes One through Four loaded. His crew and submarine were ready, but for now, they waited. Since surfacing in the lead of open water a few kilometers from the American ice camp, it had been quiet aboard *Vepr*. One of its antennas was raised to receive radio transmissions and a periscope was up to monitor activity at the American ice station.

There was no guarantee *Vepr* would be called into action, however. Their presence near the disabled American submarine was a contingency plan; one that Baczewski hoped was implemented. After all, what was the purpose of building such magnificent submarines and the thousands of hours spent training their crews if they were never used? The thought of retiring from the Navy after never firing a torpedo or missile in defense of his country grated on him. An opportunity had finally presented itself, but it remained just beyond his grasp. His orders were clear—he could not act without justification.

Baczewski continued his tour through the submarine; it was his way of pacing, relieving the nervous energy. He was about to leave the Torpedo Room when the speakers in the compartment energized.

"Captain, Hydroacoustic. Receiving underwater communications. Request your presence in Hydroacoustic."

Baczewski headed into Compartment Two, arriving at Hydroacoustic a moment later. He opened the door to the darkened room, revealing four Hydroacoustic Party members, along with Lieutenant Chaban. Baczewski had augmented each Hydroacoustic watch with someone who understood English, so underwater communications between the American ice station and their two submarines could be monitored.

Lieutenant Chaban relayed what he had heard. Spetsnaz had taken control of the American ice station and attack submarine, but someone at the ice station had managed to call for help. The American guided missile submarine was preparing to send SEALs to the ice station. Baczewski considered contacting the Spetsnaz unit, warning them of the threat from below. However, Fleet Admiral Ivanov had been clear; no details of their endeavor could be transmitted on official channels. However, if *Vepr* eliminated the SEALs, Baczewski was confident the Spetsnaz would deal with the issue at the American ice station.

He retrieved the microphone and pushed the button for the Central Command Post.

"Watch Officer, this is the Captain. Man Combat Stations. Prepare to submerge."

68

USS *MICHIGAN* • K-157 *VEPR*

USS *MICHIGAN*

Lieutenant Harrison climbed the ladder inside Missile Tube One, pulling himself through the hatches at the top into the starboard Dry Deck Shelter. Petty Officer Tim Oliver and two more SEALs followed, while in Missile Tube Two, Chief Jeff Stone led a second four-man team into the port Dry Deck Shelter.

After Commander McNeil's order, Harrison had selected the members of his eight-man squad. They would be the first to the surface, followed by the remaining twenty-four SEALs. There had been a flurry of activity, with thirty-two SEALs preparing for combat, while the other half of the detachment—Navy divers—prepared to operate the shelters, air systems, and other equipment necessary to deploy the two SEAL platoons.

Harrison climbed into the hangar where the SEAL Delivery Vehicle was stowed. After donning air tanks and fins, he climbed into the SDV along with the other three SEALs. He rendered a thumbs-up to the diver on the other side of the Plexiglas shield, and dark water surged into the shelter. After the hangar door was opened, the mini-sub exited and Harrison spotted the other SDV emerging from the port shelter. The two SDVs lifted off their rails, then passed above the Dry Deck Shelters and over *Michigan*'s bow. In the distance, the ice station lights illuminated the hole cut for the rescue equipment. Harrison adjusted course, as did Chief Stone, and the two SDVs angled toward the light.

VEPR

"Combat Stations are manned, Captain. All compartments report ready to submerge."

While *Vepr*'s crew prepared for combat, Baczewski did his best to conceal his anticipation. After waiting twenty years to engage an adversary, the wait was finally over. He turned to his Watch Captain.

"Submerge to one hundred meters."

With ice keels descending to sixty meters, Baczewski ordered his submarine deep enough to avoid them.

Seconds later, the Compensation Officer reported, "Venting all main ballast tanks."

Vepr sank into the dark waters.

USS MICHIGAN

"Conn, Sonar. Receiving ballast tank venting sounds, bearing two-seven-zero."

Lieutenant Lake acknowledged the report, then informed Captain Wilson. Intel messages had reported an Akula surfacing near Ice Station Nautilus, and the Russians must have been monitoring underwater communications. It didn't take long for Wilson to conclude why the Akula was submerging.

Wilson ordered his Officer of the Deck, "Man Battle Stations Torpedo."

Lake passed the word, and the Chief of the Watch made the announcement over the 1-MC, which was followed by the loud *bong-bong-bong* of the General Alarm reverberating through the boat. The Chief of the Watch followed up after the alarm ceased, "Man Battle Stations Torpedo."

Commander McNeil entered Control from the Battle Management Center, and Wilson filled him in. "The Akula is submerging. We need to be ready in case they attack. Where do we stand in shelter operations?"

McNeil replied, "The two SDVs have been launched and the shelter doors are shut. The remaining SEALs are entering Missile Tubes One and Two now, preparing for mass lockout."

"That'll have to wait," Wilson replied, "until we determine the Akula's intent. We're a sitting duck right now; we need speed."

Wilson called out, "This is the Captain. I have the Conn. Lieutenant Lake retains the Deck. Dive, secure from hovering. Helm, ahead two-thirds."

As the Dive secured hovering and the Helm rang up the ordered bell, Wilson checked *Michigan's* course. They were pointed south. As good a course as any, for the time being.

VEPR

"On ordered depth of one hundred meters, Captain," the Watch Officer reported. "Request steerage orders."

Baczewski checked the chart on the navigation table. Before surfacing in the lead, *Vepr* had detected the American SSGN hovering seven kilometers to the east.

"Steersman, right full rudder, steady course zero-nine-zero. Ahead two-thirds."

The Steersman acknowledged, and *Vepr* turned east, increasing speed. Baczewski kept his eyes on the hydroacoustic display, looking for their adversary. After closing half the distance to the American submarine, the expected report came across the speakers.

"Command Post, Hydroacoustic. Hold a new contact, designated Hydroacoustic two-five, bearing one-zero-zero. Analyzing frequency tonals."

Before attacking, Baczewski had to verify it was the correct target. There were two American submarines under the ice, and it would not reflect well on him if he sank the wrong one.

Hydroacoustic followed up, "Command Post, Hydroacoustic. Contact two-five's tonals correlate to Ohio class submarine."

They had found their target. "All stations, track Hydroacoustic two-five."

After determining the contact's bearing rate, Baczewski decided to maneuver for a second leg of analysis, to verify their target was still hovering, and if not, its course, speed, and range.

"Steersman, left full rudder, steady course zero-zero-zero."

69

ICE STATION NAUTILUS

Inside the command hut with Brackman and Tarbottom, Christine stead-ied herself against the edge of the RATS console. The vodka she'd consumed had kicked in, and she was feeling the effects. There was nothing for her to do at the moment, however, so she waited while Tarbottom searched for an Iridium phone battery. He had located a phone in the command hut, only to find the battery missing, and was checking everywhere for a spare bat-tery. At the hut entrance, Brackman had the door cracked open and was peering outside.

Tarbottom concluded his search. "No luck," he said. "The Iridium phone is useless."

"Doesn't matter," Brackman said. "*Michigan's* SEALs will arrive soon. I think it's time we head to the ice hole. Can we get there without being seen by the Spetsnaz at the Launch and Recovery System?"

"Maybe," Tarbottom answered. "The control station is an open-air plat-form on the port side of the LARS. He'll have a full view of the approaches, but if he's looking the other way, we should be able to sprint from the last row of berthing huts to the rescue equipment without being seen. We can then work our way to the base of the LARS, where we can wait for the SEALs."

"Sounds good," Brackman said. His eyes shifted to Christine, and a con-cerned expression appeared. "Are you okay?" he asked. "The side of your face is covered in blood."

She had apparently done a poor job cleaning up. "It's not my blood," she said, then pulled the parka hood over her head.

Brackman studied her for a moment, then opened the door wider for a better view. After verifying there was no one in sight, he led them outside.

They worked their way along the berthing huts until they reached the edge of the station, then cut across to the last row of buildings. Brackman stopped at the edge of the last hut, peering around the corner at the rescue equipment.

He turned back and whispered, "There are two men on the LARS control platform. One civilian and one Spetsnaz. They're talking, and the Spetsnaz has his back to us." Brackman added, "The PRM has returned to the surface, so there might be other Spetsnaz around. I'm going to take another look, then sprint across if it's clear. You do the same. Understand?"

Christine and Tarbottom nodded. Brackman looked around the corner again, then sprinted across the open space, stopping behind a rack of air flasks. Christine moved into position. Peering around the corner, she spotted the two men on the LARS control platform, about a hundred feet away. There were no others in sight.

She took a deep breath and sprinted across the open expanse, reaching Brackman a moment later. As she tried to stop, she lost her footing. It wasn't easy sprinting while wearing heavy boots and three layers of Arctic gear, and the vodka wasn't helping. She had trouble slowing and plowed into Brackman, who caught her in his arms.

"You okay?" he asked.

"I had a little too much vodka."

"Drinking with the enemy?" Brackman smiled.

"Something like that."

Brackman released her as Tarbottom joined them. Brackman took the lead again, working around the end of the air flasks, then down the starboard side of the rescue equipment. Brackman stopped when they reached the forward corner of the LARS. He knelt down, joined by Christine and Tarbottom, all three focusing on the ice hole fifteen feet ahead.

The massive frame of the LARS began moving, shifting from an inboard tilt to an outboard one, with the PRM suspended from the crossbeam. Once the PRM stopped swaying, it descended, disappearing into the water.

Tarbottom whispered, "I'm going to check to see if there are other Spetsnaz."

Brackman nodded, and Tarbottom climbed the starboard side of the LARS to get a clear look. He clambered down a moment later, rejoining Brackman and Christine.

"There's no one," he said. "They off-loaded equipment into the deck trans-fer lock and must have returned to the PRM."

All they could do now was wait for *Michigan*'s SEALs.

Beneath the polar ice cap, Lieutenant Harrison shifted the SDV propeller into reverse, slowing his ascent toward the disc of light. Chief Stone did the same, and the two SDVs coasted to a halt ten feet from the edge of the ice hole. Harrison turned the propeller off and the four SEALs exited the mini-sub, hanging on to the side as Harrison reached into the cockpit and ad-justed the vehicle's buoyancy. The SDV drifted toward the ice, bumping up against it.

Stone and the other three SEALs had done the same, and with both SDVs moored against the ice cap, Harrison headed toward the ice hole.

Brackman noticed it first. "They're here," he said.

Christine looked closely, spotting a small dark blob by the edge of the ice hole; the top half of a man's head, wearing a black diving suit and face mask. He was staring at them, then after scanning left and right, disappeared.

A moment later, eight small blobs appeared at the edge of the ice hole, and seconds later, eight men hauled themselves onto the ice, withdrew their weapons, and sprinted toward Christine. The men formed a single line down the starboard side of the LARS, removing their scuba gear, and two SEALs stopped beside Brackman.

"I need as much information as you can provide," one of the SEALs said.

Christine recognized the man's voice instantly. "Jake, is that you?"

He turned toward her. "Chris? What are you doing here?"

"Waiting to board *Dolgoruky*. Apparently the Russians had the same idea with *North Dakota*."

Harrison nodded, then turned back to Brackman. "Can you draw a dia-gram of the ice station, showing us where the Russians are?"

Brackman nodded and drew an outline of the station in the snow, ex-plaining where the six Spetsnaz were, although there was a seventh unac-counted for. Brackman explained there were two men on the LARS control platform, and the Spetsnaz wore white Arctic gear, while the American wore black. Tarbottom then took a moment to explain the layout of the PRM control van and where the Spetsnaz had been stationed inside.

After Harrison conferred with Chief Stone, they broke into two fire teams. One would take out the Spetsnaz at the LARS operating station, while the other team eliminated the Spetsnaz in the PRM control van.

Harrison noticed the pistol in Brackman's hand. "Are all three of you armed?"

Tarbottom shook his head while Christine answered, "I have a pistol." She tried to pull it from her pocket, but it snagged on the pocket edge. After a few tugs, she pulled the weapon free. Harrison studied her more closely. Her words were slightly slurred and there was a glassy look in her eyes. Although it'd been years since they'd been out drinking, he recognized the signs.

"What the hell, Chris. You're drunk?"

"I've had a few."

"Give your pistol to Tarbottom."

"I'm a good shot," she replied. "Probably better than him." She waved the gun in Tarbottom's direction.

Harrison reached over and grabbed the gun from her hand. "I don't want a drunk amateur firing a weapon anywhere near me."

"I'm not an amateur."

As Harrison handed the pistol to Tarbottom, Christine's irritation began to mount. Harrison was treating her the same way he had in Beijing, discounting her ability. The SEALs wouldn't even be here if it weren't for her. However, considering her current condition, she had to admit he was right this time.

Chief Stone led one SEAL fire team toward the PRM control van, while Harrison led the other team along the front edge of the LARS. Christine peered around the corner as the four SEALs halted. One of the SEALs knelt on one knee and aimed his weapon toward the LARS control platform, just around the other corner.

Christine heard the whisper of his MP7, followed by the thud of a body impacting the snow. Two SEALs moved forward and disappeared around the corner, returning seconds later dragging a body. All four SEALs returned to where Christine, Brackman, and Tarbottom waited and released the dead Spetsnaz, tossing his assault rifle onto the snow nearby.

Christine perked up and turned to Harrison. "There's an extra weapon. I could—"

"Zip it, Chris," he said. "If I need your help, I'll ask for it."

She glared at him, then sat between Brackman and Tarbottom, with her back against the LARS. A minute later, Chief Stone and the other three SEALs returned, one of them carrying a Spetsnaz over his shoulder. The Spetsnaz was deposited onto the snow beside the other, along with his weapon.

Harrison turned to Brackman, Christine, and Tarbottom. "Two down, five more to go. Since we know where four are, we'll eliminate them next, then track down the last one. Stay here, and we'll be back in a few minutes. Any questions?"

After Christine and the others shook their heads, the eight SEALs disappeared around the corner of the LARS. Brackman kept watch in the direction the SEALs had headed, while Tarbottom monitored the other direction. Across from Christine, the two dead Spetsnaz lay face up in the snow. She decided to keep an eye on them, just in case.

USS *MICHIGAN* • K-157 *VEPR*

USS *MICHIGAN*

"Conn, Sonar. Hold a new narrowband contact, designated Sierra eight-five, bearing two-eight-zero. Analyzing."

Standing on the Conn between the two lowered periscopes, Wilson acknowledged Sonar's report. Sierra eight-five was almost assuredly the Akula that had surfaced nearby, but Sonar would confirm or deny his suspicion after analyzing the frequency tonals.

In the meantime, Wilson reviewed the tactical situation. *Michigan* was headed south, with Sierra eight-five on the starboard beam. He decided to maintain course long enough to obtain a bearing rate for the contact, while Sonar determined its classification.

Sonar followed up. "Conn, Sonar. Sierra eight-five is classified Akula."

VEPR

Matvey Baczewski stood in the Central Command Post, waiting impatiently while his First Officer shifted between the fire control consoles, analyzing the data from Hydroacoustic. The American SSGN was no longer hovering; they must have heard *Vepr* submerging.

Baczewski evaluated the geographic display. Bearings to the contact drifted rapidly to the right, which meant the American submarine was headed south. Once their adversary's course was refined to within ten degrees and its speed to within a few knots, they would be ready.

Captain Third Rank Petr Lukov, Baczewski's First Officer, was hunched over the shoulders of the two men at the fire control consoles. He tapped one Michman on the shoulder. "Set as Primary." The Michman complied, and Lukov announced, "Captain, I have a firing solution."

Baczewski ordered, "Prepare to Fire, Hydroacoustic two-five, tube One."

USS *MICHIGAN*

Captain Wilson studied the sonar display, watching Sierra eight-five on their starboard beam, drifting aft. With only one leg of bearings, there was insufficient data to determine the contact's solution; it could be close and operating at slow speed, or distant and headed toward them at high speed. He was about to reverse course to determine which scenario he was dealing with when a report from Sonar came across the Control Room speakers.

"Conn, Sonar. Receiving metallic transients from Sierra eight-five. Possible torpedo door mechanisms."

Wilson acknowledged Sonar's report, then called out, "Firing Point Procedures, Sierra eight-five, tube One. Select under-ice presets. Open outer doors, tubes One and Two."

As the personnel in Control executed their checklists, Wilson added, "Helm, left full rudder, steady course north."

If the Russian crew was preparing to fire, it would be prudent to maneuver.

VEPR

"Contact maneuver," First Officer Lukov called out.

Baczewski stopped beside Lukov and reviewed the two fire control displays. Instead of bearings drifting to the right, they were now steady. Their adversary had turned to the north. It would take a few minutes to sort out their contact's exact course, but in the meantime, Baczewski would maneuver to a more favorable position.

"Steersman, right standard rudder, steady course one-two-zero."

Vepr would move behind the American submarine.

USS *MICHIGAN*

"Possible contact zig, Sierra eight-five, due to upshift in frequency."

Wilson evaluated Sonar's report. The Akula submarine had either increased speed, turned toward them, or both. After analyzing the new bearing rate, it became clear the Russian Captain was maneuvering into *Michigan*'s baffles. Two could play that game.

"Helm, ahead full. Left full rudder, steady course two-nine-zero."

The Helm rang up the higher bell as he shifted his rudder left.

Michigan's Weapons Officer, Lieutenant Marcus Benjamin, announced, "Outer doors open, tubes One and Two. Weapon in tube One has accepted presets and is ready with the exception of Master solution."

Benjamin looked over his shoulder at Lieutenant Commander Terry Sparks. The Weps could not report Weapon Ready until the XO determined a firing solution and updated it to Master. Unfortunately, they were in the middle of a melee, with both submarines maneuvering aggressively. Who lived and died would be determined by which crew determined an adequate firing solution first.

VEPR

"Contact two-five is maneuvering again," the nearest fire control Michman announced. Baczewski moved behind the Michman, evaluating the new bearing rate. It was drawing aft more rapidly than expected. The American Captain was astute, realizing *Vepr* was headed into his baffles, and was attempting the same.

With both submarines alerted to the other's presence and tactical goals, the scenario would degenerate into a circular tail-chase, each submarine constantly maneuvering to prevent the other from entering its baffles or developing a firing solution.

Baczewski decided to change tactics.

"Cancel fire," he announced, followed by new commands. "Prepare to fire, Hydroacoustic two-five, horizontal salvo, tubes One and Two. Tube One fired first."

During a circular tail-chase, it would be difficult to determine a solution with enough accuracy to shoot a single torpedo. However, he was confident the course, speed, and range of their adversary could be bracketed sufficiently for a salvo.

After evaluating the fire control display, Baczewski ordered, "Set target course to two-seven-zero, speed twenty knots. Use system range."

Baczewski's First Officer complied, then called out, "Solution updated."

"Torpedo ready," followed.

The Watch Officer announced, "Countermeasures armed."

Baczewski gave the order. "Fire tubes One and Two!"

71

ICE STATION NAUTILUS

Lieutenant Harrison crept along the outside of the plywood hut, his Heckler & Koch MP7 raised to the firing position. Following behind him were the other three members of his fire team: Tim Oliver, sniper; Brad Kratovil, breacher; and Jim Hay, communicator. Chief Stone's fire team had fanned out on both sides of Harrison's team, two men per side, each man moving down a different alley between the berthing huts. Harrison stopped at the edge of the hut to examine the next row. According to Brackman, the berthing hut containing the four Spetsnaz was directly ahead. Between the two rows of huts was an open expanse of snow—a thirty-foot trek.

Chief Stone's fire team would remain behind, providing cover, while Harrison's team moved into position for the assault. Harrison signaled his fire team, then sprinted across the open expanse, pulling up against the berthing hut. Oliver and Hay followed, lining up behind Harrison on one side of the door, while Kratovil positioned himself on the other side, standing by to open the door. It was a simple plywood door with no locks, so no extraordinary measures would be required to enter. Harrison and the two SEALs behind him raised their MP7s to the firing position, and Harrison gave the signal.

Kratovil pulled the door open, and Harrison surged into the berthing hut, moving to his right. Oliver moved to the left as he entered, providing access for Hay.

Harrison took the scene in quickly. There were four Spetsnaz in the room. Two were sitting at a small table against the far wall playing cards, while the others were lying prone on two of the six beds in the hut.

One of the Spetsnaz at the table, facing the door, reacted immediately, reaching for his AK-9 assault rifle leaning against the wall. The other Spetsnaz at the table turned toward the door, while the other two Spetsnaz, who were still awake, rolled from their bunks, also reaching for their AK-9s.

Harrison took aim at the Spetsnaz at the table, putting a bullet in his head as his hand grasped his assault rifle, while the other two SEALs put three bullets into each man rolling from his bunk. Harrison shifted his aim to the second Spetsnaz at the table, who was also reaching for his weapon. Three more bullets neutralized the threat, and Harrison shifted back to the first Spetsnaz, verifying his first shot had killed him. A quick check confirmed all four Spetsnaz were dead.

Six down, one to go. The seventh Spetsnaz was either on patrol or in a different berthing hut. Harrison decided to inspect each berthing hut, starting with the adjacent one.

After a short discussion of the plan with his fire team, Harrison led the way to the nearest hut. Using the same procedure, Kratovil pulled the door open and Harrison, Oliver, and Hay surged in. There were two dead Spetsnaz inside. One was lying on the floor, with a puncture wound in his neck and the front of his white artic gear stained red. A second Russian sat by a table, with a hole in his left temple. On the floor beside the first Spetsnaz was an ice pick.

Oliver lowered his MP7. "Nice work," he said. "I'd like to meet the guy responsible for this."

Harrison spotted a half-empty bottle of vodka on the table and recalled Christine was drunk. He was pretty sure he knew who was responsible, and it wasn't a guy. Harrison exited the berthing hut, then headed toward the next one.

Nicholai Ovechkin hitched the strap of his Izhmash AK-9 assault rifle higher onto the shoulder of his white parka as his boots crunched through the snow. It was cold tonight, but thankfully there was no icy wind cutting into his exposed face. Even so, he'd be glad when his watch was over, exchanging places with another Spetsnaz in a warm berthing hut.

Ovechkin turned the corner and stopped in his tracks. Gathered outside the Spetsnaz commander's hut were four armed men wearing black wet suits. Ovechkin moved back behind the berthing hut, pulling his radio from its holster. He spoke quietly into the microphone, attempting to contact another

Spetsnaz on duty. There was no response from Leonid. Nor Alexander or Josef. He switched channels, hailing Second Platoon at Barneo, and this time he received an answer. Reinforcements would arrive shortly.

He slid the radio back into its holster, then slipped his AK-9 from his shoulder and raised it to the firing position, looking through the optical sight as he peered around the corner. The four men were moving toward another berthing hut, but not so fast as to present a challenge. He took aim on the closest man and squeezed off two rounds, then moved to the next as the first man stumbled to the ground.

72

USS *MICHIGAN*

"Torpedo in the water, bearing two-five-zero!"

Wilson acknowledged Sonar's report, then examined the geographic display. A red bearing line appeared, radiating from Sierra eight-five, forty degrees off the port bow. He needed to turn away.

"Helm, ahead flank. Right full rudder, steady course three-four-zero. Launch countermeasure."

The Helm rang up ahead flank and twisted his yoke to right full, and Lieutenant DeCrispino launched one of *Michigan*'s decoys. A white scalloped circle appeared on the geographic display, recording the location of their countermeasure.

Wilson returned his attention to getting a torpedo into the water. His crew was still at Firing Point Procedures, but his Executive Officer hadn't determined a satisfactory solution. With *Michigan* increasing speed to ahead flank, they would likely lose Sierra eight-five due to the turbulent flow of water across *Michigan*'s sensors. They needed to launch a torpedo soon.

He stepped from the Conn and stopped beside Lieutenant Commander Sparks, examining the solutions on the three combat control consoles. With the frequent maneuvering by both submarines, the three solutions were all over the place, failing to converge on a similar course, speed, and range of their target. As Wilson evaluated his options, he was interrupted by another announcement by the Sonar Supervisor.

"Torpedo in the water, bearing two-four-five!"

A purple bearing line appeared on the geographic display. Their adversary had launched a two-torpedo salvo. Wilson responded immediately.

"Check Fire. Quick Reaction Firing, Sierra eight-five, tube One."

Wilson canceled their normal torpedo firing process, implementing a more urgent version, which forced his Executive Officer to send his best solution to the torpedo immediately. The Russian Captain wouldn't know how well aimed the torpedo was, and it was better to give him something to worry about instead of letting him refine his solution and send updates to his torpedoes over their guidance wires.

Lieutenant Commander Sparks shifted his gaze between the three combat control consoles, then tapped one of the fire control technicians on the shoulder. "Promote to Master."

Sparks announced, "Solution ready!"

Lieutenant Benjamin, hunched behind another fire control technician at the Weapon Control Console, followed up, "Weapon ready!"

"Ship ready!" the Officer of the Deck announced.

"Shoot on generated bearings!" Wilson ordered.

Wilson listened to the whirr of the torpedo ejection pump as the torpedo was impulsed from the tube, accelerating from rest to thirty knots in less than a second. Inside the sonar shack, the sonar technicians monitored the status of their outgoing unit.

"Own ship's unit is in the water, running normally."

"Fuel crossover achieved."

"Turning to preset gyro course."

"Shifting to medium speed."

Michigan's torpedo was headed toward its target.

Wilson examined the red and purple lines on the geographic display, with new lines appearing every ten seconds. The red torpedo bearings were marching slowly forward, which eased Wilson's concern until he evaluated the purple lines. The bearing to the second torpedo remained constant. The Russian captain had fired a torpedo salvo, with a *lead* torpedo fired slightly ahead of *Michigan* and a *lag* torpedo fired behind. When Wilson turned away, he had unwittingly put *Michigan* on an intercept course with the second torpedo. He needed to maneuver again.

"Helm, right standard rudder, steady course zero-seven-zero. Launch countermeasure."

Michigan turned toward the east as Lieutenant DeCrispino launched a second torpedo decoy. Wilson watched intently as the second torpedo closed on *Michigan*.

73

ICE STATION NAUTILUS

As Harrison's fire team moved across the snow toward the next berthing hut, the first indication of danger was the splatter of warm blood against his face and Kratovil stumbling to the snow. Hay lurched sideways a second later, also collapsing as Harrison and Oliver dove to the ground, sliding around and pointing their MP7s to the left, down a long avenue between two rows of berthing huts. Oliver sent a volley of MP7 rounds down the alley, although Harrison wasn't sure if he had identified a target or was firing for effect. Chief Stone's men, alerted to the presence of a Spetsnaz hiding behind one of the huts, also opened fire.

Wood splinters flew into the air as MP7 rounds tore into every hut along the avenue. Harrison lifted Kratovil over his shoulder as Oliver grabbed Hay, and the two men hustled toward the nearest cover, sliding to a halt between two berthing huts. Harrison deposited Kratovil against the side of the hut, and a quick examination told Harrison his friend was dead. He'd taken one round in the shoulder and another in his head. Hay was alive but in bad shape, with two rounds in his side.

The Spetsnaz had probably called back to the Russian ice camp for help, so Harrison spoke into his headset, ordering Chief Stone to pull his fire team back to the LARS, where they would wait for the other twenty-four SEALs, who should be emerging from the ice hole any time now. Hay wasn't ambulatory, so Oliver heaved him over his shoulder again, and Harrison did the same with Kratovil's body.

Harrison reached the LARS at the same time as Chief Stone and the rest of his fire team. He laid Kratovil's body in the snow beside the two dead Spetsnaz while Oliver propped Hay against the side of the LARS, between Tarbottom and Christine. Oliver unzipped Hay's wet suit to take a look at the wounds, but there was little they could do until they got him back aboard *Michigan*, where their Medical Officer could tend to him.

In the still night air, Harrison heard the faint, rhythmic beat of approaching helicopters. More Spetsnaz were on the way. He checked his watch. He didn't understand why the other SEALs hadn't arrived yet.

Where the hell were they?

74

K-157 *VEPR* • USS *MICHIGAN*

VEPR

After examining the solutions on both fire control consoles, Baczewski's First Officer called out, "Confirmed target maneuver, Hydroacoustic two-five. Contact has turned away again."

Before Baczewski could respond, his Weapons Officer, seated at the Weapon Control Console, called out, "Detect! First fired unit!"

Baczewski studied the fire control display. Their first torpedo had detected a contact at the location of their adversary's first maneuver. It was likely homing on a decoy. He needed to steer the weapon away from the countermeasure and put it back onto their adversary's trail. The Fire Control screen displayed an estimate of the American submarine's path. It had turned away twice; first to the north and a second time to the east.

"Weapons Officer," Baczewski ordered, "Steer both torpedoes right eighty degrees."

The Weapons Officer acknowledged, and a moment later, their torpedoes veered right.

USS *MICHIGAN*

"Conn, Sonar. Upshift in Doppler, both torpedoes. Torpedoes have turned toward."

Wilson acknowledged the Sonar Supervisor's report, then stopped behind Petty Officer Chris Malocsay, one of the fire control technicians manning the combat control consoles, and examined the torpedo solutions on the geographic plot. The Russian Captain had steered both torpedoes past

Michigan's decoys, and they were now chasing *Michigan* from behind. The bearing to the first fired torpedo was climbing up *Michigan*'s port side, which meant its course was too far to the north. The bearings to the second torpedo were steady, however, which meant its solution was dead-on.

Wilson was about to order another course change when Sonar called out again. "Second torpedo is range-gating! Estimated range to torpedo is two thousand yards."

The torpedo had detected *Michigan,* then adjusted the interval of its sonar pings to more accurately determine the target's range. It was homing.

Wilson's options were limited. An Emergency Blow was out, since they were operating under the polar ice cap. He could eject another decoy and turn again, but with the torpedo locked on to *Michigan*, the odds of it being distracted by a small decoy were low. His thoughts turned to the thin sliver of water they were traveling in. The smooth bottom of the Barents Sea offered no hiding places, but the jagged ice keels did. He needed to find one. And fast.

The Sonar Supervisor reported, "Torpedo range, one-five hundred yards!"

Wilson turned to Lieutenant DeCrispino on the Conn. "Officer of the Deck. Energize the under-ice sonar. Set range to maximum."

DeCrispino complied and the two men stared at the display, searching for a colored patch indicating a vertical surface. Just off to starboard, a red patch appeared.

"Helm, right ten degrees rudder, steady course zero-nine-zero."

The Helm complied, and *Michigan* swung to the ordered course.

Torpedo range, one thousand yards!

Wilson focused on the red patch, which was growing slowly larger. He would have to wait until it faded from the screen, indicating *Michigan* had passed beneath it.

"Officer of the Deck," Wilson said calmly. "Prepare to launch countermeasure."

DeCrispino stopped beside the Countermeasure Launch Panel, lifting up the plastic cover over one of the buttons.

Torpedo range, five hundred yards!

Wilson was about to jettison his plan—the ice keel was too far away—and eject a decoy and turn, when the red blotch faded to orange, then yellow. They were passing under the ice keel.

When the color faded to black, Wilson ordered, "Dive, make your depth one hundred feet. Use twenty up!" After the Dive acknowledged, Wilson added, "Helm, right hard rudder, steady course one-eight-zero." He turned to DeCrispino. "Launch countermeasure!"

The Lieutenant ejected the torpedo decoy as *Michigan* tilted sharply upward and twisted to starboard. Wilson followed up with another order to DeCrispino. "Secure the under-ice sonar."

As *Michigan* rose toward the ice, Wilson gambled there were no additional ice keels; that they were under a smooth ice floe, giving them a few feet of clearance to the top of the sail.

The Weapons Officer called out, "Loss of wire continuity, tube One." They had lost the wire guide to their torpedo, cut by the ice keel, but that was the least of their worries. They had no updated information to send it.

Michigan leveled off as it reached ordered depth on a course paralleling the ice keel. This was the best he could do.

It was up to the Russian torpedo now.

ICE STATION NAUTILUS

Harrison did a quick recon of the submarine rescue equipment, then deployed the ambulatory SEALs in his squad, leaving the injured Hay sitting beside Christine. Harrison took station at the forward corner of the LARS, and Chief Stone anchored the far end near the air flasks, with three other SEALs taking position in gaps between the rescue equipment. The last SEAL, sniper Tim Oliver, climbed the A-frame that launched and retrieved the PRM.

Stone and the other three SEALs worked their way to the port side of the equipment so they would have a clear view of the avenue running between the last row of huts and the rescue equipment, while Harrison remained on the back edge of the LARS, due to lack of cover if he moved to the forward corner. Harrison told Brackman and Tarbottom they'd be put to use if the situation warranted it.

The sound of approaching helicopters had faded a few minutes ago, but there was no sign of Spetsnaz until Harrison's hand went to his headset, then he took aim with his MP7. Harrison began firing, his weapon barely making a whisper. Neither the MP7 nor Russian AK-9 made much sound when they fired, but in the still Arctic air, Christine heard bullets pinging off metal rescue components and thudding into plywood huts.

Christine felt a tremor in the ice, and her's and Brackman's eyes locked for a moment. A torpedo had exploded beneath the ice cap. The Akula and *Michigan* must have engaged, which explained why the rest of the SEALs had not arrived.

K-157 *VEPR*

"Command Post, Hydroacoustic. Explosion in the water, bearing zero-nine-zero. Loss of wire guide, second-fired torpedo."

Baczewski didn't need Hydroacoustic's report to know one of their torpedoes had exploded. The sound was audible through the steel hull as the shock wave rumbled by.

Hydroacoustic followed up, "Loss of Hydroacoustic two-five. Breaking up noises, bearing zero-nine-zero."

The tension in the Command Post dissipated, and his First Officer congratulated the two men operating the fire control consoles, slapping them on the shoulders.

Hydroacoustic called out suddenly, "Torpedo in the water, bearing zero-three-zero!"

"Steersman, ahead flank," Baczewski ordered.

Their adversary must have counterfired while evading, and the torpedo had just gone active. However, it was not likely an accurate shot. He monitored the bright white trace on the sonar display, concluding the torpedo was headed southwest. Not a bad shot, Baczewski conceded. But not good enough.

"Steersman, right full rudder, steady course three-zero-zero."

The Steersman complied and *Vepr* reversed course. Baczewski monitored the torpedo bearings, which drifted rapidly to starboard. The torpedo hadn't detected *Vepr*.

Baczewski kept his submarine headed northwest until the torpedo passed astern, then ordered a new course. "Steersman, right full rudder, steady course zero-nine-zero."

Vepr turned toward the bearing of the torpedo explosion. Baczewski wasn't convinced they had sunk the American submarine. His Hydroacoustic Party had reported a submarine breaking up, but it could have been an ice keel breaking apart instead.

He needed to be certain.

Vepr surged toward the spot their torpedo had detonated.

USS *MICHIGAN*

As Wilson hoped, the torpedo had slammed into the ice keel and detonated, triggered by the contact sensor in its exploder mechanism, and he wondered if their adversary had been fooled. *Michigan* was still barreling along at ahead flank, paralleling the ice keel, and he maintained course and speed until they were two thousand yards from the explosion.

Wilson ordered, "Helm, back full. Left full rudder, steady course north."

The Helm ordered the backing bell and twisted his rudder, and *Michigan* did a 180-degree turn while it slowed. As *Michigan* steadied on the reverse course, it coasted to a halt.

"Helm, all stop. Dive, commence hovering. Set keel depth to one hundred feet."

The Helm and Dive complied, and *Michigan* maintained position where she was, with the ice keel on her port side, shielding her from the Akula hunting them. Wilson gave no further orders, and Lieutenant Commander Sparks approached him on the Conn.

"What's your plan?" Sparks asked.

"I'm hoping the Akula Captain won't want to report he *might* have sunk us. He knows that if we survived, he might regain contact if he gets here fast enough. When he arrives," Wilson added, "we'll be waiting for him."

Sparks nodded his understanding as Wilson called out, "Attention in Control." He explained his plan, and after concluding his brief, adjusted his weapon load.

"Weapons Officer. Reload tube One."

ICE STATION NAUTILUS

Sitting against the LARS between Brackman and Tarbottom, Christine listened to Harrison's communications with the other SEALs. As best she could tell from the one-sided conversation, they were seriously outnumbered. Another platoon of Spetsnaz had arrived and were interspersed along the last row of huts across from the rescue equipment.

Harrison and the five other SEALs were keeping the Spetsnaz at bay, but not without cost. The SEAL on the left side of the decompression chamber had been hit, and a moment later, the SEAL in the habitrail section stopped responding. Harrison turned to Brackman and Tarbottom.

"I need your help. Take an AK-9"—he pointed to the assault rifles lying by the dead Spetsnaz—"and take position on either side of the decompression chamber. Take the headsets off Kratovil and Hay so we can communicate."

Brackman and Tarbottom put the Spetsnaz pistols in their parka pockets and retrieved the Russian AK-9 rifles, then Brackman pulled a headset from the dead SEAL while Tarbottom removed one from Hay. The injured SEAL had his eyes closed and was either dead or unconscious. After Brackman and Tarbottom conferred, Brackman headed to the far side of the decompression chambers while Tarbottom took station on the near side. The two men hustled down the side of the LARS, disappearing into the shadows.

Harrison returned his attention to the opposing Spetsnaz as the firefight continued. Several minutes later, it became clear the situation was deteriorating when Harrison called Tarbottom and another man's name several times with no apparent response, and things took a turn for the worse when a man's body thudded onto the snow a few feet from Christine. Tim Oliver, their sniper, lay motionless in the snow, his eyes frozen open, as his MP7 ricocheted off LARS support beams as it fell.

That left only two SEALs—Harrison and Stone—plus Brackman. Christine's eyes went to Harrison as his gaze shifted from Oliver to her. "Okay," he said. "Take Kratovil's MP7 and take position on this side of the decompression chambers."

Christine scrambled across the snow and retrieved Kratovil's MP7, then hurried down the side of the LARS. After working her way through the gap between the habitrail and the decompression chambers, she reached the other side of the submarine rescue equipment, across from the Spetsnaz. Tarbottom was sprawled facedown in the snow. She lay on her stomach beside him and checked for a pulse, but found none.

She remained prone, using Tarbottom as a shield. Spetsnaz were partially hidden behind the corners of the huts, firing at Brackman, Stone, and Harrison. Propping the MP7 on Tarbottom's body, she aimed at the nearest Spetsnaz.

79

K-157 *VEPR* • USS *MICHIGAN*

VEPR

"Captain. One thousand meters to the explosion point."

Baczewski acknowledged the Electric Navigating Party Leader. They were closing rapidly on the spot their torpedo had detonated, with *Vepr* still at ahead full.

"Steersman, ahead two-thirds." Baczewski checked the nearest depth gage. They were at one hundred meters. If their adversary was hiding behind an ice keel, he needed to go deeper, to expose the American submarine sooner.

"Diving Officer. Make your depth one hundred seventy meters."

Vepr tilted down as it slowed, leveling off as it approached the explosion point.

Baczewski spoke into the microphone, "Hydroacoustic, Command Post. Do you have a regain of Hydroacoustic two-five?"

USS *MICHIGAN*

"Conn, Sonar. Hold a new contact on the spherical array, designated Sierra eight-six, bearing three-five-seven. Most likely a regain of Sierra eight-five. Analyzing."

Wilson didn't wait for Sonar's analysis. "XO, set range to Sierra eight-six at two thousand yards, course zero-nine-zero. Speed ten."

The range to the Akula was firm. The course and speed were guesses, but at this range, anything close would work.

Wilson followed up, "Firing Point Procedures, Sierra eight-six, tube One.

Select short-range under-ice tactics. Set Enable Run to minimum." With the last order, the torpedo would go active as soon as possible.

The watchstanders carried out their tasks, and the expected reports followed.

"Solution ready."

"Weapon ready."

"Ship ready."

Wilson called out, "Match sonar bearings and shoot!"

VEPR

"Command Post, Hydroacoustic. Torpedo launch transients, bearing one-eight-zero!"

Before Baczewski could react, Hydroacoustic called out, "Torpedo in the water, bearing one-eight-zero!"

Baczewski spun toward the hydroacoustic display. A bright white trace was burning in on their starboard beam. Based on the intensity of the trace, the torpedo was close.

"Steersman, ahead flank!"

As the steersman rang up maximum propulsion, Baczewski evaluated the evasion course. He decided to place the torpedo aft of the beam, so his submarine could open range while evading.

"Steersman, left full rudder, steady course zero-six-zero. Launch torpedo decoy!"

Vepr swung around quickly and a decoy was launched, which gave Baczewski hope until Hydroacoustic's next report. "Torpedo has gone active!"

The torpedo going active so soon told Baczewski it had been fired from close range, which meant it would lock on to *Vepr* before the submarine could open distance from its decoy. It would also catch up to *Vepr* soon. He had to get a torpedo out quickly.

"Counterfire, bearing one-eight-zero, tube Three! Set short-range tactics."

A target solution would not be sent to the torpedo. Instead, it would be fired down the bearing of the torpedo launch.

"Torpedo is homing!"

Baczewski remained focused on preparing their torpedo for firing. The torpedo tube was flooded and muzzle door open. All that remained was the torpedo accepting the course and preset commands.

He checked the nearest clock. He figured they had fifteen seconds left, and he turned toward his Weapons Officer, hunched over the Weapon Launch Console. Baczewski refrained from requesting a status. Forcing the Weapons Officer to reply would only waste precious time.

Ten seconds left.

The Weapons Officer finally called out, "Torpedo ready, tube Three!"

Five seconds left.

Baczewski gave the order. "Fire tube Three!"

The sound of their torpedo being impulsed from its tube greeted Baczewski's ears, followed immediately by the deafening sound of an explosion. *Vepr* jolted forward violently, knocking Baczewski to the deck. As he pulled himself to his feet, the flooding alarm sounded from Compartments Eight and Nine. The normal white lighting in the Command Post extinguished a moment later, replaced by yellow emergency lighting. Baczewski felt his submarine slow and tilt upward, as the ocean poured into the aft compartments. With two compartments flooded, not even an Emergency Blow could keep them afloat.

Vepr was going to the bottom.

USS *MICHIGAN*

Sonar made two reports over the 27-MC. The first one announced the explosion, which Wilson and his crew not only heard, but felt. As the sound of the explosion died down, a second report emanated from the speakers in Control.

"Torpedo in the water, bearing zero-five-zero!"

Wilson had already ordered *Michigan* to ahead flank and the optimal evasion course to the southeast. He ordered a countermeasure launched, then monitored the torpedo bearings. They moved steadily aft, which told Wilson the torpedo had been fired on a line-of-bearing solution, toward where *Michigan* was when Wilson fired. The bearings continued drawing aft as

Michigan opened range, and Wilson let out a sigh of relief as the torpedo passed behind them. Then his thoughts turned to Ice Station Nautilus.

He stopped by the navigation plot and ordered, "Plot a course to the ice hole." Petty Officer Leenstra complied, quickly determining the bearing.

"Helm, left full rudder, steady course three-four-zero."

80

ICE STATION NAUTILUS

Under normal circumstances, Christine was an excellent shot. But that was while firing a pistol at a stationary target, at a range of twenty-five feet or less. And sober. She had never fired an MP7 before, or an assault rifle of any type. Still, she figured the principles were the same. She wrapped her index finger around the trigger and placed her eye against the sight. She examined the berthing hut to her right, where a Spetsnaz in his white Arctic gear was partially hidden around the corner of the hut, firing his assault rifle. Christine took aim, let out a slow breath, and was about to squeeze the trigger when she felt another tremor through the ice. *Michigan* must have survived the first torpedo explosion and was dueling with the Akula.

She hoped luck was with Wilson and his crew as she focused again through the MP7 sight, exhaled slowly, and squeezed the trigger. A chunk of plywood splintered from the corner of the hut just above the Spetsnaz's head. He pulled back, out of sight. A few seconds later he peered around the corner again and Christine compensated her aim, bringing it down and to the right slightly, and squeezed off another round. A puff of snow flew up at the man's feet. Christine adjusted her aim again and was about to shoot when a barrage of bullets pinged against the side of the decompression chamber, and two bullets thudded into Tarbottom's body, only an inch below her face.

She put her head down until there was a pause in bullet impacts, then looked up again. The Spetsnaz was firing again, this time in her direction, and another bullet thudded into Tarbottom's body. Christine aimed and fired again, but this time there was no indication of where her bullet hit. She must have missed to the right, the bullet passing by in the open air.

Christine fired her MP7 each time the Spetsnaz appeared around the corner of the hut, and although she wasn't doing a spectacular job of killing

Russians, she figured she didn't need to. They were in a stalemate. Christine and the other Americans only needed to keep the Spetsnaz at bay until the rest of *Michigan*'s SEALs arrived, then the tide would turn in their favor. Assuming *Michigan* survived, of course.

Two more bullets impacted metal nearby, this time behind and just above her head. Another Spetsnaz, hiding behind a different hut, was also shooting at her. Christine alternated between the two Spetsnaz, and she thought she finally hit one, but wasn't sure. A Spetsnaz appeared a few seconds later, and she couldn't tell if it was the original man or a replacement. She took aim again and squeezed the trigger, but this time her MP7 didn't fire. She was out of bullets.

She slid down behind Tarbottom, then searched his parka pockets for the pistol she had given him. She found it, and as she retrieved the pistol, the sound of gunfire diminished, then ended, enveloping the ice station in eerie silence. A few Spetsnaz were still visible, but were no longer shooting. She wondered if Harrison, Stone, and Brackman had also run out of ammo.

The Spetsnaz disappeared behind the huts, and as Christine wondered what was going on, they reappeared simultaneously, firing a heavy barrage of bullets, which pinged off nearby metal components and thudded into Tarbottom's body. She ducked her head behind the Australian, waiting for the barrage to fade, but when it didn't, she looked up. A dozen Spetsnaz were sprinting across the open avenue between the huts and rescue equipment. She took aim with her pistol and fired twice at the nearest man, who went down. She swung her pistol toward the next Spetsnaz, but he reached the port side of the rescue equipment, hidden from her view.

There were two Spetsnaz around the corner of the decompression chamber, only a few feet away, while a third was to her right, hidden by the habitrail. It wouldn't be long before they advanced, and who survived would be determined by who had the quicker reaction time and better aim. Against three Spetsnaz, she didn't have a chance.

Christine was in an untenable position. She scrambled to her feet and sprinted back toward the starboard decompression chamber, ducking under electrical cables connecting the equipment. Upon reaching the starboard chamber, she positioned herself at the corner, her pistol extended, waiting for the Spetsnaz to advance.

USS *MICHIGAN*

Michigan was traveling at ahead flank, and Commander McNeil felt the tremors in the deck as he climbed into the starboard Dry Deck Shelter, joining the dozen SEALs inside. He would normally have remained aboard *Michigan,* but after their encounter with the Akula, he was certain the Russians on the surface had been alerted. Lieutenant Harrison and his men would soon be engaged by the second platoon of Spetsnaz, and McNeil decided every remaining SEAL, including him, would ascend to the surface.

The vibrations in the deck eased, and the lighting in the hangar extinguished, allowing eyes to acclimate to the dark water outside.

A minute later, the diver at the forward end of the hangar announced, "Flooding down."

Cold water surged through openings in the deck, rising rapidly as air was vented from the top, until the chamber was completely flooded. The hangar door swung slowly open, and the two SEALs at the front of the chamber stepped to the edge, then pushed off, surging toward the surface. The SEALs behind followed quickly in pairs. In less than thirty seconds, two dozen SEALs exited the port and starboard shelters, and McNeil followed, rising toward a white, wavering disc of light in the distance.

ICE STATION NAUTILUS

A few seconds after Christine reached the starboard decompression chamber, the three Spetsnaz appeared, working their way toward her. She took aim on the lead Spetsnaz and fired. She was certain her bullet hit him, but instead of collapsing to the ground, he moved quickly to the side, out of her view. The other two Spetsnaz retreated to her left and right, hidden by the rescue components. In the still night air, she could hear their feet crunching in the snow.

The two Spetsnaz on her left reached the other side of the decompression chamber, and she could hear the Spetsnaz on her right working his way toward her. There was nowhere to fall back to; behind her was the open expanse of the polar ice cap. She could head left, toward Brackman and Chief Stone, assuming they were still alive, or right, toward Harrison. She decided to head toward Harrison, but would have to sprint past the habitrail equipment, which didn't offer a solid shield of protection. The Spetsnaz would have a clear shot as she passed by.

She turned toward the LARS and sucked in a deep breath, preparing for the sprint toward Harrison when she heard a man's voice behind her, speaking Russian. Although she didn't understand what he said, his tone was unmistakable. She slowly raised her hands in the air as she turned around, spotting a Spetsnaz with his assault rifle aimed at her. He gestured toward the pistol in her right hand, and she dropped it onto the snow.

Two more Spetsnaz appeared behind the man, dragging Brackman between them. They had him by his upper arms, facedown, his head sagging. They deposited Brackman's body beside Christine, then joined the first Spetsnaz. Christine knelt down and checked Brackman. He was alive, but unconscious, with blood oozing from a gash in his forehead.

The first Spetsnaz pulled a radio from a holster and spoke into it. He received a response and returned the radio to its slot, then raised his rifle toward Christine. It took her only a second to realize the Spetsnaz had asked for instructions on what to do with their prisoners, and the response had been unfavorable. He didn't bother bringing the AK-9 sight to his eye; he simply pointed the assault rifle at her, and Christine heard the sound of bullets thudding into flesh.

Two of the three Spetsnaz collapsed to the ground, leaving the Spetsnaz with the assault rifle aimed at Christine. His eyes widened as he adjusted the aim of his rifle to the left. There were three more thuds and he crumpled to the snow. Christine turned around slowly. In the shadow of the LARS, Harrison and three other SEALs were approaching, their MP7s raised to the firing position, while four more SEALs were advancing behind them.

The rest of McNeil's men had arrived.

83

ICE STATION NAUTILUS

Inside the command hut, Christine listened as McNeil conferred with Vance Verbeck, Commander Ned Steel, and the two SEAL platoon leaders, Lieutenant Harrison and Lieutenant Allen. The SEALs had scoured the ice station, killing all but a half-dozen Spetsnaz who surrendered, then freed the ice station personnel bound in the huts. McNeil assimilated the information quickly, determining the most pressing issue was the Spetsnaz takeover of *North Dakota*. It appeared the Spetsnaz intended to wrap things up and return to the Russian ice camp by sunrise, erasing their tracks in the process. Exactly what they had in mind regarding *North Dakota* was unknown, but there wasn't much time to lose. It would be sunrise in three hours.

Thankfully, the Spetsnaz aboard the fast attack submarine were unaware of what had transpired atop the ice. Based on the equipment they had sent up, currently stacked in the two-story deck transfer lock, all of the submarine's tactical systems were off-line, including their WQC. However, they had heard the two underwater explosions through the hull and the attendant in the PRM had inquired. The co-pilot in the control van reported they had no idea what it was and the conversation ended there.

McNeil addressed Commander Steel. "What's the status of the rescue equipment?"

Steel answered, "The port side of the hyperbaric complex is damaged. Luckily, the decompression chambers and all essential gear are contained in metal Conex containers to make them easy to transport, and the extra layer of metal helped protect things. But the port decompression chamber is out of commission for the time being, and there are a few holes in the pressurized flexible manway we'll need to patch before we can rescue *Dolgoruky*'s crew. The Russian submarine is likely pressurized, and it would be counterproductive to rescue the crew, only to have them die from the bends. How-ever, we can retrieve the PRM from *North Dakota,* because she's at standard atmospheric pressure."

"How many men can the PRM carry?" McNeil asked.

"Sixteen, plus two attendants."

McNeil turned to Harrison. "Take two squads down and regain control of *North Dakota.*"

Harrison conferred with the other SEAL platoon OIC, selecting the fif-teen men who would accompany him. Lieutenant Allen left to round up the desired personnel, along with two sets of Spetsnaz Arctic gear. Harrison and Chief Stone would don the gear, gaining a valuable few seconds before the Russians aboard *North Dakota* realized they weren't Spetsnaz. Harrison turned to Captain Brackman, who had regained consciousness shortly after McNeil arrived; after a quick check by the Undersea Rescue Command's Medical Officer and a bandage applied to his head, Brackman was released.

"I need a layout of *North Dakota,*" Harrison said.

Brackman located a notepad and pen, then drew a diagram of the Virginia class submarine, showing the compartments and levels. At Harrison's request, Brackman noted the location of the watertight doors between the compart-ments and the ladders providing access between levels. Harrison studied the diagrams, then tore the sheets from the notepad.

Commander Steel's handheld radio squawked. It was the rescue super-visor in the control van. Steel answered and was informed the PRM was on its way up to off-load equipment.

Steel turned to Harrison. "The PRM will be back in the deck cradle in fifteen minutes."

"How many Spetsnaz are in the PRM?" Harrison asked.

Steel relayed the question, and after the rescue supervisor examined the video feed from the PRM's interior camera, he replied, "Only one."

Fifteen minutes later, Harrison stood in the flexible manway beside Chief Stone, with both men wearing the white Spetsnaz outer layer and holding Russian MP-443 pistols in their hands. One end of the manway was open, providing Harrison a view of the LARS A-frame and the ice hole beneath it, while behind him was the deck transfer lock, which provided access to the port and starboard habitrail tunnels leading to the two decompression chambers. The flexible manway was large enough for only two persons to stand abreast, so the remaining fourteen SEALs waited in the deck transfer lock.

The cursor frame that would mate with the PRM descended into the water, and a moment later, Harrison felt the subtle vibrations and heard the groan as the two heavy-duty winches began lifting the PRM. The submersible emerged from the water, its wet surface glistening under the bright ice station lights. It continued upward until it reached the top of the A-frame, where the PRM locked into the latch mechanisms. There was a jolt as the massive A-frame pivoted from the outboard to inboard position, mating the PRM with the end of the flexible manway.

The hatch ring rotated, freeing the lugs from the secured position. There was no window in the door, so it was impossible to tell who was on the other side. The door opened, revealing one of the attendants, Bob Ennis, who glanced at Harrison and Stone before securing the door on the open latch.

Ennis looked again at the two Spetsnaz, speaking dryly, "If either of you happen to understand English, you need to move aside. We've got equipment to off-load."

Neither Harrison nor Stone replied.

Ennis shook his head, then pulled back inside the PRM, and a Spetsnaz appeared in the hatch opening. He said something in Russian, then his eyes narrowed as he examined Harrison and Stone more closely.

Harrison raised his pistol and squeezed off three rounds, the first two hitting the Spetsnaz in the chest and the third in his face. The Spetsnaz fell back into the PRM and Harrison and Stone moved forward, each taking station on one side of the hatch.

"We're Navy SEALs," Harrison said to Ennis and whoever else was in the PRM. "We've regained control of the ice station. Are there any other Russians inside the PRM?"

"No," was the reply, and Ennis appeared in the hatch, examining Harrison, then Stone. He stepped from the PRM, followed by Art Glover, the other attendant.

Harrison peered inside the PRM. It was packed with electronic equipment. He turned to Ennis and Glover. "We're going to off-load the equipment, then head back down with a platoon of SEALs. What can you tell us about the Spetsnaz aboard *North Dakota*?"

The two attendants had little to offer, except that there were fifteen Spetsnaz still aboard the submarine.

"Thanks," Harrison replied. "Let's get the PRM off-loaded."

Chief Stone informed the other SEALs the PRM was secure, and the sixteen SEALs, along with Ennis and Glover, off-loaded the equipment and the dead Spetsnaz.

Ten minutes later, Harrison was aboard the PRM, sitting on a steel seat on the port side, near the hatch they had entered. There were seven SEALs to his left, while Chief Stone and the remaining seven men sat opposite them. Glover was at the far end of the PRM, while Ennis stood beside Harrison. Ennis closed the hatch, sealing the eighteen men inside, then Glover notified the control van. A moment later, Harrison felt the PRM ascend and then lurch as the A-frame shifted to the outboard position. The A-frame came to a halt, and the PRM began its descent.

PRM-1 *FALCON* • USS *NORTH DAKOTA*

PRM-1 *FALCON*

Harrison listened to the whirr of the submersible's thrusters as they adjusted *Falcon*'s descent toward *North Dakota*. Although Harrison and Stone wore the Spetsnaz white outer layer, the other fourteen SEALs wore their black insulated wet suits. Harrison and Stone had discarded the Russian MP-443 pistols, since they didn't have silencers, in favor of the MP7, hanging from a sling around each man's neck. When he and Stone boarded *North Dakota,* there were two things each man needed to conceal as long as possible: his face and his weapon. Once a Spetsnaz spotted either, he'd realize something was amiss. Still, Harrison figured they'd be able to descend the ladder before anyone got suspicious.

The whine of the PRM's thrusters increased, and the submersible's descent slowed. There was a clank as the PRM struck a metal object, and the thrusters coasted to a halt. Bob Ennis activated the low-pressure dewatering pump, which began dewatering the transfer skirt between the PRM and submarine hatches. He then opened an equalizing line between the PRM and the transfer skirt, which allowed air to flow in as the water was pumped out, and Glover bled air from the air banks into the PRM to maintain it at one atmosphere.

While they waited, Ennis explained that an initial "soft" seal had been created between the PRM and submarine by a rubber gasket on the bottom of the transfer skirt. As water was pumped out, creating a pressure differential, the final seal would be metal-to-metal as the rubber gasket was depressed. The sea pressure would force the PRM onto the submarine like a giant suction cup.

After verifying the pressure on each side of the transfer skirt hatch was the same and holding, Ennis opened the hatch, revealing the black surface of the submarine beneath six feet of seawater. He unhooked two dewatering hoses and lowered them through the hatch until they came to rest on top of the submarine, then activated two high-pressure dewatering pumps, which pumped out the remaining water.

Ennis retrieved and fastened a metal rope ladder to the top of PRM, letting it fall through the hatch. He climbed down onto the submarine and tapped on the hatch fairing with a metal hammer. He stood to the side as the hatch opened, pushed upward by a Spetsnaz with his Arctic parka removed, revealing his green mid-layer.

The Spetsnaz dropped down out of the way, and Harrison descended the ladder, with Stone following closely behind.

USS *NORTH DAKOTA*

Standing in the Command Post of the American submarine with six other Spetsnaz, Captain Second Rank Leonov heard the metal clank of the PRM mating with the submarine. That was Leonov's signal to wrap things up. They would board the PRM, with each man carrying whatever additional equipment he could fit in his lap.

But first, Leonov descended to the Torpedo Room, then headed to the forward end of the compartment, where a block of C-4 was pressed to the top of each torpedo warhead. Twenty-three of the detonators had been slaved to a master, and Leonov stopped to examine it. After verifying the timer delay was set to one hour, he reached into the duffel bag and retrieved the remote initiator, which he would activate before boarding the American submersible. He slid it into his pocket, then turned and headed toward the Torpedo Room exit.

PRM-1 *FALCON*

Harrison descended the ladder into *North Dakota,* looking down to identify the number and location of the men below. There was a single Spetsnaz, who was standing on the left side of the ladder. As Harrison landed on the deck, he turned to the right, presenting his back to the Russian so he couldn't see

his face. He unzipped his parka and retrieved his MP7, and when he heard
Chief Stone's feet hit the deck, he turned toward the Spetsnaz, as did Stone.
The man's eyes widened, but before he could react, Harrison put three bul-
lets into him.

After donning his headset from his pocket, he called into the PRM, and
the other fourteen SEALs descended. Harrison dispersed a two-man team
to each level of the Forward Compartment, joining the seventh SEAL in
his squad to form a second team in middle level, while Chief Stone led his
squad aft.

It wasn't long before they encountered a Spetsnaz, disassembling a rack
of equipment in upper level. Three whispers from an MP7 dropped the
Spetsnaz, and the lead team continued on while Harrison dropped down to
middle level behind another team. The SEALs emerged into the submarine's
Control Room, filled with a half-dozen Spetsnaz, plus what looked like one
crew member seated at the Ship Control Station. The two SEALs in front of
Harrison opened fire, taking down four Spetsnaz while the other two
Russians dove behind equipment.

Harrison moved to the starboard side of the Control Room while the first
pair of SEALs moved quickly down the port side, killing the two remaining
Spetsnaz before they could retrieve their weapons. The first two SEALs continued through the forward opening of the Control Room, while Harrison
stopped beside the man seated at the Ship Control Station. A quick inter-
rogation determined he was Chief Larry Johnson, placed on watch by the
Russians to ensure the submarine remained stable while it was being stripped.

Lieutenant Harrison remained in Control to assess the situation, listening to headset comms. Everything was going well. There were no SEAL
casualties so far and ten dead Spetsnaz. Only five more to go.

Leonov had just reached the staircase leading from the Torpedo Room when
a man in a black wet suit began his descent. It took Leonov only a second to
realize he wasn't a Spetsnaz and a split second more to realize what he was.
Leonov reached for his pistol as he ducked out of the way, but was too slow.
The advancing SEAL had his weapon raised, and fired three rounds.

Two bullets tore into Leonov's chest and a third hit him in the forehead,
snapping his head back. He collapsed to the deck as pain tore through his

body. The SEAL stepped over him and a second man removed the pistol from his grip, tossing it aside. A second later and both men were gone. Leonov lay on his stomach at the base of the ladder in agony, wondering how he was still alive. He'd been shot in the head. Slowly, he moved his hand up and located a long wound on the left side of his head. The bullet had impacted at an angle, and must have ricocheted to the outside instead of piercing his skull. Not that it mattered. He was already having difficulty breathing; his lungs were filling with blood.

The two Americans returned from where they had headed, this time at a more leisurely pace. One of them spoke into his headset, reporting the Forward Compartment, Lower Level, was secure. He asked if assistance was required elsewhere, and after a short pause, the man replied, "Understand. *North Dakota* is secure."

One of the two SEALs reached down, and Leonov closed his eyes as the man lifted him roughly to the side to examine him. He released Leonov and he fell onto the deck again. The two Americans left him behind, climbing the ladder to middle level.

Leonov could barely move, but was able to reach inside his pocket and retrieve the remote detonator. As his vision faded to darkness, he slid the protective cover out of the way and pressed the button, sending the signal to the master detonator.

85

USS *NORTH DAKOTA*

Gathered around the navigation plot in Control, Lieutenant Harrison received updates from Chief Stone and his two squad leaders. All fifteen Spetsnaz were accounted for, which translated to fifteen dead Russians, while Harrison's men had suffered no casualties. They had taken the Russians by surprise. They had also located the crew, bound in berthing, and after dispatching the Spetsnaz guarding them, they were now being freed, the plastic ties around their wrists and ankles cut. Crew members were straggling into Control, each man stopping in his tracks upon entering the gutted Control Room.

The submarine's commanding officer arrived, staring in disbelief as his eyes swept across the stripped consoles. He spotted the four Navy SEALs in the center of Control and headed over, introducing himself.

"Paul Tolbert, Commanding Officer of *North Dakota*." He wasn't sure who the senior SEAL was—no rank was displayed on their wet suits or Spetsnaz parkas, so his eyes wandered across the four men until Harrison responded.

"Lieutenant Jake Harrison." He extended his hand.

"Thanks, Jake," Tolbert said as they shook. "I can't tell you how much I appreciate what you've done."

"Just doing our job," Harrison replied. "But it looks like you've got your work cut out for you." Tolbert followed Harrison's gaze as he surveyed the gutted consoles.

"Do you know where everything is?" Tolbert asked.

"There are two shipments topside," Harrison answered. "I'll send the PRM to the surface to retrieve your equipment."

"Thanks," Tolbert said.

The submarine's Executive Officer, Lieutenant Commander Sites, plus the Chief of the Boat, Master Chief Murgo, arrived in Control, joining Tolbert and the SEALs. They were discussing how to quickly and safely reinstall the equipment when an excited report came over the speakers.

"Captain to the Torpedo Room!"

Tolbert and Harrison headed to lower level, followed by the XO and COB, stepping over a dead Spetsnaz at the base of the ladder.

The Torpedo Division Chief was there to greet them. "We got a problem," he said as he led them to the forward end of the room and pointed to the nearest torpedo. A glance across the Torpedo Room revealed all twenty-four torpedoes were wired with explosives.

Harrison examined the explosive material, which was C-4, connected to a detonator. There was probably a master detonator, with the others slaved to it, which was either on a timer or awaiting a remote signal. He glanced around the Torpedo Room, his eyes settling on the dead Spetsnaz. There was something in his grip. Harrison hustled over and opened his hand, revealing a remote detonator, the red light blinking. It'd been activated, but there was no indication of how much time was left.

Harrison sprinted back to the first torpedo, examining the detonator again. A thin wire connected the detonator to an initiating tube, inserted into the C-4.

"We need to disarm the explosives," he said to Tolbert. "This is what you need to do."

Harrison grabbed the end of the initiating tube and pulled it from the C-4, then broke the wiring to the detonator. He moved to the next torpedo while the other men assisted, each man choosing a different torpedo. They moved from one torpedo to the next, until there was only one weapon remaining. Harrison was the first to come free, and as he approached the torpedo, he noticed its detonator was different. It displayed the time, which was counting down.

Additionally, it was placed atop the C-4, with its initiator apparently protruding from the bottom. Harrison had to remove the detonator, but worried about its design. Advanced detonators included motion sensors, which would send a signal if someone tried to remove them. The other four men gathered around Harrison as he evaluated his options, eliminating all but one.

He reached for the detonator.

86

ICE STATION NAUTILUS

Inside the command hut, Brackman conferred with McNeil and Verbeck, receiving updates on repairs and on McNeil's SEALs. McNeil had lost six men during the Spetsnaz attack on Harrison's squad and the counterassault. With sixteen men aboard *North Dakota,* that left ten able-bodied SEALs, plus McNeil at Ice Station Nautilus. The ten SEALs had donned the white outer layer of Arctic gear stripped from dead Spetsnaz, as had McNeil, and were standing guard along the perimeter of Ice Station Nautilus, in case the Russians got another bright idea in the middle of the Arctic night.

Verbeck had contacted the appropriate commands, relaying what had occurred at the ice station. Commander Steel was supervising his men as they pored over the rescue equipment, repairing the leaks in the manway and damage to the port decompression chamber. To rescue *Dolgoruky*'s entire crew, they would likely need both chambers operational.

It was a few hours before sunrise, but the cooks were already busy. One of the cooks, Sally Firebaugh, stopped by the command hut, letting everyone know food would be ready soon. She noticed the blood on Christine's face, then after being assured she was okay, returned with a wet towel. It was then that Brackman noticed the tension in Christine's shoulders and the look on her face.

Christine had uncharacteristically declined to participate in the conversation with Verbeck and McNeil, and had moved to the far corner of the command hut. She was leaning against the edge of a table, her arms folded across her chest and her eyes fixed on the floor. It didn't take Brackman long to realize what she was worried about. There had been no word since the platoon of SEALs descended toward *North Dakota.*

Brackman broke away from McNeil and Verbeck and went to her.

When Christine looked up, he said, "He'll be okay."

"Is it that obvious?' she asked.

"No," Brackman replied. "But I know you well enough to pick up a cue or two."

"Good." Christine said. "Don't tell anyone. Especially Jake."

"I'm pretty sure he already knows."

His assurance didn't ease the pain on her face, and she tightened her arms across her chest. He was only trying to help, but had somehow made the situation worse. Christine's relationship with Harrison was complicated. After they ran into each other on *Michigan* last year, Brackman could tell her feelings for him had resurfaced. The problem was—Harrison was married now.

Brackman stepped close to Christine and lowered his voice so no one overheard. "You're a smart, beautiful woman, Christine, with a personality a hell of a lot more pleasant than Hardison's."

Christine laughed at Brackman's jab at the president's chief of staff, her White House nemesis. "That's not saying much," she replied.

"My point," Brackman added, "is that you can have almost any man you want. Don't dwell on Harrison. You need to move on."

"I know," Christine said. She forced a weak smile. "Thanks."

A squawk on Verbeck's radio interrupted their conversation. They listened as Commander Steel informed Verbeck that *North Dakota* had been secured with no casualties, and the PRM was on its way up with Harrison and fifteen dead Spetsnaz. Steel added that the Spetsnaz had wired *North Dakota*'s torpedoes with explosives, but the detonators had been disarmed in time. Brackman watched the relief wash over Christine.

The PRM returned to the surface, and after an update from Harrison on *North Dakota* and its crew, Brackman sent the PRM down with the first load of *North Dakota*'s equipment while Commander Steel's men continued their repairs. On the next trip up, the PRM would bring the platoon of SEALs, then return with the final load of *North Dakota*'s electronics. By then, the flexible manway repairs should be complete, so the PRM could descend to *Dolgoruky* and return while pressurized.

———

The fifteen SEALs returned to the surface, and not long thereafter, Commander Steel arrived at the command hut, approaching McNeil and Brackman.

"The manway has been repaired, but we're still working on the port decompression chamber. Some of the electrical interconnects were damaged in the firefight and we don't have enough spares. We're splicing the damaged cables together, which will take a while. However, we don't need the port chamber right away. The first two groups from *Dolgoruky* can go into the starboard chamber."

Steel finished his update with, "We're ready to commence rescue ops."

Christine zipped up her parka and stepped outside. There was an orange glow on the horizon. *Dolgoruky*'s last report stated the air in Compartment One would become toxic just before sunrise.

87

K-535 *YURY DOLGORUKY*

In the dark, bitterly cold compartment, Stepanov's head was pounding and his breathing was shallow and rapid, indications that the CO_2 concentration was approaching a toxic level. Stepanov's mind was becoming sluggish and he had difficulty concentrating. He even imagined he heard the faint rumble of underwater explosions.

In Stepanov's hand was the last functioning emergency lantern, capable of emitting only a weak yellow light. He had not turned it on for several hours, conserving the remaining energy for one more trip through the compartment, checking on his men one final time. They had abandoned the air regeneration unit, and were huddled together in small groups. Stepanov's First Officer, who had regained consciousness, was still weak, confined to his makeshift bed on one of the torpedo stows.

Stepanov's mind was playing tricks on him. He heard a faint clank against the hull. Maybe a metallic fish had bounced into the submarine. He imagined what it looked like; shiny metal scales, a tail that swiveled back and forth like a rudder, and robotic eyes looking in two separate directions. He heard another metallic sound. The fish was persistent, bouncing into the hull again. It should go around. Surely it was smart enough to figure that out.

There was another metal clank, this one louder, and Stepanov's mind cleared. He pulled himself to his feet and turned his lantern on, aiming its weak yellow beam toward the ladder leading to the access hatch. Other men stirred as Stepanov made his way through the compartment, stopping at the base of the ladder.

There were no more clanks, but he thought he heard a faint humming sound. As he wondered what it was, he was joined by his Chief Ship Starshina,

Egor Lukin. Several minutes passed, then loud metal clanks from above echoed through the compartment.

Tap codes.

Someone was on the other side of the hatch, requesting they open it.

There was no cheer from his weakened men, but Stepanov knew they were relieved. He handed the lantern to Lukin, then climbed the ladder, stopping when he was within reach of the hatch handwheel. He reached up carefully and twisted it with both hands, but it wouldn't budge, and he almost lost his footing on the ice-coated ladder. Stepanov locked his feet inside the ladder rails, gripped the handwheel tightly, then twisted it with all his strength until finally the handwheel broke free, chunks of ice falling from the hatch lugs.

Stepanov twisted the handwheel, fully retracting the lugs. He was exhausted from the effort, but he climbed one rung higher and shoved upward on the hatch. It lifted slowly, and he could see a man's hands on the edge, pulling the hatch fully open onto the latch. He shielded his eyes from the bright light above as he inhaled fresh air.

He greeted his rescuers, but the response was in English.

Stepanov froze. The fresh air helped clear his mind as he worked through the implications. Another man greeted him in Russian, explaining an American submersible had attached to *Dolgoruky,* and a Disabled Submarine Entry Team would assist in evacuating Stepanov's crew. He also explained that they had food and water for his crew, as well as atmosphere support stores to help absorb CO_2 and replenish the oxygen in the air. He then requested permission to board the Russian ballistic missile submarine.

Stepanov concurred and climbed down the ladder. Three men followed, each carrying a bag of equipment and an emergency lantern. It didn't take long for Stepanov's crew to realize the men weren't Russian. The American flag was sewn onto the right shoulder of their black parkas.

One American extracted atmosphere monitoring equipment from his bag and began taking air readings, while the other two men approached Stepanov and Lukin. Captain Kovaleski joined them as the American on the right explained he was a translator, the man to his left was a medical corpsman who could assist if there were injuries, and that the submersible would take Stepanov's men to the surface in batches of sixteen.

Stepanov informed him there were forty-five men in Compartment One and another fifty-seven men aft, and the air situation aft was slightly better. The translator replied the plan was to evacuate everyone from the forward compartment, then rescue the crew members trapped aft.

Kovaleski coordinated with the American corpsman, selecting sixteen sailors for the first journey to the surface. *Dolgoruky*'s hatch was sealed again, this time with three Americans aboard *Dolgoruky* and sixteen fewer Russians. As Stepanov waited for the rescue vehicle to complete its round trip, he retreated to the torpedo stow where his First Officer lay, motioning for his Chief Ship Starshina to join him.

Stepanov and Lukin gathered beside Pavlov, and Stepanov briefed his First Officer. Pavlov was as concerned as Stepanov, not wanting *Dolgoruky* to fall into American hands.

Lukin suggested, "Perhaps we should contact the Engineering Officer and direct him to leave armed volunteers behind, hidden in the aft compartments to prevent access."

After considering Lukin's words, Stepanov replied, "If the Americans are intent on boarding *Dolgoruky*, that would serve only as a temporary delay. We will evacuate the entire crew, and hope the Americans are not inquisitive enough to search the Missile Compartment. Let us pray instead that they let our submarine lie in its grave on the ocean bottom."

88

WASHINGTON, D.C. • MOSCOW

WASHINGTON, D.C.

It was almost midnight when the president slipped into bed alongside the slumbering first lady, and it seemed he had closed his eyes for only a few seconds when the phone beside his bed rang. It was his chief of staff, Kevin Hardison. The Russians had assaulted the American ice station and taken control of USS *North Dakota*. The president sat bolt upright. Hardison added that SecDef Richardson was on his way over with more details, and they would be ready in the Situation Room in fifteen minutes. The first lady stirred, turning toward her husband. Her eyes were still heavy with sleep when she asked him what was going on.

Fifteen minutes later, the president strode into the Situation Room in the basement of the West Wing, taking his seat at the head of the rectangular conference table. There were only two others present: Kevin Hardison and Don Richardson. Richardson had a manila folder in front of him, the contents provided by Pentagon staffers on duty, but he kept it closed. They had a better source of information. Captain Brackman was standing by via an Iridium phone.

Hardison called out to the overhead microphone, directing the Situation Room technician to put Brackman's call through. A moment later, Brackman's scratchy voice from the Iridium satellite link greeted the president.

Brackman filled in the missing details. In addition to Russian forces assaulting the American ice station and taking control of USS *North Dakota*, an Akula submarine had attacked USS *Michigan*. The good news was that

Michigan had sunk the Akula, and her SEAL detachment had regained control of Ice Station Nautilus and USS *North Dakota,* killing or capturing two Spetsnaz platoons, losing six SEALs in the process.

The goal of the Russian assault was clear; they had been stripping *North Dakota's* tactical and communication systems, sending them topside to Ice Station Nautilus. Luckily, the SEALs regained control of the station before the equipment was taken any farther, and it had already been transferred back aboard *North Dakota*. As far as Brackman could tell, nothing had made it permanently into Russian hands. Additionally, they had begun rescuing *Yury Dolgoruky's* crew, transferring them into a topside decompression chamber.

When Brackman concluded his brief, the president decided to contact President Kalinin. His eyes went to one of the clocks on the far wall, with MOSCOW labeled beneath it. It was 8 a.m. in the Russian capital. The president stood. "I'll call Kalinin from the Oval Office. Join me."

Once in the Oval Office, the call was made to Moscow and the president switched on the speakerphone, waiting for President Kalinin to be patched through. As Kalinin offered introductory pleasantries, the president cut him off and relayed what he had learned.

When he finished, Kalinin replied, "I am not aware of any Russian forces attacking Americans, and I would be advised if we were even contemplating such action. However, I will look into it."

"I'll be happy to provide evidence," the president said. "Where would you like the body bags shipped?"

"Do you have anything else to add?" Kalinin asked. The ice-cold tone of his voice was unmistakable.

"Not . . . at . . . this . . . time," the president said, unable to conceal his anger.

After a brief silence, Kalinin replied, "I will call you when I find out what happened."

There was a click on the other end, and the line went dead.

The president looked across his desk, first at Hardison, then Richardson.

"Let's hope Kalinin is telling the truth," Richardson said, "and this was a rogue operation."

"Does it matter?" the president asked. "They almost pulled it off. If *Michigan* had been sunk instead of the Akula, the Russians would have stripped *North Dakota* and likely murdered the crew and everyone at the ice station." The president's anger was palpable.

The three men sat in silence for a moment before Hardison spoke. "Christine is at the ice station with the ONI team. Do you want them to board *Dolgoruky* once the crew has been rescued?"

The president answered with a cold hardness in his voice. "Absolutely."

MOSCOW

By the time Yuri Kalinin hung up the phone, he was fuming. Russian military forces had been committed without his authorization. He picked up the phone and dialed his minister of defense. When Boris Chernov arrived at Kalinin's office, he denied everything.

"I assure you I was not involved in any way. If the American president is telling the truth, I will get to the bottom of it."

"It should be easy to verify," Kalinin replied, "if indeed one of our attack submarines has been sunk and two platoons of Spetsnaz killed or captured."

Chernov hesitated before replying, "Do you want me to go through Ivanov and Lipovsky?"

Kalinin evaluated his defense minister's question. Only Fleet Admiral Ivanov and Admiral Lipovsky, commander of the Northern Fleet, could issue orders to Northern Fleet submarines *and* Spetsnaz units. If Chernov wasn't responsible, then it was either Ivanov or Lipovsky.

Kalinin replied, "Use the proper chain of command for this query. However, I want Ivanov and Lipovsky in my office by 6 p.m. tonight."

Chernov nodded. Both Admirals would have to board flights, with Ivanov traveling from St. Petersburg and Lipovsky from his headquarters in Severomorsk.

"We have one additional problem," Chernov said. "The directive I delivered to Ivanov four days ago. Although I can determine which unit was moved into place, I do not know what instructions Ivanov has issued."

Kalinin asked, "Are we still monitoring ISMERLO communications?"

"Yes," Chernov replied. "The Americans are keeping all members apprised."

"How much longer before *Dolgoruky*'s crew is completely evacuated?"

"A few hours."

After thinking things through, Kalinin replied, "Let Ivanov issue the final order, then have him report here with Lipovsky."

89

ICE STATION NAUTILUS

Standing at the edge of the ice hole, Christine waited impatiently as the PRM returned from its final trip to *Yury Dolgoruky*, emerging from the water and rising toward the top of the LARS A-frame. The day had dragged on as Russian crew members were transferred from the PRM to the decompression chambers. The first two loads had gone into the starboard chamber, and the port chamber had been repaired and brought on-line just in time for the third load of crew members. The port chamber was filled to the gills, almost double capacity, but Commander Steel didn't have a choice. The number of men who could decompress in each chamber was limited by the number of oxygen masks, so Steel decided to use the port chamber as a holding pen, while personnel decompressed in the starboard chamber in groups of thirty-two.

The PRM would deposit the last of *Dolgoruky*'s crew into the port decompression chamber, then take Christine, Brackman, and the ONI team to *Dolgoruky*. Brackman stopped beside Christine as the LARS shifted from the outboard to the inboard position, docking the PRM with the pressurized flexible manway. Stu Berman and Greg Hartfield joined them as the twelve-member ONI team emerged from their berthing huts. Each person carried a small duffel bag and a flashlight, and Berman handed flashlights to Brackman and Christine. Commander Steel emerged from the PRM control van a moment later and stopped in front of the group.

"The PRM is all yours," he said. "Two attendants are standing by, along with an A-Gang Chief to monitor atmospheres."

He led the group to the deck transfer lock, which provided access to the flexible manway. A few minutes later, Christine was seated inside the PRM with Brackman and the ONI team, along with the Auxiliary Division Chief and two attendants.

The aft attendant, Bob Ennis, closed the PRM hatch, sealing them inside, and it wasn't long before the forward attendant, Art Glover, announced, "Standby for launch."

The submersible was lifted into the latches, then lurched forward as the A-frame moved into position over the ice hole. The A-frame halted at a thirty-degree outboard tilt, and Christine could feel *Falcon* swaying in the air.

Once *Falcon* steadied up, Glover announced, "Coming out of the latches," and the PRM began its descent. There was a gentle impact as the vehicle hit the water, and not long thereafter, Glover started calling out the vehicle's depth as it descended toward *Dolgoruky*.

ST. PETERSBURG, RUSSIA

On the third floor of the Admiralty building, Fleet Admiral Ivanov waited at the back of the Operations Center, monitoring ISMERLO voice communications and the text messages scrolling down the nearest Michman's display. The Americans were transferring *Dolgoruky*'s crew to the surface, and Ivanov learned that the submarine's Commanding Officer, Captain First Rank Nicholai Stepanov, had been transferred off on the third load, the last to leave Compartment One. The Americans then shifted to the personnel trapped in the aft compartments.

Finally, the message Ivanov waited for appeared on the screen. He listened as the operator confirmed the report. "Understand all personnel have been evacuated from *Yury Dolgoruky*. Russia sends its appreciation."

Ivanov pulled the draft message from his pocket and handed it to the Operations Watch Officer. "Transmit this message."

The man's eyes widened as he read it, then he looked up quickly at the Admiral.

Ivanov cut the man's question off. "You have your order."

The Watch Officer sat at the nearest vacant console, laying the paper beside the keyboard. He typed the radio message, then looked over his shoulder at Ivanov.

"Transmit," Ivanov ordered.

The Watch Officer turned and pressed the transmit button on his console.

K-329 *SEVERODVINSK*

Captain Second Rank Josef Buffanov stood in the Central Command Post of his nuclear attack submarine, with his arms folded across his chest as his eyes shifted between watchstanders. His crew was tense, and for good reason, but their communications remained disciplined, his men speaking in subdued tones using the succinct orders and reports they had been trained to use. His First Officer made his round through the Command Post, stopping behind each watchstander as he checked on the performance of their duties, casting an occasional glance in his Commanding Officer's direction.

Buffanov knew what his First Officer was thinking; he was wondering about the Commanding Officer Only messages *Severodvinsk* had received, messages Buffanov had not yet shared with his crew. Considering what had just transpired, Buffanov figured it would not be long before another message arrived.

A few hours ago, the shock waves of two torpedo detonations had rumbled past his submarine. *Vepr* and the American guided missile submarine had engaged. At first, there was no indication as to which submarine had survived. Perhaps neither, with both submarines sunk in a torpedo exchange. Then Hydroacoustic picked up a bottom impact, followed by the American SSGN returning to the ice hole at ahead flank speed. *Vepr* had been sunk.

Severodvinsk had been a bystander in the encounter, remaining ice-picked against the polar ice, using the VLF antenna in the conning tower to copy the broadcast as directed. As Buffanov wondered when he would receive the next message, the Communication Party Leader's voice delivered the awaited report.

"Command Post, Communications. In receipt of a Commanding Officer Only message."

Buffanov entered the Communication Post, stopping by the printers as he had done twice before. "Ready," he said, and a sheet of paper slid from the nearest printer.

Buffanov read the message. It was short and the directive clear. He returned to the Command Post, and this time did not withhold the content of the message. He stopped at the navigation table, laying the message face up on its surface.

"First Officer, Watch Officer. Join me."

Captain Third Rank Novikoff, his First Officer, and Captain Lieutenant Ronin approached the navigation table.

"Read," was all Buffanov said as he slid the message toward them.

The two men read the message, and Buffanov could tell both men read it again, surprised at the directive. They looked up, awaiting amplification.

"As you can see," Buffanov began, "we have been ordered to destroy *Yury Dolgoruky*. The Americans will not be allowed to board her and scavenge her tactical and strategic systems, weapons, and countermeasures."

"However," Buffanov continued, "we have an issue to address." He paused, hoping his two officers understood the problem.

When neither man responded, Buffanov asked, "Where is the American guided missile submarine?"

Ronin answered, "We lost her when she slowed from ahead flank, but our solution put her on a bearing of three-five-zero, near the ice hole."

"How far away from *Dolgoruky*?"

"A few hundred meters."

"Do you understand the problem?" Buffanov asked.

It took a moment, but then the light came on in his First Officer's eyes, followed by his Watch Officer. Concern worked its way across their faces.

Buffanov answered his own question. "The American submarine has already been attacked today by a Russian submarine. If we fire at *Dolgoruky* with the American submarine nearby, the American Captain will conclude we are shooting at him and counterfire."

The commanding officer of *Severodvinsk* paused, then asked a follow-on question. "Which means?"

This time, his Watch Officer knew the answer. "We must surprise and destroy the American submarine first, to ensure it cannot counterfire."

Buffanov turned to his First Officer. "Attacking the American submarine is not in our directive." He pointed to the message on the navigation table. "But it is the only way to ensure our survival. Do you concur?"

As Buffanov waited for their concurrence, he hoped they didn't see through his thinly veiled plan. *Vepr* had been sunk, and she would be avenged, regardless of the American submarine's threat.

Captain Third Rank Novikoff contemplated the question for a moment before answering, "I concur," as did Ronin.

Buffanov's eyes swept across the Command Post again. Like *Vepr*, *Severodvinsk* would engage the American guided missile submarine. However, *Severodvinsk* was no *Vepr*. The new Yasen class submarine was vastly superior to *Vepr* and the American submarine, both built in the mid-'80s of the last century. *Severodvinsk* was the more capable submarine by far, and, barring bad luck, the outcome of their duel with the Americans was not in doubt.

He directed his Watch Officer, "Man Combat Stations silently." Ronin acknowledged the order and word was passed to the crew via messengers. Buffanov followed up, "Shift to the electric drive."

In the conflicting need for stealth and maximum propulsion, Buffanov chose stealth. His plan was to approach close and leave insufficient time for the American crew to counterfire, which meant *Severodvinsk* would use her electric drive instead of main engines.

Ronin relayed the order, and a few minutes later reported, "Captain, Combat Stations are manned. Propulsion has been shifted to the electric drive."

Buffanov acknowledged, then called out, "Compensation Officer, secure from ice pick. Make your depth one hundred meters." The Compensation Officer complied, and as *Severodvinsk* drifted downward, Buffanov added, "Steersman, ahead two-thirds. Left full rudder, steady course three-five-zero."

As *Severodvinsk* turned toward the American submarine, Buffanov ordered his Weapons Officer, "Flood down and open muzzle doors, tubes One and Two."

92

PRM-1 *FALCON*

It had taken longer than Christine expected, but the silhouette of *Dolgoruky*'s hull in the video monitor finally appeared. The PRM slowed to a hover over the submarine's aft-compartment hatch, and the pilot adjusted the articulating skirt on the bottom of the PRM to match the angle of the stricken submarine. The next few minutes passed slowly as Ennis dewatered the transfer skirt.

After the seal was established, the pressure in the PRM was increased to match the last recorded pressure in *Dolgoruky*'s aft compartments, so there would be no pressure differential between the submarine and submersible. However, Christine wondered how they would open the submarine hatch, with no one inside the submarine to operate the handwheel.

Eddie Stankiewicz, the Auxiliary Division Chief accompanying them, explained there was a special tool for each class of submarine. Stankiewicz produced just such a tool, which looked like a large metal T. He climbed down the metal rope ladder into the transfer skirt and slid the end of the tool into an indentation in the center of the hatch fairing. He then twisted the tool, which rotated the hatch mechanism inside the submarine. After several revolutions, the hatch popped up an inch, and after several more turns, Chief Stankiewicz removed the tool and reached down, opening the hatch and locking it in place.

Stankiewicz looked up and said, "Normally, I'd say ladies first, but I need to check atmospheres."

He handed the tool to Ennis in return for a flashlight and an atmosphere sampling kit. Stankiewicz energized the light, then climbed down into the submarine. A few minutes later, he reappeared, his head sticking out the top of *Dolgoruky*'s hatch.

"The atmosphere isn't great, but it's good enough," he said.

He dropped back down, and Christine and Brackman prepared to join him.

"After you," Brackman said.

Christine climbed down the ladder into the transfer skirt, then descended into the darkness, guided only by the single beam of Chief Stankiewicz's flashlight.

93

K-329 *SEVERODVINSK* • USS *MICHIGAN*

SEVERODVINSK

"Steady on course three-five-zero."

Josef Buffanov acknowledged the Steersman's report. They were headed toward the American guided missile submarine, only five thousand meters away based on their earlier solution. Hydroacoustic had not yet detected its presence again, but Buffanov was not surprised. If the American submarine was hovering, there would be no propulsion tonals, and the feedwater, cooling, and lube oil systems would be running in slow speed, supporting only the turbine generators.

Four thousand meters away.

Finally, Buffanov received the report he'd been awaiting. "Command Post, Hydroacoustic. Hold a new narrowband contact on the spherical array, designated Hydroacoustic four-nine, bearing three-five-two. Analyzing."

Hydroacoustic would perform due diligence, comparing the received frequencies to their database and previous contacts. It didn't take long.

"Command Post, Hydroacoustic. Contact four-nine is classified Ohio class submarine, a regain of contact four-eight."

Buffanov called out, "Attention in the Command Post." The watchstanders turned in his direction and he continued, "We will engage Hydroacoustic four-nine once we determine an adequate solution. We will also fire simultaneously at *Dolgoruky,* in case the American submarine survives and makes our return to the area difficult. Any questions?"

After no one responded, Buffanov issued the orders. "Prepare to fire salvo from tubes One and Two. Assign tube One to Hydroacoustic four-nine and tube Two to *Yury Dolgoruky*. Tube One will be fired first."

First Officer Novikoff stopped by the navigation table. After examining the location of *Yury Dolgoruky* on the chart, he sent the coordinates to Weapons Control, then focused on determining a solution for the American submarine. The bearing was known, as was the speed, assuming the guided missile submarine was hovering. Both fire controlmen matched the bearing to the contact and entered zero knots. However, they needed to verify the range.

Novikoff announced, "Captain, request maneuver to a beam aspect."

Buffanov accommodated the request. "Steersman, right standard rudder, steady course zero-eight-zero."

Severodvinsk turned to its new course, and both fire controlmen matched the new bearing rate to the American submarine, developing identical solutions. The contact was 3,200 meters away. Novikoff tapped one of the men on the shoulder and ordered, "Send solution to Weapon Control."

Novikoff announced, "Captain, I have a firing solution on Hydroacoustic four-nine, and the coordinates for *Yury Dolgoruky* have been entered into Weapon Control."

USS *MICHIGAN*

It was just past noon aboard Wilson's submarine, and the two off-going watch officers—the Officer of the Deck and Engineering Officer of the Watch—had just delivered their after-watch report to Wilson and were sitting down for lunch. Wilson was at the other end of the wardroom table, finishing a cup of coffee before heading to Control to relieve his Executive Officer, who was stationed as Command Duty Officer.

It was obvious that the Akula had attacked *Michigan* to prevent the SEAL detachment from interfering with the Spetsnaz's attempt to scavenge *North Dakota*, and now that the Russian plot had been thwarted, there seemed no reason for Russia to attack again. As a precaution, however, either Wilson or his Executive Officer would be in the Control Room 24/7 until he became convinced there was no further threat or *Michigan* departed the area.

Rescue operations on *Dolgoruky* had wrapped up, but *North Dakota* needed a tow from under the ice cap, and *Michigan* had been tagged. NAVSEA was working on the problem, manufacturing the tow cable and figuring out how to attach it to both submarines. In the meantime, *Michigan* would wait. Wilson took a last sip of coffee, then headed to the Control Room to relieve his XO.

SEVERODVINSK

Buffanov stopped beside his First Officer, evaluating the solution to Hydroacoustic four-nine. The American submarine was hovering three thousand meters away. He retreated to the rear of the Command Post, where he had a clear view of all stations and awaited the remaining reports.

His Weapons Officer announced, "Ready to Fire, tubes One and Two."

Severodvinsk's Watch Officer followed. "Countermeasures are armed."

Buffanov ordered, "Steersman, prepare to shift to the main engines." He examined the solution for the American submarine and the distance to *Dolgoruky* one final time.

Satisfied that all parameters were optimal, he announced, "Fire tubes One and Two."

USS MICHIGAN

Wilson had just stepped from the Wardroom when he heard the 1-MC announcement.

"Torpedo in the water! Man Battle Stations Torpedo!"

The loud *gong, gong, gong* of the submarine's General Emergency alarm reverberated throughout the submarine as Wilson ascended the ladder to Control two steps at a time, entering as the Chief of the Watch repeated the announcement on the 1-MC. The XO, Lieutenant Commander Sparks, was hunched behind one of the fire control technicians at a combat control console, and the Officer of the Deck, Lieutenant Lake, was on the Conn. Wilson stopped beside the OOD and scanned the displays in Control, assimilating the data.

He could feel the tremors in the submarine's deck, indicating the main engines were coming to life, and a glance at the Engine Order Telegraph by the Helm confirmed Lieutenant Lake had ordered ahead flank. The navigation repeater confirmed what Wilson already knew; *Michigan* was on course three-four-zero, depth three hundred feet.

As Wilson turned toward the sonar display, another announcement blared from the Conn speakers.

"Second torpedo in the water, bearing one-seven-two!"

Wilson examined the two white traces on the display. Both torpedoes had been fired from the south. *Michigan* needed to turn east. He didn't wait for a turnover from his XO or Officer of the Deck.

"Helm, hard right rudder, steady course zero-nine-zero."

The Helm twisted his rudder hard right, and *Michigan* turned slowly to the evasion course. The eighteen-thousand-ton submarine had accelerated to only five knots thus far, and *Michigan* would evade the incoming torpedoes only if they had been fired from long range. As Wilson wondered how far away they were, the announcement over the Control Room speakers gave him an indication.

"First-fired torpedo is homing!"

Wilson cursed under his breath. The first torpedo was within two thousand yards and had locked on to *Michigan*. With the torpedo already homing, a decoy would do little to distract it from the 560-foot-long submarine. However, it could still be jammed.

"Officer of the Deck, launch acoustic jammer!"

Lieutenant Lake complied, launching one of the five-inch counter-measures, then Wilson tackled the problem of where to place *Michigan*. The torpedo would be momentarily blinded, but once it passed the counter-measure, ahead would be clear water. And *Michigan*.

"Helm, all stop. Back emergency!"

Wilson decided to stop-and-drop. Rather, stop-and-rise. The best way to prevent the torpedo from locking on to the submarine was to stay near the acoustic jammer and get as close to the ice canopy as possible, hoping the jammer and sonar reflections from the ice would sufficiently confuse the torpedo. Unfortunately, *Michigan* was moving too slowly to drive to the surface quickly enough. The Hovering system wasn't an option, either; it would adjust *Michigan*'s depth gradually. Wilson needed a radical depth change.

"Chief of the Watch, Emergency Blow all main ballast tanks!"

The Chief of the Watch stood and activated the mechanical levers above the Ballast Control Panel, porting high-pressure air to the main ballast tanks. The sound of air rushing into the tanks drowned out the conversations in Control, and Wilson felt *Michigan* rising toward the surface.

With the ballast tanks full of air, the submarine's ascent would be un-controlled, and it would smash into the ice above. They were either going to mangle the sail, or if the ice was thin enough to break through, they might shear off the fairwater planes on the sail. This wasn't going to turn out well, but he had no choice.

After *Michigan* began rising rapidly, Wilson ordered the Chief of the Watch to secure the blow, then flood all variable ballast tanks, bringing on weight to decrease the rate of ascent and lessen the submarine's impact with the ice. As the Chief of the Watch flooded water into the tanks, Wilson turned his attention to the incoming torpedoes, and the submarine that fired them.

Sonar did not hold a contact, so there was no target solution to send to the torpedo. The best they could do was get a torpedo in the water ASAP, ramming it back down the throat of whoever had attacked them.

Wilson called out, "Quick Reaction Firing, tube One, bearing one-seven-two!"

The Control Room was fully manned now, and as the Fire Control Party prepared to launch a torpedo, Wilson checked the submarine's depth. *Michigan*'s keel was at one hundred feet and rising rapidly. They were going to smash into the ice cap any second.

Wilson grabbed on to the Conn railing as he called out, "Brace for impact!"

94

K-329 *SEVERODVINSK* • K-535 *YURY DOLGORUKY*

SEVERODVINSK

Buffanov stood behind his Weapons Officer, monitoring the status of his out-going torpedoes. The first torpedo was homing on the American submarine, while his second torpedo had descended to a search depth of 175 meters, as close to the bottom as possible, which would increase the probability it detected the sunken ballistic missile submarine. A rocky ocean bottom would have been problematic, but the smooth bottom of the Barents Sea should present no issue. The announcement from his Weapons Officer confirmed his assessment.

"Detect, second fired torpedo!"

Buffanov listened to the next report; their torpedo was performing as expected.

"Second fired torpedo is homing!"

On the Weapon Launch Console, the parameters updated as the torpedo increased speed and angled down toward its target.

YURY DOLGORUKY

As Christine descended the ladder into the abandoned Russian submarine, cold, stale air greeted her. Chief Stankiewicz waited on the deck below, shining his flashlight around the deserted compartment, its surfaces covered in a thin layer of ice. Christine reached the bottom of the ladder and stepped onto an angled deck. As she shined her flashlight around, she realized the Russian submarine had settled on the bottom of the Barents Sea at a twenty-degree down-angle and fifteen-degree list to port.

They were in the center of what looked like the Engine Room, standing on a walkway suspended in the air. She leaned over the railing and shined her flashlight below; it looked like they were on the upper of two levels. Beneath her sprawled the submarine's main engines and reduction gears, and in the distance toward the stern of the submarine, she could see the shaft, with water trickling into the submarine from around the shaft seals.

She moved forward to create room for Brackman and Berman, and after the two men landed on the walkway, they continued forward to make room for the rest of the ONI team. Brackman led the way toward a watertight door, open on the latch. He stepped into the next compartment, followed by Christine and Berman, the white beams from their flashlights cutting through the darkness.

Christine heard it first. Faint, high-pitched pings. She'd heard the noise before, while aboard USS *Michigan* off the coast of China. The pitch of these pings was a tad higher, but unmistakable nonetheless. Brackman heard the noise as well, stopping on the walkway, his head cocked as he listened to the distinct sound, growing gradually louder.

Berman heard it next, and as he stopped to listen to the unusual noise, there was a deafening explosion behind them and the submarine jolted, knocking Christine and the two men to the deck. There was a pressure transient and pain pierced her ears, and the roaring sound became muffled.

Christine pulled herself to her feet, as did Brackman and Berman, and as all three turned their flashlights toward the compartment behind them, a torrent of water blasted through the watertight door opening, hitting Berman and knocking him backward. He ricocheted off Christine and tumbled over the upper-level walkway, and his impact and the surge of water knocked Christine the other way. She hit the waist-high railing and flipped over it, but managed to grab on to the metal bar with one hand.

As she dangled from the walkway, her grip started to slip, so she released the flashlight and grabbed on to the railing with her other hand. She tried pulling herself onto the walkway, but the water surging into the compartment buffeted her with too much force. Her left hand lost its grip and she clamped down hard with her right, but the railing slipped away and she tumbled into the darkness.

95

USS *MICHIGAN* • K-329 *SEVERODVINSK*

USS *MICHIGAN*

Michigan shuddered as she slammed into the polar ice cap. The air was filled with the groan of twisting metal as water sprayed from both periscope barrel seals, dousing Wilson on the Conn. He moved to the port side of Control, turning back to examine the damage. A quick glance told him the flooding was within the capacity of the drain pump, but the bigger concern was that the seawater was spraying on the combat control consoles. The dual screen consoles were water resistant, not waterproof. The watchstanders remained at their consoles, processing the Quick Reaction Fire command as the sound of an explosion rumbled through *Michigan*'s hull.

Checking the nearest sonar display, Wilson noted the second torpedo had disappeared from the screen, while the bearing to the first torpedo remained constant, which meant it was on an intercept course with *Michigan*.

Sonar called out, "Estimated range to torpedo is five hundred yards."

Wilson focused again on firing preparations as seawater doused the four combat control consoles. Petty Officer Malocsay at the Weapon Launch Console was making final preparations, sending presets to the weapon, when his console began to spark. Lieutenant Benjamin and Malocsay stepped away as the XO directed one of the other fire control technicians to reconfigure his console for Weapon Control. As Benjamin moved behind the reconfiguring console, the three remaining workstations dropped off-line.

Wilson stared at four dead consoles. They could not shoot back.

"Two hundred yards to incoming torpedo!"

Their only hope was that the acoustic jammer and *Michigan*'s proximity to the ice canopy would confuse the torpedo enough.

"One hundred yards to incoming torpedo!"

Wilson grabbed on to a nearby piping run, bracing himself for the explosion.

He counted down the distance, finally reaching zero.

There was no explosion.

He waited a few more seconds, then Sonar made the report he'd hoped for.

"Conn, Sonar. Torpedo bears three-five-zero. Down Doppler."

The torpedo was on the other side of *Michigan* and heading away. However, the Russian submarine was still out there, and its Captain would soon realize his torpedo had missed. It would not be long before he steered the torpedo back toward *Michigan* or fired another one.

SEVERODVINSK

Josef Buffanov stood at the back of his Command Post, listening to the report from his Weapons Officer.

"Second-fired torpedo has homed to detonation on *Yury Dolgoruky*."

Buffanov was pleased with the report, but destroying a submarine lying on a smooth ocean bottom was not challenging. His first torpedo, however, faced a more difficult task. The Americans had ejected a powerful acoustic jammer, and Hydroacoustic had reported air transients, followed by a loud metallic transient. The American Captain had emergency blown and hit the ice, hoping his proximity to the ice cap would fool the incoming torpedo.

The Weapons Officer announced, "First-fired torpedo bears three-four-zero, range three-five hundred meters. No detection."

Buffanov joined his First Officer, examining the fire control solution. The American submarine was at a range of 3,200 meters. Their torpedo had passed it. He decided against a steer; it would turn their torpedo around, headed not only toward the American submarine, but also toward *Severodvinsk*. It would be better to launch another torpedo, and keep them both heading away.

The lack of counterfire from the American submarine was comforting. It must have experienced Command Post damage from the ice impact. Buffanov decided to approach even closer before firing his next torpedo, leaving the America Captain with insufficient time to react, just in case he had another trick up his sleeve.

Buffanov examined the bearing to Hydroacoustic four-nine, then ordered, "Steersman, left twenty degrees rudder, steady course three-four-zero. Slow to ahead one-third."

Severodvinsk turned toward its target, slowing to reduce the sound of its approach.

Buffanov ordered his Weapons Officer, "Reload tubes One and Two. Make both tubes ready in all respects."

96

K-535 *YURY DOLGORUKY*

Christine fell through the darkness, expecting to break her legs when she hit the metal deck. Instead, she plunged into ice-cold water. She kicked her way to the surface and flailed about, hoping to grab on to something. But her heavy boots and Arctic clothing became waterlogged and started to pull her under. Just before she slipped beneath the water, she took a last gasp of air.

As she sank toward the bottom of the compartment, she ripped off her gloves and tore at her bootlaces, pulling the second boot off as her back hit the deck. She planted her feet and pushed upward, ascending only a few feet before sinking again. Terror tore through her mind when she realized she could not reach the surface while wearing the heavy Arctic clothing, and there wasn't enough time to remove it; she already felt lightheaded.

She tried once more, squatting low and thrusting upward, kicking with her legs and pulling herself up with her arms, but a moment later her feet hit the deck again. As she searched frantically for a solution, a light plunged into the water, traveling quickly to the bottom. The light scanned from left to right, and as it illuminated her profile, Christine repressed a scream when she spotted Stu Berman floating beside her, his eyes frozen open and blood flowing from a gash in his head.

The light grew brighter, then moved past her. There was a tug on her parka hood, dragging her backward. The light extinguished and she was hauled upward, and just when she thought she couldn't hold her breath any longer, her head was lifted above the surface.

As she gasped for air, she heard Brackman's voice in the darkness, a few feet above her. "Grab on to the ladder."

Christine felt the ladder behind her and twisted around, grabbing the cold

metal and gaining a foothold. Brackman released her parka, then withdrew
the flashlight from his pocket and shined it around. They were halfway up
the compartment and the water level was rising rapidly; it had already reached
her chin again. Brackman aimed the light upward, following the ladder until
it reached a walkway in upper level. He began climbing and Christine followed.

She reached the walkway and followed Brackman toward an open watertight door, illuminated in the distance. After entering the next compartment, Brackman tried to shut the door, but the door latch was encased in a
layer of ice. Water began surging through the door opening as he hammered
the latch with the back of his flashlight, knocking off chunks of ice, and it
finally broke free.

Brackman tried to close the door, but was unable to overcome gravity
and the force of water rushing through the opening. *Dolgoruky* had settled
with a twenty-degree down-angle and fifteen-degree list, and both were
working against him. Christine joined in, pushing with her hands while
Brackman put his shoulder into it, and the door began closing. But their
feet slipped on the sloping deck, and the door started to inch in the wrong
direction.

With the water level halfway up the door opening, Brackman shouted
over the roar of the inrushing ocean. "Hold on to the door!"

Brackman gradually let go, and Christine's feet slid across the deck as the
door opened, until her right foot hit a stanchion. Brackman stuck his flashlight in her parka pocket, bulb end out, and he pulled himself through the
door opening into the adjacent compartment.

Brackman turned around and grabbed the handwheel in the center of
the door from the other side, bracing himself with both feet on the bulkhead. It took a second for Christine to realize what he was doing. They had
no leverage pushing the door shut, their feet slipping on the angled deck. So
he had climbed into the adjacent compartment where he could use the
strength of his back and legs, pulling the hatch closed. The problem was—
once the door was shut, Brackman would be on the wrong side.

Christine refused to help, shouting through the door opening instead.
"What are you doing?"

"Push the door shut!" Brackman shouted.

"No!"

"This is the only way!"

The terror Christine felt moments earlier as she was about to drown returned, but this time she feared for Brackman. She was unable to will her body into motion; to sentence Brackman to death.

"No!" Christine replied. "Let's try from this side again."

"It won't work," Brackman shouted. "Either I die, or we both die. There's no other option!"

Christine realized she had to make a decision. Her strength was fading, while the force of water they were pushing against was increasing.

Reluctantly, she concluded Brackman was right.

She lowered her shoulder and pushed against the door. It moved slowly closed until there was only a fraction of an inch remaining, water spraying out from around the watertight door seal. Christine twisted the handwheel, and as the lugs dogged down, the water spraying past the door seal slowed to a trickle, then stopped.

Christine dropped down to the circular glass viewport in the door, illuminating Brackman on the other side with her flashlight. The water level had risen above the watertight door, and with the downward angle of the submarine, the only pocket of air would be on the far side of the compartment; too far for him to swim to in his bulky Arctic gear.

She stood frozen at the watertight door in disbelief. As she struggled to accept Brackman's fate, the realization of what she had done settled low and cold in her gut.

Brackman remained on the other side of the door, his eyes locked on hers as he held his breath. He finally exhaled, and Christine watched him choke as he inhaled icy seawater into his lungs. His hands remained on the door handwheel until his eyes glazed over and his grip loosened. Slowly, he drifted into the darkness.

97

K-329 *SEVERODVINSK* • USS *MICHIGAN*

SEVERODVINSK

"Captain, Torpedo Tubes One and Two are reloaded, flooded, and muzzle doors reopened. Both tubes are ready in all respects."

Buffanov acknowledged his Weapons Officer's report as they approached their target. Fire Control's new solution held the American submarine a few hundred meters away from its original position, stationary, hiding near the ice. However, Buffanov's Yasen class submarine was up to the task, with the most advanced sensors ever built into a Russian submarine. His Hydro-acoustic Party was also well trained, with significant experience under the ice, and they had locked on to their target's main tonals from among the ice reflections.

There had still been no counterfire from the American submarine, which meant it was either damaged or its crew had not yet detected *Severodvinsk*. Buffanov examined the distance to his target.

Two thousand, five hundred meters.

Another three minutes before they closed to two thousand meters.

The American submarine would not get away this time.

USS *MICHIGAN*

With the Russian torpedo on the other side of *Michigan* and speeding away, Wilson focused on the flooding and dormant combat control consoles. The Chief of the Watch had lined the drain pump to the Operations Compartment bilges, and the pump was keeping up. Water sprayed from both periscope barrel seals, and Auxiliary Division personnel were on the

Conn, adjusting the packing glands around the barrels. Thankfully, the top of *Michigan*'s sail was at a depth of only ten feet, up against the bottom of the ice cap, and the pressure of the water spraying past the periscope barrels wasn't dangerous.

Both periscopes were out of commission, and a glance at the Buoyancy Control Panel told Wilson the sail had suffered extensive damage. They had lost the Down indication on several masts and antennas, indicating they'd been jammed downward during the collision and their magnetic indicators were misaligned. However, the damage to the sail was inconsequential compared to the loss of *Michigan*'s combat control consoles.

The breaker to the submarine's BYG-1 Combat Control System had tripped, and tripped again each time it was reset. Something was shorted out and it would take time to determine the affected component and isolate it. The entire Fire Control Division was working on the problem, but there was little hope they could solve it while seawater sprayed onto the consoles.

Wilson's thoughts were interrupted by the Sonar Supervisor's report. "Conn, Sonar. Hold a new narrowband contact on the spherical array, designated Sierra eight-seven, bearing one-six-zero. Analyzing."

Wilson examined the narrowband display. There was a weak fifty-Hertz tonal; standard Russian fifty-cycle electrical machinery. As the tonal grew stronger, two more tonals appeared, followed by a fourth.

A moment later, the Sonar Supervisor followed up. "Conn, Sonar. Sierra eight-seven is classified Yasen class nuclear attack submarine."

A pit formed in Wilson's stomach. They were going up against one of Russia's newest attack submarines. Additionally, the tonals were growing stronger.

The Russian submarine was moving in for the kill.

SEVERODVINSK

Range to their target was now two thousand meters. Close enough, Buffanov decided. Their torpedo would detect the American submarine as soon as it went active.

Buffanov called out, "Prepare to Fire, Hydroacoustic four-nine, torpedo salvo from tubes One and Two."

As his crew readied two more 533-millimeter torpedoes, Buffanov evaluated his adversary's possible responses; he intended to ensure at least one of his torpedoes homed to detonation this time.

With the American submarine up against the ice, its captain could not pull the same trick as before, launching an acoustic jammer and then emergency blowing to the ice canopy. If he launched a jammer, it would eject into the water only a few meters away. True, the jammer would mask the fainter sounds of the submarine, but it could also be used as a beacon.

Buffanov ordered, "Weapons Officer. Preset torpedo in tube One to Home-on-Jam."

If the American crew ejected another jammer, it would draw Severodvinsk's first torpedo close enough to activate its magnetic field exploder. If the American Captain evaded, leaving his acoustic jammer behind, his submarine would be snapped up by Buffanov's second torpedo.

The expected reports flowed from his watchstanders.

The First Officer called out, "Solution updated."

"Torpedoes ready, tubes One and Two," his Weapons Officer announced.

The Watch Officer reported, "Countermeasures armed."

Severodvinsk was ready.

Buffanov moved to the rear of the Central Command Post, placing himself where he would have a clear view of the hydroacoustic and fire control displays. One final scan convinced him of the pending outcome.

His adversary would not get away this time.

As he prepared to issue the Fire order, he was interrupted by a report from Hydroacoustic, blaring from the Command Post speakers.

"Torpedo launch transients, bearing two-seven-zero!"

Buffanov's eyes locked on to the hydroacoustic display, trying to figure out what was going on. The American guided missile submarine was to the north, yet Hydroacoustic reported a torpedo fired from the west. It took only a second for Buffanov to understand what had occurred, and his face paled when he realized his failure.

98

USS *NORTH DAKOTA* • K-329 *SEVERODVINSK*

USS *NORTH DAKOTA*

"You forgot about us, didn't you?"

Commander Paul Tolbert wasn't sure whether he spoke the words aloud or just thought them. A few hours earlier, the electronic components scavenged by the Russians had been reinstalled and all tactical systems restored, and Commander Tolbert now stood in the Control Room of a fully operational Virginia class submarine. There was the propulsion issue, but the front end was fully functional.

Sonar had picked up the Yasen class submarine, and Tolbert's crew had monitored its approach toward *Michigan*. Once the Russian Captain's intentions became clear, Tolbert had manned Battle Stations and determined a firing solution. With his submarine a sitting duck, Tolbert would normally not have engaged, since counterfire from the Russian submarine would have resulted in the destruction of his submarine. However, he couldn't stand by as *Michigan* was sunk, plus he was optimistic the Russian Captain would have insufficient time to counterfire. The Yasen class submarine had maneuvered close to *North Dakota,* and Tolbert's torpedo, closing at High One speed, would hopefully detonate before the Russian crew could respond.

Tolbert watched his outbound weapon merge onto the bearing of Sierra one, which was less than a thousand yards away from the torpedo now.

He called out, "Command Enable tube One. Shift speed to High Two."

His Weapons Officer complied, transmitting the new orders over the torpedo's guidance wire. Not long thereafter, the Sonar Supervisor reported the expected indications.

"Own ship's unit has gone active. Increasing speed to High Two."

A few seconds later, the Weapons Officer called out, "Detect!" followed almost immediately by, "Homing!"

North Dakota's torpedo was performing well, but Tolbert decided to prepare another one just in case.

"Firing Point Procedures, Sierra one, tube Two."

SEVERODVINSK

"Incoming torpedo is homing, bearing two-seven-zero!"

Buffanov's thoughts went in several directions, but he settled on the two most important issues: evading the incoming torpedo and counterfiring.

"Eject torpedo decoy!"

The Watch Officer complied, ejecting a decoy into the water, and Buffanov focused on increasing speed, putting distance between his submarine and the decoy. Unfortunately, *Severodvinsk* was still operating on the electric drive, which was capable of only ten knots.

"Steersman, shift propulsion to the main engines!"

It would take a minute to complete the shift, and in the meantime, Buffanov prepared to counterfire. Although *Severodvinsk* had ten torpedo tubes, only two were 533-millimeter ones loaded with torpedoes designed to kill submarines. The torpedoes in both tubes were assigned to Hydroacoustic four-nine, and Buffanov needed a torpedo to fire to the west.

He called out, "Cancel Fire, Hydroacoustic four-nine. Prepare to Fire, tube One, bearing two-seven-zero."

His crew responded quickly, canceling the solutions sent to the two torpedoes and sending a new firing bearing to the torpedo in tube One. However, precious time was lost resetting the torpedo's guidance system. Through the submarine's hull, Buffanov heard the faint sonar pings from the incoming torpedo, growing louder.

The Weapons Officer finally announced the torpedo in tube One was ready to fire. As Buffanov issued the command, his order was drowned out by an explosion that jolted *Severodvinsk* and knocked him to the deck. A geyser of ice-cold water surged into the Command Post from the level below, shooting up the access ladder and ricocheting off bulkheads and consoles. The wail of the Flooding Alarm filled Buffanov's ears, followed by emergency reports detailing flooding in Compartments Two and Three.

As Buffanov watched the ocean pour into his submarine, he realized there was little he could do; the flooding was beyond the capacity of their drain pumps, and an Emergency Blow with two flooded compartments would do no good, even if they hadn't been under the ice.

Severodvinsk was going to the bottom.

Buffanov's submarine tilted downward and increased speed as it descended. Buffanov struggled to his feet, fighting against the water surging into the Command Post, already waist high. As he clung to the starboard periscope barrel, he glanced at the digital depth detector. Its glowing red numbers increased as *Severodvinsk* plummeted toward the bottom.

With a jarring impact, water and men surged forward as the attack submarine's bow plowed into the ocean floor. The screech of twisting metal filled Buffanov's ears as *Severodvinsk*'s bow crumpled like paper-mache. The Flooding Alarm, which had fallen silent a moment earlier, wailed again, this time followed by a report of flooding in Compartment One. With flooding on both sides of Compartment Two, Buffanov and his men in the compartment were trapped. As the water level rose above his shoulders, he realized there would be no escape.

USS *MICHIGAN*

"Explosion in the water, bearing one-six-zero."

Wilson acknowledged Sonar's report, but in the complex under-ice environment, what he didn't know was whether *North Dakota*'s torpedo had homed on the Russian submarine or a nearby ice keel. Sonar's next report provided the answer.

"Mechanical transient, bearing one-six-one, consistent with bottom impact."

The immediate threat had been eliminated. However, *Michigan* had been attacked by a second Russian submarine, and a third might arrive soon. The reason for the first attack was clear; the Akula Captain was trying to stop *Michigan*'s SEALs from interfering. But why had the second Russian Captain attacked? To avenge the Akula? Wilson then recalled the Yasen Captain had fired two torpedoes and both had exploded. The other torpedo hadn't hit *North Dakota,* so what had it hit?

Petty Officer Malocsay looked up as Wilson stopped by his console and examined the bearings to the second torpedo. Wilson directed Malocsay, "Give me an estimated course for a fifty-knot torpedo at a range of three thousand yards.

Malocsay adjusted the scale of electronic speed strip to fifty knots, lining up each bearing with the appropriate time. He finally got a perfect fit and looked up as Wilson's eyes narrowed. The torpedo course passed directly over *Yury Dolgoruky.*

K-535 *YURY DOLGORUKY*

In the bitterly cold compartment, Christine peered through the portal in the watertight door, watching Brackman's body disappear in the murky water. It had happened too fast; she had pushed the door shut, sealing Brackman to his fate. She remained at the door, staring into the darkness as her grief broke, tears falling from her cheeks, her sobs echoing in the deserted submarine. She began shivering, and it took a moment before she realized her predicament.

Hypothermia was setting in. The wet clothing and the twenty-nine-degree temperature were sucking the heat from her body. She wiped the tears away and shifted her focus from Brackman's death to her own survival. She needed dry clothing. A quick examination of the compartment revealed auxiliary machinery. She pointed her flashlight forward, spotting an open watertight door leading to another compartment.

She was in the seventh of nine compartments. Compartments Eight and Nine behind her were flooded, as were Compartments Two and Three, leaving Compartments Four through Six to explore. If ONI intel was correct, Compartment Six contained the reactor, and Compartment Five was the missile compartment. She prayed Compartment Four contained crew berthing, where she might find something dry to change into. Her bare hands were already numb.

She moved quickly through the watertight doorway and found herself in a long passageway, which she presumed was the Reactor Compartment Tunnel. She continued into the next compartment, where two rows of missile tubes stretched into the darkness.

Christine headed down the starboard side of the compartment, past eight missile tubes, until she reached another open watertight doorway. As she stepped through, her flashlight illuminated electronic equipment on each side of a narrow passageway. She continued forward, finding a ladder, which she followed down to a berthing level filled with several rows of bunks. A search of the crew's lockers produced coveralls, underwear, socks, and shoes. Still shivering, she shed her wet apparel and donned two sets of clothing and a pair of shoes, then used a blanket to dry her hair.

Having temporarily staved off hypothermia, she evaluated the prospect of being rescued. The PRM had almost certainly been destroyed, and she wasn't aware of a replacement. Refusing to concede defeat until the air gave out or she froze to death, she decided to put her time aboard *Dolgoruky* to good use. She headed aft into the missile compartment, where the missile tubes and associated equipment resembled that aboard USS *Michigan,* and searched for the Russian version of Missile Control Center.

There wasn't one at either end of the compartment, so Christine returned to Compartment Four, stopping in the passageway lined with equipment. On the inboard side of the passageway was a door with a five-button cypher lock. She pushed the cypher lock buttons, hoping by sheer laziness the combination was something simple, like 1-2-3 or 1-2-3-4, but each attempt failed. The door remained locked.

An ax. If she could find one, maybe she could break through the door. A search of the missile compartment produced fire hoses and extinguishers, but no ax. With her hope of gaining access to *Dolgoruky*'s Missile Control Center fading, she headed forward to check Compartment Four.

As she passed by the missile tubes, her flashlight beam reflected off a small circular window in the side of a missile tube. She stopped and scraped the ice from the glass with her flashlight, then peered inside. To her surprise, the tube appeared empty.

There was an access hatch on the side of the tube. She wedged the flashlight between a piping run, then twisted the hatch ring open slowly, in case the tube was flooded. The hatch cracked open, and after no water came out, she spun the handwheel and pulled the door back, then peered inside.

There was no missile. She looked down and spotted a lead ballast can instead. She moved to the next missile tube, clearing the ice from the portal. It too appeared empty, and an inspection of the tube produced the same result. She checked the next missile tube and the next. Neither contained a missile; only lead ballast.

She leaned back against the missile tube.

So *this* is Russia's big secret?

The United States had been worried about the warheads carried by the new Bulava missile, and especially the possibility it carried advanced anti-ballistic missile countermeasures. But that wasn't what Russia was hiding. The problems plaguing the Bulava missile had not yet been solved, and with the last Typhoon and remaining Delta submarines reaching their end of life, Russia had been left with no survivable leg of their nuclear triad. *Dolgoruky*'s deployment had been a ruse, designed to fool America into believing the Borei class submarines and their new ballistic missiles were operational.

Christine had no idea how long she leaned against the missile tube, but decided it was prudent to get moving again. The excitement of uncovering Russia's secret was wearing off, and she was starting to feel lethargic. She could no longer smell the stale air, but she could tell the carbon dioxide concentration was high; her head was pounding. Still, the greater threat was the low temperature. Despite the dry clothing, she was shivering more violently than before. Finding a heat source was critical.

She decided to head aft to the auxiliary machinery compartment. Upon entering the reactor compartment passageway, she slowed, hoping to sense heat from the bulkheads. They were cold. She continued into the next compartment, pausing at the walkway running across upper level. As she examined the equipment, she wondered why she was bothering to look for a heat source. There was no power to run anything, and it wasn't like she was going to find a stack of firewood, kindle, and a match to light it with. Even so, she decided to check lower level. After finding a ladder near the aft bulkhead, she climbed down, and another search with her flashlight produced the same result. Nothing but machinery.

Christine started climbing the ladder to the upper level, but pulling herself up was more challenging than the descent. Her hands were numb and she had difficulty gripping the metal rungs, and had to resort to wrapping an arm around the ladder before moving each foot up. The going was slow and her strength was fading, but she finally reached the upper level and pulled herself onto the walkway. She rolled onto her back and caught her breath for a moment, her exhale turning to white mist in the frigid air. As she wondered if she would freeze to death aboard *Dolgoruky*, she realized she wasn't shivering anymore, and knew it was a bad sign.

Pulling the flashlight from her coverall pocket, she examined the compartment again. She was back where she started, beside the watertight door she and Brackman had shut. She pushed herself to a sitting position with her back against the bulkhead and pulled her knees to her chest. After considering her options for a moment, she wrapped her arms around her legs, placed her head on her knees, and closed her eyes. There were no options.

She could hear the subconscious screams—if she fell asleep, she would never wake up. A surge of adrenaline lifted her head and she opened her eyes, examining the cold, dark compartment again. The flashlight on the deck was already starting to fade, a fitting analogy for her life. Death wasn't something she feared; it was unavoidable. But this wasn't how she had envisioned her life ending. As a child, she pictured herself as an old woman, spending the last moments of her life in bed surrounded by her family, holding the hand of her granddaughter. But she had no family. Only regrets.

Regrets for the missed opportunities; for the poor decisions she'd made throughout her life; guilt for what she had done moments earlier in this very compartment. There was no fear, only regret. And fatigue. Her eyelids began drifting shut. She placed her head on her knees again, closed her eyes, and yielded to the inevitable.

101

BARENTS SEA

Near the bottom of the Barents Sea, a bright shaft of light descended through the darkness. Inside the Atmospheric Diving Suit, Navy Diver Roy Armstrong peered through the murky water as the light affixed to the cage he was in panned back and forth. He'd been descending for fifteen minutes, lowered by a cable attached to the ADS Launch and Recovery System. The topside controllers had informed him he would reach the bottom any time now, and through the bulbous vision dome of his diving suit, the bottom of the Barents Sea came into view.

Armstrong called to the LARS atop the ice, communicating with personnel through the umbilical attached to the top of his suit, that the bottom was in sight. The cage Armstrong was descending in came to a halt twenty-five feet above the bottom. Armstrong powered up his thrusters and the light on his right shoulder, and after topside lowered the crotch support, he flew down and out of the cage. After several thruster adjustments, he landed gently on the ocean bottom.

He checked his compass. Based on his earlier trip to *Yury Dolgoruky* before commencing rescue operations, the ballistic missile submarine lay on a bearing of one-seven-eight. He rocked the right foot pedal inward, activating the lateral thrusters attached to the back of his suit, and he turned slowly until he was headed south. Directly ahead, the outline of *Yury Dolgoruky*'s propulsor appeared in the distance, illuminated by the light on his suit. He leaned forward on the right and left foot pedals, activating the thrusters, and he began gliding toward the Russian submarine.

As Armstrong approached *Yury Dolgoruky,* it became obvious why the PRM's Launch and Recovery System had retrieved only a severed umbilical cable. There was a gaping hole in the stern of the submarine. One of the

Russian torpedoes had indeed been fired at *Yury Dolgoruky*. The Compartment Nine hatch, where the PRM would have been attached, was open, but there was no sign of the PRM.

Armstrong hovered near the hole in the stern and examined the jagged edges of the hull, bent inward from the torpedo explosion. He activated the lateral thrusters again. The light from his suit cut through the darkness as he turned, and the PRM came into view. The submersible was lying on its side next to *Dolgoruky*. The pressure wave from the explosion must have broken the suction seal between the PRM and the submarine, shearing the PRM's umbilical in the process. Armstrong leaned forward on both foot pedals again and flew toward the PRM. A closer inspection revealed the transfer skirt hatch was open. The inside of the PRM was flooded. There would be no one alive inside.

He turned back to the hole in *Dolgoruky*'s stern. Compartment Nine was flooded, which left Compartments Four through Eight. Before descending, Anderson had learned the Russians kept the aft watertight doors open on the latch, so that a greater volume of air could absorb the increasing carbon dioxide level. That being the case, all of *Dolgoruky*'s aft compartments were likely flooded.

He could not proceed inside to check, however. The bulky metal ADS wouldn't fit through the watertight door into Compartment Eight. Plus he couldn't risk entering Compartment Nine, potentially cutting his umbilical, his only source of power and communication, on the sharp metal edges of the hole.

Instead, Armstrong tilted his left foot pedal backward, and he rose toward the top of *Dolgoruky*'s hull. After several thruster adjustments, he landed on the deck and headed forward to the missile compartment hatch. If there were survivors, they would be waiting below the hatch for help to arrive.

After reaching the hatch, he leaned forward and tapped on the fairing with his manipulator—a metal claw, on the end of his right hand.

There was no response.

He tapped again, harder this time. After no response, he banged as hard as he could.

Still no response.

The conclusion was grim. There were no survivors.

Armstrong called to the LARS, informing them he was ready for retrieval.

A few seconds later, the slack in his umbilical was removed and he flew back into the cage, and the crotch support was raised. The cable attached to the cage retracted, and Armstrong began his ascent. As he rose, the lights from his suit and cage illuminated *Dolgoruky* and the PRM until they faded into the darkness.

WASHINGTON, D.C.

Seated across from the president in the Oval Office, Chief of Staff Kevin Hardison listened as the president's phone call drew to a close. Based on the president's comments, Hardison learned SecDef Richardson was on the other end, informing the president that a second Russian submarine had attacked USS *Michigan* and the guided missile submarine had been damaged during its torpedo evasion. More troubling was that the Russian submarine had fired a torpedo at *Yury Dolgoruky* with Christine, Brackman, and the ONI team aboard, and there had been casualties. With a grim expression on his face, the president hung up the phone, then filled in the missing details.

"Christine and Brackman are dead."

Hardison sat frozen in disbelief as the president added, "They were aboard *Yury Dolgoruky* when the Russian submarine torpedoed it. We lost the entire ONI team and the rescue submersible crew as well."

Hardison digested the president's words. It was difficult to accept the death of Christine and Brackman, with whom he had worked for the last three years.

After a long silence, Hardison asked the critical question.

"How do you plan to respond?"

The president answered, "I prefer not to go down a path that takes additional lives. However," he added, "I want to hear Kalinin's explanation first."

The president picked up the phone.

ICE STATION NAUTILUS

Standing in the command hut beside Verbeck, McNeil, and Commander Steel, Lieutenant Harrison listened intently to Steel's report.

"*Falcon* is flooded. *Dolgoruky*'s hull has been breached and it appears all aft compartments are flooded as well." Steel turned to Harrison. He had quickly realized the SEAL had a special interest in the personnel who had boarded *Dolgoruky*. "I'm sorry."

"She could still be alive," Harrison said.

He had meant to say "*They* could still be alive," but the one word had come out wrong.

Harrison continued, "The Russians are preparing to rescue survivors from their two attack submarines, and they could send their submersible to *Dolgoruky* first, accessing the submarine through the missile compartment hatch."

"The ADS pilot checked the hatch," Steel replied. "There was no response. That means anyone inside either can't make it to Compartment Five or they're already unconscious from hypothermia or carbon dioxide toxicity. Either way . . ."

Harrison knew quite a bit about both dangers. The air should have been able to last several more hours, plus the effects of hypothermia varied by individual, as well as their ability to recover. If Christine was alive, even if she was unconscious, there was still a chance.

"There's only one way to know for sure," Harrison argued. "We need to check. If the missile compartment is flooded, then we have our answer. If not, we need to board *Dolgoruky* and verify there are no survivors."

Steel considered Harrison's request. If there were survivors aboard *Dolgoruky,* they had far less time than the men aboard the two Russian attack submarines. If it was his decision alone, he would give it a go. However, he would need to discuss the issue with his Russian counterpart, Julius Raila, and attempt to redirect their rescue efforts.

"Okay," Steel replied. "I'll try to talk the Russians into checking *Dolgoruky* first."

He pulled a handheld radio from its holster and contacted the Russian ice camp. It wasn't long before Raila and a translator were on the other end, and Steel made his case, requesting the Russian submersible investigate *Dolgoruky* first. Raila was hesitant to agree; the odds of survivors aboard *Dolgoruky* were extremely low, and there were over two hundred men on the two Russian submarines whose status was unknown. A delay in their rescue efforts could be catastrophic.

Harrison began to fume. One of those Russian submarines had torpedoed *Dolgoruky,* creating the situation they were in. Commander Steel was about to acknowledge defeat when Harrison grabbed the radio in his hand, pressing the transmit button.

"You owe us," he said.

There was silence on the other end for a moment, then the translator responded, "Our ice hole is not yet ready. If you allow us to use yours, we will send AS-34 to *Dolgoruky* first."

Harrison handed the radio back to Steel, then stepped outside to let off some steam in the cold air. In the distance, the PRM Launch and Recovery System was inactive. The large A-frame was still in the outboard position, with the sheared umbilical cable swaying in the light Arctic breeze, a stark reminder of the PRM's fate.

104

AS-34

Mikhail Grushenko leaned forward in the Priz class deep submergence rescue vehicle, watching the sonar display over the pilot's shoulder as the submersible descended toward the ocean floor. Seated beside Grushenko and
behind the co-pilot, their medic, Pavel Danilov, kept himself busy, checking for the fourth time the atmosphere monitoring equipment they would
use at the end of their long journey. As they approached the bottom of the
Barents Sea, a white blip appeared on the sonar display, just ahead and a few
degrees to starboard. The pilot activated the forward port thruster, and
AS-34 turned slowly toward the object.

The angle of the submersible finally leveled off, and AS-34 cruised thirty
meters above the ocean floor. Grushenko shifted his eyes from the sonar
screen to the video display as the co-pilot brought the camera and external
lighting systems on-line. In the distance, *Yury Dolgoruky* slowly materialized,
its bow buried in the silt and the stern rising from the bottom.

AS-34 passed slowly over *Dolgoruky* from astern, the bright lights from
the submersible aimed downward, illuminating the stricken submarine. As
they glided above, Grushenko spotted a large hole in *Dolgoruky*'s stern, the
jagged and twisted edges of the hull bent inward. AS-34 continued forward,
slowing to a hover over the Fifth Compartment hatch, where the co-pilot
adjusted the angle and list of the submersible until it matched that of the
submarine. The pilot lowered AS-34 onto the submarine's deck, then the co-
pilot pumped the water out from the cavity between the submersible and
submarine hatches.

It was not long before the hatch beneath AS-34 was opened, and Grushenko dropped down onto *Dolgoruky*'s hull. Danilov handed him a hammer,

and Grushenko banged on the submarine's hatch, transmitting the prescribed tap codes.

There was no response.

Danilov passed the hatch-opening tool to Grushenko, who inserted it into the center divot of the hatch fairing. He twisted the tool firmly, and the hatch mechanism broke free. Grushenko turned the tool slowly until the hatch popped open a fraction of an inch.

There was a whistling sound as stale, cold air flowed into AS-34.

Grushenko monitored the inflow of air with concern. The submarine compartment had been pressurized, which meant it was at least partially flooded. If the compartment pressure had equalized with the ocean depth, they would not be able to gain access; Grushenko and the other men in AS-34 could not be pressurized to twenty atmospheres.

The pressure inside the submersible increased, approaching the limit where they would have to abandon their effort and shut AS-34's lower hatch. But then the rate slowed and pressure steadied at five atmospheres absolute. The compartment below was only partially flooded.

Grushenko resumed twisting the T-bar until the hatch popped open a few inches. He reached down and lifted it to the open-latched position, then aimed his flashlight into the darkness.

There was no one.

He lowered the sampling tube into the submarine and Danilov activated the atmosphere monitoring equipment. The oxygen and carbon dioxide levels were marginal, but sufficient to allow access. Grushenko felt his way down the ladder into the dark, frigid compartment.

Grushenko landed on the sloping deck, and he panned his flashlight slowly around the compartment, the beam of light reflecting off ice-coated surfaces. At the forward end of the compartment was an open watertight door; another one aft. While he waited for Danilov, he called out, then listened for a response. Only a low, metallic groan greeted him. The submarine was above crush depth, but its hull had been compromised by the explosion. They had to move fast.

Danilov descended, then headed forward while Grushenko checked each level of the compartment they had entered. There was no one present. He headed aft, into the Reactor Compartment Tunnel. The bulkheads were cold—there was no residual heat from the reactor. He traveled farther aft, straining to detect signs of life. As he entered the next compartment, his flashlight illuminated a human figure at the end of a long walkway, sitting on the deck beside a closed watertight door. The person was leaning against the bulkhead, knees drawn to their chest and head resting on their knees.

Grushenko hurried down the walkway and knelt beside the figure. He lifted the person's head up—a woman. Her eyes were closed and her face was pasty white; her lips blue. In the minus-two-degree air, her skin felt warm. He checked for a pulse on her wrist. There was none.

He placed the woman's head on her knees again, then pulled the radio from its holster and called Danilov.

"I found someone," Grushenko said.

As he waited for the medic, he shined his light over the edge of the walkway. The compartment was partially flooded, water almost reaching the deck plates. He brought his light back to the upper level and examined the closed watertight door beside the woman. Water was seeping past the door seal. The compartments aft were completely flooded.

A shaft of light approached, cutting through the darkness. Danilov stopped beside Grushenko.

"Did you find any survivors?" Grushenko asked.

"There is no one else," Danilov replied.

His light examined the human figure on the deck. "Is it the woman?"

"Yes."

"Is she alive?"

"I could not find a pulse, but she is still warm."

Danilov knelt beside the woman, checking for signs of respiration as he placed two fingers against her carotid artery. After a moment, he said, "She has a pulse. Very faint, only thirty beats per minute."

Grushenko slid his flashlight into his pocket, then lifted the woman from the deck, cradling her in his arms. The two men headed toward the escape hatch, with Danilov illuminating the way.

105

MOSCOW

An hour after receiving the American president's phone call, Yuri Kalinin stared across his desk at Fleet Admiral Georgiy Ivanov, Commander-in-Chief of the Russian Navy, and Admiral Oleg Lipovsky, Commander of Russia's Northern Fleet. Along the side of his office sat Boris Chernov, Russia's minister of defense. One of these men was responsible for deploying the Spetsnaz unit and *Vepr*'s attack on *Michigan*.

It was Lipovsky who professed his innocence first. "I assure you, Mr. President, that I was not responsible for issuing these orders. These units attacked without my direction."

"You expect me to believe," Kalinin replied, "that a Polar Spetsnaz unit deployed to the ice cap, and a Northern Fleet submarine was operating in the vicinity of the ice camps without your knowledge?"

"That is a different question," Lipovsky replied. "Of course I was aware of their movements, but I was not aware of their assignments."

Kalinin leaned forward. "Then who gave the orders?"

Lipovsky ran his finger along the inside of his shirt collar while he searched for an appropriate answer. Finally, he replied. "I do not know."

Kalinin leaned back in his chair. Lipovsky was lying. He had either given the orders or knew who did, and was crafting his answers to avoid implicating the guilty party.

"Let me rephrase the question," Kalinin said. "Besides you, who else could have given those orders?"

Kalinin watched Lipovsky carefully. The obvious answer was one of the two other men in the room. But Lipovsky did not glance in Ivanov's direction, nor did he look at Defense Minister Chernov. There was another possibility, however. Rear Admiral Leonid Shimko, Commander of 12th

Squadron, could have given the order to *Vepr*. The submarine was under his command. But that scenario was more alarming. The Polar Spetsnaz unit was not under his purview, which meant there was at least one other person involved; a conspiracy willing to use military force without the president's authorization.

Fifteen seconds passed and Lipovsky still did not reply. The Admiral's face grew flush and beads of sweat formed on his brow.

"I'm growing impatient," Kalinin said.

Lipovsky sputtered, "I cannot say for sure."

Kalinin slammed his fist on his desk. "Answer the question or I will relieve you of command!"

"I gave the orders."

Kalinin turned to Fleet Admiral Ivanov. The older man sat in his chair calmly, with no hint of distress. Ivanov had cleared Lipovsky. But not Chernov. Kalinin watched Chernov from the corner of his eye as he directed his next question at Ivanov.

"Why did you give those orders?"

"The potential gain was worth the risk."

"What risk?" Kalinin asked. "The loss of *Vepr* and two Spetsnaz platoons?" Kalinin's anger built as he continued. "A direct attack on the United States?" The Russian president's anger crested as he leaned forward, adding, "The end of your career and your incarceration!"

"Yes."

Kalinin glared at his Fleet Admiral, who remained unfazed, wondering why Ivanov was so calm. Was he following orders, preparing to absolve himself with his next statement? Kalinin glanced at Chernov. The Defense Minister seemed nervous, changing his position in his chair, his eyes shifting between Ivanov and Kalinin.

Kalinin followed up, "Were you following orders, or did you come up with this idea by yourself?"

"It was my idea," the Admiral replied. "No one else was involved."

Kalinin noted Chernov's reaction. His Defense Minister seemed relieved, but that could be because Ivanov was covering for him or because he had been worried Ivanov would falsely accuse him. Kalinin could not be sure, but with Ivanov accepting full responsibility, there was little more to probe.

"Fleet Admiral Ivanov," Kalinin replied. "You are relieved of your command and reduced in rank to Admiral pending disciplinary action."

There was no visible reaction from the former Fleet Admiral. He sat there, staring at Kalinin as he awaited further direction.

"You are dismissed," Kalinin added.

Ivanov pushed himself to his feet, then left without a word, glancing briefly at Chernov as he passed by.

Kalinin turned to Lipovsky. "You are now the acting Fleet Admiral. Attend to this mess and keep the defense minister informed of all issues. You are dismissed."

The relief in Lipovsky's face was apparent as he rose and left the president's office, closing the door behind him. Kalinin shifted his gaze to Chernov.

"I will call the American president and let him know what I've learned, then come to an agreement as to what will be made public. Our task is more difficult, as we have to explain the loss of two attack submarines. Do you have a recommendation?"

It appeared Chernov had been contemplating the matter, because he replied immediately. "I suggest," he began, "that we be truthful about the collision between *Dolgoruky* and the American submarine. These things happen, and it would be difficult to conceal the damage to the American submarine when it returns for repairs. Regarding *Vepr* and *Severodvinsk,* they collided while searching for *Dolgoruky,* and the reason for the Spetsnaz deaths can be easily concealed.

"That leaves the American casualties to explain, and I am sure an *understanding* can be reached. As a concession to America, we will credit them with the rescue of *Dolgoruky*'s crew, and praise their assistance as we rescue survivors aboard *Vepr* and *Severodvinsk.*"

Chernov added, "We will highlight that during this difficult time, our two countries have put aside our political differences and are working closely together, strengthening the bond of our unique relationship." Chernov smiled.

Kalinin absorbed Chernov's words as the defense minister added, "We will brief all parties involved on our side, so that only the official story is released. The American president will have to do the same."

After a moment of reflection, Kalinin nodded his approval and picked up the phone.

106

USS *MICHIGAN*

Christine's eyes opened, then fluttered shut in the bright light. She opened her eyes again, this time just a tad, letting them adjust to the light as she tried to figure out where she was. She was lying on a bed somewhere with a heated blanket wrapped tightly around her. As her surroundings came into focus, she noticed an insulated IV Warmer hanging from the bulkhead beside her, with the clear plastic tubing running out the bottom and tucked inside the blanket on her left side. She could feel warmth radiating up her left arm.

"Welcome back to the living, Ms. O'Connor."

Christine turned in the direction of the man's voice, spotting Commander Joe Aleo standing beside her. She realized she was aboard *Michigan,* in Medical—Doc's office, lying on the single bed against the bulkhead. It was in this same office that he had stitched her arm up after being shot on the way out of Beijing. Aleo pulled a pocket flashlight from his coveralls and examined her pupils.

"Can you talk?"

"Yes," Christine replied.

"What's your name?"

"Christine."

Doc asked several more questions, and she saw the relief on his face when she answered them correctly.

"How do you feel?"

"Tired," she replied, "but okay otherwise."

"You gave us quite a scare," Aleo said. "You were rescued from *Dolgoruky* just in time. You were about to turn into an ice sculpture."

Christine asked what happened, and Aleo explained how they had used the Russian submersible to rescue her. It had then surfaced in a nearby lead along with USS *Michigan,* where she was transferred aboard the guided missile submarine so she could be placed in one of the Dry Deck Shelter hyperbaric chambers to decompress, and had been released a few hours ago.

"How's your hearing?" he asked.

"A little muffled," Christine replied.

"Your eardrums are ruptured," he explained. "It must have happened when *Dolgoruky* was torpedoed, from the pressure transient when the submarine flooded. Most eardrum ruptures heal with no loss of hearing, but my bigger concern is hypothermia. You're out of the danger zone now, but there might be some permanent damage. I won't know for another day or two. We'll see how things go and I'll do my best."

"Thanks, Doc."

"You should thank Harrison," Aleo replied. "He was the one who talked the Russians into checking *Dolgoruky* before rescuing their two submarine crews. If you had been down there much longer, you wouldn't have made it."

Before Christine could respond, Aleo said, "Wait right here." He smiled, realizing she wasn't going anywhere. She was wrapped tightly in the heated blanket. "I'll let everyone know you've regained consciousness."

Aleo stepped from his office, and as Christine waited for his return, she wished he had turned off the lights. She was already feeling drowsy, and the bright lights were annoying. She was about to close her eyes when the door opened and Jake Harrison entered, stopping beside her.

"How are you doing?" he asked.

"Remarkably well, considering the circumstances."

Harrison nodded. "You certainly manage to get yourself into difficult situations."

Christine smiled. "I appreciate your help, convincing the Russians to rescue me."

Harrison didn't respond, so Christine decided to be more direct. "Thank you for saving my life."

"I would have done it for anyone."

Under normal circumstances, Harrison's response would have irritated her. But she was too tired. Instead, she said, "Why can't you just say *You're welcome?*"

Harrison stared at her for a moment, then leaned over near her ear. "You're welcome." He kissed her on the cheek, then stood erect, a grin on his face.

"Don't try stealing any real kisses," Christine replied. "I'm completely at your mercy." Her arms were pinned against her sides with the blanket tucked under her.

Harrison started to lean over when the door opened. This time it was Lieutenant Commander Kelly Haas, *Michigan*'s Supply Officer. As she stopped beside Harrison, Christine noticed her height again; she was nearly as tall as Jake.

"Welcome back aboard *Michigan,* Ms. O'Connor," she said. "I'm rounding up some clothes for you." She offered a warm smile, then added, "It looks like you'll need to borrow some underwear again. We were going to throw yours in the laundry, but noticed you were wearing men's underwear. Exciting times down there?"

Christine laughed. "Yes, very exciting."

Captain Wilson stepped into Medical. It was getting crowded in Doc's small office.

"Welcome back aboard *Michigan,* Christine."

"Thanks for the hospitality," she replied. "Is the food still as good?"

"You bet." Wilson grinned. He glanced at the IV bag. "We'll get you out of here and eating normally as soon as possible." He added, "Commander Aleo will make sure you're stable and don't have any frostbite or other issues. When you're ready, the SEALs can take you back to Ice Station Nautilus in one of the SDVs, or, if you want, you can remain aboard until we return to port. But it'll be a while. We've been assigned tow-truck duties for *North Dakota.*"

Doc Aleo returned to his cramped office. "All right, everyone. I've got work to do. Move along now." He looked at Wilson. "Respectfully, sir."

Wilson patted Aleo on the arm as he exited.

Kelly Haas left, leaving Harrison and Aleo in Medical with Christine. The Doc stared at the SEAL, waiting for him to depart.

Harrison turned to Christine. "I'll see you around."

"Thanks for stopping by," she said.

After Harrison left, Christine asked, "What's the plan, Doc?"

"Give me another day or two to make sure you're fully recovered, and in the meantime, why don't you get some sleep? Hypothermia takes a toll."

Christine could hardly disagree. Her eyelids were getting heavy. She closed her eyes as she replied, "Aye aye, Doc."

ARLINGTON, VIRGINIA

A light snow was falling from a gray, overcast sky as a cold March wind swept up the green slopes of Arlington National Cemetery. Christine O'Connor stood behind a row of vacant chairs alongside an open pit that would become Captain Steve Brackman's grave. Standing beside her was Kevin Hardison, along with other members of the president's staff and cabinet, with others arrayed in several rows behind them. Navy divers had retrieved Brackman's body from *Dolgoruky,* and in the distance, working its way up the curving road toward the gravesite, was the horse-drawn limber and caisson carrying his flag-draped casket. Following closely behind was a procession of cars carrying the president and Brackman's family.

Positioned alongside the road, awaiting the arrival of the burial procession, was the six-member honor guard who would serve as Brackman's casket team, led by the Officer-in-Charge of the ceremony. One hundred feet from the foot of Brackman's grave stood the firing detail, a seven-member rifle team that would fire three volleys at the appropriate time. Not far away, up the slope of Arlington National Cemetery, the solitary bugler stood ready.

As Christine waited for the ceremony to begin, her thoughts drifted to the events of the past two weeks. After a few days aboard *Michigan,* she had returned to Ice Station Nautilus, then began the long journey home to Washington, D.C. During the trip, she was painfully aware of the vacant seat beside her that Brackman would have occupied.

Upon arriving in Washington, her first stop after briefing the president was the Office of Naval Intelligence. ONI personnel had been surprised at her revelation of what *Dolgoruky* carried. The Bulava missile's poor performance during flight tests was originally thought to have been the result of inadequate quality control of critical components, which had been corrected.

After reassessing their intel, ONI concluded the Bulava missile had a serious flaw that would require an extensive redesign, resulting in a gap of operational submarine launched ballistic missiles as the last Typhoon and Delta submarines reached their end of life. Russia was about to lose its only survivable leg of their nuclear triad, a fact they were desperately trying to conceal.

It had cost Russia two of their nuclear attack submarines. Russia was able to rescue the survivors aboard *Vepr* and *Severodvinsk,* but the death toll had still been high; forty-five Russian sailors and almost two full platoons of Spetsnaz, not to mention Brackman and twenty-four other Americans.

The president was still evaluating Kalinin's proposal; it would be difficult to permanently conceal so much carnage above and below the ice, but so far, the details had been withheld from the media. In the meantime, Kalinin had agreed to include inspections of Russia's Borei class submarines and Bulava missiles in the follow-on nuclear arms treaty, and the president was wringing additional concessions from Kalinin on a number of international issues, holding the threat of going public with what Russia had done over his head. The president was still seething, searching for other ways to punish Russia.

The limber and caisson carrying Brackman's casket pulled to a halt just past the six-man casket team, and the president and Brackman's family stepped from their sedans. Although there were over a hundred persons in attendance, there were only three members of Brackman's family: Brackman's mother, father, and older sister, Lisa. Brackman's wife and daughter were not present, having died three years earlier.

The president and Brackman's family stopped alongside the road, and the ceremony OIC signaled the casket team, who moved into position behind the caisson, marching slowly in unison. Brackman's casket was removed from the caisson, and the chaplain took station at the head of the casket team, leading the procession up the slope to the gravesite. Brackman's family and the president followed.

Brackman's casket was placed atop the supports that would lower his body to its final resting place, and the casket team remained standing at attention, three men on each side. The chaplain moved to the head of Brackman's grave while Brackman's family took their seats in the chairs alongside the gravesite. The president remained standing, stopping behind the chairs, next to Christine.

The casket team lifted the American flag from Brackman's casket and held it waist high, stretched taut over Brackman's casket, and the chaplain began the committal service. As the chaplain read the scripture, approaching the final moment when Brackman would be lowered into his grave, Christine grappled with her guilt; her responsibility for Brackman's death.

It was her recommendation that resulted in Brackman joining her on the trip to the polar ice cap. Compounding her culpability, Brackman would have already transferred to his next job if she hadn't convinced him to remain the president's senior military aide for another year. Her motive had been selfish. She and Brackman agreed on almost every issue, and she didn't want to lose her dependable ally in the political wars waged among the president's staff. Finally, she had closed the watertight door and sealed Brackman in Compartment Eight.

There was no avoiding it. Brackman was dead because of her. She wondered how many people gathered around Brackman's grave understood her guilt. She glanced at Brackman's parents and his sister. They were seated in front of her, looking away toward Brackman's casket, and Christine was grateful she did not have to look them in the eye during the ceremony.

The chaplain stepped back from the gravesite and the OIC signaled the firing detail, ordering them to attention. The president and military personnel saluted as the firing detail fired three volleys. As the echo of the last round faded, the bugler sounded taps. The long, lonely notes from his bugle filled the air. Christine knew only the first line of the lyrics:

Day is done, gone the sun.

She looked up into the overcast sky, the sun hidden by clouds. The weather, at least, was appropriate. As the last note from the bugle faded, the chaplain resumed his position at the head of Brackman's grave and offered the benediction. The casket team folded the American flag they had held over Brackman's casket, then handed it to the president, who presented the flag to Brackman's parents.

"On behalf of a grateful nation and proud Navy, I present this flag to you in recognition of your son's years of honorable and faithful service to his country."

Brackman's mother accepted the flag as tears streamed down her cheeks. The president stepped back and saluted, then the casket team marched away from the gravesite. The OIC signaled the firing detail, who also turned and headed down the slope.

The president offered his condolences, followed by members of his staff and cabinet, as well as Brackman's friends from the many commands he served on. Christine remained behind, searching for the right words, but they eluded her. The line of mourners wound down, and when there was no one left, she could put it off no longer.

Christine stopped in front of Brackman's parents, and as they met her gaze, she decided to keep her condolences short. "Your son saved my life. I cannot thank him, so I thank you."

Brackman's parents nodded their appreciation.

Christine wanted to say more, but wasn't sure if they harbored resentment toward her. After all, their son had traded his life for hers.

Brackman's sister stood and offered Christine a hug. As Lisa pulled away, she said, "We understand why Steve did what he did. He spoke highly of you." It looked like there was more she wanted to say, but then she noticed Christine's pain. Lisa hugged her again, this time whispering in her ear, "Don't feel guilty. It was Steve's decision, not yours."

She had stopped by to offer condolences, but it was Lisa who did the consoling. Her words helped, and the lump in Christine's throat diminished. Brackman's family stood, then headed down the slope to their sedan. The president also departed, as did his staff and cabinet, followed by Brackman's friends, leaving only Christine, the chaplain, and the OIC. The two men bid her farewell, then joined the congregation making its way toward the cemetery's exit.

Christine remained behind, standing at the foot of Brackman's grave. She thanked him one final time, then looked up into the dark gray sky, blinking as heavy snowflakes hit her face. The snow was falling harder now. She pulled the collar of her overcoat around her ears, then tucked her chin down as she headed into the bitter wind.

* * * THE END * * *

COMPLETE CAST OF CHARACTERS

AMERICAN CHARACTERS

UNITED STATES ADMINISTRATION
Kevin Hardison, chief of staff
Christine O'Connor, national security advisor
Don Richardson, secretary of defense
Dawn Cabral, secretary of state
Lars Sikes, press secretary
Steve Brackman (Captain), senior military aide

PENTAGON
Michael McFarland (Admiral), Chief of Naval Operations
Gary Riley (Rear Admiral), Director, Undersea Warfare Division (N97)

COMSUBFOR / COMSUBLANT
Bob Tayman (Vice Admiral), Commander, Submarine Force
Rick Current (Captain), chief of staff
Vince Harms (Electronics Technician Second Class), Communications Center Watchstander
Marc Arsenault (Chief Electronics Technician), Communications Center Supervisor
Joe Ruscigno (Commander), C4I Watch Officer
Andy Wheeler, C4I Watchstander

USS *NORTH DAKOTA* (VIRGINIA CLASS FAST ATTACK SUBMARINE)

OFFICERS

PAUL TOLBERT (Commander), Commanding Officer

GEORGE SITES (Lieutenant Commander), Executive Officer

ROGER SWENSON (Lieutenant Commander), Engineer Officer

MARK LIVINGSTON (Lieutenant), Weapons Officer

SCOTT MOLITOR (Lieutenant), junior officer

JP VAUGH (Lieutenant), junior officer

CHIEFS

PAUL MURGO (Sonar Technician Master Chief), Chief of the Boat

MIKE MORAN (Electricians Mate Chief), Electrical Division Chief

LARRY JOHNSON (Machinist Mate Chief), Auxiliary Division Chief

TONY SCALISE (Machinist Mate Chief), Machinery Division Chief

BOB BUSH (Sonar Technician Chief), Sonar Division Chief

PETTY OFFICERS AND SEAMEN

ART THOMPSON (Electrician's Mate First Class), Electrical Division

TIM BRANDON (Electrician's Mate First Class), Electrical Division

ALLEN TERRILL (Electrician's Mate Second Class), Electrical Division

SCOTT TURK (Machinist Mate Third Class), Engine Room Forward Watch

BOB HORNSEY (Electronics Technician Second Class), Quartermaster

JOE HIPP (Electronics Technician First Class), Propulsion Plant Operator

TOM PHILLIPS (Fire Control Technician Second Class), Plots Operator

REGGIE THURLOW (Sonar Technician Second Class), Broadband Operator

DAVID LORMS (Seaman), Phone Talker

USS *MICHIGAN* (OHIO CLASS GUIDED MISSILE SUBMARINE)–CREW

MURRAY WILSON (Captain), Commanding Officer

TERRY SPARKS (Lieutenant Commander), Executive Officer

KELLY HAAS (Lieutenant Commander), Supply Officer

MARCUS BENJAMIN (Lieutenant), Weapons Officer

BARBARA LAKE (Lieutenant), Junior Officer

MARK DeCRISPINO (Lieutenant), Junior Officer

PAT LEENSTRA (Electronics Technician Second Class), Quartermaster

CHRIS MALOCSAY (Fire Control Technician Second Class), Fire Control Technician of the Watch

USS *MICHIGAN*-SEAL DETACHMENT

JOHN MCNEIL (Commander), SEAL Team Commander
JAKE HARRISON (Lieutenant), SEAL Platoon Officer-in-Charge
LORIE ALLEN (Lieutenant), SEAL Platoon Officer-in-Charge
JEFF STONE (Special Warfare Operator Chief), fire team leader
TIM OLIVER (Special Warfare Operator First Class), sniper
BRAD KRATOVIL (Special Warfare Operator Second Class), breacher
JIM HAY (Special Warfare Operator Second Class), communicator
JOE ALEO (Commander), Medical Officer

UNDERSEA RESCUE COMMAND

NED STEEL (Commander), Commanding Officer
MARLIN CRIDER (Lieutenant Commander), Executive Officer
PETER TARBOTTOM, lead contractor for Phoenix International
BOB ENNIS, Pressurized Rescue Module (PRM) Attendant
ART GLOVER, Pressurized Rescue Module (PRM) Attendant
EDDIE STANKIEWICZ (Machinist Mate Chief), Disabled Submarine team member
ROY ARMSTRONG (Navy Diver First Class), Atmospheric Diving Suit pilot

ARCTIC SUBMARINE LABORATORY

BOBBY PLEASANT, director
VANCE VERBECK, technical director
PAUL LEONE, ice pilot

ICE STATION NAUTILUS

ERIC DAHLENBURG (Vice Admiral), On-Scene Commander
MIKE NAUGHTON (Captain), Coordinator, Rescue Forces
NED STEEL (Commander), Rescue Element Commander

VANCE VERBECK, ice camp Officer-in-Charge (OIC)
PAUL LEONE, ice pilot
ALYSSA MARTIN, above-ice sonar array operator
SCOTT WALWORTH, RATS operator
FRANK SALIMBENE, Casa C-212 pilot
SALLY FIREBAUGH, cook

OFFICE OF NAVAL INTELLIGENCE

PAM BRUCE, supervisor
GREG HARTFIELD, Borei class submarine expert
STU BERMAN, Bulava missile expert

RUSSIAN CHARACTERS

RUSSIAN FEDERATION ADMINISTRATION

YURI KALININ, president
BORIS CHERNOV, minister of defense
MAKSIM POSNIAK, director of security and disarmament, Ministry of
    Foreign Affairs

FLEET COMMANDERS

GEORGIY IVANOV (Fleet Admiral), Commander-in-Chief, Russian Navy
OLEG LIPOVSKY (Admiral), Commander, Northern Fleet
LEONID SHIMKO (Rear Admiral), Commander, 12th Squadron

K-535 *YURY DOLGORUKY* (BOREI CLASS BALLISTIC MISSILE SUBMARINE)

NICHOLAI STEPANOV (Captain First Rank), Commanding Officer
DMITRI PAVLOV (Captain Second Rank), First Officer
ANTON TOPOLSKI (Captain Third Rank), Navigating Officer
MIKHAIL EVANOFF (Captain Lieutenant), Central Command Post Watch
    Officer

IVAN KHUDOZHNIK (Senior Lieutenant), Torpedo Division Officer

ANDREI POPOVICH (Senior Michman), Torpedo Division Leading Petty Officer

OLEG DEVIN (Starshina First Class), Torpedo Division Petty Officer

ERIK GLINKA (Michman), Electric Navigation Party Technician

EGOR LUKIN (Chief Ship Starshina), Senior Enlisted

IVAN KOVALESKI (Captain of the Medical Service), Medical Officer

K-157 *VEPR* (AKULA II CLASS NUCLEAR ATTACK SUBMARINE)

MATVEY BACZEWSKI (Captain Second Rank), Commanding Officer

PETR LUKOV (Captain Third Rank), First Officer

LUDVIG DOLINSKI (Captain Lieutenant), Central Command Post Watch Officer

EUGENY CHABAN (Lieutenant), Duty Officer

K-329 *SEVERODVINSK* (YASEN CLASS NUCLEAR ATTACK SUBMARINE)

JOSEF BUFFANOV (Captain Second Rank), Commanding Officer

ANTON NOVIKOFF (Captain Third Rank), First Officer

DMITRI RONIN (Captain Lieutenant), Central Command Post Watch Officer

ICE CAMP BARNEO / *MIKHAIL RUDNITSKY*

DEMIL POLESKI, ice camp director

JULIUS RAILA, Chief of Search and Rescue Services

POLAR SPETSNAZ UNIT

JOSEF KLOKOV (Captain First Rank), Commanding Officer

GLEB LEONOV (Captain Second Rank), Executive Officer

ERIK TOPOLSKI (Captain Lieutenant), platoon leader

KIRIL BOGANOV (Captain Lieutenant), platoon leader

NICHOLAI OVECHKIN (Starshina First Class), patrol

AS-34 DEEP SUBMERGENCE RESCUE VEHICLE

MIKHAIL GRUSHENKO, rescue team member

PAVEL DANILOV, rescue team member

OTHER RUSSIAN CHARACTERS

DANIL KRASINSKI (Michman), Operations Center Radioman

EDUARD DAVYDOV (Captain Second Rank), Intelligence Center Watch
  Officer

AUTHOR'S NOTE

I hope you enjoyed reading *Ice Station Nautilus*!

This was both a fun and difficult book to write, in that it allowed me to explore a region where submarines do not routinely operate, taking the reader both above and below the ice. Although I have not operated below the ice, I was fortunate to have visited a base camp atop the polar ice cap a few years ago while two submarines were shooting exercise torpedoes at each other, and I assisted with the torpedo recovery through the ice. I broke my hand while I was up there, and I'd like to say it was while saving the ice camp by wrestling a polar bear, but the truth is less exciting.

There are a lot of technical issues I did not explore in *Ice Station Nautilus*. I only scratched the surface with respect to the issues USS *North Dakota*'s crew would have to deal with if trapped beneath the polar ice cap without power. You could write an entire book covering the plethora of problems that would arise and how they would need to be addressed, plus there are issues with reactor cooling and recovery that make my head hurt when I think about them. Addressing every issue and how each would be resolved would have bogged *Ice Station Nautilus* down with technical details that are more appropriate for a nonfiction book on the topic rather than a novel, where the focus is plot and pacing.

Also, some of the tactics described in *Ice Station Nautilus* were generic and not accurate. For example, torpedo employment and evasion tactics are classified and cannot be accurately represented in this novel. The dialogue also isn't 100 percent accurate. If it were, much of it would be unintelligible to the average reader. To help the story move along without getting bogged down in acronyms, technical details, and other Navy jargon, I simplified the dialogue and description of shipboard operations and weapon systems.

For all of the above, I apologize. I did my best to keep everything as close to real life as possible while developing a suspenseful, page-turning novel. Hopefully it all worked out, and you enjoyed reading *Ice Station Nautilus*.